AMIDST FALLEN ANGELS

A BOOK IN THE STANDALONE SERIES INNER DEMONS AND
FALLEN ANGELS

REBECCA JOSE

FREE DOWNLOAD!

https://mymeshara.wixsite.com/nethersouls/landing-page

THIS BOOK CONTAINS GRAPHIC
SCENES CONTAINING VIOLENCE,
FOUL LANGUAGE, AND SEXUAL
CONTENT AND MAY NOT BE
SUITABLE FOR CHILDREN.

PARENTAL DISCRETION
IS ADVISED.

Rebecca Jose

Author of steamy fantasy adventure romance

TRIGGER WARNINGS

- STALKING, BUT FOR A GOOD REASON

- BLOOD AND GORE

- TALK OF MURDER

- DEPRESSION AND ANXIETY

- AGGRESSIVE SEX, INCLUDING SPANKING, BREATH PLAY, AND BONDAGE

- MORE BONDAGE

- INSOMNIA AND HALLUCINATIONS, AND NOT THE FUN KIND

- CONTROVERSIAL OPINIONS ON RELIGION, PLEASE KEEP IN MIND THAT THIS IS A WORK OF FICTION, AND MAY NOT REFLECT THE VIEWS OR OPINIONS OF THE AUTHOR. IT IS SIMPLY A STORY TOLD FOR ENTERTAINMENT PURPOSES ONLY.

- FOUL LANGUAGE AND EXPLICIT SEX SCENES (BUT I FIGURED YOU ASSUMED THAT FROM THE AGGRESSIVE SEX WARNINGS)

THIS BOOK IS DEDICATED
TO ALL OF MY FANS. YOU
HAVE MADE ALL OF THIS
POSSIBLE. I APPRECIATE
EACH AND EVERY ONE OF
YOU.

OTHER BOOKS BY REBECCA JOSE

THE NETHER SOULS (BOOK ONE OF THE NETHER SOULS SERIES)

TIME AND TIME AGAIN (BOOK TWO OF THE NETHER SOULS SERIES)

FOR THE LOVE OF DAWN

FORCE OF THE IMMORTALS (BOOK ONE OF THE DRAGONS OF DESTINY TRILOGY)

WITCHBALL

SHATTERED APPARITIONS

SHADOW MIRROR – A Horror book in the standalone series *Inner Demons and Fallen Angels*

CHAPTER 1: MIA

Moving shadows that come alive, reaching for me with shadowy arms, filling my ears with malicious whispers that promise violent things.

That is what I see and hear all around me whenever I close my eyes. They taunt me with their threat of a night full of horrors I cannot even imagine until they show up in my nightmares.

Sometimes, they even show up when I'm not asleep, especially when I look in a mirror.

It is always like this when I don't sleep, which happens to be a lot. I have always had trouble, but it has become a significant problem lately.

I haven't slept in days, and the stress and strain on my brain is starting to show. The shadows are beginning to come alive in my head again.

They are terrifying in my nightmares, where my subconscious is ignorant of the fact that they are not real. In waking hours, I mostly disregard them since I am smart enough to know that they are just hallucinations brought on by my sleep-deprived brain.

I can ignore them without fear when I am awake, but how much longer will I be able to function like this? Coffee and other forms of caffeine are not going to sustain me forever. I will have to nap sometime.

I am sitting in my office on the second floor of the abandoned building I bought shortly after coming to Daisville, Kentucky. I needed someplace to work and live here temporarily, maybe longer if I decide to stay.

I cleaned this office on my first day here so I would have a nice workspace. The desk sits on the back wall before a large window, so I can turn in my chair, open the slatted blinds, and see the street below.

The now-clean walls are stark white to match the concrete tiled floor with a few paintings I had found and salvaged from the first floor.

The large bookshelf on the right wall sits empty for now, but I will fill it with my collection if I decide to stay permanently. My heavy eyes drift back to my desk, and I sigh as I glance at the half-empty mug of coffee sitting on my desk. Even caffeine isn't going to help if I keep drifting off before I can drink it. Pencil in hand, I turn my attention back to the paper I was working on before my mind had started to wonder, and I groan in frustration.

If the substantial fucking mistake I just made on this form is any indication of my sleeplessness, I don't know what is. One fucking number. That is all it took to ruin three days' worth of work, and now I have to go back and do it all again.

This never happened to me back home, even though I had trouble sleeping there too. I have always had insomnia, but back home, I learned to live with it. It goes along with stress and anxiety, which is part of my job. But back home, I never saw the shadows.

Why the hell did I ever leave Phoenix?

For Sophia, that's why.

My messed-up younger cousin, Sophia, needed someone to take care of her stupid restaurant after she got herself locked up in a mental hospital for trying to commit suicide. She suffered a mental break when she lost her mom, my Aunt Katrina, Dad's sister.

Sophia is my Dad's favorite niece…well, she is his only niece. Plus, Dad loves restaurants and has always wanted one of his own. There was no thinking about it for my Dad. He was ready to go the second he got the call.

For me, it was all about the guilt.

I was a shitty cousin to Sophia growing up. I pretty much tortured her during our entire childhood simply because I was jealous of her. I was older, but she was always more competent and more mature. She was prettier than me, too. I thought I hated her, but as I got older, I realized it was simply petty jealousy that drove me to be horrible to her.

I felt awful when Sophia lost her Dad, and then she lost her mom, too. The guilt of how I treated her eats at me even to this day, even though Sophia has told me she holds no ill will toward me since we have both grown up.

However, I still hold myself accountable. I have a lot of making-up to do with Sophia.

So, of course, I also decided to come when Dad came galavanting to her rescue. My father took over the restaurant while I took over Sophia's finances.

Then, Sophia ended up falling for her doctor. She almost married him, but he died of a heart attack before she could. However, he left her his entire estate, which included a substantial bank account and two hospitals. One of which is a Victorian mansion-turned-mental facility where Sophia now lives.

That gave me an entirely new set of financial assets to add to her portfolio and more work to do for her. But I was happy to do it. However, Sophia may not need me much longer.

She completed her therapy plan and is now mentally stable. She has a board of trustees that runs her private medical hospital and is now running her dead fiance's mental hospital all on her own. Thanks to my competent teaching, she manages her finances independently.

Give a man a fish, feed him for a day; teach him how to fish, feed him for life. That was my philosophy when I taught her, and she has hardly had to call me lately.

The only reason I am still here is because I still handle the account for the restaurant for my Dad after Sophia gave it to him, and he has decided to stay here permanently to look after his new restaurant. However, he is rapidly learning how to keep up with the books on his own.

So that leaves the question, do I stay or do I go?

I have my business back in Phoenix to run, even though it doesn't need me there in person to run efficiently. My business has been established for years. I have a competent board of directors and a senior management team that does an exceptional job.

If they need me…well, that is what video conferences are for.

So why am I still here?

I could open a branch here and expand my business, but do I really want the extra stress? Dad wants me to stay, but what do I want?

Something in my periphery catches my attention, drawing me from my thoughts. The shadows around me move restlessly, and I fidget in my seat. They are not ordinary shadows that follow you around as the sun is setting. These shadows writhe and move, even though the light is still. They have no form or purpose. They are simply black, smoky blobs that coalesce around the corners of the room.

It is getting harder to ignore them the longer I am awake. They seem to grow and fill the room more and more as time passes. But at

3

least they snapped me back to reality. Once again, I have let my mind wander and have lost focus.

Dammit, I have got to get some shut-eye.

Maybe I should check myself into Sophia's mental hospital. I could get free care since my cousin owns it. Maybe then I could relax and get some much-needed rest.

My eyes drift shut of their own accord for about the one thousandth time today but are jerked back open by a loud banging sound coming from downstairs.

This building had been cheap because it was rumored to be haunted, so I bought it. If I decide to stay, I will need an office building like this to open my new branch. Given that the building used to be apartment housing, it also has a penthouse apartment, so I will have a place to live as well.

If I decide to go? Well, then I will leave it to my Dad. He can live in the penthouse, rent out the apartments, and have a second source of income. He would be set for life.

A door slams downstairs, jerking my eyes open again, and the sound of running footsteps travels through the building. I wonder if the building really is haunted or if I am only having sleep-deprived hallucinations.

The only spaces in the building I have had repaired and cleaned are the one apartment on this floor I am staying in while I wait for the penthouse to be redone and this office. The other five floors are still full of two years of abandoned messes that will take me some time to clean up, so there shouldn't be anyone down there thumping around.

The banging of another door comes from the floor just beneath me, and I slap my pencil down on top of the paper stack before me. Tossing my long, black hair over my shoulder, I stand and shove my office chair back, intending to take a much-needed walk and investigate the annoying noises.

I rush out into the hallway. The elevators are still being repaired, so I turn toward the other end of the hallway to the stairs. The heavy metal door used to be set with an alarm, but the alarm system has long been disabled. So, there is no noise other than the sound of the heavy door opening when I enter the dark stairwell and start down the stairs.

"Don't go down there," That little voice in my head says as I stare down into the darkness.

Sometimes, I hate that voice.

"I am going, and you cannot stop me," I say snippily. "I am not afraid."

Running footsteps echo through the stairwell, echoing off the walls as I grip the metal rails. My step quickens, hurrying to get out of the darkened stairwell until a blood-curdling scream fills my ears. I stop in the middle of the stairs as my heart stops with fear. Tiny slivers of icy terror climb up my spine, raising the hair on the back of my neck. My breath quickens, filling my lungs with the stifling air in the stairwell.

The scream continues, drawing out long and loud and ending on a...

Laugh?

What the fuck?

My body unfreezes, and I move again, flying blindly down the last few steps and busting through the first-floor metal door.

The entryway is empty, and the glass doors to my left are darkened by the night outside. The bright lights inside illuminate the entryway, casting a stark light on the abandoned mess within.

Before me, the former front desk, ragged and broken down on one side, sits empty as always, dust and cobwebs covering every corner. The old metal mailboxes, the numbers long since faded, are sat on the wall beside the desk and house God knows how many spiders and bugs. To my right is the elevator, its metal doors gleaming dully under the fluorescent lights and a doorway leading down a long, lighted hallway beside it.

I look around, confused, but then I hear the laughter coming from one of the many rooms down the hallway to my right. Apartment doors line either side of the hallway, all hanging open the way I had left them. The apartments are dark inside and all empty.

I walk swiftly, looking left and right as I glance into each open door down the hall. The light from the hallway shines into each door, lighting the front room of each apartment enough to see halfway inside. My high-heel boots clack along the marble floors and echo off the empty, dry-walled walls.

The laughter stops suddenly as I draw closer to the apartment at the end of the hallway, and a light shines from the door out into the hallway. A tentative voice calls out through the open door.

"Hello? Anyone there?" A young male voice calls.

"I told you I heard footsteps earlier," A young female voice says.

A sudden, wicked idea hits me, and I quickly dodge into an empty, dark apartment to my left. I don't need a couple of teenagers breaking into what they believe to be a still abandoned building for their damn make-out sessions. I have other things to worry about. Hopefully, my plan will scare them off for good.

I duck behind the open door of the apartment, kneeling to quietly take off my boots. I hear the footsteps of the two teens coming down the hall slowly, and I can tell they are trying to be stealthy.

And failing.

"Stay behind me, I'll protect you," The boy whispers.

"There isn't anybody out here," the girl answers. "But I know I heard something."

"Maybe it's the ghosts," he says humorously.

The boy lets out an 'oomph' sound, and the girl says, "That's not funny."

"Shhh! Quiet!" The boy chides.

I wait, holding my breath in my stockinged feet until the pair is right by the door I hide behind. I push hard, slamming the door fiercely and casting the apartment into darkness. The sound echoes through the empty living room where I stand, and I can imagine how it sounded in the extra-loud hallway.

I turn and run, quickly and silently, clutching my boots in my hands, and leap into an empty closet. I don't need lights to guide my way in the small room. I knew the closet was here since I scoped these apartments when I first bought this building.

I close the sliding, slatted door of the closet I am hiding in, opening the slats just a hair so I can see out into the room, but not enough that anyone would be able to see inside the closet if they turn on the lights.

I hear the girl scream from the hallway when the door slams, but the boy does not utter a sound. I expected that. Boys are harder to scare.

The apartment door opens, flooding the small room with light from the hallway. A young boy steps cautiously into the doorway of the room, glancing around suspiciously with slanted, probing eyes. He is younger than I expected, maybe 14 at the most. His puberty-ridden body is thin, with the tiniest hint of muscles that will undoubtedly pop up as he ages. His face is pimpled, his dark hair disheveled, and his face is amazingly handsome for a youth.

He will most likely be a heartbreaker when he finally fills out.

"Josh, is that you in here messing with us? I told you guys to stay downstairs and give us some privacy," The boy says bravely, but I heard the slightest inflection of fear in his voice.

His hand fumbles along the side wall, no doubt searching for a light switch.

"Come on, man, this ain't funny no more," The boy says, and I can undeniably hear the anxiety in his tone this time.

"Danny?" the girl says from the hallway. Her pitch is uncertain and cautious as she steps slowly into the still-dark room behind him. "Do you see anyone?"

He looks behind the door, then around the room one more time before turning to look over his shoulder at the girl.

"No," The boy answers. "It was probably just the wind from that broken win…"

"GET OUT," I interrupt loudly, disguising my voice as deep and scary as possible. I cup one hand around my mouth and place it as close to the slats of the closet door as I can to make my voice echo through the room. I hold the closet door closed with my other hand, just in case one of them is brave enough to investigate.

Neither of them says anything as they stand, frozen in place at the doorway with wide, terror-filled eyes. I slap a hand over my mouth to stifle a giggle as I watch through the slats.

"D…d…Danny?" The girl squeaks. "Let's get outta here, please."

Danny backs out of the door with the girl clutching his shoulder and moving with him.

"Yeah, let's go back outside with the others," He says shakily.

I cup my hands around my mouth again and shout, "GET OUT," one more time, this time louder and adding, "ALL OF YOU."

The girl lets out a high-pitched scream, turns, and runs out the door. Danny screams almost as high-pitched as the girl and follows. Laughter bubbles in my chest, and I wait until I am sure the kids are out of earshot before I bust out of the closet, bent over in heaving laughter.

I laugh so hard that my eyes water and my stomach hurts. My boots lie on the floor in front of me. I am bent over with my hands on my knees, and my knees are slightly bent as I laugh at my own antics. I am no longer paying attention to the still-open door.

That is until a voice calls out from the doorway.

"Does scaring kids amuse you that much?" the intensely masculine, smoothly sexy voice asks.

My laughter fades as I rise to stand, holding my aching stomach as I shoot a questioning look at the door.

That voice was way too deep and masculine to be a teenager.

I clear my throat and wipe the moisture from my eyes with my fingertips. My breath catches in my throat when I see the man standing in the doorway, the light from the hallway almost blocked out by his huge frame.

How does he even fit in the doorway?

He turns on the light, and I blink as my eyes adjust to the sudden brightness.

His broad chest and shoulders are the first thing I notice. His suit jacket is bursting at the seams from all that muscle. I can see the hint of tattoos peeking out from the collar of his button-up shirt, just above the knot of his red tie, which is only a few shades lighter than his hair.

It is cut in a pompadour style and shaved on the sides with lined designs. The dark, brick-red color stands out against the man's tanned skin and bright green eyes, the color of sparkling emeralds.

The red color of his hair is natural unless he has dyed his strong brows the same color. They arch humorously over round eyes, emphasizing the balled eyebrow ring in his right brow. His straight, strong nose sports a looped, silver-colored septum that matches the stud in his brow. Strong cheekbones, a powerfully massive jawline, and a rounded chin complete his extremely handsome face. A neatly trimmed goatee and thin mustache the same color as his hair and brows polish it all off nicely.

My eyes save the best feature for last, which is the sensual, kissable lips that are framed by all that sexy, goateed goodness. My tongue darts out, running across my own lips as the strongest urge to kiss those lips and run my tongue over the silver lip ring on the right side curls through my mind.

A shiver runs through me as I imagine the tickling sensation of his mustache and goatee running lightly over my skin as he kisses me passionately.

My fingertips ache to run through all that magnificent red hair, and my palms long to feel the smooth hardness of all that glorious muscle underneath the suit and tie as I trace the lines of his glorious tattoos.

I blink several times to clear my vision, wondering if my sleep-starved brain just sent me an illusion of the sexiest man on earth. It has been a while since I have had a sexual encounter, so it is a possibility.

"I'm sorry," He says when I continue to stare open-mouthed instead of answering him. "I did not mean to startle you, even though you scared those poor kids witless."

8

He crosses his massive arms over his even more massive chest, chuckling as he leans against the doorframe, looking sexy and luscious. The erotic sound of his voice enters my ears, shooting tendrils of delight through my shattered nerves.

Nope. He is definitely real.

And sensually dangerous.

I shake my head to clear it, clearing my throat and snapping my mouth shut as I step forward and pick up my boots.

I put on my best annoyed tone as I finally answer, "Not that it is any of your business, but those kids broke in and caused a nuisance. Since I have not had a chance to clean the place properly, it is dangerous. I don't want to be held liable for a bunch of trouble-making kids getting hurt, so I was hoping to scare them away for good."

He quirks one dark red brow and says, "Well, I think that might have done the trick."

I put on one boot, hopping to keep my balance as I say, "Can I help you with something, or do you always trespass on private property and stick your nose in business that does not concern you?"

His brow remains quirked as the corners of his succulent mouth rise. His deep, sensual tone sends sparks of desire through my veins as he answers, "Your cousin, Sophia, sent me here. She said you were the best financial advisor in town and were considering starting a business here. I was hoping you would give me a job. I'm a decent accountant."

With one shoe successfully returned to my foot, I pull the other one on as I intelligently answer, "Oh."

He stands patiently for a moment, waiting for me to get my other shoe on and stand back up straight before responding with a sultry smirk, "Is that all you are going to say?"

Was that all I was going to say? What the hell is wrong with me? Is it being sleep-deprived or sex deprived that has me acting with the intelligence of a clam? I take a deep, steadying breath and pull myself together, shaking off the evasive thoughts of imagining what this man looks like naked.

"I am sorry, Mister…?"

"Maleck. Deklan Maleck," he answers.

God damn, even his name evokes sensual thoughts. The image of me, under all that muscle, screaming that sexy name…

Don't stop, Deklan…oh God, Deklan…fuck me, Deklan…

While he pounds his massive cock into me hard and fast and…
STOP IT!

I push those thoughts aside as I step closer and try to hide my nervousness, extending my hand for a shake and saying, "Nice to meet you, Mr. Maleck. I am Mia Dominquez-Garcia."

"Mia, what a beautiful name," Deklan replies as he grasps my hand and shakes it softly.

My knees weaken at his touch when he grasps my hand. His skin is like silk. The touch of his hand is heavenly, shooting sparks of intense longing through my entire body. It stimulates thoughts of how those sensually soft hands would feel running all over my naked body.

I jerk my hand back, wiping it on my shirt as if I can clean off the desire flowing through me.

I clear my throat, trying to keep my voice steady as I say, "I am sorry for my rudeness earlier. My office is nowhere near ready to be open yet if I even open it at all. I have not decided whether or not I am staying in Kentucky."

Deklan's smirk fades into disappointment. "So, you may be leaving soon?"

"Maybe. I need some time to wrap up some things, decide if I am staying, and get this office ready if I do stay," I answer with an apologetic smile. "However, if you still need a job in a month, please come back by and check. I will be happy to help you then."

Deklan nods as he runs a hand through that sexy knot of hair on the top of his head, smoothing it back as he says, "That's too bad. I was looking forward to working with you."

"I'm sorry," I say apologetically, holding my smile in place.

"It is quite alright, Mia Dominquez-Garcia." My name rolls off his tongue, toe-curlingly dark and seductive, like forbidden dark chocolate coating the sweetest sensual strawberry.

I shudder at the sensation as he continues to speak.

"I am disappointed, but I understand. Maybe I will see you in a month." He offers me another knee-weakening smile, and my panties instantly moisten.

Without another word, he turns and walks out the door.

My eyes catch a glimpse of his ass, round and firm and downright dreamy in his black dress slacks. I almost like the view from behind as much as the front.

Almost.

It's too bad I won't be seeing it anymore, but I do not need that kind of distraction in my life right now.

But, damn, it would be an incredibly pleasurable distraction.

CHAPTER 2: DEKLAN

Sophia is in big trouble when I get my hands on her. I need to be close to Mia now, not a month from now. She failed to mention that Mia might not even be staying in Kentucky. And she certainly did not tell me how absolutely fucking sexy and distracting Mia Dominquez-Garcia is.

Sophia is a beautiful woman, so I should have expected her cousin to be as well. But I did not expect Mia to set my loins on fire with a flame so hot that a thousand cold showers won't make my dick go down.

Those fucking, sultry chocolate-brown eyes set in a heart-shaped face stared into my soul. Her full lips begged to be kissed while her round hips called out for me to grab them in my large hands, digging my fingers in while I fuck her. The long, silky-looking black hair that cascaded down her back and shoulders beseeched me to grab it, balling it into my fist while I lavished her dark brown skin with my mouth and tongue.

The entire time I spoke to Mia, I was envisioning her laid out naked and tied up on my bed while I fucked her hard until she screamed my name. Watching her bounce around in that short skirt while she had put her boots back on had not helped matters in the slightest. The fantasies stick in my mind and refuse to go away.

Fuck this God damned human body. I'm gonna have to jack off to get rid of this fucking erection.

Or go back into that room and just take her.

Hell no. I can't do that. I am not going to fuck up this assignment, even if she does make me want to sell what is left of my fallen, broken soul to Lucifer himself if only she would let me fuck her one time.

I could just give her a good fuck and be done with it, but I have a feeling that it wouldn't be that simple with Mia Dominquez-Garcia. The way my loins cry out for a taste of her is nothing like I have experienced before. She would get under my skin, and I don't need the distraction right now.

I may as well just keep to myself and continue to seek random pussy when I feel horny. I just have to put those thoughts of Mia out of my mind and concentrate on finding another way to watch her so I can, hopefully, pay my debt back to Sophia and Harper.

I was supposed to have helped Harper with his inner demon when I first arrived in this dimension. He had been my very first assignment. But instead of helping him, I spent most of my time drunk and out of my head.

That was a dark time for me. I had just been sent down here, assigned to be the leader of a bunch of fallen souls who just want to earn their exoneration and return home.

However, when I finally got my shit together, Harper had already made peace with his inner demon on his own. The Powers That Be had failed to tell me he was a witch and was capable of handling demons with spells and incantations. And not only had he tamed his demon, but he was helping others tame theirs. One of those people was Sophia, who I helped him with whenever I wasn't drunk.

Eventually, I got clean and was put on probation, and The Powers That Be started to employ witches to work with the Fallen Angels. Since Harper had done such a superb job with his demon and helping other people, he was assigned as the Children of the Mystic Moon Coven's leader, the coven that worked with the fallen angels.

Despite being still under probation, I remain the leader of the fallen angels, so I work closely with Harper. In addition to being my closest friend, he had also offered me and some of the other fallen angels jobs as guards or nurses' assistants at his new facility. I still work there, and I help him and Sophia. It keeps me out of trouble.

But now Harper is trapped in the Demon Dimension because he fell in love with her and gave himself up to save her from Jeremy, a twisted person who used his inner demon for evil deeds because he had no angel to help him. I had dropped the ball big time. My assignment was stuck in the Demon Dimension, and another poor soul was not given an angel because I was too drunk to notice that he even had a demon.

And now he and his demon are dead.

I have had two assignments since then, which I completed in record time. My confidence is slowly being restored. Then, Sophia personally asked me to help Mia, her cousin. How could I refuse when I was responsible for Harper getting stuck in the Demon Dimension in the first place? However, after meeting Mia, I am not sure I can take this one. It has not gone all that great so far.

Sophia gave me a way to get in touch with Mia so I could begin to get to know her, but how the hell am I supposed to concentrate on helping her with her demon when all I want to do is take her to bed?

I am pulled from my thoughts when I reach the overrun courtyard of the old building and notice the teenagers gathered in a huddled circle, whispering and pointing toward the doors I had just come out of. One of them spots me as I come out.

"Hey, mister. Were you in there just now making noises and yelling at us to leave?" He asks.

I frown, putting on my best angry face as I answer, "No, and you shouldn't be poking around inside that building. That's private property."

"Yeah, private for the fucking ghosts," One of the other boys says with a snicker.

I point my finger, speaking sternly as I say, "Watch your mouth, kid. Go home, all of you."

I puff out my chest to look threatening, like when I'm working at the hospital and a patient becomes unruly.

"You can't tell us what to do," The first boy says, but they are already scrambling to get on their bikes.

"Yeah, we don't have to go home if we don't want to," The other boy says as he jumps on his bike and pedals away quickly.

The rest of the kids follow suit, leaving me shaking my head with a chuckle. Just like all teens, they can talk the talk but can't walk the walk.

Not that I would have done anything to them anyway. I don't hurt kids. Or let anyone else hurt them.

I walk down the sidewalk to my own bike, but I don't have to pedal mine. It runs on gas. I start it up and rev the engine several times, enjoying the feel of the rumbling machine under me. I glance up at the building again, thinking of something else I'd like to have under me.

Or on top of me.

Or on her knees in front of me.

I speed off, heading back to the hospital where I am currently living. I opted out of wearing my helmet. I allow the wind to whip through my hair as I ride, clearing my head of Mia fucking Garcia.

When I reach the hospital, my hair is beyond repair until I wash it, and my suit is wrinkled and dusty. Good thing it wasn't an expensive one. It was a waste of time to wear a suit anyway. Soph seemed to think it would impress Mia, but Mia didn't even give me a second glance.

I pull at the knot, loosening the tie and pulling it over my head. I unbutton the top button of my shirt as I stroll through the Victorian mansion-turned-hospital's grandiose reception area.

The used-to-be-foyer is cheery and bright. Comfortable modern furniture is placed strategically throughout the room. A large reception desk takes up most of the right side of the room, and there is a locked door behind the desk that leads into the turret where Sophia's private living quarters are located.

An arched doorway on the right wall beside the desk has signs that say 'kitchen and cafeteria' and 'classrooms'. Another arched doorway on the opposite side of the room has a sign that says 'living areas'.

A grandiose staircase takes up the back wall, with an open landing, cherry-colored wood railings, and a floor sign that sits beside the staircase. It reads, 'office space' in big, bold letters, but I know it is more than just office space.

My room is up there, along with the rooms of the three other guards who are fellow fallen angels, and a triple-locked, secured, private room that Soph often occupies when not attending to hospital business. Soph is speaking with Nurse Cora about something when I come up to the desk. Nurse Cora turns her blue eyes to me, tossing her blond hair over her shoulders as she gives me her full attention. Soph quirks a dark eyebrow at me as she stares questioningly with her almost-black eyes.

"Well, how did it go, Hulk Number One?" she asks.

That was her nickname for me. When she first came to this facility, she had an 'encounter' with me and the three other security guards. She called us hulks because of our size. She numbered us one through four; I was lucky enough to be number one.

"You didn't tell me she was thinking about leaving," I snarl. "She practically shooed me out the door."

Soph raises her eyebrows in confusion. "I didn't know she was thinking of leaving. I thought she was moving here with Uncle Vinny. Did you tell her I sent you?"

"Yes, and that did not seem to matter to her. She told me to return in a month after she had time to think of her next move." I run my hand through my hair, hoping to smooth out the mess. "I can't wait an entire month to start the assignment. It may already be too late by then."

"Hmm," Soph says thoughtfully and then turns to Cora. "Didn't you say that Clark mentioned he needed help at the bank yesterday?"

"Oh, yeah," Cora says, turning to Soph. "When I went to deposit my paycheck, he said that one of his tellers quit. They moved back to Florida to take care of their mom. Clark seemed quite desperate to replace him quickly. As it turns out, the person who quit is the one who handles the accounts for the restaurant."

"What a coincidence. It's a good thing Clark owes me a favor," Soph says with a smile. "His sister is a patient here. I comped her stay since Clark's money went to paying her court fees, fines, and restitution after she ran through that building with no insurance when she was drunk."

"Yeah, that's a pretty big debt. This hospital isn't cheap," Cora quips. "So Clark owes you a big favor."

"I guess I'll be working for the bank then?" I ask sarcastically, tossing the tie on the desk so I can shrug out of my suit jacket.

"Can't you wait until you get back to your room to get undressed?" Soph asks.

Nurse Cora chuffs. "You can get undressed here. I don't mind." She smiles slyly before adding, "Although you better get used to that suit and tie if you're gonna work at the bank."

"Yes, get used to the suit," Soph responds, shooting Cora an exasperated look before turning back to me. "Particularly since you will be in charge of my…er…Vinny's restaurant accounts. The same accounts that Mia manages."

"You are devious sometimes, you know that, Soph?" I say to her, ignoring Cora's sly comment. "No wonder you were able to tame an inner demon so easily."

Sophia winks one dark brown eye as she says, "I had good teachers."

I wave her comment away draping my suit jacket over one arm and heading for the staircase. Harper had been her teacher for most of it; I had stepped in later.

"See you later, handsome hulk," Nurse Cora drawls as I make my way up the staircase.

That woman has been flirting with me since I started working here. Maybe I should take her up on her offer. It would certainly help with the not-so-subtle bulge in my pants, caused by thoughts of Mia and hidden by the suit jacket. That was the real reason I took it off.

How the hell my dick can still be throbbingly hard after all this time is beyond me. I hope the cold shower I plan on taking when I get to my room helps.

I take a second glance when I reach the second-floor landing. Cora stares up at me with sultry blue eyes, and she waves with a wiggle of her fingers when she sees me glance down at her. She tosses her wavy, silky blond locks over her shoulder and turns away.

I scoff contemptuously. Cora sure is full of herself, but she is nice enough. Still, she's not my cup of tea. I don't like women who are conceited, and I don't like blonds.

Maybe I won't be easing my libido with her after all, especially since my cock goes a bit softer at the thought of Cora naked. So, I picture her naked on purpose to tame the monster in my pants. It seems to work, and I breathe a little easier as I finally reach my room.

I cast the thought of Cora from my mind, shuddering at the image of the blond hair that would cover her mound if she were a natural blonde. I imagine her pussy would be nicely trimmed or even shaved, knowing how prissy Cora is.

I don't like that either. I like hair; even a light sprinkling is better than none at all. A woman should have hair. Course, tickling my nose when I lick her delicious pussy, and not blonde either.

I like a darker, more exotic look.

Like Mia.

I wonder what her pussy is like? Probably beautiful, delicious, tight, wet…

Fuck. There goes my dick again.

If I don't get that woman off my brain, I will have to learn how to perpetually live with a hard-on.

Particularly since the cold shower does not help and I have to go to my bed rock-hard. How am I ever going to get any sleep like this?

CHAPTER 3: DEKLAN

I look in the mirror with wide, surprised, emerald eyes. Sophia is a fucking genius when it comes to makeovers. My usual pompadour is styled into a long shag, parted over the side, and combed neatly. My neck tattoos are covered with special make-up so that none shows over my shirt collar.

All of my piercings are gone. My nose ring, eyebrow ring, and lip ring are gone, with the holes made less noticeable by some trick of the light Sophia created with her talent for contouring.

The only piercings that remain are my earrings, which are gauged and hard to disguise. They are not overwhelmingly large, but big enough that I cannot cover them. However, the black, simple tunnel plugs she placed in the holes are stylish enough not to detract from my professional look.

I actually look like a bank teller.

I smile softly at my reflection. I look rather dashing. I wonder if Mia will like it. I sigh and mentally punch myself in the fucking face. Stop thinking about Mia! Think about something else, like the fact that the color of my tie is all wrong. I fiddle with the red tie and cringe at the contrast between it and my dark red hair.

"Don't you have any other color tie?" I ask Sophia.

She is standing at the side of the mirror in the secret, triple-locked room, watching me. Soph never stands in front of mirrors except for when Harper appears, and this would be the mirror he appears in. Hence, the reason for the triple-locked, private room; to hide the elaborately decorated, gilded-framed mirror that is actually a portal to the demon realm for those who can go through it.

She frowns and answers, "I suppose I can lend you one of Harper's. They are in his room in the turret. I'll be right back."

I nod as I pull the knot loose and remove the offending tie. Maybe I will dye my hair a different color. I am picturing myself with auburn hair when the mirror's reflection begins to swirl and change.

I sigh in frustration.

Now is not the time for a visit from the Boss Witch.

"Hi, Boss Witch," I say in a bored tone before Harper can even form. "Sophia just left if you were looking for her."

"I always know where Sophia is, thanks to Jewel and Lucien," Harper says as his form solidifies in the mirror's reflection.

I chuckle knowingly.

Lucien and Jewel are Sophia's inner demons. Jewel belonged to Harper before he got stuck in the Demon Dimension. Now, Jewel is attached to Sophia and bonded to Lucien.

"So you are here to see me, then?" I ask, even though I know the answer.

"Yes, actually. You look rather dashing, by the way," Harper says, and I hear the humor in his tone. "You let Sophia get a hold of you, didn't you?"

I hold my arms out at my sides and turn around. "She does great work."

Harper chuckles. "That she does. However, I didn't come to discuss my future wife's talent for makeovers."

Future wife. I don't know how Sophia is supposed to marry Harper when he now lives in another realm, but I am sure they have something up their sleeves knowing those two.

I sigh as I roll my eyes. "Fine. What do you need from me?"

"I was checking on your progress and telling you that you may want to hurry."

I look into the mirror with a frown. "What do you mean?"

Harper clears his throat. "I mean that her demon is getting stronger. She may not have much longer. It has manifested already, even though she has ignored it. I have had Jewel and Lucien keeping eyes on her, and they told me they saw the demon. Its eyes are turning purple, Deklan."

Fuck…

The color of an inner demon's eyes says a lot. The first color of any demon is red. Red means that the demon is newly formed and untrained. Then, the color can go two ways from there.

If the demon's eyes change to shades of purple, that is a bad sign. That means that the owner does not have complete control over the demon. Most of the time, it is because the owner is immoral, which leads to the demon being evil, too.

Other times, as in Mia's case, it is a sign of insufficient training. The owner either does not know how to tame the demon or ignores it entirely because they do not know about it or do not want to face their inner demons.

However, this situation is exceptionally rare since a demon must be trained to gain enough power to manifest to a state that can interact with the living. It means the demon is strong enough to gain power on its own, which is very dangerous to the person carrying the demon.

In this case, the demon could completely take over the owner, sending the person's soul to the deepest corner of their mind. I swallow hard, thinking of Mia having to live in darkness for eternity.

"So, you're saying Mia is in danger?" I say, my voice catching in my throat.

Harper nods. "Yes, that is exactly what I am saying. And your soul is in danger, too."

Double Fuck…

"What do you mean?" I ask as tension soars through my body. "What have you heard?"

"The Powers That Be found out that you took Mia on yourself as a favor to Sophia. They have told me that if you fuck this one up, then your soul is forfeit and will be sent to oblivion. In simple terms, you will no longer exist.

"You have maybe three months before her demon takes over, and then it is over for the both of you. If that happens, they will start looking for new leaders.

"Deklan, you have to succeed. It isn't just about us losing our leadership. I don't want to see my friend wiped from existence."

Triple fuck. Son of a bitch, I am running out of fucks.

"Let's hope Sophia's plan works, then," I say around the lump in my throat.

"Three months?" a broken female voice says from behind me.

Harper and I both startle.

Sophia steps out from behind me, hands me a blue tie, and moves to the mirror, placing her hand on its surface as she draws shaky breaths. Harper places his hand on the mirror where Sophia's hand rests.

"Don't worry, baby girl. Have faith in Deklan. I have faith in him."

Pride and sadness flash through me as I loop the tie around my neck. I don't deserve such a compliment from Harper. As I tie it expertly, I clear my throat and school my features to hide my jumbled emotions.

I place a hand on Sophia's shoulder and say comfortingly, "Don't worry, Soph. This will work."

Sophia's eyes dart between Harper's and my reflections as she says, "It's not Deklan's abilities I'm worried about. It's Mia. When I told her about my inner demons and all I had endured after being sent away, she told me to get my act together. She didn't believe a word of it.

"She's very…tied to reality. She has no imagination, and getting her to believe in anything is hard. You will never get her to believe in inner demons and fallen angels."

"You mean she's stubborn like you?" Harper says affectionately.

Sophia scoffs. "That's different. I had you to convince me, and you are very convincing."

Harper smiles, and I make a retching sound. "You two are making me sick."

Sophia turns and slaps my shoulder playfully. "Shut up, Hulk. One day, some girl will come into your life and strip all that hardness right out of you."

"Hey, are you saying I'm soft now?" Harper asks.

"Oh no, baby. You are very hard when it counts," Sophia drawls, turning to the mirror with a seductive waggle of her eyebrows.

"Alright, that's it. I'm leaving," I say.

"Wait," Harper says. "We need to discuss a plan of action before you leave."

"I promise we will behave," Sophia adds.

I sigh.

Gods, they are insufferable when they are together.

"Fine. Make it quick," I say, crossing my arms over my chest and leaning against the wall.

Thirty minutes and several sexual innuendos later, even though Soph had promised to be good, I turned and hurried out of the room, leaving her and Harper to their machinations. At least Harper can only appear in the mirrors since he is stuck in the Demon Dimension, else I would be worried about my sheets.

I take my car instead of my bike since I don't want to mess up the hairstyle Sophia has worked so hard on. It is a nice enough ride, even if it isn't a motorcycle. I open the door to my little red sports car and squeeze inside.

I got to the Daisville National Bank in time for my interview with fifteen minutes to spare, even though I thought I would be late. I don't know why I need a damn interview if I already know I am getting the job, but Clark says it is part of the hiring process, so here we are.

I sit in the conference room, waiting for Clark to come in for my interview. My mind wanders, thinking of the nerve-wracking time when I will have to see Mia again. Harper has no idea how much his plan has my emotions scrambled. It will undoubtedly be loads of fun as long as I can keep myself from becoming obsessed.

I am in the process of adjusting my crotch just thinking about it, when the object of my semi-erection walks by. She doesn't see me as she walks by the glass-walled room, but I certainly see her.

My cock throbs.

She keeps her chocolate-brown eyes straight ahead as her shapely legs move in a confident stride, her black high-heeled boots clacking along the tiled floors. Her profile is perfection, with high cheekbones, a small straight nose, pouty lips, and a perfect chin. Her straight, long, black hair hangs down her back, and wisps of it flow behind her as she walks.

Her perfectly round ass sways just right in her short, black pencil skirt as she strides by. Her perky breasts jut out from her silky blue blouse as she walks with her shoulders back in a confident stance. She holds a stack of papers tucked to the side under one elbow. The other arm swings loosely at her side.

I frown as I realize that is the same outfit she wore yesterday when she scared those kids out of her building. Had she not slept last night? Or showered? Or changed clothes…

Shit, I should not have thought about her changing clothes or taking a shower.

Son of a bitch…

I swallow hard as my mind goes crazy with the need to see all that luscious nakedness, water streaming down that perfect body, dripping off of perky nipples.

This will be the most distracting assignment, and if the way my human body responds to her is any indication, my human heart is in major trouble.

Oh, and let's not forget about the fact that my soul is in danger as well.

I am running out of fucking time…

CHAPTER 4: MIA

I hate coming to the bank. The lines are horrible, the staff is wretchedly over-friendly, and the air is stuffy from the crowd breathing all the air. I was not made for being inside a bank.

I hurry past the tellers and down the hallway to Joseph's room, hoping to avoid the afternoon crowd. I just need these papers filed for my Dad's restaurant account immediately. I had stayed up all night to get them done after my stupid mistake, and I am ready to drop.

I need a shower and a bed, stat. Even though I probably will not sleep. My nightmares always keep me from sleep.

Which is probably why I am hallucinating about the sexiest man on Earth again. That, plus the fact that I fantasized about him all night, made it hard to concentrate on my work.

Which is why it took me all night in the first place.

Nevertheless, there he sits in the conference room, looking all delectable in his black suit jacket, white dress shirt, and blue tie. I can see him out of the corner of my eye as I walk by the room, but I do not turn my attention to him. I pretend I do not see him, even though I can feel his eyes on me. If I turn to look, I will feel obligated to go in and say hi.

Nope.

I do not want to face the object of last night's fantasy, especially since he looks extra appealing today with the new hairdo. No, it would be better to keep walking and pretend I do not see him with his piercings gone and his face clean, looking extra sexy.

It would be simpler not to notice his new blue tie and the way it accentuates the green of his eyes, making them seem almost turquoise. It would be easier to pretend I don't see how stimulating his clean neck looks, even though I also like the tattoos.

I do not want to remember how I imagined those muscled arms holding me close with his luscious lips pressed against mine. I do not need to think about what his mouth would feel like if he kissed down my neck. It would be dangerous to envision his hands sliding along my naked skin as I lay beneath him. And I certainly do not want to recall my fantasy of his cock penetrating my pussy, stretching and filling me as I writhe underneath him and scream out his exotically stimulating name.

Nope, I do not need that at all.

"Mia?" The darkly sensual voice drifts into the hallway as I walk by the open door.

Dammit.

I had almost gotten past it.

I plaster on a smile and turn toward the room.

"Oh, hello, Mister...?" I respond, pretending to forget his name.

Honestly, I just want to hear him repeat it. It sounds so sensual coming from his mouth, almost as sensual as when he says my name.

"Maleck. Deklan Maleck," he says, and my heart stutters.

I keep my voice as boringly casual as possible as I answer, "Oh, yes, Mister Maleck. The man who can't keep his nose in his own business and rudely calls women he does not know well by their first names."

Deklan smirks and rises from his seat. "Yes, that's right. And you are the scary child abuser who doesn't even know if she is staying in Kentucky and who doesn't know mutual instant attraction when she sees it."

I gasp at his audacity. How rude.

Even though it is true.

And how utterly seductive to hear that he finds me attractive as well.

I scoff as if offended, looking him up and down with mock disgust.

Holy shit. The suit he wears today fits better than yesterday's, showing every cut of his muscled body under the suit. His hair seems darker today, parted to the side and hanging down on his face. His green eyes sparkle with mischievousness as he smiles seductively at me.

I swallow the lump in my throat and try to sound insulted as I respond, "First of all, you are not my type. Secondly, those children do not need to be hanging around a spooky abandoned building anyway, and I am sorry that I have a life in Phoenix that I need to get back to."

"Firstly, you're a bad liar, Mia," he accentuates my name, making my pussy walls throb.

"Secondly, Phoenix, huh? What is so exciting in Phoenix that could keep you away from here?" He asks with that fuck-me-now smile.

My fingers itch to smack that smile off his face.

Or maybe they are itching to run through that silky-looking mess of hair. I am confused as to which itch to scratch.

I ball my hands into fists to keep from doing either of those things.

"Oh, I don't know, Mister Maleck," I retort, putting just as much emphasis on his name. "My house, my company, my friends, just to name a few."

"I noticed you didn't mention a boyfriend," Deklan says.

I fold my arms over my chest, careful not to drop the papers I worked so hard on last night.

"That is absolutely none of your business, Mister Maleck," I answer sternly.

"I'll pick you up at seven this evening since you don't have a boyfriend," He says with a shrug.

Did he just order me to go out with him?

"Now, hold on a minute. You can't just…," I start, but Clark, the bank president, enters the room from a side door and interrupts me.

His attention is focused solely on Deklan when he enters the room, so he does not see me standing in the opposite doorway.

"Mister Maleck, I presume," He says, holding his hand out to Deklan.

"You must be Clark," Deklan says, shaking the offered hand. "It is a pleasure to meet you. Soph has told me a lot about you."

Soph? Deklan has a nickname for my cousin?

"All good things, I hope," Clark says with a chuckle as he smooths his hands down his suit jacket, a nervous tell he has had since I have known him. He pushes his spectacles up his straight nose, another nervous tell.

I am wondering what Clark has to be so nervous about when he suddenly realizes I am standing in the doorway to the hall. "Oh, hello, Miss Garcia," Clark says to me, then frowns. "Are you here with Mister Maleck?"

"Absolutely not," I answer a bit too forcefully.

Clark's frown deepens as his gray eyes flick between Deklan and me in confusion. He runs a hand over his blond hair, smoothing his cowlick down into place.

I clear my throat and answer in a calmer tone. "I was just passing by and stopped to say hello. I met Mister Maleck yesterday when he stopped by my building."

Clark's frown melts away with my explanation. "Oh, I see. Well, I am glad you two have met. Mister Maleck here will be taking over the La Hacienda account."

I frown. "The restaurant? But that's Joseph's account. I was just about to bring him this month's revenue. I just finished the report last night."

"Ah, yes. I am sorry to say that Joseph left us quite suddenly. His father fell ill in Florida, and he moved there to care for him," Clark explains as he pushes his wire-rimmed spectacles up his nose.

"I guess we'll be working together after all," Deklan says, that stupid smirk still on his face. "I'll see you at seven tonight."

"No…but you…I can't…," I sputter, but Deklan turns and follows Clark out of the room and down the hallway before I can spit out anything.

The fucking nerve of that man. Does he think he can just order me to go on a date with him? Who does he think he is? I'll show him. I will not be ready at seven or at any time after, for that matter.

I start to turn and stomp down the hallway in the opposite direction, but then I realize I am still carrying the damn papers under my arm that I was supposed to deliver to Joseph.

Sighing defeatedly, I turn back and walk down the hallway toward the office that used to be Joseph's. The maintenance man is already taking the nameplate off the door. I wait until he is done, which only takes a few minutes, and then I knock on the door.

"Yes? I am in a meeting," Clark's voice calls out through the half-open door.

"I'm sorry, Clark. It's Mia again," I call out through the crack. "I forgot to give you the revenue report for La Hacienda."

"Ah, yes," Clark says from inside the room. "You can give the file to Mister Maleck. He will be taking over your father's account."

The door opens, and Deklan stands in the doorway. He looks down at me, literally since he is about a foot taller, and smiles seductively.

"Couldn't stay away?" He asks in a whispered tone.

"I just need to give you this report," I answer through gritted teeth, shoving the stack of papers toward him. "And I am not going out with you tonight."

"Thank you," He answers with a smug smile as he jerks the papers from my hand. "And, yes, you are. Be ready at seven if you don't want me to punish you. Also, call me Deklan, or the punishment will be worse."

I sputter a curse, but the door blocks the sound as he pulls his bulk of a frame back into the room and shuts the door in my face. I ball my hands into fists at my side and make a frustrated sound through clenched teeth. I look around to see if anyone heard my tantrum before stomping down the hallway toward the central area of the bank.

I am livid by the time I reach the bathroom, and I slam the stall door as I go into one of the stalls.

Fuck him and his orders. I don't care how mouthwateringly erogenous he is. I will not let him treat me like some kind of whore that he can just order to go on a date with him or be punished.

Of course, being punished by him might not be such a bad thing. I can just imagine those massive hands cupping my ass, leaving the cheeks red as he smacks each one. Maybe he could shove a finger inside my pussy while he spanks me…

NO…

ABSOLUTELY NOT…

God dammit I need to get this man out of my head, and going out on a date with him is totally not the way to do that. I just need to go home, shower, and climb into my soft, warm bed.

Yes, that is what I will do.

Maybe I will even get some sleep.

I finish my business in the restroom and head out the door. My building is only two blocks away, so I head in that direction on foot as I ponder Deklan being in charge of the restaurant's financial accounts. He must be good at his job if he has enough skills to work in a bank and manage large accounts.

Come to think of it, he must be good if my cousin sent him to me for a job. I regret not hiring him now. At least I would have been able to have some control over whether I had to interact with him or not if he had been working for me.

Now, I have no choice.

He seems to know Sophia well. I will have to set up a lunch date with her and ask her about him. Strictly for business purposes, of course, since I will be working with him on Dad's account.

It has nothing to do with wanting to know him more.

When I get to my building, I notice a couple of bikes leaning up against the brick siding. I sigh in annoyance. I will lose it if I run into those kids on my way to my apartment. Fortunately, no kids were found, so I let it go this time. Let their parents deal with them.

I unlock the door to my apartment, turn the lights on, and enter my living room. I'm just about to settle in when my office a few doors down beacons me. There are a few more things to settle before I can completely relax, so I may as well get it over with.

Besides, I tell myself glancing at the clock on my living room wall, I will mess up my sleep schedule if I go to bed too early. It's only two in the afternoon. I have already messed it up by missing an entire night, so I need to stay awake for at least a little while to fix it.

I walk the short way down the hallway to my office, settle at the desk, and get to work. It takes a few hours of crunching numbers on several files before my eyes start to drift shut, and I can no longer focus. I get up, fix a cup of coffee at the coffee station I put up in the office, and then get to it again.

Finally, my body starts aching all over, and I decide that I need to stop for the day. I stand from my desk and languidly stretch out my muscles. I smirk victoriously when I realize that I had not thought of Deklan Maleck even once while I had been working. See? I can go a long time without thinking about him. It won't be hard to completely forget him.

Until I turn in more work for the restaurant at the bank.

I shrug the thought away. I will deal with that when the time comes. I stroll back to my apartment, glancing toward my bedroom as my bathroom shower calls my name. The clock on my bedside table reads six-thirty, but I decide it is late enough to shower and go to bed. I rummage through my drawers and find a gown and panties as I fantasize about the new rain fixture I had installed in my shower last week.

I carry my clothes to the bathroom, turn on the hot water, pull a towel out of the linen closet, and undress. I am as naked as the day I was born when the noises start. Footsteps running up and down the halls, squealing screams and laughter, and doors slamming shut or against walls as they are flung open ring through my bathroom, coalescing into one cacophony of sound.

That's it.

I am taking care of this problem once and for all.

I wrap the big fluffy towel around me that I had pulled out earlier, glancing longingly back at the hot, steamy water cascading from the rain fixture. I open the door to my bathroom, which I hate doing when the hot water is on. I like the bathroom to get all steamy and warm so that I don't freeze my ass off when I get out of the shower.

Steam rolls out the door as I stomp over to my bedside table where I had left my cell phone. I dial the number to the local police station. Good thing I had put the number on my speed dial after buying this place. One can never be too careful when dealing with old buildings.

I tell the lady who answers the phone my problem, and she promises to send someone out to investigate. With that problem solved, I shut myself back inside my bathroom, fold the towel back onto the sink, and step into the hot, heavenly, absolutely luxurious water.

This is what I needed.

I bask in the sensations of the flowing water as it cascades over me from the shower head before me and the rain fixture over my head. The curling tendrils of steam caress my naked skin, seemingly as if they are alive. The steam fills the shower, and I breathe in the heated air, filling my lungs so completely that it is almost stifling.

But I like it.

I am so engrossed in my shower that I fail to detect the tendrils of steam subtly wrapping around me. I do not notice when their hold tightens ever so slightly. The sensation does not capture my attention until it is too late, and I am wrapped up in hot, snake-like, filmy limbs of steam so tightly that I can no longer move.

My arms are trapped over my chest where I had been holding them as I enjoyed the heat of the water. My wrists are crossed over one another, and my elbows are lowered to my sides. My breasts stand up over the framing of my forearms, the nipples hardened by the water that flows over them.

My heart flutters in my chest at the awareness that I am effectively trapped, and my breathing kicks up a notch.

What the fuck?

I struggle against the surprisingly strong hold of…well, nothing…there is nothing there but puffs of steam curling around me and holding me in place. I strain to move my arms to no avail, and I step to the back of my shower as I start to feel suffocated by the heat instead of soothed.

My foot slips on the wet tiles, and I feel myself falling. But I cannot catch myself. I am helpless. My head comes dangerously close to the hard, tiled wall when I feel arms catch me and bring me back upright.

The freezing, arctic cold of those arms run through me, chasing away the heat from the shower and the breath from my lungs. My heart stops for a breath of time, captured in a moment of terror so intense that my throat closes, stealing the scream that had built in my chest.

My eyes are too wide, and my mouth is open in that silent scream as a figure of absolute darkness comes into my full view. This shadow does not play in the periphery of my vision as the shadows around me usually do.

This one is right in front of my face, staring at me with glowing, purplish-blue eyes. Its freezing grasp holds me by the shoulders with its abyss of a mouth open wide, showing an abyss of a hole that threatens to suck me in and trap me forever.

"Hello, Mia," A soft, musical voice floats through my mind. *"You are mine now."*

The breath is suddenly released from my lungs, expelling in a half scream before sucking in a deep, horror-filled breath. My heart pumps wildly against my breasts as I let out a louder scream, and suddenly all goes dark.

The hold on my arms is released, the shadow person disappears, and my arms flail as I feel myself falling. I manage to stay upright somehow, catching myself against the shower walls. The water is still hot and steamy, streaming over me as I blink rapidly.

Reality comes back into view as I realize I had fucking fallen asleep, standing up in the damn shower. It was a good thing I had a nightmare that woke me up. God, I need to sleep before I kill my fool self.

I soap up quickly, keeping myself busy so I don't drift off again. I am shampooing my hair when I hear footsteps echoing through the building. They must be close to hear them over the running water.

I think nothing of it, however. The officers are probably gathering up the unruly teenagers. Maybe they will finally stay away. I ignore the sound of the footsteps and turn back to my shower, rinsing the shampoo from my hair.

I quickly massage some leave-in conditioner into my wet hair before turning off the water and opening the shower door a crack to reach for my towel. My bathroom door is suddenly flung open, causing me to jump violently as It crashes against the doorstop with such force that it bends it slightly.

I let out a startled scream and watch in terror as a dark figure enters my bathroom and stalks over to the shower. The shower door opens completely, revealing one large, glaring, terrifyingly angry Deklan

Maleck.

My heart hammers in my chest.

His eyes have darkened to the clearest jade, his cheeks are flushed, blending with the red color of his mustache and goatee, and his carved muscles bulge with tension. The piercings are back, one on his eyebrow and one on the corner of his lower lip. The tattoos stand out over the collar of his shirt in stark contrast to the copper color of his flushed skin.

He is fucking exquisite when he is mad.

"I thought I told you to be ready at seven," He seethes as his flashing jade gaze roves up and down my naked body. "I hope you are prepared for your punishment."

CHAPTER 5: DEKLAN

The sight of Mia standing naked in the shower sets my entire body on fire, especially after the fantasy I had earlier at the bank. But my fantasy did not do the sight of Mia in the shower justice.

The flames lick along my nerves as I take in the perky breasts with beads of water dripping from perfect nipples, staring at me as if begging to be licked and sucked. Her luscious curves beckon me to run my hands over them, feeling the smooth, wet skin. Her plump hips call to me to dig my fingers in the tender flesh, holding them steady as I push my cock between the apex of her thighs, running my shaft between her lips and over her entrance.

My blood heats, boiling in my veins as those thoughts run through my mind. What the Gods has Harper gotten me into with his insane fucking plan? I can barely contain my erection in my jeans.

I am supposed to get her sexually attracted to me, but I am already hooked. Harper seems to think that tons of sexual energy will bring out her demon, and then I will be able to deal with it.

I argued that I didn't have the time to seduce Mia gently, and if I did it my way, I might break her, but Harper seemed to think it was the only way since we were on a time crunch.

Sophia believes Mia doesn't have it in her to fall for anybody. She says Mia has just gotten out of a relationship and isn't ready to settle for another man, so she should be fine with my...let us say...rougher methods.

I failed to tell Harper and Sophia that it wasn't only Mia I was worried about. I have my share of women who would fall at my feet if I gave them a chance, but I never give them a second thought.

But Mia?

Whatever this is that I feel for Mia, it is different somehow. I burn for her more than I have for anyone, even before I fell from the Divine Dimension. I have a feeling that I will never be able to get her out of my head if…no, when…I actually fuck her.

I have to play this very carefully.

I give her my best angry smolder, and then I notice the steamy tendrils floating around her. The tendrils had blended in with the steam from the shower, so I had not noticed them, but now I see them. They are darker than the steam, moving around her seemingly unnoticed, writhing and reaching for Mia.

Fuck no.

There is no more time to be worried about consequences and feelings. I have to get that fucking demon to manifest solidly while I am present, and there isn't much more time if those tendrils are any indication. If the demon manifests while I'm not around…

I must get her away from its reaching tentacles. Seeing them swirling around Mia's tempting form boils the blood in my veins, causing my already present anger to spike dangerously.

I am already angry at Harper for sending me on this fool mission.

I am angry at myself for being so damn stupid over a fucking woman.

And now I find that Mia's fucking demon tried to mess with her before I got here, and it is the fucking demon's fault that I am even here in the first place.

My anger consumes me, and I hang on to that rage, playing the villain as I look Mia up and down salaciously.

She glares at me with those entrancing chocolate eyes, but I ignore her contemptuous look as I reach for her wrists. Electric sparks dance along my fingers when my skin comes into contact with hers, and I hear her audible hiss as my hand closes around her wrist.

She feels it, too.

Her eyes may hold anger, but the flush of her skin and the way she is biting her lower lip tells a different story. She doesn't stand a chance against my punishments and rewards, judging from the look on her face. By the end of this day, she will be putty in my hands, and the demon will be put to sleep, ready to be tamed.

"You are not ready," I drawl in my best sexually charged yet angry voice as I pull her from the shower. "Did you think I was just spouting bullshit? Did you think I wouldn't punish you? I don't make threats I don't carry out, Mia."

Mia tugs at her wrist in an attempt to pull away from me as she screams, "Let me go, you brute! Who the fuck do you think you are, Mister Maleck?"

She had emphasized my name, taunting me as if she wanted her punishment to be worse. She balls her petite hands into fists, lashing out at me with her free hand. I have had mosquito bites that hurt worse. She digs into the tile floor with her heels, which is fruitless since her feet are wet from the shower, and they just slide along the floor.

I pull her into my body, wrapping one arm around her waist as I answer roughly, "I am your fucking salvation, Mia. Now be a good girl and say my name, and I may lighten your punishment."

"Fuck you, asshole!" she yells as she pummels me with her tiny fist.

My hand, the one not wrapped around her waist, still holds one of her wrists, and I catch the other one in that same hand, stopping her strikes. Her wrists are so tiny that I have no problem holding both of them tightly in one of my hands.

I back her into the wall beside the shower and press my body into hers. I pull her arms over her head and trap her wrists against the wall. The feel of her body struggling against me turns my already heated blood into molten lava.

Her cheeks are flushed as I lower my face to hers, breathing across her skin as I whisper, "Fine. If that's how you want it, stay still and take your medicine, Mia."

She shudders against me, hardening my cock as she tries to hold an angry visage. She is not fooling me. I can tell how turned on she is. I can see her speeding pulse in the fluttering skin of her throat, and I can see the rise and fall of her chest with her rapid breathing, bringing attention to her heaving breasts with the hardened nipples. I can see the twitch of her lips when I draw closer as if preparing for me to kiss her.

She wants me, and it makes my dick even harder to think that I have her at my mercy right now. I could do anything to her, but she could do nothing to escape. My gaze darkens on hers as those thoughts run through me, and her eyes widen with fear.

"Let me go!" She demands, and I can hear the quiver in her voice.

"Not until you say my name and then take your punishment for disobeying me," I say darkly as I come closer to those kissable lips.

"What are you going to do to me?" She asks, and her tone is frightened.

But still, she refuses to say my name.

Her fear spikes the desire flowing through me as I trap her against the wall and pull my arm free from around her waist. I then place my hand on her flat, firm stomach. I run my hand up to the underside of her breast, growling deep in my chest at the sensation of her silky-soft, wet skin against my palms.

Her skin is even softer than I imagined it to be.

She shudders again, the skin of her stomach fluttering under my touch. She struggles against me yet leans into my touch at the same time. A whimper of longing tinged with terror escapes her throat and sends a coil of yearning through my soul.

"Please," She squeaks as I graze her nipple with my palm, the bud hardening under my touch.

I smile deviously and respond, "You can beg all you want, Mia. You disobeyed, and you must accept your punishment."

My hand travels even further up until I reach her neck. I curl my large hand around her tiny throat. It fits perfectly as if my hand was made to fit around her neck. I squeeze just a little bit, enough to let her know I could crush her if I wanted to, but not enough to cut off her air supply. She whimpers, and the sound intensifies the yearning running through me.

I am barely hanging on. It is all I can do to keep from turning her around, bending her over, and shoving my cock deep into her core. I have to keep it together, though. I am on a mission right now, and I cannot have my desire to fuck her messing this up.

I have to hold on.

"Deklan, please," Mia squeaks around the hold on her throat, and the sound of my name falling from her lips, begging me, does me in.

"Yes, that's right. Say my name, baby. Such a good girl," I say.

She whimpers again, and it is my undoing. With a needy growl, I capture her lips with mine. Gods, she tastes good. The sensation of her lips against mine is glorious. I have to resist the urge to squeeze even tighter with my hand, which makes the entire experience even more intense.

I move my lips against hers, thrusting my tongue against her mouth, but she denies me entrance. The denial brings me back to myself.

Fuck.

I am supposed to make her want me, not vice versa. Refusing to admit defeat, I play this into my punishment scheme.

I pull away from her lips and growl, "Kiss me, Mia. Kiss me, or the punishment will be worse."

"Fuck you," she rasps, her eyes narrowing as she stares up at me.

38

"I said your name, dammit."

I tighten my hold on her throat just enough to let her know I mean business. She can still breathe, albeit very tightly. I can hear her rasping as she strains to breathe.

"Fine, Mia. Don't say I didn't warn you," I say in a sultry tone.

This is going to be enjoyable. I pull her arms down and release her throat. She takes in gasping, deep breaths as I pull her with me into her bedroom. I am glad I am still wearing the blue tie.

I loosen it and take it off with one hand. Mia struggles against my hold, pulling on her wrists in an attempt to pull away from me. I tighten my grip and pull her into my body once more.

"If you don't stop struggling, you will have bruises on your arms tomorrow," I chastise.

"Then let me go!" She screams, jerking her arms for emphasis.

"Not yet, Mia. You still have to take your punishment," I say roughly, looping the tie around her wrists.

"What are you doing?" She wails as she continues to try and pull her arms away from me.

I get the tie around her wrists and tie it in a firm knot. It was not an easy feat, with her struggling every step of the way. I toss her to the bed angrily when I finally get the knot tied. She lands on her back, bouncing a couple of times before she quickly flops over, slides down until her feet hit the ground, and then tries to run away.

I chuckle as I grab her around the waist before she can get two steps away and sling her back onto the bed. This time, she tries to roll to the other side of the bed and slip away, but I am too fast for her. Still laughing maliciously, I flop down and capture her around the waist again before she can even get off the bed.

I fling her over my knee with her butt in the air and give her a good, firm slap on her naked ass. The slap sounds through the room, mingling with her indignant scream.

She struggles to get away from me, but I hold her firm as I give her another hard slap. Another scream and more struggling, her legs kicking and her tied-together hands flailing. This time, instead of slapping her ass, I run my hand down between her legs and find the lips of her sex.

Her struggles cease, and she freezes.

Yes. That is precisely the response I was looking for. I have her now. The problem is, I have made myself want her even more. The slick feel of her sex has my heart pounding fiercely in my chest, my breathing ragged and hurried, and my dick hard as stone.

But I have her.

I smile deviously as I slide my fingers between her folds and find that bundle of nerves right above her entrance. I swirl my fingers around the sensitive bud, and satisfaction runs through me when I hear her moan of pleasure.

I pull my finger back, finding her entrance and plunging it inside, smiling with pleasure as Mia's hips writhe in my lap.

Mother Fucker she is tight.

And hot.

And soooo wet.

My dick jumps in my pants with longing, and the need to ram my cock inside that heavenly hole almost overwhelms me.

The rest of Mia's body goes limp in my lap as she concedes defeat. Still, her hips continue to writhe against my touch as I fuck her with my finger, one thrust, two, three, then pulling my finger out and torturing her clit with the swirling of my finger.

Her sweet moans and cries of ecstasy grow louder as I continue to torture her quivering, heated pussy. My dick grows harder as my finger experiences the tight, wet pocket of heaven that my cock begs to fill. I can feel the trembling of her pussy walls around my finger grow more intense with every thrust.

She is close, so close.

"Say my name again, baby," I rasp, wanting to hear my name as I feel the suckling of her pussy that signifies the start of an orgasm.

"Deklan, please," She cries, and I almost give in to that plea.

But I resist.

I pull my finger away from her suddenly, and her moan of protest tells me that my timing was exquisitely perfect. This isn't about satisfying her. This is a punishment, and orgasms are rewards.

"Good girl. Now, take your punishment, Mia," I rasp.

I pull her up and place her on the bed on her back. She doesn't try to get away this time. She stares at me with those chocolate eyes, lidded and glazed with prohibited release. It would be too easy. All I would have to do is touch her one more time, swirl my fingers around that spot, or push my cock into that tight wetness inch by delicious inch, and she would go.

And so would I.

But I'm not going to let her cum until I am ready for her to cum.

I climb on top of her, straddling her right below the apex of her thighs. With her legs held down by my weight, I place one hand on her sternum between her breasts, holding her down on the bed.

With my free hand, I unbutton and unzip my jeans. I watch her eyes widen as she gazes down her body to see what I am doing. She whimpers with need when I pull my massively hard cock out of my pants, freeing it from its prison.

I know I am well endowed, and I smile at the look of utter longing on Mia's face when she sees my enormous dick. It throbs and jumps in appreciation of being free as Mia's big, brown eyes widen further, showing too much white as I begin to stroke myself while she watches.

I make a show of it, throwing my head back and moaning with pleasure as I pump my hips in time with my stroking hand. The head of my cock comes dangerously close to the apex of her thighs with every stroke, and her whimpers of longing grow ever louder with each thrust of my hips.

The sensation is amazing. Watching her watch me sends shooting rivulets of pleasure coiling through every nerve ending in my body. The feel of my hand stroking my dick as I imagine it is her slick pussy I am pumping into drives me ever closer to that sweet release.

Her choked cries of protest grow louder as I let go of my cock to slide my hand between her thighs. The absolute inferno leaking from her entrance almost burns my palm as I run my hand up her sex. My hand comes away wet with her juices, and I rub those juices onto my hard, throbbing cock.

The heat throws my head back, and the moan of absolute pleasure is no longer for show as I stroke my cock with her heat covering my palm. I thrust my hips, coming ever closer to that sweet spot that promises such heavenly pleasure, but I do not enter.

Instead, I brush the head of my cock ever so lightly over the top of her mound without touching her entrance. I barely graze her lips with my head as I stroke myself harder and faster, my breathing ragged and my heart pumping a fierce beat in my chest.

I cry out my pleasure as I come to my release, and my seed covers her thighs and top of her mound as my dick throbs. Tides of pleasure ride through me with every beat of my heart, and I ride the tide as I watch her face.

Her eyes are wide, her mouth hanging open, and her cheeks are flushed with color. Her breathing is almost as ragged as my own, and she writhes under me with whimpers of protest as my orgasm subsides.

I curse under my breath as I look around for dark tendrils coming from her body and find none. It hadn't worked. The demon did not manifest despite Mia's intense desire and my own uninhibited lust. Maybe it will take more than once to bring it out.

That thought sparks my desire again as I ponder new ways I can torture Mia. I glance down at her and suck in a breath at the utter devastation on her features.

Mia's chocolate eyes stare up at me, sparkling with unshed tears. Her mouth is turned down, and her lips thinned to a hard line. Her breasts rise and fall with her rapid breathing. A lump forms in my throat as the realization hits that I did this to her.

I swallow hard.

Stay strong, Deklan. It will all be over soon, and then maybe you can have her for real and turn that look on her face into a look of blissful pleasure.

Wordlessly, I reach up and untie the tie from her wrists, climb off her, and pad silently to the bathroom. I find a washcloth and wash myself before putting my cock back where it goes and refastening my jeans.

I walk back into the bedroom with a fresh, wet washcloth to find Mia lying where I left her, tears flowing down the sides of her face. My heart stutters with regret, but I brush it away. I have to stay firm when it comes to her.

Both of our souls are on the line.

I toss the washcloth on her chest.

My tone is firm as I say, "Clean up and get dressed, Mia. And the next time I tell you to be ready…be ready."

"I hate you," she says, her voice weak as the tears stream down.

"I know," I say, smiling cruelly and trying to sound nonchalant.

Deep inside, my heart crumbles to my feet.

CHAPTER 6: MIA

The cold cloth Deklan tosses my way hits my stomach, and I flinch. Deklan's cold words hit my ears, and my heart clenches. The tears streaming down the sides of my face are a mixture of longing, humiliation, and the denial of release.

Fuck him and his stupid…massive…utterly dreamy cock…God Dammit, I want him more than ever now. Watching him pleasure himself and yet denying me release filled me with a yearning so intense that my pussy is still throbbing.

How fucking sick is that?

The coils of need still have me in their grip, and I can't stand it. How the fuck can he make torturing me, violating me, and utterly humiliating me seem so fucking erotic. And how the fuck am I supposed to function with this intense need riding me?

Still, I do not want to be at his mercy any longer…or do I?…no, I do not want to be punished again.

Well…at least not right now.

I clean myself up and roll off the bed.

Fuck, I am even more exhausted now than I was before.

Sniffling, I shuffle to the bathroom and wash my face. My knees are weak, and my pussy still throbs with need. I stumble to my closet, shooting Deklan an angry glance. He sits on the bed, smirking in victory like the cat that just ate the mouse.

"Put on a skirt," Deklan orders. "Or a dress. Preferably a skirt."

I scoff in irritation as I turn to my closet. This is fucking insane. Why am I letting him push me around like this? I barely even knew the man, and yet I was just up close and personal with his massive manhood.

"Stop letting him push you around. Let me out, and I will deal with him," The annoying voice screams in my head.

What…the…fuck?

The voices in my head are becoming more than annoying. They are moving into the category of delusional and psychotic. Do I have a hidden bad side somewhere inside me? Is that what I am supposed to *let out*? I would let it out if I wasn't so afraid that Deklan would completely destroy my sanity with his sexual games. He seems to be better at them than I could ever be, even if I did have a bad side.

On the other hand, maybe losing that game wouldn't be so bad. On the contrary, it could be rather pleasurable. Maybe I could...

NO!

What the hell is wrong with me?

Scoffing in disgust at myself, I shake my head to clear it as I pick out a cute, tiny pink mini-skirt that one of my few friends in Phoenix bought me for my birthday. I slide the elastic waistband up my legs, the pleats parting perfectly as I place it low on my waist. Next, I grab a white gypsy top with cut-out shoulders and flowy sleeves.

I put on a lacy pair of black panties and the matching bra, then put the top on, pulling my hair out of the neckline and letting it hang loose down my back and over my shoulders. I found a pair of strappy black heels that I had not worn in a while and put those on. I go to the bathroom and run a brush through my hair, glancing in the mirror to check the results.

My reflection startles me.

My dark eyes are even darker, like the color of coffee with a bare touch of cream. My skin is washed out from lack of sleep, and there are bags under my eyes as well.

I look like hell.

Fine. I don't care. He is the one who insisted I get dressed, so here I am. This is as good as it is going to get. I march up to Deklan, holding my arms out to my sides as I turn a slow circle.

"Does this meet your expectations?" I ask sarcastically.

His emerald gaze runs up and down my body, the emerald green darkening to the color of a stormy sea. The silver stud glints in his brow.

His growl of approval rumbles in his chest, coalescing with his voice as he answers, "Very nice, Mia. You will receive your reward later."

I gulp. Can I have it now? My pussy still tingles with longing. But I don't ask. Instead, I stand and wait for his next demand, my eyes narrowing as he stands. He stalks across the floor to my location, and I shudder at the look of absolute eroticism on his face.

He towers over me as he takes my chin between his massive fingers and tilts my head up. He bends down, almost touching his nose to mine. His goatee tickles my chin as he blows a breath over my skin.

It flows over my face, hot and heavenly, as he says, "Kiss me, Mia."

I swallow hard.

He had begged for my kisses, and I had denied him. I had wanted to punish him in return. But the way he says it now, erotic and sensual, as if the kiss promises to be laden with dreams and star shine.

I close my eyes and open for him as he tilts his head and plants his lips on mine in the most erotic kiss I have ever had.

His lips move over mine expertly, the lip ring teasing the sensitive skin of my lips. His thin mustache tickles my nose as his lips slide over mine. His tongue violates my mouth, swirling around in an exotic dance with mine and sending tendrils of desire coursing through me. The strokes of his tongue are long and languid, eliciting a moan from my throat as he threads his fingers in my hair.

The kiss lasts for what seems like forever as time and reality disappear, leaving me frozen in a space where only Deklan and his sensual kiss exist. The pleasure coursing through my veins stimulates the pulsing of my pussy walls once more, and I writhe against Deklan as I sigh with pleasure.

It is over too soon, leaving me reeling with tension and an unreleased climax. He releases me suddenly and turns away, and I swear I caught a glimmer of…something…in his gaze. I'm unsure what I saw, but it piques my curiosity.

"Deklan?" I ask uncertainly, saying his name on purpose because I know he likes it.

He doesn't turn around to look at me. He answers with his back still turned, and his tone is strained and full of some dark emotion that drives rivulets of pleasure through my soul.

"Good girl, Mia. Now, follow me."

He walks away without a look back.

I sigh and follow.

We reach my front door when he stops and turns to me. Whatever I thought I saw in his face earlier is gone, replaced with a look of utter mischief. My throat tightens at that look. What is he going to do to me now?

"Before we leave, I have something to give you," Deklan says impishly. "And you must wear it for the rest of our date. Do this for me, and your reward will be very…pleasurable."

He emphasizes the word *pleasurable*, causing my knees to go weak. My eyebrow quirks in curiosity.

"Wear what?" I ask.

He reaches into his back pocket and pulls out what looks like a pair of thongs attached to a little plastic set of butterfly wings. I frown in confusion.

"What the hell is that?" I ask.

Deklan hands it to me. "Put this on under your regular panties or in place of them. Whichever you prefer. But make sure the butterfly wings go in front with the...um...attachment...in between your juicy lips."

"What attachment?" I ask, but when he hands me the 'panties', my question is answered.

The 'butterfly wings' have a small, oval-shaped bulb attached to them that sticks out horizontally from the wings. If I put the contraption on like panties, then the attachment will fit right in place, sticking in between my pussy lips and sitting right over that sensitive spot above my entrance.

"Put them on," Deklan says, and his voice carries the promise of dark, erotic pleasure.

I gulp as I slide my panties off and put the butterfly panties on. The sensation almost brings me to my knees as the hard bulb hits my clit, especially since that little bundle of nerves has been overstimulated with no release. My heart thunders in my chest as my breathing grows ragged.

"Good girl," Deklan drawls, snatching my former panties from my grasp. "These are mine, now."

He shoves my panties in his jacket pocket with a smirk and then asks, "Are you ready to go?"

"You expect me to walk with this thing on?" I ask, my eyes going wide as I swallow hard.

How am I supposed to walk when the sensation is already going to make me explode just standing still.

Deklan smirks as he says, "If you falter, I will carry you."

Hell no. I will walk on my own.

Then his tone goes dangerously dark as he rasps, "But you better not cum."

I glare at him and lift my chin in defiance. "I will walk, but I cannot guarantee that I won't cum."

Deklan chuckles maliciously and opens the door, motioning me forward with a sweep of his hand. "Go ahead, Mia. I love punishing you."

His sexy tone sends tendrils of desire coursing through me at the promise of more punishment. Fuck. I have to get it together.

I take a deep breath and steel my nerves as I take a tentative step forward. My movement brushes the contraption over the sensitive bud, and I almost stumble at the sensation.

Deklan's hand reaches out to catch me, but I straighten and brush him off. My anger and frustration help brush away some of the lust running through me as I take a few more steps, making it out into the hallway with Deklan close behind me.

I can do this.

I focus on breathing as I pick up my pace, and I am a bit calmer when we reach the stairs. The sensations curling through me have dulled, and I smile in victory as I take my first step down.

My smile fades.

Walking down the stairs is a totally different set of problems. The different movement shifts the contraption to a different area of my still-throbbing sex, coming dangerously close to my entrance with every step.

There is no ignoring the desire curling through me as I grip the handrail so hard my knuckles turn white, and that is a big feat considering the darkness of my copper skin.

Sweat breaks out along my skin, my heart thunders in my chest, and my breathing turns ragged. The throbbing of my pussy walls intensifies as the pressure of the orgasm that has built inside my core comes dangerously close to spilling over. Every muscle in my body is tense, and a fine trembling starts in my legs. A moan of absolute desire escapes my throat as I take another step down.

Deklan stops me with a hand around my elbow. He steps down before me until his face is even with mine. He pierces me with an intense stare, and his tone matches that stare as he speaks.

"If you cum I will punish you again. You are not allowed to cum."

God damn him.

I swallow hard, and every nerve in my body quivers. I narrow my eyes and am so tempted to spit right in that smug face, but I do not. I fear what he would do, and I do not know how much more I can take.

The anger helps. It rises inside me, hotter than anything I have ever experienced. I have never been this livid. The mixture of the anger, along with the intense need that still throbs in my veins from the infernal contraption strapped to my sex, is almost too much to bear.

Tears prick the backs of my eyes, but I do not give him the satisfaction. I blink rapidly to keep them from falling as I move forward defiantly.

Deklan chuckles and moves aside to allow me to pass, keeping a firm hold on my elbow. Good thing, too, since I stumble a couple of times when the sensations threaten to overwhelm me.

But I make it to the bottom without exploding, and my poor pussy quivers. I am sweating profusely now, and my hot pussy juices soak the contraption held to my body.

My poor heart feels like it will never slow down, and my lungs burn from too much exertion. Deklan moves in front of me as we reach the bottom of the stairs, pushing me backward until we are hidden from sight, away from the front windows.

"That was very good," He drawls seductively, pulling something else from his back pocket. "Time for one of your rewards."

God help me.

Curiously, I watch as he waves whatever he has pulled from his pocket in front of my face. It is some sort of remote with a few buttons. Deklan smirks salaciously and pushes one of the buttons.

"Oooh…Ah!" I cry out as the bulb suddenly vibrates against my clit, shooting extreme pleasure throughout my entire body and causing an instant orgasm.

My knees go out, but Deklan catches me and holds me against his chest as the powerful sensations ride me. The denial of release makes the climax stronger when it hits, and it rolls over me like a tidal wave, crashing through me as my pussy walls throb to the beat of my pounding heart.

I cry out over and over, clinging to Deklan's suit jacket and calling out his name as the pleasure intensifies, crashing into another orgasm more powerful than the first as the tiny bulb vibrates again.

"Oh God…fuck…Deklan!" I cry as the second orgasm rides me, and I writhe in his arms.

He holds me against his chest until the sensations fade, and I am left a quivering mass of nerves, lying limp in his embrace. I cannot move or speak, and my eyes flutter closed of their own accord.

Deklan hauls me up until his lips are against my ear and whispers, "Such a good girl. Remember that, Mia. I have complete control of your pleasure right in my hand."

I am too weak and tired to say anything. Deklan picks me up in his arms and carries me like a baby, and I am powerless to stop it. I don't know where we are going, nor do I care.

If he gives me more orgasms like that, he can take me anywhere he pleases.

CHAPTER 7: MIA

I actually drift off to sleep in Deklan's arms, but I am jolted awake when my butt hits something soft, cushiony, and leathery. My eyes fly open, and I look around in alarm. Deklan's face is in my vision, smiling victoriously as he holds me steady.

"Wake up, Mia. You will need to be awake to hold on," He says.

My heart pounds as I realize we are outside and I am sitting on a motorcycle. A big, blue, powerful motorcycle. Deklan hands me a helmet, and I reach out with shaking fingers to grasp it.

"I have never...I don't...Deklan, I have never ridden a motorcycle before," I say, stuttering over my words nervously.

My hands shake so bad that Deklan places the helmet on my head for me. His sparkling emerald gaze pierces mine as he straps it under my chin.

"Don't worry, Mia. It isn't that hard. Just lean the way I lean and hold onto me. Most females enjoy it." His tone is suggestive, and I frown with suspicion.

However, I don't respond. I swallow the lump that has formed in my throat and nod, the helmet tilting slightly with the movement. The feel of it on my head is foreign but not particularly uncomfortable. The chin guard on the strap actually feels nice. It is plush and soft against my skin.

"Oh, and one more thing. We may want to take this off."

My eyes widen as he reaches under my skirt and slides his fingers behind the butterfly. His knuckles brush against my sex as he fiddles with the contraption, sending electric currents of desire licking through my veins.

I moan as the sensations ride me, writhing my hips against his hand as he pulls the contraption away from the butterfly with an audible click. He pulls his hand and the small hard bulb out, both covered in my juices.

The realization that I am still drenched in my own juices hits me, and I squirm uncomfortably. I really need a shower. Suddenly, a devious thought enters my mind, and my squirming takes on a purpose.

I smile wickedly, pointing at Deklan's messy fingers as I say, "You're going to have to wash your seat soon."

Deklan throws his head back and laughs, startling me as my wiggling ceases. I stare at him questioningly.

"My wicked little Mia," he drawls as his laugh fades and his eyes grow dark and dangerous. "I will be happy to clean your seat…"

He pauses, and my eyes widen as I watch Deklan bring the bulb to his lips as he holds my gaze.

"With my tongue," he adds, and his tongue darts out and licks the contraption clean, making appreciative 'mmm' sounds as he does.

Then, he licks his fingers clean one at a time, swirling his tongue around each digit. The eroticism of the gesture sends intense longing coursing through me, and I wonder what that tongue would feel like swirling around my clit like that.

I blink rapidly when he slides the entire contraption into his mouth, suckling it like the juiciest piece of candy, then letting it slide back into his fingers. He tucks it into his back pocket with a heated look.

"You taste divine, Mia," he purrs. "I will taste from the source soon."

"I hate you," I respond in a quivering tone as my entire body shakes with longing.

He chuckles. "I know."

He turns and mounts the bike, swinging his leg up and over to avoid hitting me. Then, my arms automatically go around his torso as he settles into place. He instructs me on where to place my feet, shows me what to avoid touching with my bare legs, and then starts the engine.

The rumbling of the machine underneath me startles me and fills me with a dreaded sense of danger and...

Oh Gods. Now I know why he took the vibrator off. The vibration of the machine against my almost-naked sex does the job tenfold.

I squeeze my thighs tight against Deklan's hips, my skirt bunching up in front of me. I squirm and hear Deklan chuckle even over the rumble of the bike's engine.

He turns his head to me and yells over the noise, "Remember, lean the way I lean and hold on. Oh, and enjoy the ride."

With a salacious wink, he turns back around and revs the engine several times. I bite my bottom lip to stifle the moan that tears through my throat, just as the bolt of electric ecstasy tears through my soul.

My heart rockets in my chest, my breathing becomes hurried and shallow, and my pussy walls flutter as Deklan takes off. I hold on tight as the motorcycle shoots forward, my hands fisting Deklan's shirt.

I am scared out of my mind and turned on as hell at the same time. The conflicting emotions ramp up the pleasure ricocheting through me. I writhe on the seat behind Deklan, squeezing his hips tight between my thighs as we barrel down the highway.

My body trembles with adrenaline as I watch the scenery whip by, and my heart lurches with a thrill of excitement. Deklan takes an exit off the highway to a winding country road, and I remember what he said about the turns.

I lean when he leans, learning to anticipate which way he will move by watching the road before us. I even grow confident enough to let go slightly so I can sit up straight and feel the wind whipping around my torso as we go a bit faster. The sensation is freeing, and I imagine this is what a free fall would feel like.

After a few more minutes, I find the courage to sit back a tiny bit further to see the entire scenery before us. It is exhilarating, exciting, and absolutely the most fun experience of my life.

We turn onto a straight road with very little traffic, and he guns it. The bike takes off, speeding down the road and making my heart race with exhilaration. The sensation builds in my chest, and I throw my arms up and whoop with excitement.

Deklan laughs at my antics. I can feel the rumble of his laughter vibrate against my breasts as I wrap my arms around his torso and press myself against him again once more. I feel amazing. I feel free. I feel alive.

I have not felt like this in…maybe ever.

The thrill of the ride runs through me as we slow down to take a few twists and turns before coming to an even smaller country road. Deklan slows the bike as we turn onto yet another tiny road, and then finally, we come to a beautiful Victorian mansion-turned-mental-facility, the one that belongs to my Cousin, Sophia.

I frown in confusion as Deklan parks his motorcycle right in the center of the roundabout, in front of the front doors, as if he owns the place. My curiosity is peaked, and I want to know more about his relationship with my cousin.

Sophia and I did not have the best relationship growing up, but I have tried to atone for that. However, the stresses of running my business long-distance, keeping up with the restaurant accounts, and helping her with all her accounts has kept me busy. I have not had time for social visits, but we do speak on the phone from time to time.

Deklan turns the motor off, kicks the kickstand down, slides off the side, then offers his hand to help me down.

"Why are we here?" I ask accusingly. "This is Sophia's place."

Deklan smiles. "Yes, it is. I am surprised you know it, given how little you talk to your cousin. Have you ever actually been here at all?"

I wave his hand away angrily as I slide down on my own, then growl in frustration when I stumble in the stupid heels, and Deklan has to catch me.

"I am busy, and she knows this," I say huffingly, jerking away from his touch as I smooth down my skirt and blouse. "Not that our relationship is any of your business, but I stay in touch despite not having time for social visits. Despite what you may think, I care about and am helping her."

"Right, and now she wants to help you," Deklan mumbles under his breath as he steadies me and then lets me go.

"What do you mean? I don't need help with anything," I say. "What could Sophia possibly want to help me with?"

Deklan waves his hand and says, "Forget it. We are not here for Sophia, anyway."

"Then why are we here? Why did you make me get dressed up if we aren't going anywhere?"

"I was planning on taking you somewhere, but then you fell asleep in my arms. You are dead on your feet, and you need sleep. I am going to make sure you get some."

My heart pounds in my chest. "You are checking me in to the mental facility?"

Deklan barks a short laugh as he answers, "No, Mia. We are here because I live here as well, and I am going to put you in my bed."

My eyebrows raise in surprise. "You live here? Just what kind of relationship do you have with Sophia?"

"I work security for her, so she provides me with a place to live," he says with a shrug.

"But I thought you were going to work for the bank?"

"I am. I have worked here for a long time, but this was never my trade. Sophia knew this, so she helped me finally finish my schooling and earn my degree, and then she helped me get the job at the bank.

"She sent me to you first, but you were unsure how long you would be here. Your cousin is quite the philanthropist, and I owe her a lot," Deklan explains.

I say nothing as I follow him to the front entrance, but I am smiling on the inside. Mia has always had a kind heart, and I am slowly learning how wrong I was to treat her the way I did.

Deklan opens the door for me, and I step in. He places a hand on the small of my back and guides me through the reception area. He towers over me as he walks beside me. The pretty blond nurse at the desk gives me a once-over as we pass by.

"Hello, handsome," she croons with a saccharine smile as she waves with a wiggle of her fingers in Deklan's direction.

Then, her eyes narrow on me as she says in a derisive tone, "What kind of stray have you brought in this time."

"Careful, Cora," Deckland says hotly, shooting the blond an angry glare. "This is Mia, Sophia's cousin."

"Oh," is all she says as Deklan leads me toward the staircase at the back of the room.

"Tell my cousin I'm here," I call out before Deklan can push me out of earshot.

If Sophia knows I am here, she may come looking for me. It would give me an excuse to get away from Deklan. God knows what Deklan's plans are. Fear lances through me at the thought of him taking me up to his room and doing unspeakable things to me.

Or maybe it is something other than fear.

I push that thought aside. I am not ready to face the fact that I have inexplicable feelings for a practical stranger who has already violated and abused me. I also am not ready to admit to myself that I enjoyed it.

"Sophia knows you are here," Deklan says, interrupting my train of thought.

"How does she know?" I ask, shying away from his touch.

Deklan smirks as he answers, "I knew the first time I saw you that I wanted you. After I left your building that day, I returned here and told Sophia that I was going to take you."

I scoff. "And what did my cousin have to say about that?"

"She thought it was about time you had someone to take care of your stubborn ass. I told her I was taking you out tonight, and then bringing you here."

"But you're not taking me anywhere," I argue. "You're taking me to sleep."

"You need to sleep, Mia," He says. His tone is harsh, and I raise my eyebrows defiantly.

"Why the fuck is it your business whether I sleep or not?"

Deklan stops and grabs my elbow, turning me to face him as he answers sharply, "Because I take care of my own. You are mine now whether you like it or not, and as such, you will be taken care of whether you like it or not."

He turns me back around and pushes me slightly, beckoning me to climb the staircase before us as he speaks in harsh tones.

"This means you will get the proper amount of sleep, eat right, and exercise daily. If you cannot care for yourself properly, I will do it for you. And if you fight me, you will be punished. Do as I say, and you will be rewarded."

The nerve...

"I belong to no one," I say stubbornly, trying to pull myself free of his hold. "I can do as I please."

He tightens his hold on my elbow, stopping me in the middle of the staircase and turning me to face him.

"Wrong answer," he growls, bringing his face close to mine. His emerald eyes shine with the heat of his anger, burning into my soul as he challenges me.

"Do you want to try that statement again?" He asks ominously.

Gulp.

I do not answer, so after a heartbeat, he growls, "Tell me, Mia. Tell me you understand that you are mine."

He moves around me, hiding me from Nurse Cora's sight as she stares up the stairs questioningly. He reaches around to his back pocket and brings into my view the pod-like contraption that attaches to the butterfly I am still wearing.

"Tell me and be rewarded," He says seductively as he reaches under my skirt.

I gasp and try to move away, but he traps me against the stair railing and runs his hand from my elbow up to my neck. He squeezes like he had before in my bathroom.

It had both excited and scared me simultaneously, and it has the same effect now. The knowledge that he could crush my throat with the slightest tightening of his massive hands but doesn't is oddly erotic.

My throat cries out from the abuse, but I can still breathe. I focus on that fact, willing the oncoming panic away. I had panicked before, and my throat had paid the price.

This time, I force myself to relax and focus on what he is doing. I turn my attention to the hand that is reaching under my skirt and away from the hand that is choking me.

He slides the contraption behind the butterfly, and the slight brush of his knuckles against my sex sends an electric sensation through my core. There is a slight clicking sound as he connects the pod to the butterfly base and positions it right against the bundle of nerves above my entrance.

His hand smooths my skirt down and then grasps a handful of hair. He tugs tightly, eliciting a constricted gasp of pain. Even the gasp hurts as his other hand tightens around my neck.

He brings his face in close and whispers, "Tell me, Mia. Tell me you are mine."

He releases my neck, reaches into his back pocket again, and brings out the little remote that promises intense pleasure. My pussy walls throb with anticipation.

I pull in a long, deep breath, relishing the freedom of breathing fully. It does not hurt like it did last time.

"I am yours," I rasp as I stare defiantly into those jade eyes.

He jerks my head back with the handful of hair he still holds. "Say my name when you say that."

I swallow, narrowing my eyes. The urge to spit in his face is overwhelming. "I hate you."

He growls and pulls harder. "I know. Now, say it."

I gasp in pain and hiss through gritted teeth, "I am yours, Deklan."

"Mmmm, yes," He breathes erotically. He pushes against me even harder, pushing my breasts into his hard chest. "Now, tell me like you mean it."

His fist in my hair tightens, and he brings his face in close. Our noses are touching, his mustache hairs tickling my upper lip, and his breath blows across my heated skin as he breathes. He flicks his tongue out, licking along the side of my lips as he makes that 'mmm' sound that drives me absolutely insane with need.

Fuck it.

I make my voice as sultry as possible and say, "Take me, Deklan. I am yours."

A flicker of surprise runs through his jade eyes, and he covers it quickly.

But not before I saw it.

He schools his features as he purrs, "Good girl."

He crushes his lips to mine, kissing me fiercely as he leans even further into me. I open to him, afraid he will crush my lips against my teeth if I don't. The lip ring teases the corner of my lips as his tongue thrusts into my mouth, swirling fiercely with mine as he kisses me like his life depends on it.

The stair railing digs into my back so hard that I am afraid it will break under the pressure. I squeak in protest and push against his chest, but he only growls and continues kissing me. He wraps his free hand around my waist, keeping the hold on my hair as he pulls me away from the railing. He lifts me in his massive arms, and my feet dangle in the air as he carries me the rest of the way up the steps, down the hall, and stops at one of the doors.

He breaks the kiss as he lowers me to the floor so he can open the door. He picks me back up, piercing me with lust-filled eyes as he carries me into the room and backs me into the wall beside the door. He releases me, and I slide down the wall until my feet hit the ground.

He reaches to the side and shuts the door firmly, holding my gaze as we both breathe raggedly. He smiles maliciously as he raises his hand, and my eyes widen when I see the remote.

Please push the button…please push the button….please push the button.

He pushes the button.

I scream in absolute, torturous pleasure as the intense orgasm rips through me, bringing me to my knees on Deklan's carpeted floor. He doesn't catch me this time.

Instead, he allows me to go down on hands and knees and kneels on the ground behind me as the orgasm…no, orgasms…continue to ride me. I am useless. I fall to my stomach, unable to stay up on my hands and knees. All I can do is wantonly thrash against the floor as the orgasm flows through me.

I hear the rustle of Deklan's movements as I continue to writhe on the carpet. The vibration of the contraption stops, allowing the orgasms to drift away slowly, leaving my pussy walls quivering with the release of so much tension.

My skirt has ridden up over my thighs, leaving my ass bare save for the tiny strip of the g-string. My shirt is bunched up under my breasts, leaving my stomach bare to the carpeted floor. It burns with minor carpet burns as my struggles come to a stop.

I am barely able to catch my breath before Deklan's hands grab my hips, pulling my ass up into the air with my legs still stretched out straight. One of his hands falls away, causing me to gasp when his fingers pull the strap of the butterfly panties away from my pussy.

Something presses against my entrance, eliciting a moan of pleasure from my lips as I lift my head up enough to look over my shoulder.

Deklan is on his knees behind me, straddling my outstretched legs. He is naked and glorious, his muscles rippling in the dim light of his apartment. He must have undressed while I was riding out the tail-end of multiple orgasms on his carpet.

He holds my ass up in position with one hand and the strap of my panties away from my bared pussy with the other hand. His massive cock is hard and throbbing, and he has the head pressed against my entrance. At this angle, his massive cock will probably go in deep. It will most definitely hurt.

I gasp, managing to cry out, "Wait!"

I tense in preparation since I don't know if he will listen to me at this point, but to Deklan's credit, he doesn't press any further.

His tone sounds tortured as he groans, "Mia, I may be a demanding asshole, but I am not a rapist. Tell me now if you really don't want this."

I swallow hard, shaking my head in denial. "No, you don't understand. I...I..."

I stutter, not wanting to admit how much I love this. I don't want him to stop, but I don't want it to hurt, either.

Plus, other things need to be taken into consideration.

"What, Mia. Tell me," Deklan urges through gritted teeth, pushing against me enticingly. "Tell me you really don't want this cock inside you, and I'll stop."

"Yes, I want you inside me," I say admittingly, then add quickly, "But I'm afraid you'll hurt me in this position. Plus, I am not on birth control."

I hear Deklan release a chuckle of relief as he responds, "Don't worry about that, angel. You won't get pregnant, and I will be very gentle until you are comfortable. I promise."

"How can you promise that I won't get pregnant?" I ask

breathlessly, rivulets of pleasure shooting through me as he presses his cock against me more firmly, begging for entrance.

"Just trust me, angel, please," he rasps.

I don't know why, but I do.

Nodding my consent, I arch my back, pressing myself more firmly against him as I say, "Just be gentle."

"Thank the Goddess," he moans.

His fingers, still holding the scrap of string of the butterfly panties out of the way, shift slightly, causing the contraption to move against my clit as he pushes the head of his massive penis into my entrance.

I cry out from the exquisite sensation, writhing against him, silently begging for more. It doesn't hurt at all yet.

His fingers dig into my hips as he gently pushes himself further into me, and I can feel my pussy walls milking his dick as pleasure ripples through me. Still, there is no pain, causing me to grow bold.

"Deklan!" I cry out. "More. I want more!"

He pushes further into me, moving slowly and carefully. I push my ass up further, bringing my stomach off the ground as I moan with frustrated pleasure.

It still doesn't hurt, and I am desperate to have him fully inside me.

"More, Deklan. Give me all of you, please!" I cry.

And then I am screaming with pleasure as he thrusts suddenly, sheathing himself the rest of the way into me with one stroke.

"Fuck, Mia!" He cries out. "God dammit, you are so tight."

I whimper and writhe as pleasure tears through me and Deklan's fingers dig further into my hips. The fingers holding the panties at bay twitch, causing the silver contraption of pleasure to rub against the sensitive bundle of nerves above my entrance.

The mixture of so many sensations is almost too much to bear, and I whimper out another ecstatic moan as Deklan pulls halfway out and then pushes in again, this time faster than before but still torturingly slow.

"Are you ok, baby?" Deklan asks breathlessly.

"Yes, Deklan," I rasp desperately. "Please, just fuck me."

"God dammit," He breathes, pulling out and pushing in even faster.

He lets out a choked sound somewhere between a moan and a growl as he pulls out and thrusts back in one more time.

"I'm sorry for this, baby, but I am not going to last," He rasps above me, and I can hear the tension in his tone. "I promise I will make it more pleasurable next time."

He reaches for something on the floor as he pulls out, leaving only the head inside me. He picks up the remote for the butterfly orgasm-maker.

Holy…fuck.

I brace myself for the intensity, curling my fingers into the carpet to hold on. And then, I am lost in a world where only pleasure exists as Deklan pushes the button and sheaths himself into me, picking up a rhythm with his hard, fast thrusts as he cries out in ecstasy.

The force of the sensations ripping through me is nothing like I have experienced before as my pussy walls throb so hard against Deklan's cock that I think it may break us both.

Deklan only thrusts a few more times before he roars his pleasure through the room, the sound mingling with my screams as we ride our releases together into blissful oblivion.

How the hell can he ever make that more pleasurable? If he does, I may die from bliss. I am barely aware of Deklan turning off the contraption, pulling out of me, and collapsing onto the floor beside me.

When I come back to myself, Deklan is lying on the carpet, breathing heavily with his arms flung out beside him. He is staring at the ceiling, and I wonder what he is thinking.

I almost ask, but he suddenly moves, rolling over and coming up to his feet in a move so fast I wonder if he hurt himself. He bends down and pulls me from the floor, wrapping his massive arms around my waist as he turns me to face him.

My nose meets hard chest just before he picks me up, my feet dangling in the air as he lifts me so that my face is level with his. I grip his shoulders and wrap my legs around his waist, gasping as I marvel at the strength he possesses even after that tryst. How does he do it?

Then I am gasping for a different reason as I lock gazes with him, his emerald gaze boring into mine with an intense look I can only describe as reverence. He kisses me softly, like the touch of a butterfly's wings fluttering against my lips.

I swallow hard as he draws back and pierces me with that look again before moving with me in his arms. He walks me through what I assume is his living room. I peer over his shoulder and catch a glimpse of a simple sofa, chair, and coffee table, all in black. I don't have time to see much else as he carries me out of the room and into the next room.

I turn my head to the side when we enter the next room, straining to see over my shoulder. The beautiful four-post bed catches my eye, telling me Deklan has carried me into his bedroom. I almost struggle to get out of his hold, ready to protest at being brought into his bedroom. I'm not ready to sleep yet.

Deklan's hold on me tightens as he ignores my struggles, carries me further into the room, and turns so that I can see the bed clearly. I freeze, and the protesting words I was about to say die in my throat when I take in the sight of the glorious bed.

It stands in the center of the room, an island of comfort draped in mystery, so stunning that I fail to take in any other thing in the room besides that bed. Filmy material hangs from a canopy, cascading down like a waterfall of gossamer, silvery threads. The gauzy, see-through fabric shimmers in the soft light of the bedroom, swaying gently with a slight breeze that seems to come from nowhere, creating an ethereal dance of light.

The delicate veil of fabric envelops the bed on all sides, offering a sanctuary that seems to exist between dreams and reality. It reminds me of a place where secrets are whispered, and the world outside fades into a distant memory, leaving only the promise of restful slumber and sweet dreams.

I would give anything to sleep and have good dreams, uninterrupted and complete, surrounded by that curtain of translucent cloud. Deklan moves me toward that vision of heavenly bliss, pulling back the filmy fabric and gently laying me on the bed's surface.

I sink into a cloud-like softness as I run my hand over the silky bed linens. The silk comforter is a deep, velvety blue, reminiscent of the midnight sky. The pillows are a soft, creamy white, like clouds resting against the dark expanse of that sky. Together, they create a harmonious blend of tranquility and dreams that invite me into their soothing embrace, cutting off any protests I may have had about not wanting to sleep.

Now, in this heavenly slumber-inducing bed, all I want to do is sleep.

Deklan slides into the nest-like bed and sits gently beside me, removing my strappy heels from my feet one at a time. He pulls my skirt down my legs, my shirt over my head, and removes my bra. He takes off the butterfly panties and takes the pod-like contraption out of them, leaving me completely free of my clothing and the vibrating orgasm-maker.

The silkiness of the blanket caresses my bare skin as I roll over onto my side. I sigh with utter contentment as Deklan pulls the comforter from under me, leaving me lying on the softest silk sheets I have ever felt. My naked skin cools against the silk, and I rub against it reverently.

Deklan bundles several pillows around me as he covers me with the warm comforter, and I burrow into the cloudy softness of the comfortable bed. The bed dips and a cool breeze hits my backside with the raising of the covers.

The pillow at my back is tossed away, and the hot hardness of Deklan's body presses against me, replacing the pillow's softness and stealing the cold from my body. The sensation is heavenly, so I do not mourn the loss of the pillow. I would much rather have the smooth, solid muscle against me, warming me as I cuddle into blissful rest.

I have never been so relaxed, so drained of all tightness. My muscles twitch with the sensation as Decklan curls against me, spooning me as he throws one massive arm around my waist and pulls me in close to him.

"Sleep, baby. I will keep the demons away," Deklan whispers in my ear.

I sigh with blissful contentment as every muscle in my body liquifies into relaxation. I want to ask Deklan what demons he is speaking of, but I am gone into dreamland before I can even ask.

CHAPTER 8: DEKLAN

I fucked up. I realized I had fucked up as soon as my cock entered that heavenly pussy. I realized just how bad I had fucked up when my traitorous heart lurched at the sight of Mia writhing under me as I entered her. Then, again when I pulled her perfect body against me, and she fell asleep in my arms.

I will always want to sleep like this. I will always want to prop up on my elbow with my head resting on my fist as I watch her sleep, thinking of how beautiful she looks as she dreams.

My heart is gone. My soul is hers. There will never be another. She is mine, and I am hers. Her willful spirit, delightful laugh, and smart-ass mouth both irritate and intrigue me. I have to have her, and I have to know more about her.

She is mine.

And the fucking demon still has not shown its face.

It is personal now.

Mia is my woman, and no demon will mess with my woman.

I will just have to think of another way to lure it out.

I startle when Mia takes in a deep breath and whimpers in her sleep. Is it the demon? Is it messing with her in her dreams? It is pure torture that I cannot do anything to ease her nightmares.

Well…I could do something…but then the demon would never come out, and Mia might suffer the consequences. No, that would be unacceptable. I will just have to endure this; I have to wait and see if the demon will come to the surface so we…no…so I can do something with it.

I don't know how I am going to endure it.

I brush a tendril of hair from her face and lay a gentle kiss along her cheek, longing to take the nightmare away. Maybe I can without any abilities if she genuinely feels safe with me…

"I'm here, baby," I whisper into her ear. "You are safe."

I smile victoriously when her whimpers grow quiet, and her eyelids stop the infernal fluttering. She relaxes against me once more, and I sigh with contentment.

I have to speak with Harper. I have to find another way. This is not working, and we are running out of time.

And I have already lost my heart.

Gently, oh-so-slowly, I pull away from my sleeping sweetheart and climb out of bed. I pull on a pair of sleep pants, tie the string, slip on my slippers, and pad silently out of the room.

I go to the locked room down the hall from my suite first. That is usually where I can find Sophia in the middle of the night. That is where she can be with Harper while she dreams.

The room is usually sealed with several locks, one in particular that can tell me if Sophia is in there or not. The giant, steel-enforced padlock is not in its place, so Sophia must be there. She never leaves the padlock off when she is not there.

I pound loudly on the door, placing my lips close to the door and yelling, "Sophia, open the door! I have to talk to you and Harper ASAP!"

I wait for a heartbeat before pounding on the door again. My nerves are on edge as I wait, my patience gone. Every muscle in my body sings with tension.

I raise my arm, about to pound on the door again when it is flung open, and Sophia blinks at me with her almost-black, sleepy eyes.

"What the hell is so important that it could not wait til in the morning?" She complains in a whiney voice. "And where are your clothes?"

"I couldn't get the demon out," I say, my voice rough with emotion. "But I did finally get her to go to sleep."

Sophia's eyebrows rise. "She's here?"

I nod.

"In your bed?"

I nod again.

"Hmph."

I frown in irritation. "What?"

Sophia smiles teasingly as she responds, "Oh, nothing. I just never thought the big, tough Hulk number one would ever have a lady in his bed overnight, much less my cousin."

"I told you I was bringing her here to sleep," I say in irritation.

"Mmmhmm," Sophia says with a mischievous smirk. "And you could just as easily shown her to my room in the turret to sleep, but nooo. She is in your bed down the hall."

"Fuck, Sophia, I don't have time for this. This is serious. Where's Harper?" I say grouchily.

Sophia holds her hands up surrenderingly. "Alright, alright, Mister Grouch. Come on in."

She moves aside and opens the door. I don't waste a second, moving into the room and toward the mirror as soon as the door opens wide enough to allow my bulk of a frame to enter.

"Jewel, bring Harper here, now!" I shout at the shadow waving at me in the mirror.

"Jeez, Deklan, calm down before you piss off a demon," Sophia scolds as she comes up behind me.

"Oh, I'm going to do more than piss one off. I'm going to force the fucking thing out and wipe it from existence," I say roughly, balling my hands into fists.

"You know you can't do that," Jewel's voice flows through my mind. *"Mia won't make it. The demon is too strong now and will pull her down with it."*

"You can't kill Mia!" Sophia yells at me in a panicked tone. "She's my family!"

I turn to Sophia. "I'm not going to kill Mia. I'm going to take it the way Harper took Jewel. I just need him to tell me how."

Sophia frowns in confusion. "What? What the hell are you talking about, Deklan?"

Shit. I must have said too much. I had just assumed Sophia knew.

"Thanks, Fuck Head," Harper's voice says.

I turn back to the mirror to see Harper standing beside Jewel with an irritated look on his face.

"I haven't had a chance to tell her that particular secret yet," Harper says.

Sophia turns to the mirror. "What secret?"

Harper sighs. "It's a part of my past I have kept hidden. I was going to tell you eventually."

Sophia folds her arms over her chest. "So, tell me now."

"You're an asshole," He says, piercing me with an angry look. "I didn't want to revisit this piece of my past, especially not with Sophia. At least, not yet."

Sophia's eyes soften, and she relaxes her angry stance. She steps toward the mirror and places a hand on its surface.

"Harper, you know how hard it was for me to talk about my horrid past, but I did. You supported me and helped me through it, and I will do the same. I'm not going anywhere, no matter how horrible your past is, so you may as well tell me," Sophia says in a calming tone.

Harper's visage falls in defeat, and he takes a deep breath.

He turns to me and says, "Fine. I don't know if you can pull it off like I did, but I can tell you what happened, and you can decide what you want to do from there."

"Take me to Harper," Sophia says to Jewel. "I want to be with him while he revisits his past."

Harper's blue eyes fill with love and relief as he watches Sophia walk across the room to the bed that always sits in the corner. The mirror, bed, and recliner in front of the mirror are the only pieces of furniture in the room.

I watch as Sophia's body drifts off to unconsciousness as Jewel floats out of the mirror and pulls Sophia's soul from the crown chakra at the top of her head.

Sophia's form flickers through the slats of time and reality as Jewel pulls it through to the other dimension and into the mirror. Sophia reforms on the other side, appearing next to Harper with Jewel's arms wrapped around her waist.

"Thanks, Jewel," Sophia says weakly. "Just give me a minute to reorient myself before you let me go."

I sit in the recliner, facing the mirror, waiting for Harper to start his story. Sophia, now able to touch Harper, wraps herself around him, burying her head into his body.

"I missed you," She says, her voice muffled against Harper's muscled chest.

"You see me every day," He says with a chuckle.

"But I don't get to touch you every day," She says.

"Sophia, you know it isn't good for a human soul to spend too much time here in the Demon Dimension," Harper says chidingly. "Your soul gets weaker the longer you are here, and if you are not careful, you could fade away and die."

"But you live here," she says. "I could, too, if you would let me."

"No, absolutely not. I will find a way back to your world," Harper says.

"But you're here," Sophia repeats. "And your soul hasn't faded away yet."

"You know that is only because a piece of Thorn attached itself to my soul while I was controlling him," Harper says. "Which is also the reason I am stuck here in this dimension."

"I know," Sophia says sulkingly. "If we could only find a way to extract it…"

"We will," Harper interrupts, pulling Sophia close and stroking her head soothingly.

"That's not the entire truth," I say with a smirk. "Tell her the whole story of why you're stuck and why your soul doesn't fade away."

"You're still not being truthful?" Sophia asks with a lilt, pulling away from Harper slightly. "Please enlighten me, Harper. Tell me the rest of the story, and please tell us how you *took* a demon while your fiancé was under the impression that you were born with one like she was."

I chuckle. I already know this part of the story, but watching Sophia's reaction to it will be hilarious. She's not gonna let Harper off easily if I know Sophia.

Harper pinches the bridge of his nose between his thumb and forefinger as he shakes his head and says, "I didn't take a demon like Deklan is implying."

"So, tell me," Sophia says, letting go of Harper and placing her hands on her hips.

Harper releases his nose and opens his eyes before responding, "I really did have a demon, but I…well I…"

"You what?" Sophia asks with narrowed eyes.

"I…" Harper sighs in defeat. "I'm a witch, Sophia. You know this."

"What does that have to do with Jewel?" Sophia asks, crossing her arms over her chest.

I snicker, and Harper shoots me a silencing look before continuing.

"Jewel's owner was having a hard time taming her, so I cast a spell to separate Jewel from her owner. However, the spell didn't quite work as planned, and Jewel attached to me and became mine."

Sophia's eyes widen, and she looks between Harper standing before her and me sitting outside the mirror. The look on her face is priceless. I should have brought some popcorn.

"Do your spells ever work the way you plan them?" Sophia asks, throwing her hands up in the air and then letting them fall back to her side dramatically.

I can't contain my barking laugh, and Harper shoots me an evil glare.

"You think this is funny, angel?" Harper growls.

"Yes, I do," I say between guffaws. "I think it's funny that you haven't told her any of this, yet she never questioned you about why your soul never faded in the Demon Dimension."

My laughter fades as I sit back in my chair.

Sophia frowns. "What happened to your demon, Harper? After you took Jewel, I mean?"

Harper huffs and crosses his arms, refusing to answer.

Jewel steps up beside him with a regretful look on her shadowy face.

"I killed him," she says remorsefully. "I was not yet tame and angry at being pulled away from my master. I wanted to kill Harper by killing his demon, but it didn't work. I ended up bound to him instead."

Sophia puts her hand out and touches Jewel on her arm comfortingly. "It's alright, Jewel. I'm not going to judge you based on your actions before you became the wonderful inner demon you are now."

Jewel smiles and bows, saying, "Thank you, Sophia. You are a wonderful master as well."

Sophia's eyes harden as she turns her attention back to Harper. "Now, tell me the rest. Why doesn't your soul fade?"

Harper runs his hand down his face and glares at me.

I sit up on the edge of my seat in anticipation. Here comes the part where Sophia lets Harper have it for keeping things from her.

Harper takes a deep breath and says, "I am stuck here because the spell that backfired and caused a piece of Thorn's soul to attach to me also turned me into an inner demon. I can't return to your world until I go through the process."

Sophia's eyes narrow dangerously as she backs further away from him and hisses, "You need to repeat that because I could have sworn you just said that you're an inner demon."

"He will have to be assigned to a human before he can return," I answer for Harper. "Once placed inside a human, he will lose himself and all of his memories. He will never know who he was or remember his life as a human."

Sophia's eye twitches as she looks to Harper for confirmation.

"I will figure this out," he says softly. "Please, don't worry."

"How am I supposed to not worry, Harper? What…are you going to cast another spell to make yourself human again? Your spells never work!"

I slap my hand over my mouth to stifle another laugh.

"I'm getting better," Harper mumbles indignantly. "The spell I cast to make myself corporeal instead of shadowy seems to work."

"Yeah, well, you better get perfect because we have to save my cousin!" Sophia says. "And we may need your spells to do it!"

"And you!" she adds, turning her attention to me. She jabs her pointer finger at me and says sternly, "Stop picking on Harper and figure out how to save my cousin!"

"I would be glad to," I say, rising from my seat and gesturing toward a defeated Harper. "I just need Harper to teach me that spell so I can take her demon."

Harper turns to me with a severe look. "It is similar to the spell I did to take Thorn over when I had to save Sophia from Jeremy, but you see what happened to me after that one."

"But this didn't happen when you took Jewel," I say, frowning. "What was different?"

"Jewel didn't have a name; she was still new and red-eyed. The spell I did to take Jewel was to steal a new demon, not to take over one already matured demon. Mia's demon may not have a name yet, but it already has purplish eyes. The spell could be dangerous for you and Mia with a slightly matured demon."

I run a hand through my fiery hair. "I have to try, Harper. Besides, I am no human. I am an angel, so the spell may not have the same effect on me as it did on you. Not only will I not be stuck since angels can travel into the Demon Dimension freely, but the demon may not be able to attach itself to an angel.

"Angels' natural abilities only allow us to subdue or kill an angry demon. Subduing a demon is temporary, and I can't kill it, or I risk Mia. I can't just take a demon like you did without using spells and magic, So I have no choice but to try that."

"While all that is true," Harper responds, his tone laced with empathy. "You still take the risk of killing Mia if you pull an almost-matured demon from her."

I let out a frustrated sigh, holding the bridge of my nose between my thumb and forefinger as I whisper fearfully, "Then it is hopeless. I can't lose her."

Fuck, I hadn't meant to say that aloud or with such emotion, but it's too late now. Harper pierces me with a knowing look, and I know he knows before he even says anything.

"Fuck me, Deklan, you fucking fell for her, didn't you?" Harper says.

I sit back in the recliner, resting my elbows on my knees and placing my head in my hands. "I think I did."

"Out of all the bleeding-heart fallen angels that could have lost their hearts to Mia, I thought you would be the one to resist falling in love," Harper says. "That's why Sophia wanted you specifically to help Mia. She doesn't want some lovesick fallen angel fawning all over her cousin."

I sit up defensively. "It was your bright idea to try to lure the demon out with sexual energy. Did you think I could just play with Mia and not grow any sort of feelings for her or her for me?"

"Yes!" Harper exclaims. "You are the master of this game with a string of broken hearts behind you. You do it all the time to other women. And Sophia has assured me that Mia isn't looking for any kind of relationship right now. I thought it would be the perfect match with no strings attached."

Harper is right about me, but...

"Mia is different," I say, completing my thought aloud. "She's ...hell, I don't know how to explain it. There's just something about her that sets my soul on fire. And I think Mia feels it, too."

"How sweet," Sophia purrs with a sardonic smile. Then, her tone and visage grow stern as she adds, "But I still don't want to see you or Mia get hurt. I know how you are, and Mia's already been through enough."

"Like I haven't?" I shoot back, unable to control my temper any longer. "I know heartbreak like you will never experience in your pathetic human life. I'm taking the bigger chance here."

"Watch how you talk to her, Deklan," Harper warns with a dangerous hiss.

I run a hand through my hair and take a calming breath, pulling back the reigns on my tattered emotions.

"Sorry, Soph. I'm just on edge right now. You know I didn't mean that. I know how hard it was for you to lose your parents."

"I know," Sophia says, giving me a compassionate smile. "I know you have been hurt, too. I shouldn't have disregarded your feelings like that. You will have to tell me about what happened to you someday."

"That's a story for another day," I sigh, then turn to Harper and continue. "I don't even know her, but I feel this connection with her. It's even stronger than the connection I had with..."

My voice breaks, and I bury my face in my hands again. I mumble through my fingers, "I can't go through it again, Harper."

Harper's tone softens as he responds, "Look, I will help you with the spell if you want, try to perfect it so there is no danger. But let's save it as a last resort. Let's try to get it to come out first," Harper says in understanding. "You can subdue it and put it to sleep, giving us time to tell Mia about her demon and teach her how to tame it before it wakes up. We won't let anything happen to Mia."

"Alright, fine. I will continue my present course and hope for the best," I say. "Maybe it will take a few more times."

"Look on the bright side," Harper says. "When Mia falls for you, you won't have to break her heart."

"No, just the hearts of all the other women that were hoping for a chance to snag him up," Sophia says with a chuckle.

"Mia says she hates me," I say with a shrug. "I don't believe her, but if she does, that's okay. As long as we can tame that fucking demon, I will be happy. I would rather her be safe and hate me than the alternative."

"At least she is finally getting some sleep," Sophia says. "The weaker her body, the easier it will be for the demon to take over."

Harper's eyes light up with shock, and I have an idea I know what he thinks since the same thought enters my mind. We lock gazes, our eyes narrowing. Sophia looks back and forth between us.

"What?" She says.

"That's what it's doing," I say through gritted teeth. "I didn't even think about that until you said it."

"That's exactly what I was thinking," Harper says.

I smack my forehead with the palm of my hand as I shout through gritted teeth, "God, I'm so stupid!"

Sophia looks confused, her gaze flicking between me and Harper. "Someone needs to tell me what I said because I'm confused."

"It's wearing her down, making her weak so it can take over. It won't come out until it's ready," I answer, the anger growing in my gut again.

If that demon has messed with Mia while I was away…

I don't want to think of that right now. I need to get to her. I rise from the chair as Sophia speaks, her tone alarmed and panicked.

"Hurry, Deklan! Go to her! It's probably messing with her right now through nightmares. I'll be right behind you as soon as I return to my body."

I am almost to the door, Sophia's words still hanging in the air when the screams start. Despite us being in the middle of a mental facility and hearing screams from mental patients nightly, I know the screams are Mia's. I can feel her fear deep in my bones.

My heart leaps into my throat as I run out the door and head to my room, where I left her asleep and vulnerable to a fucking demon. But it doesn't stand a chance against me. I am a fucking fallen angel, and I will help Mia tame this damn demon.

Or I will die trying.

CHAPTER 9: MIA

The shadows in my room are alive, twisting and writhing around me. I am apparently hallucinating again. I know that it is inconceivable for shadows to be alive. I know that there are no such things as monsters under the bed.

But here we are, the infernal visions pulling me from my sleep again. I take in my surroundings, my eyelids fluttering sleepily, and realize I am not even in my room. Where am I, and how did I get here?

The bed is unknown to me. It isn't like my firm mattress in my apartment. It is fluffy and soft, like lying on a cloud. Even a filmy material surrounds me as if I actually am floating in the sky. If only I truly was high up in the sky, away from these scary shadows that keep haunting me.

Anger consumes me. Anger at the damn wisps of darkness that keep pulling me from the desired bliss of rest my body seeks. I was finally able to fall asleep after…

Memory slices through me as I suddenly realize where I am and how I got here. I was in Deklan's heavenly bed, but…

Deklan…

Where had he gone? I no longer feel his presence at my back. Instead, another presence presses closer, and I squeeze my eyes shut to keep from seeing them. They had left me alone when Deklan had been here.

Maybe he had gone to the bathroom. Hopefully, he will be back at any moment. He can keep the demons away. He promised he would. I heard him whisper it in my ear just before I had drifted off to sleep, and I wondered what demons he was protecting me from.

Now I know. He meant my own demons.

But now he is gone, and the shadows are closing in.

I slit my eyes open and peep through the narrow opening. I can see them writhing around, curling up the sides as if they are coming from under the bed. They coalesce in the empty space before me, and the chill from their icy presence seeps into my bones.

The darkness continues to swirl around lazily, and my eyes fly wide when I realize that they are taking on a shape…no…not a shape…a form. The form of a human body!

It materializes right before my eyes, and suddenly, a shadowy person is lounging on the bed beside me. It turns its head toward me, glowing purplish-blue eyes piercing my gaze.

"Hello, Mia," A sinister, wispy voice says, flowing through my mind and icing my brain like an arctic breeze.

I open my mouth and scream long and loud, the terrifying sound echoing in the room. I scramble toward the other side of the bed, away from the shadow woman and off the other side. I land on my ass on the floor with a loud thud, tearing a piece of the filmy fabric from the canopy frame attached to the bedposts. It floats to the floor, bunching up beside me and flowing over me as I land.

"Oomph," I puff out, stopping my screams and stealing the air from my lungs.

My horrified gaze darts all around as I flail wildly to pull the fabric off my head. Finally getting my head and arms free from the translucent material, I look back up toward the bed's surface to see if the shadow lady followed my movements. My eyes shoot to each side of me to see if she is coming around the bed after me.

I am trapped between the wall at my back, a bedside table on one side, and the bed before me. The other side remains open to me with only a pile of light fabric I can easily climb over if I can unravel myself from the piece I managed to entangle myself with. Still, I dare not scramble out from my little cubby I accidentally put myself in for fear that the shadow lady will be waiting when I come out.

My heart thuds against my ribs even though my lungs are paralyzed from having the breath knocked out of me from my fall off of the bed. I sit where I fell, pressing up against the wall to make myself as small as possible, praying to whatever God is up there for invisibility. My lungs scream for oxygen as I struggle to breathe.

Finally, my lungs spasm, and I take a gasping breath. The room is silent, other than the sound of my ragged breathing as I try to catch my breath, and my heartbeat echoing in my own head.

"Don't be afraid, Mia. Just let me take all your worries away," The shadow woman whispers in my mind, soothing promises that do nothing to ease my fears.

"Leave me alone!" I scream aloud, pressing further against the wall.

"I am part of you. I will never leave you alone," She whispers, her voice changing from soothing to menacing.

The shadowy darkness drifts toward me, coming from the bed's surface and drifting down to where I still sit, huddled on the floor and entangled in the bed's canopy. I try to scramble away, bumping into the nightstand and halting my escape.

"Get away from me!" I scream.

The terror inside fills me, overwhelming me with emotion. It spills out with my tears, great sobs wracking my body as I helplessly watch the shadows come alive and form into the shadow lady once again.

Only this time, she stands before me as I sit helplessly on the floor, reaching shadowy fingers toward me. The eerie sensation of...I don't know how to describe it...like my soul is being torn from my body...overtakes me. I fight against the feeling, clinging to myself desperately.

But I am so tired.

The exhaustion of the last week consumes me, and the fight to stay in my own head dwindles. I am fading, and my mind is slowly going dark. My vision goes fuzzy at the edges, and I see the glowing, purplish eyes of the shadow lady before me.

My sobs go quiet as the sensation intensifies. An overwhelming sense of peace suddenly comes over me, as if nothing matters any longer. My entire life was so insignificant, just a speck of sand in the entirety of space and time. Cold nothingness surrounds me, beckoning me with its icy fingers, pulling me from my mind and dragging me into the dark abyss of surrender.

"Mia!"

The sound of Decklan calling my name echoes through the room, kickstarting my heart and reverberating through my ears. My heart thuds solidly and rapidly against my chest, reviving me and crashing my thoughts back into reality. I take in a great gulp of air, realizing that I had ceased to breathe.

"Deklan," I call out, but it comes out as a hoarse whisper.

The shadow lady jerks back from me, taking with her the iciness of her presence. I feel a strange sensation in my gut, like a rubber band that had been stretched taut and snaps back into place suddenly.

"I got you now, fucker," Deklan's voice calls, and I see a bright light sear across the shadow lady's body, consuming her in its brightness.

Her purplish eyes dull to a bluer shade, and she opens her abyss of a mouth and lets out a scream. The sound grates against my nerves, filling my ears and threatening to burst my eardrums. I place my hands over my ears to block out the sound, but nothing blocks out the pain.

It radiates through my head as she screams, flowing through me as I watch her fade away. Her shadowy figure disappears into the bright light, and the light fades as she does until, finally, there is nothing left.

The sound of her screaming and the sensation of her icy presence is gone, the place where she stood empty as if she had never existed. But I know that is wrong. I know she was there, and there is no more denying that the shadows I thought were in my mind are real.

And they…or it…are part of me.

I can feel it inside me, writhing angrily in my gut. The sensation makes me sick, and I heave as I clutch my arms around my stomach. The sensation is gone as fast as it had come, leaving me quivering with the fading of adrenaline.

"What the fuck!" I cry out in relief, denial, and a bit of anger. "What the fuck was that?"

Tears are streaming down my face, and I reach a hand up to wipe them away. My breathing is rapid and shallow, and my heart feels like it is about to tear its way out of my body.

Deklan's hulk of a form comes into view, squeezing between the bed and the wall, trampling the delicate fabric of the formerly beautiful canopy into the carpet as he bends over, grasps me under the shoulders, and hauls me to my feet. I try to ignore the fact that he is shirtless until he begins to peel the entangled fabric away from my naked body.

"That, my dear, was an inner demon. A nasty one, too," He says as he pulls at the fabric. "And, unfortunately, it is yours."

I bat at his hands with one of mine, trying to fend off his attempts to pull the silky material from my naked form as I grasp it tightly with my other hand.

"What?" I ask blankly, the words bouncing off the awareness of my brain as I stare at his massively muscled chest. I feel my cheeks heat as I avert my gaze.

Frowning questioningly, Deklan stops pulling at the bed canopy still wrapped around me. He pulls the silky top sheet from the bed and wraps it around me instead, giving up the fight and allowing me to keep the flimsy covering while adding a better one.

"I have subdued her for now, but she will be back, which is why you need to keep up your strength. You need to learn to control it before it takes control of you, and I can help you with that." He says, lifting my chin and forcing me to look into his…

His eyes!

His eyes are glowing! The emerald light cascades over me as he stares down at me.

"You need rest, a proper diet, exercise…" Deklan continues. "This is why I have been fussing at you to care for yourself. It is important that you…"

His eyes are glowing! It is all I can think of as the mantra repeats in my head, and the rest of Deklan's words get lost in the swirling mess of my thoughts.

"Mia, are you in there?" He asks, shaking me gently. "Did you hear anything I said?"

"Your eyes," I say, my voice coming out a hoarse whisper. "Your eyes are glowing."

"Yes. That's what happens when an angel smites a demon," Deklan says nonchalantly as if he is talking about the weather or last night's football game.

I blink.

"What did you say?"

Deklan sighs and runs a hand through his fiery red hair, causing the pompadour to become mussed. It looks adorable. He looks amazing.

The muscles of his naked chest move under his skin as he moves. My eyes roam down his cut abs, leading down to low-hung sleep pants that sit just right on his hips. My mouth waters at the thin sprinkling of hair trailing from below his navel and down to…

I swallow hard, thinking of what lies beyond the v-shape cut muscle that leads into the elastic band of those pants. The thought of what those black cotton sleep pants hide at the end of that sprinkling of hair cuts through my thoughts, heating the blood in my veins as a thrill of desire shoots through my soul.

"Mia!"

I shake my head to clear it and try to concentrate on his words. "Did you hear anything I said?"

"Something about angels and demons?" I say uncertainly.

"I guess I have some explaining to do," He says in a defeated tone as he runs his hands through his hair again and blows out a long breath.

The door to the bedroom is slung open, and my cousin walks…no runs…into the room. Her panicked, almost-black eyes are wide as they search the room, relief filling them when they land on me. Sophia's dark auburn, wavy hair is frazzled, and she wears a long, white, silky nightgown and slippers.

Even sleep-tousled and frightened, Sophia is beautiful, and that old jealousy flares in my chest. I tamp it down when I see the worry-turned-relief flare in her visage as she shoves past Deklan to get to me.

"Mia, are you alright? What happened to you?" She asks hurriedly, grasping my shoulders and looking me up and down.

"I…I'm not sure. The shadows…," I stop speaking and just shake my head.

Sophia looks to Deklan. "She's completely out of her head and wearing a sheet. What happened?"

"The demon tried to take her," He says, turning to a tall chest of drawers against the wall at the end of the bed. "She almost had Mia when I got here. I took her out with my light, but I know she will be back."

"She? The demon is female?" Sophia asks, taking an offered shirt that Deklan had pulled out of one of the drawers.

My eyes widen. Did Sophia just say something about a demon? Wasn't Deklan just talking about a demon?

"Yes," Deklan answers. "Do you think Jewel could talk some sense into her?"

Who the fuck is Jewel?

"I don't know. I can ask," Sophia answers, pulling the sheet off me. She frowns when she sees the filmy material tangled around me underneath the sheet.

I allow her to pull at the material, feeling confident that her body in front of me is hiding me from Deklan's heated gaze. Finally free of the bed canopy, Sophia helps me put Deklan's oversized shirt over my head and my arms through the sleeves. It swallows me, hanging almost to my knees.

"Well, ask her, and make it quick," Deklan says authoritatively. "If that attack was any inclination, we are running out of time."

Sophia gently pushes me down until I sit on the bed. I am left sitting there, now dressed in Deklan's shirt, with my brain swirling in confusion, disbelief, and utter shock.

Sophia and Deklan continue their discussion like I am not even here as my gaze bounces back and forth between them, my eyes wide and my mouth hanging open.

"Obviously, whatever you did worked," Sophia says. "Maybe you should continue whatever you were doing,"

"Soph, we already discussed that," Deklan mutters, slanting a look my way. "It wasn't me that did anything. The demon was waiting for her to be worn down. Besides, I can't continue what I was doing without consequences. She already hates me."

Sophia glances at me with a smirk. "She doesn't look like she hates you right now. She looks like she was naked in your bed."

"Trust me, she hates me. We need to get her to Harper. If she doesn't believe in the demon by now, she will believe when she sees him," Deklan says as he turns his attention back to Sophia.

Harper? Isn't he dead? What the hell? Anger takes over the shock and confusion in my brain, and I come crashing back to reality. I ball my hands into fists and slam them down on the bed on either side of me.

"Stop talking about me like I'm not here!" I shout. "And one of you tell me what the fuck is going on! Why are you talking about angels and demons, and how the hell is Harper still alive?!"

They both stop speaking and turn to me. Sophia quirks an eyebrow at me, and Deklan just looks…worried?…scared?…I am unsure what that look in his eyes means, nor do I care right now.

"The shadows are real, Mia," Sophia says to me. "I told you that the day I was released from the hospital after I was rescued. But you didn't want to believe me."

She crosses her arms over her chest defiantly.

"That was no shadow," I hiss. "That was…was…I don't know what that was, but it was no shadow."

"You're right," Deklan says. He leans against the wall and crosses his feet at the ankles with his arms hanging loosely at his sides. "That wasn't a shadow. Like I was trying to tell you before, it was a demon."

"A demon?" I scoff derisively. "And you are what? Some kind of angel, right?"

My coldly logical mind struggles with the urge to expand my reality. I am comfortable living in a world where demons and angels are things of fantasy or part of a religious dogma, and I do not want to admit the reality of what I saw with my own eyes.

The lady formed out of darkness…I saw it myself…her purplish, glowing eyes that seemed to see into my soul are now burned into my memory. The light that made her disappear and Deklan's glowing eyes afterward will forever be etched into my mind. It all makes a liar out of the logic swirling in my brain.

I cannot deny what my eyes have seen, no matter how much I do not want it to be true. But even as I replay the scene over and over in my mind, a part of me clings desperately to the belief that there must be some rational explanation. Maybe it was a trick of the light, a hallucination brought on by stress and fatigue. Anything but the truth that threatens to shatter my carefully constructed worldview.

I think back to the stories Sophia told me of her adventures here in this hospital, and my heart lurches at the newfound knowledge that they were all true. Poor Sophia. Things, horrible, terrifying things, that I thought to be made up by her confused, shattered mind, had really happened to her. Sophia was never crazy, after all.

And neither am I. But accepting this new reality means admitting that everything I believed in, everything I trusted, is flawed. I am not ready to let go of my logical world, not yet. But I have to eventually.

After all, I have a fucking inner demon to tame.

My hands relax, and the anger drains from my body. I move quickly, surprising Sophia as I jump from the bed and collide into her, wrapping her in my arms. I hug her hard.

"I am so sorry, Sophia. For everything. For when we were little, and I was a jealous little bitch. And for now, because I didn't believe everything you told me and all you have been through. I'm sorry. I'm so sorry, cousin."

My words end in tears as I hold her to me, and after a moment, she throws her arms around me and returns my hug.

"You two can play kiss-and-make-up later," Deklan's voice cuts into our emotional hug. "There isn't much time left to get this demon under control."

I break away from Sophia, brushing the tears away with the backs of my hands as I sniffle loudly.

"Tell me what I have to do," I say with resolve.

"We need to get you to Harper," Sophia says as she tenderly brushes a strand of my hair behind my ear. "Remember the stories I told you of how he is trapped inside the mirror? Well, those stories were true as well. He will know how to help you."

"But first," Deklan says, coming up off the wall and brushing Sophia away so he can take her place before me. "You need a full night's sleep. Your mind and body are exhausted, and you need to recharge."

I shudder at the memory of the shadows drifting around me as I lay in bed. "I don't know if I can go back to sleep."

"I won't leave you this time. I will keep you safe," Deklan says, then smirks seductively.

Deklan leans in, placing his face close to mine as he adds huskily, "I can even help you fall asleep if you like."

My heart flutters and my stomach twists in knots as my gaze drops to his amazing lips. I swallow hard as I suddenly realize that he is still shirtless, and I am wearing nothing but his shirt.

"And on that note, I'm going back to bed," Sophia says, giving Deklan a pat on the shoulder before heading toward the door. "We will deal with all this tomorrow. Good night, Mia."

I don't respond. My gaze is still locked on Deklan's lips as coils of longing curl through my veins. The memory of his cock entering me from behind roils through my brain, and I gasp at the electrified sensations that run through me.

The door to the room closes, and I suck in a breath as I realize that I am now alone with Deklan, and he is staring at me as if I am his last meal.

By the Gods, but he is so fucking sexy. And no wonder. He's a fucking angel. A fallen one, but still an angel.

My angel.

"Mia, you are zoning out again," Deklan smirks. "If you keep looking at me like that, we will never sleep."

Fuck me, I cannot believe I'm saying this...

"I don't want to sleep."

"Mia," Deklan says, my name spilling from his lips like a prayer. "What do you want?"

"You," I say.

Why won't my mouth shut up?

"I've been bad, Deklan. I need to be punished," I say, grasping the hem of his shirt and pulling it up and over my head.

What the fuck am I doing? My body has taken over my brain, and I am out of control.

"Mia, for fuck's sake. You gotta get some sleep," Deklan says in a tortured tone.

I reach out and run a hand up his muscled chest, relishing in the feel of the hardness rippling under his soft skin. My fingers trace the lines of his tattoos like I have wanted to do a hundred times before.

I waggle my eyebrows suggestively and say, "I touched you without permission. Aren't you going to punish me?"

He growls, the sound rumbling up from his chest as he says, "Fuck it. We'll sleep later."

He grabs me, pulling me to him and slamming me against the wall. I give in to my body's urges and decide to just enjoy it.

Maybe he will fuck me into oblivion, and I will finally get some sleep.

And I will enjoy every second of it.

CHAPTER 10: DEKLAN

Yep, I definitely fucked up. The minute she pulled the shirt off, revealing that perfect body with those perky breasts, I was a goner. There was no way I was going to be able to resist her.

Powers That Be save me...

Then she asked me to punish her, and that was the end of my resolve.

I have her up against the wall, her legs wrapped around my waist. The only thing separating my throbbing dick from that celestial pussy is the cloth of my sleep pants. It would be so easy to reach between us, pull it from its prison, and pound into her.

But she wants to be punished, and I want nothing more than to please her.

Gripping her thighs to steady her on my hips, I lean in and capture her lips with mine. My mouth moves over hers, and she opens to me. I take the offer, swirling my tongue with hers slowly, languidly, savoring the taste and heat of her kiss.

Her tongue traces my lips, twirling around the lip ring in the corner of my mouth. Her soft little moan makes my cock throb with longing. I rock my hips against her, the cloth of my pants rubbing against her naked entrance. I can feel the head of my dick pushing against the fabric as I rub myself against her. I moan for emphasis, making the sound as erotic as I can as it vibrates against her lips.

My mouth moves away from hers so I can taste the heated skin of her jawline, moving up to her earlobes and then down the side of her neck. I lick and suck my way to her breasts slowly, savoring every stroke of my tongue as I taste the sweetness of her skin.

"Deklan," She whispers, arching her back and pressing her breasts closer to me.

"Mmmm, baby, are you enjoying that?" I ask sensually against her skin.

"Yes, Deklan, oh yes," she sighs as she writhes against me.

I stop, pulling away from her with my upper body while I press her more firmly against the wall with my hips. I feel her thighs flex as she holds on, and she slaps her palms flat against the wall on either side of her for balance.

"You are not supposed to be enjoying yourself. You are being punished," I say harshly, and I watch as excitement mixed with a bit of fear flickers in her chocolate eyes.

I run my hands up her sides slowly as I stare into her eyes menacingly. I slide one hand around her neck and squeeze, watching her eyes widen as my dick gets harder. I love playing with her like this, relishing the fear and loving the way she looks as I take her to the edge of pain.

Her cheeks flush beautifully, her chocolate eyes shine with a mixture of pleasure, pain, and fear, and her lips part sensually as she moans and whimpers.

My hand tightens around her neck as the other hand plays along each breast in turn, pinching her nipples firmly and rolling them between my thumb and forefinger. Her eyes flutter and roll back when I lean forward and take one in my mouth, biting down on the nipple until I hear a squeak of protest escape her parted lips.

"Deklan, please," She rasps.

I bring my face close to hers and tighten my grip ever so slightly. "Please, what?"

I can tell she is close to having her air cut off by the wheezing noises she makes when she breathes. Her eyes go wide with fear as I squeeze just a bit more, cutting off her air.

I capture her lips while her breath is cut off and smile against her mouth when I feel her kiss me back despite being choked. She likes airplay, and I like that she likes it.

I count off the seconds in my head as I kiss her, practically tasting the fear radiating from her. I get to ten and then release my hold. I break the kiss, watching the relief fill her eyes as she pulls in gasping breaths of air.

"Please, what?" I ask again, rotating my hips and driving her harder into the wall.

The fabric of my sleep pants violates her entrance just a tiny bit, and I growl at the sensation. I can feel her juices soaking through to the head of my cock, hot like an inferno.

"Ah!" she cries out, her eyes rolling back into her head.

I pull back, pulling my sleep pants and the head of my dick out of her sweet pocket of heaven. I grasp her hips and throw her onto the bed. She lands on her back with a squeal and tries to scramble away from me, but I see the sassy set of her eyes and lips. She is toying with me. She wants me to chase her.

I smirk, my tone malicious as I say, "Where do you think you are going, angel? You have not had your punishment yet."

I lunge for her, catching her ankle and dragging her back to the center of the bed. She fights, kicking and throwing her fists at me in desperation. I laugh as a few of her hits connect against my hard chest and arms, brushing off the punches like insect bites.

"Let me go!" She screams in mock viciousness as I pull her under me and pin her to the bed, but I see the corners of her mouth quirk in a suppressed smile.

I straddle her legs with mine, my knees on either side of her upper thighs. I grab her wrists and pin them to the bed above her head, leaning my face down close to hers.

"Never," I whisper. "You are mine, Mia. I will never let you go. Now, take your punishment like a good girl."

I grasp both her wrists in one hand so I can reach over to the bedside table with my other hand. I pull open the drawer and draw out a long piece of rope. She watches me trepidatiously, shuddering slightly as she watches me bring it up to her trapped wrists.

"What are you going to do to me?" She asks, her voice quivering with anticipation. I can feel the heat coming off her skin as I lean over and wrap the string around her wrists several times.

"Anything I want to," I answer maliciously.

I tie her wrists tightly, but not too tight. I loop the other end of the rope to the headboard, pulling slightly on the knot I made to be sure it will hold. I raise off her legs, holding them down as I pull out another length of rope.

"If you let me tie your legs to the bedposts, I will give you a nice reward after your punishment is over," I say, raising my brows suggestively.

She doesn't answer and only nods, spreading her legs out so I can tie each ankle to the opposite bedpost. My dick hardens almost painfully as her divinely sweet pussy is laid bare for me. My cock throbs with desire as my gaze travels over the pink perfection of her tiny vagina. My tongue darts from my mouth, licking my lips as I watch the swelling of her sensitive bud and remember the taste of her juices.

My gaze travels up to her eyes, shining with trepidation and anticipation. Her lips are parted, and her tongue darts out to moisten them nervously. She is practically panting, her chest rising and falling rapidly. Her perfect breasts move with each breath.

A devious idea lights up in my mind as I lock gazes with her. I pull one more item from the bedside table and lean over her.

"Raise your head up," I order.

She does, and I tie a blindfold around her eyes, blocking off her vision. Her breathing speeds up, and I can see her pulse bounding rapidly in her neck. Smiling, I lean down to lick that pulse, and Mia startles with a surprised whimper.

"Are you ready for your punishment?" I whisper into her ear and smile when I hear her gulp.

"Yes," She answers in a raspy whisper.

"You are not allowed to cum until I say. Do you understand?" I ask.

"Yes." She answers.

"That is your punishment. And if you do cum, you will get a spanking. Do you agree to my terms?"

I run my hand down her stomach, and she gasps. Her stomach quivers as I stroke across her navel and then dip further until my fingers brush the sprinkling of hair over her mound.

"Yes," she answers shakily, her voice breathless as I continue to play with her pussy hair.

"Good girl," I drone, running my fingers through her nicely trimmed pussy hair. I love that she has hair. "Now, I need you to pick and remember a safe word. If this all becomes too much, you say the safe word, and it stops immediately. Do you understand?"

She nods, her lips thinning out as she releases a soft "mmm" sound when I run my hand between her legs, cupping her sex momentarily, then returning to her heavenly mound where my fingers play with her pubic hair.

"I understand," Mia says, and her voice is barely a shaky whisper.

"What's your safe word, baby?" I ask, growling deep in my chest at the sensations of Mia's black nest of softness as I run my finger through it, finding my reward at the end of it.

"Angel," she says with a gasp just as I dip my finger into the lips of her sex. She thrusts her hips against my finger, begging for more.

"Angel it is," I say as I pull my finger back, grasp her hip, and roll her until her ass cheek comes off the bed. I slap it firmly with my other hand, and Mia cries out.

I release her hip and let her body roll back as I hiss, "Do not move, Mia."

She whimpers as I move my finger back to the spot it had been before, stroking the sensitive spot above her entrance. Her thighs quiver as she whimpers, and I smile at the knowledge that she is struggling to remain still under my ministrations.

I thrust my finger into her tight pussy, swirling it around as I drive it in.

"Fuuuuck," Mia cries, ending with a squeak as every muscle in her body tenses.

I watch her, reveling in her torture. I momentarily regret the blindfold as I wish I could see the lust shining from her eyes. She pulls at the bindings on her wrists, throwing her head back as she trembles. The effort to lay still and not arch her back in pleasure tears another moan from her as I pull my finger out and repeat the thrust. Mia arches her back and writhes against my hand, unable to hold back any longer, and I smile.

I love to punish her.

I roll her over to deliver another slap to her ass, my cock hardening to stone at the sound of her hiss of pain.

"I said don't move," I say through gritted teeth.

"I hate you," She whimpers shakily.

"I know," I say softly as I thrust my finger inside her again.

"Deklan!" She cries, but she resists the urge to writhe. Every muscle in her body quivers with the effort.

I pull my finger out and place it on her lips. She flinches at the unexpected touch but relaxes when I speak.

"Suck it," I say. "See how sweet you taste."

She parts her lips, and I shove my finger in, relishing the feel of her tongue swirling around it.

"Yes, Mia," I moan seductively. "Suck it good. Such a good girl."

She sucks harder as I pull my finger out as if she is trying to prevent me from leaving her sweet mouth. I chuckle.

"I will give you something bigger to suck, baby."

She whimpers, and I smile, moving off the bed to remove my sleep pants and slippers. I climb back up onto the bed, holding onto the headboard as I place my knees on either side of her head.

"Deklan?" she asks uncertainly.

"It's ok, baby. Trust me," I rasp, lowering myself to her sweet mouth. "Open wide, baby."

She does, and I groan in ecstasy as I watch the head of my cock slide into that sweet mouth. Mia gasps in surprise at the first taste of my dick, and then she sucks me into her as if begging for more.

"Sweet Goddess," I rasp as I slide further down into her mouth.

"Mmmm," Mia murmurs around my cock and swirls her tongue around my head.

Mother of God that feels divine.

"Fuuuck, Mia," I groan. "Such a good little cock sucker."

I slide into her further and am surprised to see almost half of my huge dick inside her mouth. I can feel my head pressing against the back of her throat, but she makes no sounds of protest.

For the love of all that is holy, she has no gag reflex.

She hums around my dick again, the sound vibrating through every nerve in my body as she sucks my cock appreciatively.

I throw my head back and cry out. Goddess, I won't last inside that sweet mouth. I dip a bit further in until my head is past the back of her throat.

Now she protests, pressing her head back into her pillow as if trying to pull away. I look down into her blindfolded face. I can't see her eyes or tell if she is panicking for air in this position, and my cock is too far down her throat, so she cannot say her safe word.

This could be dangerous.

I pull out.

Mia takes in a gasping breath and then rasps, "More."

I had half expected her to say the safe word.

"Fuck, baby," I say as I give her my cock again.

I only give her a little this time before pulling back out and then dipping in again. I fuck her mouth slowly, sliding in until I feel the back of her throat against my head before pulling back out again.

Her moans vibrate through me, and I grip the headboard so hard it mottles my knuckles. The sweet pressure of release builds within me, my balls shriveling in preparation to release their load.

"Baby, I'm not gonna last. I have to stop," I grind out as I pull out of her mouth.

She whimpers in protest, but I climb away from that heavenly mouth.

"You still have a punishment waiting," I say huskily, trying desperately to keep my voice steady. "Maybe another day I will let you swallow my load as a reward."

I keep my tone nonchalant, as if unbothered by the fact that she just sucked my cock. I am glad she is wearing the blindfold so she cannot see my face to tell what a lying asshole I am. I know how flush my skin must be from coming so close to release and then denying myself. My legs shake with the effort it took to hold back as long as I did. But I play it cool, allowing her to think it doesn't affect me to play this game.

I position myself at the bottom of the bed this time, placing my hands on her hips. Mia startles at my touch and then moans in ecstasy as I slide my hands down each leg, unhooking the ropes from the bedposts but leaving the tie around her ankles. I roll her over on her stomach and retie the ropes to the bedposts, spreading her legs out once more.

I run both hands over that delectable ass, relishing the softness of her skin and the firmness of her cheeks. I lean down and kiss each cheek lavishly, smiling at Mia's gasps with each touch of my lips.

"Mmm, Such a nice ass," I say appreciatively. "I'm going to enjoy spanking it."

Mia whimpers. I smack her ass.

Hard.

Hard enough to elicit a cry of pain from Mia's lips as she buries her face into the mattress. I smack the other cheek just as hard, my dick hardening even more as I watch her entire body jerk with the force of my hit. She screams again.

I run my hands over the red marks I left on her ass, kissing each one and lavishing the tender spots with my tongue. Mia moans and writhes under my attention, and I smile in victory.

"Good girl," I croon seductively. "Only a bit more, and then you will be rewarded."

I am so glad she hasn't said the safe word yet.

I repeat the process, hitting harder this time. I groan my pleasure at her cries of pain. I repeat the process one more time. She still has not even attempted to utter her safe word.

"You take your punishments so well, baby," I say seductively as I stroke her red ass cheeks. "Now, time for your reward."

I unhook the ropes from the posts again, turning her over to her back once more before taking the ropes off her ankles. Tears stream down Mia's face from under the blindfold, and her sobs coalesce with her moans as I lavish her with kisses and soothing strokes.

I remove the blindfold, and she blinks rapidly before gazing up at me with red-streaked, tear-soaked eyes. The tears roll down her cheeks as she blinks, dripping to the pillow under her head.

I keep the rope attached to her wrists.

"Let me fuck away those tears," I say as I lean over her, settling myself between her legs.

I keep most of my weight off her by balancing on my elbows as I lean down and capture her lips with mine. I kiss her softly, tenderly, moving my mouth over hers slowly as I caress her tongue with long, languid strokes.

She moans into my mouth, sending rivulets of shooting pleasure coursing through me. I answer her moan and deepen the kiss, digging my fingers into the mattress. I writhe on top of her without entering her, grinding my hips against hers in an exotic dance of ecstasy, pain, and intense desire.

I break the kiss to lick and suck my way across her jawline, to her ear, and to the thumping pulse at the base of her neck. Her breath hitches as I bite there, and then she moans as I soothe the bite mark with my tongue.

I move down her body, lavishing both breasts with my attention, then moving to her stomach and down to her navel. She moans and writhes as I finally get to her mound and blow a breath over her sex.

"Deklan!" She cries, my name coming from her mouth like a prayer.

I wrap my massive arms around her upper thighs as I settle onto my stomach between her legs. She rests her heels on my shoulder blades and rotates her hips, begging for the touch of my mouth on her.

"My Mia," I whisper reverently as I take my first lick of her delicious pussy.

"Mmmmm," I growl as my tongue licks from the bottom of her opening to the top and then up between her lips, swirling over her clit before going back and doing it again.

Over and over, I stroke her with my tongue as she moans my name and cries out her pleasure. I lavish her clit with attention, swirling my tongue around and around the sensitive bundle of nerves as I insert a finger into her opening. She screams in pleasure, and her hips writhe, bucking and rotating as I strain to keep my tongue in place over her clit.

I move my finger in and out of her sweet pussy, fucking her opening with my finger as I fuck her clit with my tongue. Her cries grow louder, and I can tell she is close by the sensation of her pussy walls milking my finger as they flutter around it.

"Deklan," Mia moans as she draws closer to orgasm. "God…oh, God…Deklan."

I pause and say, "Go, baby. Cum in my mouth. Let me taste those juices."

Then I fuck her with my mouth and fingers…hard…pumping two fingers into her roughly as I lick, nip, and suckle her clit.

"God, Deklan," She screams, and then she cums.

Her pussy walls milk my fingers as her hot, sweet juices flow. I place my mouth over that delectable pussy and gather all those delicious juices into my mouth. I swallow her down before lavishing her with my tongue, cleaning her pussy of every last drop before climbing up her body and settling between her legs once more.

"Fuck, Mia, you taste so good," I whisper. "Let me show you how good you taste," I add before capturing her lips with mine.

I reach above her as I kiss her, releasing the knot around her wrists with one hand. When her arms are free, she grasps my shoulders, her nails digging into my flesh as I continue to kiss her.

I reach between our bodies and settle the head of my cock against her entrance. I push into that sweet pussy, pushing just the head in as I settle into position. I run my arms under her shoulders so I can grasp handfuls of that soft, black hair in my hands and kiss her while I fuck…

No…

While I make love to her, sinking into her torturously slow.

She wraps her legs around my waist, trapping me between her thighs and resting her heels on my ass cheeks. She moans against my lips and bucks her hips up to mine as her fingers dig into my shoulders.

I pull slowly out and then push in again, matching her strokes with every buck of her hips. I bury myself to the hilt with every thrust in, grinding against her clit before pulling out and doing it again.

I keep a slow, torturous rhythm going as I kiss her long and lazily, enjoying every sensation of my dick pumping slowly in and out of that sweet, throbbing pussy as her nails dig into my flesh and she moans against our lips.

I break the kiss, placing my forehead against hers so I can stare into those chocolate orbs. She stares back, her eyes hooded with passion as I continue to move in and out of her. That sweet pressure builds as I see the pure ecstasy in her gaze. She grasps handfuls of my hair, holding onto me as I hold onto her.

Our breaths mingle as we both breathe raggedly, holding onto one another as if we are all that is keeping each other bound to this world.

And maybe we are.

I am nothing without her now. She has my heart, my body, and my soul. I am all hers, and she is mine.

"Mia," I whisper her name like a prayer as the pressure builds torturously slow inside my core.

"Deklan," She rasps as her hands tighten in my hair. "You feel so good inside me."

"Oh, Mia. I would live inside that sweet pussy if I could," I whisper.

I capture her lips again, kissing her more urgently this time. I pump into her faster as the pressure builds in my core, and her moans of pleasure against my lips drive me even faster.

"Yes, Deklan. Oh, yes. Please let me cum," She cries against my mouth as I drive into her faster still.

I could die right now, and I would be forever happy.

"Yes, Mia. Cum for me, baby," I answer against her lips as the pressure builds and builds, higher and higher, threatening to spill over like hot, molten lava and burn me up from the inside.

Her moans of pleasure come faster, and her walls quiver around my cock. I feel the suckling of her pussy as her orgasm starts, and it throws me into my own.

I break the kiss, capturing her shining gaze and holding it as we ride our orgasms together. Our eyes lock, our cries coalesce, and our bodies dance together as the erotic, intense sensations of our release take us to another world where only she and I exist.

We come down slowly, the world around us drifting back as we relearn how to breathe. I pull myself out of her slowly and roll onto my back beside her. I stare at the ceiling as my heartbeat slows and the euphoric sensations fade.

"Deklan?" Mia whispers.

"Yes, baby?"

"Will you stay with me and not leave me this time?" She asks.

My heart swells for her even more, if that is even possible.

"I promise I will stay until you tell me to leave," I whisper, leaning over to kiss her forehead.

"Okay," she says, rolling over and cuddling into my side.

She sighs in total contentment, settling in as if she is trying to climb inside me. I turn to my side, facing her, and pull the covers over her. I wrap my arm over her protectively and smile as her eyes drift closed.

I watch her for a long time. Her eyes flutter behind her eyelids, and soft little snores escape her lips.

My heart has been stolen by her, and I want to know all there is to know about her. I look forward to getting to know her and hearing her history and stories of her youth. Nothing she could tell me would keep me away from her, though. I will forever be hers. The pleasure of getting to know her is merely a bonus.

She is well and truly asleep by the time I finally feel sleepy, and I lay my head on my pillow when my eyes flutter shut.

"I love you, Mia," I whisper just before I drift into a long, deep sleep.

CHAPTER 11: MIA

I sigh contentedly and cuddle into the naked body at my back. Deklan's hard muscles cradle me as I dig in, and something else presses against my ass.

I smile as memories of last night whisper through my mind. It would be so easy to get him riled up this morning. However, it had been a while since I had had sex before Deklan, and he was a tad too big for my tight walls.

Needless to say, I am sore. I need to soak in a bath, and I desperately need some clothes. I have been naked too long. But, Gods, it was worth it all.

And what's worse, I think I may be falling for him. I know he is supposed to be my guardian angel of sorts, but does that mean I can't have him as my lover as well?

I don't want the answer to that question right now. I am afraid of the answer and what it will do to me. I am afraid it would shatter me.

Fuck I'm in trouble with this man. The punishments and rewards…the way he fucked my mouth…the way he ate my pussy. God dammit he feels so good.

But none of that compared to the way he…he…it wasn't just fucking. The emotion in his eyes as he stared down at me was more than that. The look on his face as he…made love to me…that was just…more.

It's the only way to describe what we shared in the end.

And I could have sworn he whispered he loved me as we fell asleep. This is all happening so fast, too fast. I don't even know this man, but already he holds a piece of my heart, and apparently, I own a piece of his as well.

I probably dreamed that he said he loved me, though. My body was so exhausted that I fell asleep almost instantly. And man, did I sleep! I slept like a bear in winter, and now I am as hungry as a bear in spring. Other than that, I feel so much better.

I hear Deklan's breathing change and know he is awake. I feel his body tense behind me as I move slightly, and his dick against my ass throbs. I smile deviously and writhe against him, stretching my arms over my head and pretending to stretch. I make sure to stick my ass right over his hardened cock and rub languidly against it.

My smile widens when I hear Deklan's tortured groan.

I 'stretch' some more as I rasp out sleepily, "Good morning, asshole."

Deklan growls, the sound rumbling against my back as he grounds out, "Asshole, am I? Sounds like you need another spanking."

Fuck. I shouldn't have tried to play with him. The spanking is another reason I am sore. I am not sure my ass cheeks can handle another round of that.

I scramble away from him, or at least I try to. Instead, I get tangled up in the sheets, and Deklan's strong arm hauls me back to him. Fear skitters through me as I struggle, loving the thrill of it when it mixes with the longing to have his dick inside me again.

"Let me go...ah...," My protests are interrupted by Deklan's hand around my throat as he licks up the back of my ear.

"Stay still, Mia, and take your punishment, and I just might let you cum," he whispers, his breath blowing across my skin and making me shudder.

I instantly go motionless.

"Good girl. Now bring your leg back and drape it over my hips."

I do as he says.

"Good, baby. Now don't move, and if you listen, I will let you cum," He drawls as his free hand travels across my flat stomach and down to...

Fuuck. I will never be able to hold still in this position. The head of his glorious cock is right against my entrance. All I have to do is pivot my hips back slightly, and it would go right into my pussy. But I cannot move, or I will be punished.

And would the punishment be so bad? I love his punishments almost as much as the rewards.

How sick am I?

"Oh, Mia, you are such a good girl," Deklan drawls as he rubs the head of his dick over my entrance enticingly and strokes my clit with one finger.

And that is why I obey him. I love to hear him tell me what a good girl I am. It entices me almost as much as his dick rubbing over my pussy.

I moan, my hips quivering with the need to move. Deklan's hand tightens around my neck for a moment while his other hand cups my mound as his finger swirls around that bundle of nerves above my opening.

My entire lower body trembles with the need to move, but still, I hold my place. I cry out in painful pleasure as Deklan's finger dips inside my entrance and begins that torturous swirl inside my walls.

"Mia," Deklan moans. "Tell me I'm yours."

My breathing turns ragged as my heart runs like a rabbit behind my ribs.

"You are mine, Deklan," I rasp as his finger comes back to trace lazy circles around my clit, and his dick rubs against my entrance again.

"Tell me you want me," he grates, breathing faster.

"I want you Deklan," I whimper.

"Tell me to take you," He says, and I can tell by his tone he won't last.

"Take me, Deklan," I cry.

"Mia," he rasps and then pushes his way inside me. "Move with me, angel."

Thank the Gods.

I move, crying out my pleasure as his dick forces its way inside me. The soreness is forgotten with the different angle as he pumps in and out of me from behind. His hand on my neck tightens, and I lock a hand around his wrist.

I can feel the tension in his arm. He is fighting not to choke me for real, and the thought of how much danger I am in if he loses it excites me. The sensation of the excitement and his finger swirling around that magic spot builds the pressure of an orgasm, but I hold it back.

I'm not allowed to cum unless Deklan lets me.

It builds and builds as he continues to fuck me while he strokes me, and then his rhythm begins to falter. His hand tightens even more, and I pull at his wrist as my breath is cut off.

Fuck, I can't breathe, but it only excites me more. I won't be able to hold back much longer. The tide of pleasure crests, threatening to overtake me. Every nerve in me quivers with the need for release, and my lungs scream for oxygen. But still, I hold back.

"Deklan," I rasp, pulling in the tiniest breaths around my closed throat. "Please."

"Cum for me, Mia," Deklan cries out roughly as he lets go of my neck, and the dam breaks inside me.

Waves and waves of pleasure roll over me, throwing my head back against Deklan's chest as I suck in deep, gasping breaths, crying his name like a mantra.

"Deklan, God Deklan, yes Deklan," I cry as the orgasm rides me.

I feel Deklan's cock throbbing inside me as my orgasm fades and his hips pump faster and harder. His hands grasp my hips, holding me in position as he continues thrusting into me, building yet another orgasm in my core. His rhythm falters, his breathing stutters, and finally, he cries out.

"Mia! Fuck Mia," He screams, and the sound of my name pouring from his throat like a plea tears the second orgasm from me, this one more intense than the first.

I scream, my cries mingling with his as we come to climax together. His hot seed fills my pussy in decadent streams as his dick throbs inside me, and my pussy walls milk his cock dry.

The sensations fade, and I sigh in utter happiness and contentment.

I had finally gotten sleep, woke up to the sexiest man on earth cuddled at my back, and had two mind-blowing orgasms in a row. How much better could life get?

But my happiness is short-lived with the ringing of Deklan's alarm.

"Shit!" He exclaims as he reaches over and turns it off.

He gently pulls out of me, takes my leg off his thigh, and places it back on the bed.

"I have to go to work," he says disappointedly. "It's my first day at the bank."

I groan in protest. "Can't Sophia call in a favor and get you out of it?"

Deklan chuckles. "She could, but then how would I support my human self? It's not like we angels have an endless supply of money."

"Well, you should," I say poutingly.

Deklan smacks my ass as he rolls away from me, and I let out a surprised squeal. I duck under the covers to avoid any other assaults until I feel the bed shift as his weight leaves the bed.

"Come out from under those covers, baby," Deklan chuckles. "Don't make me late."

I groan and throw the cover off my head to look at him. "Can't I just sleep in? Sophia can take me home later."

He turns away from the dresser where he had been rummaging through one of the drawers. His jade eyes turn serious, the playfulness leaking away.

"I don't want you to be alone, Mia. I was going to suggest we go to your place, get you cleaned up, and then you can come to the bank with me under the guise that we will be working on the restaurant files today. Then we can go see Harper afterward."

I raise my eyebrows. "Seriously? Deklan, you can't keep eyes on me twenty-four-seven. I have work to do. We can go see Harper, but do I really need to go to work with you?"

I swallow hard when I spot his jaw clenching and his eyes narrowing. Will he be angry with me just because I do not want to be watched over constantly like a toddler?

I try to be angry, but it is hard when he is standing there looking so damn hot. His fiery red hair is adorably disheveled. His jade-green, angry eyes are hooded with the aftermath of mind-blowing sex, the eyebrow ring glinting in the morning sun streaming in from the window.

His muscles ripple under his tanned skin, causing the black tattoos to writhe over his toned chest, upper arms, and neck. The tattoos are a mesmerizingly beautiful pattern of swirls and wavy lines that dance along his skin. I linger on those as my eyes travel down his body.

I stop again below his stomach, Marveling at his massive member hanging limply. Even soft, he is enormous, and I wonder how he had fit all that delicious muscle inside me.

"See something you like, angel face?" Deklan's seductive voice says.

He reaches down and grasps his massive member, wrapping his large hand around it and stroking slowly. He instantly hardens. My eyes swing back to his face, and I gasp. The flash of anger is gone, replaced with a dangerous carnal lust that sends sparks of yearning all the way to my toes.

"If you are a good girl and do as I say today, I will give you some of this as a reward later," He says, holding his cock up as he stalks seductively toward the bed.

"That's not fair," I breathe as I watch him move toward me, a predator stalking its prey.

And I am the prey.

"Or I can just punish you for being a naughty girl," He adds as he comes up beside the bed. "Your choice, my wicked angel."

"I hate you," I say to him as he stares at me with that smoldering heat in his jade eyes.

He smiles softly. "I know."

But does he? Does he know that whenever I say I hate you, I am really saying I am falling for you? Fuck, I am in so much trouble with this man.

"I'm getting up," I say in defeat, even though I would love some punishment right now to go along with my reward later. It makes the orgasms so much more...intense.

He grasps one of my wrists and pulls me up, hauling me off the bed and to my feet roughly. I catch myself on his rock-hard chest as I stumble. He grasps my shoulders and pulls me into his hardness, and I gasp when I see the dark look in his eyes.

"I so hoped you would make it more difficult, angel. I love punishing you," He growls low and seductively.

For the love of all that is holy. My pussy instantly moistens. But I am slowly learning his game, and it is time I started playing.

I put on my best erotic face and say alluringly, "Well, then maybe I will find something bad to do today. Just for you, baby."

I smile wickedly when I see the surprise flicker across his visage. He quickly tried to hide it by schooling his features, but I caught it.

"Fuck, woman, you are going to make me late," He says with a growl.

After two painful yet pleasurable spankings and a quickie-but-not-so-quickie in the shower for my reward later, we are dressed and ready to start our day. Sophia loaned me an outfit after coming to check on me and seeing me dressed in my now-wrinkled pleated skirt and gypsy top I had worn last night.

It was simple yet chic, with black dress slacks, dress flats, an undershirt, and a flowy, sheer top with bell sleeves and a lovely paisley pattern in fabulous fall colors.

Deklan is dressed in the same suit and tie he had worn the day I had seen him in the bank, and I blushed profusely when I recognized the blue tie he had used on me that night. He smirked when he caught me staring at it, waggling his eyebrows suggestively and causing me to blush even harder.

I had mouthed 'I hate you' at him, and of course, he mouthed back, 'I know'.

Now we sit in his mini kitchen, having a cup of coffee and buttery bagels before leaving. I am surprised we even had time for breakfast since we had difficulty keeping our hands off each other this morning. I am even more surprised that we are keeping our hands off each other now.

Especially since Deklan seems to make every sip of coffee and bite of bagel so erotic. He swallows the bite of bagel he has now, piercing me with that lustful stare. He brings the coffee mug to his lips and blows softly. Then, he takes his tongue and swirls it around the rim, making those 'mmm' sounds that drive me crazy with need. Lastly, he takes a small sip, staring at me over the rim of the cup with lust-filled, jade eyes.

"Stop it!" I say as he salaciously licks a drop of butter from the corner of his mouth, swirling his tongue over his lip ring. "You're insufferable!"

"Only when it comes to you, angel face," He says seductively. "I will always want you."

I get up from the table quickly with a huff of annoyance.

"You shouldn't say stuff like that if you don't mean it," I say. "You might give a girl the wrong impression."

I move to take my mug to the sink, but Deklan's hand clamping around my wrist stops me. Damn, he's fast! I didn't even see him move! He pulls me back as he stands and pulls me against his body.

He grabs my chin between his fingers, bringing my gaze to his angry, jade eyes as he growls, "What do you mean by that, Mia?"

My name sliding from his tongue angrily has my blood heating in my veins.

"I mean, we are just having sex, right? This…," I gesture toward him and then back toward me. "This is just two adults having consenting, albeit mind-blowing, sex while you try to teach me to tame my demon before it takes me over."

I swallow as his eyes turn dark, his fingers tightening on my chin. "I will protect you from your demon. But this is a lot more than just sex, Mia, and you know it."

I lower my eyes and mumble, "You don't mean that."

He growls deep in his chest, bringing my gaze back up to his. "Who says I don't mean it?"

I gulp. There is no humor or lying tell in his serious gaze.

"You don't even know me," I whisper in a quivering voice.

"I'd like to remedy that," He responds softly, planting a tender kiss on my lips.

"Deklan…I…but you're an angel."

Deklan chuffs. "So? What does that have to do with anything? I am mostly human when I am here on Earth. I may not age like a human, but that doesn't matter to me. I'd like to be yours forever, Mia. Or at least, as long as you'll have me."

Is this really happening? The sexiest man on Earth wants me?

"But, I am just a boring human. I never do anything exciting, I'm a fucking financial advisor, for God's sake, and I am anti-social. Why would an angel want to be with me?"

Jeesh, when did I get so down on myself? When I met Deklan fucking Maleck, that's when. Do I want him? Absolutely. Am I sure he wants me? For now, sure. Later? Absolutely not.

It may seem good for now, but he will tear my heart out when he gets to know me and realizes how utterly boring and hopeless I am.

Just like the other man I mistakenly fell for.

The muscles in Deklan's jaw tic as he stares down at me. His eyes are hard, but his touch is tender as he cups my face in both hands.

His tone matches his eyes as he says, "Who hurt you, Mia? Give me a name, and you will never have to worry about them again."

"No one hurt me," I lie. "I just know what I see in the mirror."

Deklan's eyes widen in disbelief. "You're a fucking Goddess, Mia. Why would you even say that?"

"I'm not talking about my looks," I say, dashing the sudden tears that spill down my cheeks with the back of my hand. "I'm talking about me. I am nothing special. I'm just…nothing."

"Mia, you are not nothing. You wouldn't have a demon to tame if that were true. You just need someone to show you how special you really are. Let me be that someone."

"Don't say things you don't mean," I say shakily. "Just to save my feelings. Just help me tame this demon and we can go our separate ways."

"Mia, dammit."

He lets me go in a huff, stepping back and running his hand over his face. He looks at me like he doesn't know what to do with me. His jaw does that tic again, and his jade eyes look like they could pierce my soul.

"We will finish this conversation later. We have to go before we are late," He says. "We will take my car today. And when we return after work, we will see Harper about your demon."

My face falls in disappointment. The motorcycle was scary, but I liked it. But he is right. We are too dressed up to ride a motorcycle.

I follow Deklan out of his apartment and down the grand staircase to the hospital's reception area. The blond nurse is there again, and she narrows her eyes at me when she spots me coming down the stairs.

"She really doesn't like me," I whisper to Deklan.

He turns and looks over his shoulder at me as he whispers, "She is jealous. That firecracker has been after me for a while now."

I raise my eyebrows at him, surprised that he would divulge that information to me.

"So, why did you turn her down? She's stunning," I say.

"She's not you," He says with a shrug.

I frown. "You haven't even known me that long."

"I may not have known you that long, angel. But I have been waiting for you for an eternity."

He turns back around without another word and continues down the steps. I blow out a breath and follow him.

Why the fuck does he have to be so God damn sweet?

But I must admit there is a little spring in my step as I follow him out the door, smirking victoriously at the blond behind the counter.

CHAPTER 12: DEKLAN

Mia slept in my bed last night. Mia was there when I woke up this morning. Mia's pussy was divine every single time I took her. Mia…Mia…Mia.

She consumes my mind, my body, my soul. She is all I can think about, want, and need.

And she thinks she is not good enough.

Where the fuck had that come from? Mia is a strong, independent woman with her own company. It runs so well that she doesn't even have to be there. She is grounded, so grounded in fact that she didn't even believe in angels and demons until she saw us with her own eyes.

She is sexy as hell with a perfect body. She is intelligent, driven, and funny at times. Not to mention absolute fire in bed; she loves being punished.

She is the perfect woman.

So why does she think she is less than perfect?

I knew she was lying to me when she said no one had hurt her. I know the signs. I know the pain that consumes a broken heart when happiness threatens to take over. I know the sensation of grief and guilt that consumes a soul over ever wanting someone else. It makes us crazy and confused when we love someone else after falling out of love with the one who hurt us.

I want to get my hands on the bastard that hurt Mia and tear his fucking throat out for making Mia feel this way. Did he not see what he had?

Or maybe I should shake his hand and thank him for being a stupid moron since his loss is going to be my gain. Either way, I will show Mia how perfect she is. She will never doubt herself again.

Of course, we have to get rid of this fucking demon first. My light will only keep the thing quiet for a limited time. But I am not about to leave Mia alone. The next time it comes out, I will be there waiting. I will smite the bitch as much as necessary until we find out how to tame her or get rid of her without hurting Mia.

Mia sits beside me in my sports car, staring out her side window. I wonder what she is thinking? She hasn't said a word to me since we left the hospital, and I am starting to get nervous about it. I won't let her know that, though. I will just sit here and play it cool and...

Just fuck it...what's the worst that can happen just from trying to start a conversation?

"What are you thinking about?" I ask, giving her a quick glance.

Of course, my stupid, infatuated, school-boy-lovesick mouth would say something simple and stupid like that. I kick myself mentally as I grip the wheel, waiting for Mia's answer.

She turns to me with those big, chocolate-brown eyes and answers, "Did you really mean everything you said?"

Without taking my eyes off the road, I answer, "I absolutely did, Mia. Why do you doubt me?"

I watch her through my peripheral vision as she picks at an imaginary piece of lint on her black dress pants and answers, "I don't really know you. How do I know you don't say that to get girls into your bed?"

"Well, if that was true, you fell for my schemes," I say jokingly, but she doesn't laugh.

"I fully admit I may have messed up. That's why I'm worried," Mia says, and I hear the slight tremble in her tone. "I couldn't resist you, and I may have..."

Her words cut off as she huffs.

"You may have what," I ask softly, not wanting to spook her. She is actually opening up to me, and I do not want to do anything to scare her away from that.

"I think I might be falling for you. There, I said it."

She huffs again and flops back. Her back hits the plush back of the seat with an audible poof sound, and she crosses her arms over her chest.

My heart soars and I cannot stop the wide, happy smile that stretches across my face. I try to school my features, but it is no use. This smile will be on my lips for the rest of the day.

"Oh, baby, you just made me a very happy angel," I say as I reach over and grab her hand. "You are gonna get one hell of a reward tonight."

I bring it to my lips and kiss it with a reverent brushing of my lips, all while keeping my eyes pinned to the road.

Mia gulps so hard I hear it echo through the tiny sports car, and her hand trembles in mine. "Well, are you going to tell me how you feel?"

I laugh happily. "Mia, did you not hear anything I said this morning? Do you not see the smile plastered to my face or hear me say how happy you made me just now?"

"I wanna hear you say it," She says stubbornly, her voice trembling.

"I have already said how much I want you," I say, frowning in confusion.

"No, that's not what I mean," she says, pulling her hand from mine. "I want to hear you say what I just said. I want you to say you are falling for me, too."

"Isn't that what I said?" I ask, still confused.

"Not really," Mia answers, crossing her arms over her chest. "You just said you want me and want to keep me for a while. That could mean just sex. I want to hear you say you are falling in love with me."

Fuck, she's gonna make me say it. Despite her earlier words of self-doubt, she put herself out there and made herself vulnerable. So, why does the thought of me doing the same make me nauseous? My Mia is so brave, yet I am a fucking coward. I grip the wheel hard.

"But only if you mean it," she says at my hesitation. Her voice is a tiny whisper, her tone wavering.

Fuck me.

I am no longer smiling. The corners of my mouth draw down, my mouth slightly open, and my brows furrow as my visage slips into a look of absolute terror. Sure, I had said the words to her last night, but she had been asleep. She hadn't heard me. To tell her to her face, laying myself bare before her? Can I allow myself to be that vulnerable?

The air in the car is suddenly stifling, making breathing difficult. A trickle of sweat breaks out along my forehead, and I wipe it away with the back of my hand. My hands are trembling slightly as I grip the wheel. It's safe to tell a sleeping woman I love her, but this...

Can I put myself out there with the risk of having my heart broken again?

"Deklan?" My name slips out like the most desperate of pleas.

Goddess, I hope she isn't looking. But I know she is because she is waiting for my answer. The words are stuck in my throat, frozen by fear of the unknown. She says she is falling for me, but will she stay around?

I'm a Fucking coward.

By some sweet grace of mercy from The Powers That Be, we pull into the bank parking lot. I park the car and scramble out rapidly, pulling in deep breaths of fresh air and trying not to vomit. The bagel and coffee we ate and drank this morning is in danger of leaving my stomach.

I walk unsteadily around to Mia's side, opening her door and offering her a hand. She turns and looks up at me, her chocolate-drop eyes shimmering with unshed tears. The rims are red, her cheeks flushed, and her lips tremble.

God dammit she is going to cry, and that will break me. She brushes my hand away, and my heart plummets to my feet. She pulls herself out of the tiny car and gets to her feet. She takes a breath and opens her mouth as if to speak but turns without saying a word.

"Mia," I rasp around the massive lump in my throat.

But she doesn't look back. My heart thuds as I watch her walk away.

Molten-hot fury at my fucking dumb self flows suddenly through me. My hands ball into fists as my entire body trembles with it. Mia disappears into the bank, and I let out my fury with a scream, turning and punching the side of my beautiful, red car.

Of course, it dents.

God, I am an asshole. Why the fuck couldn't I just say the words? Would it have been so hard to say, *"I'm falling for you too, Mia"*? I could have made her extremely happy by saying, *"I am completely and totally heads-over-heels in love with you, Mia"*, which would have been the truth.

But instead, I fucking choked. I am a giant fucking coward.

I take a steadying breath and run a hand over my face. I have to tell her. I cannot stand the fact that I have hurt her. The look on her face as she got out of the car replays in my mind. She had been so brave, holding back her tears so I wouldn't see her cry.

The thought that she may be in my office waiting for me and crying her heart out breaks something inside me. It fills me with a sudden resolve to tell her everything; why I fell from my Goddess and why it is so hard for me to speak those words to anyone. I have never told another, but I will be brave for her. For her, I will face my past and find my future.

I straighten my stance and walk with purpose toward the bank. I am going to tell Mia everything. She deserves to know. I straighten my suit jacket and tie as I walk in the door and head to my office. One of the tellers stops me as I walk by.

"Mister Maleck. Miss Garcia said to tell you she had to visit the restroom and that she would meet you in your office. Oh, and welcome to the company," The teller says with a wide smile.

Fuck, she is probably in there crying.

Schooling my features, I nod and say, "Thank you…Sarah, was it?"

Her smile widens. "You remembered! And you are very welcome."

I return her smile tightly and move on, walking down the short hallway to the side of the tellers' desks. I open the door that says *employees only* at the end of the hall, which leads into a more extensive, larger hallway.

Clark is waiting for me in my office when I walk in.

"Welcome to the Daisville National Bank, Mister Maleck," He says, standing from the chair behind the desk and offering me his hand.

I take the offered hand and shake it. "Thank you for the opportunity, Clark."

"Well, you came very highly recommended by Sophia, so you can't be all bad," Clark responds humorously.

I chuckle. "I will try not to disappoint."

"I'm sure you won't, Deklan. I have a good feeling about you. I trust you can get settled in here on your own?"

"Yes," I say, gesturing toward the door. "I have actually brought my first order of business to work with me. Miss Mia will join me when she is done in the restroom to get me caught up on the restaurant portfolio."

Clark pushes his spectacles up onto his nose with a flourish and smiles. "Ah, excellent! I love the initiative. Keep up the good work, Deklan."

"Yes, sir," I say with a nod as Clark moves around the desk and heads out the door.

I sigh heavily and move around the desk to take the chair Clark had just vacated. I plop down in the chair, looking around at my new desk. I have a computer, an adding machine, a blank nameplate, and a cup of pens and pencils. Not bad to start.

I start pulling the drawers of the desk out and rummaging through them. The top drawer contains office supplies like rubber bands, paper clips, sticky note pads, white-out, and other random things. The bottom drawers are filing drawers with empty hanging file folders that I will be expected to fill soon.

This could be a promising gig. I may keep this job even though I only took it to get close to Mia. I am good at numbers and organization, so I may be great at this job.

Too bad I'm not just as good at relationships.

I am just beginning to wonder where Mia ran off to when my cell phone buzzes in my pocket. I pull it out and look at the screen. It's Sophia.

"Hiya, Soph," I answer, hoping she believes the perkiness in my tone.

"Where's Mia?" Sophia says, and the urgency in her tone raises the tiny hairs on the back of my neck.

"She's in the bathroom. Why?" I say, standing from my seat and going around the desk. I prepare to bolt out of the office and run towards the bathroom.

"You left her alone, around mirrors?" Sophia says, her voice going high and squeaky.

"I can't very well go in the bathroom with her, Soph," I say defensively.

"Well, you need to watch her closely, Deklan. I found out something disconcerting today."

I swallow hard as concern rockets through me. I am almost too afraid to ask, but I do anyway.

"What did you find out?"

Sophia doesn't answer for a long moment, but I can hear her breathing on the other end of the line. My concern grows as I ponder what could be going on.

Finally, she says, "Jewel told me that she sensed Thorn's presence last night when you were dealing with Mia's demon, and not just the part of him that lives inside Harper," Sophia says worriedly. "I asked Jewel what it could mean, and she said that sometimes traces of a demon can be left behind when they die, especially a very powerful demon.

"It's kind of like energy spirits, you know, when something tragic happens, and it leaves behind an energy signature which may or may not turn into a spirit?"

She pauses, waiting for my answer, so I say, "Yeah, I know what you mean. The spirits that aren't really the spirits of certain people but are simply spirits formed from the traces of energy that person left behind because they died in a highly emotional state, like being terrified, happy, or sad."

"Yes, exactly!" Sophia says. "Jewel said that she thinks Thorn may have left traces of energy behind, which is what lives inside Harper. That energy may have merged with other untrained demons, one of which is Mia's demon. Mia was in town when all this happened, so it is possible that her demon was around when it all went down."

"Wait, are you telling me that Mia's demon may carry traces of Thorn like Harper does?" I ask.

"Yes," Sophia says, her voice lowering to a worried whisper.

"Soph, Harper has more than just an angry energy signature inside him. You don't know what he goes through just to keep that part of him dormant. If it was just a simple energy signature, then it wouldn't be so strong, and Harper could have cast it out of himself by now."

"So, what are you saying, Deklan?"

I sigh and run a hand through my hair before answering. "I'm saying that Thorn didn't exactly die that day. We don't know if he did it on purpose somehow, or if he was simply so overpowered that it was a phenomenon that just happened. Whichever it was, Thorn somehow lives inside Harper.

"Therefore, if what you say is true, then Thorn would have had to split himself into pieces. I have heard of other entities doing some type of soul-splitting thing, but I have never heard of an inner demon doing it. But it could be possible if Thorn was powerful enough."

"So, Jewel's theory may not be too far off the mark?" Sophia asks.

"No, except if Mia's demon does have a piece of Thorn, it is actually Thorn and not an energy signature."

Sophia's hard swallow is audible over the phone just before she replies, "You know what will happen if that's true. He will take over Mia. She isn't strong enough to fight a demon as powerful as Thorn."

"I won't let anything happen to Mia, Soph. You know that."

"I know you will try. Also, what about you? Your ass is on the line over this. If we fail, then you will cease to exist."

Sophia's tone is worried, so I try to sound calm. "I know you're worried, Soph, but try to have some faith in me."

"I did have faith in you, Deklan, but look what happened."

"I know you are worried about our relationship as well," I say with a huff. "I'm going to make it right. I promise."

"That's not the point, Deklan, and you know it," Sophia says, and I hear the beginnings of anger in her tone. "I asked you to help with

Mia because…"

I cut her off before she can continue. "Because you and Harper knew I wouldn't fall for Mia since I am an unfeeling asshole, but you also knew I would work extra hard to help her despite my lack of caring since she-who-shall-not-be-named will obliterate me if I don't tame Mia's demon."

"Exactly, and now look what's happened," Sophia retorts. "Obviously, Harper and I were wrong, and now your heart is on the line as well as your existence. I told you Mia wasn't ready for any kind of relationship, but you went and fell for her anyway, and you probably haven't even had the guts to tell her yet, have you?"

But I don't answer because Sophia's voice is drowned out by another one…

"So that's why you want to keep me around so badly," Mia's voice comes from the doorway.

I had not even heard her come in. I turn my head toward the door and capture her angry stare as my heart sinks to my feet.

"You don't care about me at all. That's why you couldn't say the words. You feel nothing for me at all. You only care about taming my stupid demon to save your own ass," Mia hisses.

She stands in the doorway with her raven-black hair hanging loose over her shoulders and down her back. Her chocolate-kissed eyes are narrowed dangerously, flashing like copper fire in the overhead lights of the office. Her cheeks are flushed, and her lips are curved down.

I can't help but notice how dangerously beautiful she looks when angry. But the observation is nothing compared to the stark terror that rises within me when I realize that the look on her face is not anger.

It is complete and utter devastation.

I can't lose her…and yet, I am about to.

The phone drops from my hand, bouncing on the carpeted floor harmlessly. I turn to her, taking a step toward her as I hold out a hand.

"Mia, wait. Let me explain…"

She interrupts me, backing away as she holds up a hand to ward me off. "No, don't try to lie to me anymore. If sex was all you wanted, I would rather you had been honest with me, but you pretended to care with all your pretty words. You didn't have to do that, Deklan. You didn't have to hurt me."

And with those words, she turns and flees my office, taking my heart with her.

CHAPTER 13: MIA

Stupid, stupid, stupid. I don't know what I had been thinking when I told Deklan that I was falling for him. I must have been out of my mind. What the fuck was I thinking?

I wasn't thinking. That had been the problem. I was letting my fucking neglected pussy do the thinking for me. Jeesh, I go for over six months without dick, and suddenly I am falling for the first man that fucks me?

Pathetic.

I guess it really had been a dream when I thought Deklan said he loved me as we fell asleep last night. That thought ran through my head as I ran from the bank, not knowing where I was going or how I would get there.

And I really didn't care.

I know it was foolish of me to care, to allow myself to fall for him. But he had been so damn…irresistible. The way he somehow knew when to be rough and when to be gentle. The way he seemed to care for me even when I didn't care for myself was all so fucking alluring.

And I fell for it.

Stupid, stupid, stupid. I had known all along. I had told myself that I was in danger, that it would be a mistake to fall for him. I had not listened to myself.

When we arrived at the bank after my startling revelation, Deklan still had not spoken to me. I was hurt. I thought at first that maybe I had caught him by surprise and he had needed time to absorb what I had said to him, so I had waited for the excruciating rest of the ride.

But when he remained silent even after parking, getting out of the car, and opening my door, my heart began to fall to my feet. I knew I had made a mistake.

I got out and ran away as fast as I could. I had hidden in the bank's bathroom like a coward, trying to put my face and heart back together so I could face him again.

Then, I had walked back into the room and heard him say that he would never fall for me. He only wanted me near to tame my demon and save his own ass. I didn't know who he had been talking to, nor did I care.

It had destroyed me, and I ran from him.

Again.

Truthfully, I was running from myself as well. Running from my own stupidity. Running from my past mistakes that I somehow continue to make over and over. Running from my own bleeding, hopeless romantic heart.

Running from myself.

But I can never get away. No matter where I go, I am always there. No matter how far I run, I still let my heart overrule my better instincts.

I am still an introvert, distancing myself from the people who love me most. I am still a bitter bitch, thinking if I am angry all the time, people will not want to get to know me and leave me alone. I am still striving for perfection that doesn't exist, thinking that if I attain perfection, then everyone will love me.

I am a fucking catch twenty-two that will never be fixed.

I am pathetic.

Now, I am walking down the sidewalk of Main Street, which isn't very extensive here in Daisville. The town is so tiny that I could probably throw a rock across the entire city. The sun is shining despite the storm clouds roiling in my darkened heart, and the morning mist rises, lending moisture to the already stifling day.

The buildings of the small town are older and poorly maintained, and some are boarded up with signs in the window that read *closed* or *out of business*. The sidewalks are cracked and broken due to a lack of repair, and the ancient crosswalk signs no longer work. Not that there is any traffic to watch out for anyway.

Even so, the open, cared-for buildings are beautiful, cozy, and full of down-home country charm, including a little honky-tonk bar in the middle of town across from the courthouse.

My building is only two more blocks away, so it wouldn't hurt to go in, have a drink and a good cry, and take the edge off before heading home.

And never seeing Deklan Maleck again.

I go in and look around, my eyebrows raising in surprise. I had expected a small, seedy-looking place, and while the bar is small, it is modern-looking and clean. The cushioned barstools look comfy and inviting, sitting before the shiny bar with the cherry finish. The mirror-backed shelves behind the bar showcase a multitude of liqueurs and spirits, spotlighted by stage lights fastened above the shelves.

There are a few tables scattered throughout the floor, but they are all empty. It is early, so I hadn't expected anyone to be here, but there are a few patrons sitting at the bar.

They all look my way when I walk in and take a seat at the bar. The man at the end of the bar looking up at me curiously captures my attention. He looks hot in that stifling leather jacket but doesn't seem to mind the heat at all. He is big and burly, with tattoos that almost cover the surface of his bald head. His eyes are hidden behind dark sunglasses, even though the bar's interior is dark.

He looks like someone I would not want to piss off.

I turn my attention away from the colossal man and glance at the other patron. He sits at one of the booths along the far wall, but he does not pay any attention to me other than the brief look he gave me when I walked in. He holds his coffee with both hands, staring down into the mug and mumbling something unintelligible.

I turn back to the bar and almost jump out of my seat when the burly man fills my vision.

"Can I help you, ma'am?" He asks in a deep, dark tone.

Oh. He must be the bartender.

"Y…y…yes," I stutter. "Give me something strong."

The bartender chuckles, the sound rumbling through the empty room. "Yes, ma'am. Rough morning, huh?"

"You could say that," I mumble, looking down at the bar.

If I drink myself into oblivion, maybe I can escape this excruciating pain that radiates through my chest.

"Wanna talk about it?" The man asks.

I don't answer and only shake my head. Tears prick the backs of my eyes, and I blink rapidly to keep them from falling.

The man shrugs. "Suit yourself. Here's your drink."

He slides a small shot glass my way, filled with clear liquid. He places a lime wedge on a napkin beside the glass and slides me a salt shaker.

"My name's Duke. If you need anything, just ask," He says.

"I'm Mia," I say, my voice quivering with unshed tears.

"You're Sophia's cousin," Duke says.

It isn't a question, so I don't answer. I don't think I could, anyway, around the huge golf-sized lump in my throat. I simply nod.

"Well, it's nice to meet ya, Mia," Duke says, then resumes his place at the end of the bar.

I look at the drink Duke left, the pressure in my chest expanding painfully. The tears threaten to spill over as I pick up the glass and bring it to my lips. The sharp smell stings my nose, but I ignore it and toss the drink into my mouth, swallowing quickly before I lose my nerve.

I never drink. I can't stand losing control of my thoughts and actions. It terrifies me. Therefore, I never drink and have never in my life been drunk. This is the excuse I use for the sudden bout of coughing that seizes my body as the excruciatingly burning drink sears its way down my throat and into my stomach.

That was nothing like it is in the movies when they shoot their drinks and they act all cool and together, slamming the shot glasses back down on the bar. I never see anyone fall into a coughing fit.

Duke looks down at me in concern, but I wave him off with a flourish of my hand as I inhale a deep breath to relieve the burn. It doesn't work and only leads to more coughing. My eyes are watering, my chest is on fire, and I feel like a fool.

The burn eases somewhat, and I concentrate on breathing normally. Finally, the coughing fit subsides, and I wipe the tears from my eyes.

"Next time, try some salt before you put the drink in your mouth, and then try sucking on the lime right after you swallow," Duke says with a chuckle as he stands and moves my way.

He gives me another small glass of the burning liquid, along with a glass of water this time.

"This one's on the house," He says with a smile.

"Thanks," I mumble as I reach for the glass.

I sprinkle some salt onto my tongue before tossing the drink down this time and then shove the lime wedge in my mouth after swallowing.

It still burns like fire.

Gasping, I pull the lime out of my mouth and take a long pull of the water. The tears spill down my cheeks as I swallow it down. I blame it on the fiery drink, but it's not the case. The pressure in my chest erupts, coming to the surface in a sob that I stifle by placing a hand over my mouth.

"You okay?" Duke asks as I struggle to breathe around the sobs.

"B...b...bathroom?" I rasp.

"Around the corner that way," Duke says, pointing to the end of the bar where he was sitting when I first came in.

I jump from the barstool and practically run around the corner. I look around and spot the sign for the bathrooms. Clutching my chest, I run into the ladies' room and to the sink. I grasp the edge of the sink with both hands, leaning my head down as I let out a gut-wrenching sob.

Dizziness causes me to pitch forward, and I struggle to remain upright. My thoughts jumble together as my vision goes blurry, and my lips go numb. I raise my head and look into the mirror. My eyes are bloodshot, my nose red, and tears streak down the sides of my face.

I try to stifle the emotions tearing through me and shut them all away like I have always done, but I cannot. The tears come freely; the pain in my chest overwhelms me. What the hell is wrong with me?

"You are drunk," A voice says inside my head.

My demon. It's awake. But how?

"Being drunk weakens your system, which allowed me to come out of the stupor that fucking angel put me in," My demon answers me, even though I did not ask the question aloud.

My eyes widen as I watch the swirls of shadow surround me in the mirror's reflection. The form of my demon comes drifting from the shadows, superimposing over my own reflection as its eyes glow a purplish-blue.

"If you let me take you, I will take all the pain away," She says aloud, her shadowy hair falling around her dark shoulders.

I swallow hard. Her voice sounds...different... more eerie when she speaks aloud. "Weaf me awone an go back whurr yew came fom," I say, dramatically slurring my words.

Fuck. I really am drunk, and I only had two shots. And it was only minutes ago. Whatever the bartender gave me works fucking fast.

"Come on, Mia. Don't you want to get revenge on Deklan for hurting you?" The demon says as its translucent form solidifies just a bit.

Revenge? That word never crossed my mind when it came to Deklan. I did not want to see him hurt just because he had hurt me. I shake my head emphatically.

"At least let me take your pain away," The demon says as its form wavers slightly.

I shake my head harder, backing away from the mirror unsteadily.

My vision is blurrier, and my dizziness worsens as I move. My breath comes in uneven, ragged pants as my heart patters in my chest.

I stumble and almost fall, but I grab the paper towel holder on the wall beside the sink. My eyes widen as I see my demon come dangerously close to the surface of the mirror. Her form solidifies to the point that she blocks out my reflection entirely, and I feel that pulling sensation in my gut again.

No, no, no.

Terror fills my bones, which has an instant sobering effect. I am suddenly hyperaware of everything around me, and I cling to my soul as the demon tries to take it away.

I have to fight. I can't let my demon take me. Deklan's words play in my mind.

"Because you and Harper knew I wouldn't fall for Mia since I am an unfeeling asshole, but you also knew I would work extra hard to help her despite my lack of caring since she-who-shall-not-be-named will obliterate me if I don't tame Mia's demon."

Deklan may have obliterated my heart, but that does not mean I want him to be obliterated, too. Even though I will never be with him, I couldn't imagine a world without him in it.

"Just let go, Mia. I will take good care of you," The musical tones of my demon whisper to me, her tone comforting and inviting.

"No," I say, but it comes out in a whisper instead of the commanding tone I had intended.

The pulling sensation strengthens, and I feel myself slowly slipping. My vision goes dark around the edges, and I wobble on my feet. My hands grip the paper towel holder tightly as I make my way back to the sink.

"L..l..let…m..m..me…GO!" I stumble over my words through gritted teeth as I hang on to the sink with mottle-knuckled hands.

"Never," She whispers in my head. *"I will take your soul and leave it lost in the void between space and time, and then I will have your body for my own."*

By some base instinct I hold deep in my soul, I tighten my muscles and imagine pulling back on whatever is pulling me forward. I grind my teeth hard with the effort, and my body actually moves back a few inches as if physically pulling something. My body trembles from the struggle.

The terror inside ignites into an inferno of horror as I watch my demon's form coalesce in darkness and shadow through the mirror, flowing in an ocean of black fog into the bathroom, where I stand huddled over the sink. Her form materializes fully before me, with her purplish eyes glowing like a beacon of evil.

The pulling sensation grows too strong for me to fight it any longer. My clenched muscles tremble with the effort to hang on, but I am not strong enough. I feel my soul slipping from my body as the evil laughter of my demon fills my head.

I grab for my demon, reaching out and grasping her wrist even as she grasps mine with her free hand. We hold onto each other that way, neither of us letting go as I am pulled from my body.

She struggles against me, but I hang on. If I am going to be pulled from my body, she will not have it. If she takes me, I will take her with me. The pulling sensation continues, and I can no longer feel my body. The sensation is oddly soothing due to the lightening of the pressure in my chest.

My pain dissipates with the departing of my soul. Darkness fills my vision as I slip away, and my demon's icy fingers hold my upper arm as my soul is pulled free. She makes one final effort to pull away from my hold, but I grip her arm with all my might.

I may not be able to feel my physical body, but I can still experience the sensation of my fingers wrapped around my demon's arm. It is as if I am nothing but my thoughts and those fingers that I so desperately keep clamped around that arm.

Sadness and regret fill my departed soul as my demon pulls me into the void along with her. Her screams of rage fill the empty air. She has failed to disengage me from her, and she is with me now somewhere in the space of nothingness.

I smirk in victory. Now, we are both lost.

CHAPTER 14: DEKLAN

I am frozen in my grief as I watch Mia walk out of my life. My throat closes, cutting off my breath and my oxygen. My heart threatens to burst from my ribcage. My ears pop, and sound comes rushing back to me.

"Deklan? Deklan! Deklan, are you there?" The tinny sound of Sophia's voice coming from the phone I had dropped on the floor floats in the empty air of my office.

I bend over, moving in slow motion, and pick up the phone, placing it to my ear with Soph's voice still coming out of the speaker.

"Deklan, what is happening?"

"Mia walked in and heard the last thing I said," I explain calmly, even though my chest is a melding pot of emotion, and I feel as if I am about to explode. "Now she thinks I only want to be around her because I don't want to die."

"Did you explain to her that..."

I cut off Sophia's words. "She didn't give me a chance to tell her anything. She just walked out."

"Well, go after her!" Sophia says urgently. "She shouldn't be alone right now!"

I run a hand through my hair and sigh into the phone. "Soph, she told me she was falling for me today, and I choked. I didn't say anything back, and now she thinks I don't reciprocate her feelings."

"For fuck's sake, you ignorant, moronic Hulk!" Sophia yells into the phone.

I pull the phone away from my ear to save my eardrums for the rest of the rant.

"Do you know what you have done? Do you know what a chance she took by putting herself in a vulnerable situation like that?

"I never thought she would ever want to be with another man again, but you got to her somehow. And now you have gone and ruined it!

Goddess, now she will never open up to anyone!"

"Don't you think I know I hurt her, dammit?" I yell back. "Don't you think I'm hurting too?"

My Goddess's face flashes in my mind, beautiful and ruthless, just like the last time I saw her.

The day she threw me out of her realm.

And now I have been rejected once more.

"I'm sorry, Deklan," Sophia says, her voice quiet and sympathetic. "I forget sometimes that you have been hurt too."

"It's fine, forget it. We can fight later. For now, I have to go find Mia. If anything happens to her, I will never forgive myself."

"Then go! I will call and handle Clark. I'll tell him I had to call you in here for some emergency. Call me when you find her," Sophia says, and I hear the beep signifying the call has been cut off.

"Fuck me," I mutter to myself as I run my hands through my hair and then down my face. "Where the hell do I even start looking?"

My phone vibrates in my hand, and I look at the screen questioningly. I frown.

Duke, one of my Fallen Angels, is calling me.

I used to frequent his bar back in my earlier days here when I wanted nothing more than to drink my human life away, party, and see how many women I could get into my bed.

Duke always had a seat for me at the bar, plenty of patrons I could socialize with, and the women loved going there. The women who frequented Duke's bar were pretty much a sure thing anyway. Plus, Duke shared a love for motorcycles, and we would often ride together.

Then, I sobered up and stopped going to the bar. Now, I only talk to Duke when I have an assignment for him. But he never calls me. What could he want?

I hit the answer button and place the phone to my ear. "Deklan here."

"Hey Boss, aren't you the one helping Sophia's cousin, Mia?" He asks.

Hope blossoms in my chest. "Yes, I am. Have you seen her?"

"Absolutely. She is here now, in the little girl's room," Duke answers. "That's why I'm calling. She was acting weird, so I thought I would call."

"Thanks, Duke. Good job. Don't let her leave. I'll be right there."

"Yes, Boss," he answers.

I hang up and bolt out of the office and down the hall. I can only assume Sophia has held up her end and called Clark because I am not about to stop and explain why I am leaving.

I reach my car and peal out of the bank's parking lot, straight down Main Street, and stop in front of Duke's bar. My heart lurches with anxiety as I park on the curb in front of the bar. There is an ample-sized parking lot out back, but I don't want to take the time to drive around the block to the back of the store.

Every nerve in my body vibrates with energy as I walk up to the door. Mia will probably not want to speak to me, and I will probably have to force her into the car to take her back to safety.

We have set back to square one of our relationship, but this time, there will be more resistance on her part. But I am okay with that. I just want Mia safe for now, and we can deal with the rest later.

I walk into the bar and find Duke sitting in his usual spot at the end of the bar.

"Where is she?" I demand as I walk up to him.

"Still hasn't come out of the bathroom," Duke answers with a shrug, running one hand over his bald, tattooed head.

Alarm and fear crash through me, sending my gut into a tailspin of nausea.

"And you didn't think to go check on her?" I ask angrily.

"You said not to let her leave, so I figured as long as she is in the restroom, she would be here," Duke answers defensively. "Besides, I figured she was probably puking or something since she had a hard time handling the two shots of tequila she had."

I growl in frustration and run toward the restrooms.

Looking over my shoulder, I call out, "Call Sophia. Tell her what's happening and that I am bringing Mia there."

I stall when I reach the bathroom door, wondering if I should barge in and play the overbearing jerk who doesn't know how to take no for an answer and likes forcing women to play his naughty reward and punishment sex games, or knock and be myself so I can pour my heart out and tell her that I am falling for her too. The second one is the one I should do, but the fear spikes when I think about saying the words.

Fuck this. I need to get in there with Mia now. I'll just have to play it by ear and see what happens.

I fling the door open.

"Mia, what the hell were you thinking..."

My words freeze in my throat, and my heart falls to my feet.

Mia lies on the floor unconscious, her arms flung out to her sides and her hair surrounding her head like a silky black halo. Her legs lie sideways and are bent at the knees. Her eyes are closed, and there is no fluttering of her lids as there are when she sleeps. She lies utterly still.

"Mia," I rasp as I fall to her side.

I fumble nervously at her neck, pressing my fingers to the site where her pulse should be. I watch her breasts closely, looking for the rise and fall of her breath. Relief floods my system when the pulse plays at my fingers, and her chest rises and falls, but the relief is short-lived.

It hits me like a spear to my gut, sharp and swift as the sensation runs through me. Angels are attuned to the human soul like electricity to wires, especially when we are in human form. Therefore, I can feel the emptiness of the body lying before me. The heart beats, and the lungs work, but no soul is inside.

Mia's soul is gone.

"Oh, Mia," I say, my tone filled with misery as I gently pick her up and lay her in my lap, holding her close to my body like a tiny baby.

I place my hand on her chest, where her heart beats against my palm. I close my eyes and concentrate on that spark that should be inside her body if her demon is there. There is nothingness.

The fucking demon bitch is gone too. She's probably taking Mia's soul far away, across time and space, maybe even somewhere in the Demon Dimension. Anywhere where she could hide Mia long enough to take over Mia's body.

If the demon shows its face in Mia's body, I will annihilate it and damn the consequences. Then, I will burn the heavens, Earth, and dimensions to find Mia and bring her home.

A scream of pure rage and grief rips through my soul and exits my throat. Why am I such a fuck up? Why can't I get just one thing right? Why do I destroy every person I get close to?

Shake it off, I tell myself. *There is no time for a pity party now. You have got to save Mia.*

Duke comes running into the bathroom, undoubtedly because he heard my scream. He looks wide-eyed at Mia and crosses himself as he mutters something in Latin. Duke is a fallen angel of Jehovah's line, but his God cannot save Mia now. Nor can he help with the demon.

"Should I call an ambulance?" Duke asks nervously.

I shake my head. "No. I'm taking her to Sophia, and Sophia can decide what to do."

"How the hell are you gonna get her there? She can't hang on a bike like that," Duke says worriedly.

"My car is right out front," I respond.

"But it's a two-seater," Duke says.

"I'll lay the seat back," I answer. "Why are you adamant about giving me a hard time?"

"I'm not trying to give you a hard time, Boss, but you must stop and think. Do you even have a plan?" Duke says, wringing his hands nervously.

"Just let me get Mia out of here, and we will be out of your hair, Duke," I say as I attempt to push past him.

Duke holds his hands up in surrender. "Fine, fine. I'll call Sophia and tell her you are on your way."

I carry Mia past Duke and toward the front door.

"Damn demons always ruining everything. The entire race needs to die," Duke mutters as I walk by him.

I ignore him and keep walking, holding Mia's body close to mine. I just want to get Mia's body somewhere safe and figure out how I am going to find and save her soul.

I struggle to get Mia's limp, unresponsive body in the car and settled for the ride to the hospital, but I do. Walking around to the driver's side, I try to get a grip on my emotions. It won't do Mia any good if I panic, drive like a maniac, and get myself killed and her body destroyed.

I need her body so I can bring her back.

By the time I settle into the driver's seat, I am calmer than when I had slid into the parking lot earlier. I drive faster than the speed limit, but not too fast. Nothing that would draw unwanted attention.

I make it to the hospital, sliding to a stop in front of the covered porch. Sophia is waiting in front of the Victorian mansion-turned-hospital with Gabe, Caleb, and Pierce, my three fellow hulks.

Gabe, hulk number two, steps forward and opens the passenger-side door of my car before I can even open my door. His short, blond hair shines in the noonday sun as he leans into the car. He glances at me with his topaz-colored eyes, raising his eyebrows in concern.

"I got her, Boss," He assures me when he sees me flinch.

Gabe picks Mia's body up gently and turns to the other two hulks.

"Caleb, help Gabe with Mia, please," Sophia calls to hulk number three.

He jumps to do her bidding, brushing a hand over his bald head as he salutes Sophia. I like that they respect her, especially since she is their boss just as much as I am.

"Pierce, guard the turret door when we go in. No one goes in after us, no matter their clearance," Sophia says as I jog to catch up after hefting myself out of the car.

Pierce falls in line behind Sophia, brushing his black bangs out of his amber-colored eyes. I catch up to them and follow Pierce as we approach the small doorway behind the reception desk.

Cora stares at us with wide, concerned eyes as we pile in the front door and approach the small door behind her desk. Pierce closes the door behind us after we enter one by one, staying back with Cora to guard the turret door as Sophia had requested.

The wide hallway that leads to the turret is longer than I would like it to be. The anxiety that expands my chest threatens to burst out of me in waves of fury the longer we wait to get to wherever Sophia is taking us. The line moves agonizingly slow around the corner and into the pristine, white-marble hallway with the sterile white walls and spotless windowed rooms.

Gabe, still carrying Mia's body, leads us into one of the rooms after Caleb unlocks the door and holds it open so we can all pile in. The monitors that show different parts of the hospital line the wall on the far side of the room. The desk and chair in front of the monitors usually holds a guard, sometimes two, but it is suspiciously empty now.

Caleb walks over to the desk and pushes on the surface. A panel opens, and Caleb pushes the hidden button underneath. The whooshing sound from the other side of the room causes me to flinch slightly, and I turn quickly toward the sound.

The sterile whiteness of the wall is broken by the hidden door that is revealed as it slides open. I curiously approach it as Gabe ducks inside with Mia's body cradled in his arms.

I know of the hidden rooms. We all do since we diligently guard the place and know all the secret tunnels and hide-outs. Sophia made us memorize them all after she had been kidnapped, her soul taken, and her body hidden in one of the secret tunnels.

Even though Harper had made Thorn tell us where her body was while he had control of Thorn, It had still taken hours to find her body. The tunnel system was confusing because we didn't know the names of the passageways or rooms.

Despite all of that, I have never been inside this particular hidden room until now. I knew about it but have never been inside. It was new, built and placed here by Sophia after Harper's death.

"Deklan," Sophia says, placing a hand on my arm to stop me from entering the new room.

I turn questioning eyes to her, the impatience in my gut threatening to spell over.

"You must not let anyone know what I have in that room, understand?" Sophia says sternly. "It is of the utmost importance that this room remains hidden. Also, you must not be angry with me. It was Harper's idea not to tell you because he didn't want to get your hopes up."

I frown. "What the hell do you have in there?"

"Don't freak out when you see what's there. Just concentrate on Mia, and know that she will be safe," She says, and my heart skips a few beats at her mysterious words.

"Sophia, let me in that room now," I say, my tone dangerously low.

She gestures toward the room. "Be my guest. Just don't freak out."

I turn and duck inside the small door, straightening on the other side and looking suspiciously around. The room is sterile and starkly white, just like the other rooms. However, this one is extra sterile, like a hospital room.

In fact, it is exactly like a hospital room.

Several gurneys are placed along the wall on one side, each with an IV pole, different monitors, and those metal hospital dressers where the doctors keep all the medical supplies.

Caleb carefully places Mia's body on one of the beds, covering her with the blanket and gesturing toward the other side of the room in a come-over motion.

I turn my attention that way to find a table and chairs on the other side of the room where two men and a woman, all wearing scrubs, sit at the table, raising questioning eyebrows.

The woman and one of the men get up and stride quickly toward Caleb. The other man's eyes dart nervously toward one of the other beds, and my eyes follow his.

I freeze in my tracks as I recognize the body lying on that bed, hooked up to several of the monitors and a plethora of IV bags, tubes, and wires.

"What the fuck have you done, Sophia?" I whisper as I walk closer to the bed.

Sophia places her hands on her hips and answers, "What I was told to do. I told you not to freak out."

Freak out does not begin to describe my emotions as I look at the body lying in the hospital bed. There are multiple wires and tubes hooked up to different places on his body. His once-shiny dark hair is dull, and his skin has lost its color. My heart sinks as I look upon my friend in this state. It is a shock to see his body still alive.

"But, I thought Harper died," I say to Sophia. "This makes no sense. You cannot revive a body after it has been dead for so long, and it was hours after he had the heart attack before the paramedics were called. Is Harper trying some kind of necromancy spells?"

"Harper's body didn't die," Sophia says.

"Yes, he did. He died of a heart attack after he completed that spell that took all of his energy," I argue.

"No, that's just what everyone thinks," Sophia says. "Only the other three hulks and I, and now you, know the truth, and we want to keep it that way.

"The backlash of the spell only forced Harper's soul out of his body and back into the Demon Dimension. It didn't kill him. His body was frail when the paramedics found him. They took him to Harper's hospital initially.

"However, I made them bring him to this hospital and then told everyone he died. I paid these doctors here who are still taking care of his body to write up a death certificate, and they provided me with an urn of ashes so I could have him a ceremony for his family."

"But why?" I ask.

"Harper left me a note providing instructions in case anything happened. He didn't want to give up his body until he absolutely had to, but he also didn't want his family trying to take everything away from me since he would have technically still been alive.

"This way, I would inherit everything, and his family couldn't do anything about it since his will can't be contested. Also, it leaves me in charge of everything so I can guard the mirror portal."

I frown in confusion. "So you have been keeping his body alive this entire time in hopes he would find a way back? And you thought he was only stuck due to his spell fucking up."

Sophia smiles sadly as she answers, "Yes. Now you see why I was so upset that he had not told me until last night."

"This is all my fucking fault," I say, running a hand through my ruby hair.

"No, Deklan, it's not. And I am fucking tired of hearing your self-pity moans about how everything is your fault. Dammit, Deklan, everyone is responsible for their own decisions. Stop carrying the weight of those decisions on your own shoulders.

"Yes, the first time was your fuck up because you chose to drink yourself to death instead of step up and do your job. However, Harper chose to do everything independently even after you came to work for him and was helping him, so that was his own fault.

"Now, can we focus on how we will save Mia? In the meantime, Her body will be safe here."

I stare at Harper's body. "Are you still going to keep his body alive, even knowing Harper may never be able to go back to it?"

"Of course I am. He didn't give up even knowing that, and I won't give up either. We will find a way to get Harper back," Sophia says stubbornly.

I smile at her optimism. I wish I had some.

The steady beeping of a heart monitor fills the room, and I turn to see the doctor and nurse hooking Mia's body up with wires, sticky pads, and an I.V.

"We will take good care of her," Sophia says. "Now, go and find out how to save my cousin."

CHAPTER 15: MIA

Time means nothing. Space is an irrelevant thing. My demon still has me in her grip as we fly through nothingness, clinging to me just as I cling to her shadowy form. Pieces of my life start to flash before my eyes as we travel through time, and I ride the sensations the memories induce as I hold onto my demon.

Sophia and I are playing in my room during one of her visits, and I am angry at the dolly she is playing with. Daddy gave it to her as a welcome gift. Where was my present? Why does he pay so much attention to her whenever she is around?

The boy of my dreams sits before me during our first date. I couldn't believe he had actually asked me out. The night was perfect and wonderful, and I had lost my virginity to that boy.

The next day, I was the harlot of the school after he had bragged to his friends how easy it had been to convince me to have sex with him. That was the beginning of my introversion.

I had made it. I opened my own company, gathering clients from years of working freelance. Still, my father talked about Sophia and how proud he was of her accomplishments. I would never add up to Sophia's standards.

But the man who lived in the apartment across the hall thought I did

and then some. He loved me wholly and unconditionally, and we
would be married.

It was the most horrific day of my life. I had stopped by after my
bachelorette party to see my fiancé. I needed some moral support,
being depressed because my maid of honor and best friend had not
made it to the party. She had come down with a headache at the last
minute, but it was apparent my future husband had the cure.

I stood frozen in his bedroom doorway as they scrambled to find
their discarded clothing after I had walked in on them having sex. He
kept saying how sorry he was, how she didn't mean anything to him,
that he only loved me.

Then why the fuck did he have sex with her?

It was the second time my heart had been shattered.

I never trusted anyone after that.

Except Decklan.

My soul screams for the visions to stop. I cannot take anymore.
The pain I experienced when I heard Deklan casually dismiss me as if
I were just another booty call still holds me in its clutches.

Three times is the charm, they say. But this was not a charm for
me. This was outright torture.

And I wasn't even good enough to be just a booty call. He had no
choice but to seduce me. His existence was on the line over me, so he
had to get close to me.

Pain and grief washed over my soul at this thought. Someone
would find my unconscious body in the bathroom, and Deklan's life
would be forfeit. That, more than anything, fills my soul with misery.

Deklan may be a pompous, controlling, self-centered asshole who
had torn my heart out and stomped it into the ground, but I don't want
him to die over me.

However, there is no way to get back to my body. I would not even
know how.

Besides, my fucking demon still has a death grip on my arm.

Literally.

"Let me go, you idiot, before someone takes your body away and I cannot find it," My demon says to me, and I hear it aloud as if her voice is no longer in my head.

Yet her mouth does not move. It is strange, but I am too angry to pay attention to that now.

"What, so you can have it to yourself? No fucking way," I hiss at her, tightening my grip on her arm.

"It is better than both of us losing it, is it not?" She asks.

"No, you pompous fucking demon!" I answer harshly. "I would rather die than let you have my body."

"Fucking humans," The demon seethes. "Always so possessive over your fucking bodies when they are nothing but weak little shells that do not even last that long."

"Then why do you want it so bad?" I ask sarcastically.

"Because it's better than nothing!" She shoots back.

I do not respond and only huff as I cross imaginary arms over a chest I no longer have. At least, in my imagination, I still have a body.

Suddenly, I notice that we are no longer moving through space, and I look around. It is dark in this place, wherever we are, and I cannot see anything except the glowing eyes of my demon.

"Where are we?" I ask nervously.

"We are somewhere in between the lines of time and dimensions. Your unwillingness to let me go so I could get us back to your body has gotten us lost," My demon answers in an accusatory tone.

"You didn't want to get us back. You just wanted to get yourself back," I say harshly. "You were going to leave me here and take over my body."

"You would have been fine," She says, dismissively waving her free shadowy hand. "Eventually, you would have just faded away into nothingness. It would not have even hurt. In fact, you may still fade away into nothingness. Human souls don't last long here."

"Neither will you," I say in a derogatory tone.

"Just shut up so I can figure out what to do," She snaps as her eyes glow brighter.

The demon snaps her fingers, and suddenly there is light. Sensations flood my soul, and I realize I must have somewhat of a body if I can see and feel. I lift my free hand and try to see it, but nothing is there. I move my hand back and forth, and the air wavers where my hand should be.

Am I invisible? The sensation is strange, and it makes my stomach roil. I drop my hand back to my side as I turn my attention back to the hand that still clutches my demon.

I can see a faint outline of that hand as it contrasts starkly against the darkness of my demon's shadowy form. It trembles slightly from the effort to hang on, but I do not let go.

My demon huffs in irritation. "I guess we should go back since you are a stubborn brat. I will have to find another way to take your body."

I frown. "Why can't we just get along and work together?"

The demon scoffs. "Yeah, right. I do not want to be ordered around by some stupid human."

I shrug. "Who says I would order you around? Sophia doesn't order her demons around. From what I have heard from Sophia, they are all friends and work together."

"I don't believe that," My demon says with a roll of its glowing eyes. "Sophia is an evil bitch."

"You are the evil bitch," I shoot back harshly. "Besides, how do you know Sophia?"

My demon frowns for a moment before answering. "I am not sure. I just know that she...well, she...

"I have these memories of her for some reason. Her face, cold and calculating, watching helplessly as she ordered me to...No, she didn't order me. I was forced by another human, her mate. They ordered me...I had no choice but to...My former master was torn apart.

"I tore him apart, forced by Sophia and her mate. Then I...I...That's all I remember."

My heart beats wildly in my chest as I listen to my demon's story, and the stories Sophia told me swirl around my brain. I go over the details in my mind, but...What the fuck? No...it cannot be...my demon is female, and Sophia's kidnapper, Jeremy's demon, had been male.

But the story...that is what had happened...that is what Sophia had told me.

Could it be possible?

"Thorn?" I ask softly.

Recognition lights up my demon's purplish eyes. "Yes, that's my name...er...that was my name...it isn't anymore."

My demon pauses, a look of contemplation blooming over her features. She frowns as she continues to speak.

"I am not that demon, but I have a piece of that demon inside me. Something happened to me when that demon was vanquished, but it is all just a blur when I try to remember what happened."

Her head whips around, and she looks at me with a frown still on her face. "When you said the name just now, it sparked something inside me. I...I am separated from that piece of demon inside me. He is asleep inside me. How is this possible? Who was the demon called Thorn?"

"I don't know how this can be happening, but strangely, I do happen to know who Thorn was and what happened to him," I say, tightening my grip on My demon's arm. "And I can tell you right now that Sophia was not the one that was evil."

"But how can someone who isn't evil stand there and watch someone be torn apart so coldly?" The demon asks.

She pauses, taking a breath as she says, "I remember it all so vividly, as if the memory is my own instead of Thorn's. I can feel the sensation of Thorn tearing his master's limbs from his body while the woman just stood there and watched. I remember Thorn's helplessness at being unable to stop as he was controlled by another."

She pauses again, looking at me with tortured eyes set in her shadowy face. The blue and violet colors battle against each other as they flash.

Her hoarse voice is barely a whisper as she says, "Why did they force a demon to tear his master apart if they were not evil?"

My face softens as I look into the demon's questioning eyes. My tone is less angry as I say, "I'll tell you what happened, but first, you have to promise to take me back to my body."

She huffs. "Fine. I promise I'll take you back. Now, tell me what happened."

"Ha. Do you think I am stupid? Take me back first, and then I will tell you."

My demon growls. "How do I know you will tell me when I take you back and not just have your angel put me to sleep like he did Thorn?"

I shake her slightly with the hand that still grips her arm. "You are so infuriating!"

She seems unbothered by my anger and simply stares at me, her eyes flashing alternatively between purple and blue.

I growl frustratingly. "How about we move and talk at the same time?"

"Fine," The demon says, moving slowly and pulling me with her. "So, talk."

So I do as my demon pulls me through space and time.

I tell her the story that Sophia told me, which I did not believe when I first heard it. I had thought it was the imaginings of a sick mind that had seen its fair share of strange hallucinations, but now I know that is not true.

It all really happened.

Jeremy kidnapped Sophia and used his demon, Thorn, to help rape and torture her. He tried to force her into bonding her demon, Lucien, with Thorn. Jeremy planned to take control of both demons and use them to gain immense power.

Fortunately, Harper knew Thorn's name. He knew of a spell allowing him to take over a demon using the demon's name. He took over Thorn and used him to rescue Sophia and kill Jeremy. And now Harper is trapped in the Demon Dimension because the spell backfired.

When I finish the story, my demon stops moving. She stares at the fog-covered ground in front of her with a look of shame on her face.

"So, Thorn and Jeremy were the evil ones," She whispers to herself. "The human and her angel acted out of anger, vengeance, and protecting Sophia when they forced Thorn to tear Jeremy apart."

"Yes," I say.

We continue walking, moving in silence for a moment, as my demon stares contemplatively ahead. Finally, after a few awkward moments, I break the silence.

"So, have you been controlled by Thorn this entire time?"

She nods her shadowy head, wisps of smoky hair flying around her with the movement. "While I have been inside you, yes. I don't know how this happened to me. I can vaguely remember being assigned to you. I was excited about it and loved the idea of helping someone.

"Then, suddenly, I was flooded with those memories and the idea that I WAS Thorn. I knew I wasn't, but sometimes it was hard to tell myself apart from Thorn, and it would all get jumbled inside my head."

"Maybe if you helped me now, Thorn's influence might fade," I say softly.

"Yes, I agree," She says.

She turns her head up and looks at me, and I gasp as I watch the purplish color leak from her eyes. The cornflower blue color that is left reminds me of a sky just before a rainstorm, and the color shines with the force of the brightest streak of lightning.

"Your eyes changed," I say reverently.

"Is that a good thing or a bad thing?" She asks shakily.

"I don't know. We must ask Deklan when we return, even though I don't want to talk to him." My grip on my demon's arm begins to slip as I sigh with resignation.

"He is your guardian angel, isn't he?" The demon asks. "The one who put me to sleep before?"

I nod. "Yes."

"He broke your heart," she says, and I swear I hear compassion in her tone.

I raise my eyebrows in surprise and look over at her. Her hand has slipped from my arm so that we both walk alone, side-by-side. Fear grips me as I realize that she could easily leave me here at any moment.

But she doesn't.

Instead, she moves closer to me and slides her arm around my shoulders, pulling me close to her in a sideways hug. The frigid coldness of her body seeps through me, but it is oddly comforting.

"I am sorry," She says softly. "I never meant for you to be hurt. Before Thorn, I wanted to help you. I have always wanted to be connected to someone, to be an inner demon. Now, I have my chance."

Is it possible to cry without a body? My chest expands with a plethora of emotion, even though I have no chest to contain it. Tears threaten to spill out of my eyes, even though I have no eyes and no face for the tears to fall down. A sob escapes a mouth I do not have, but the sound reverberates around the space nonetheless.

"Don't cry," My demon croons. "You will never be alone again. You have me now."

I sniffle and wipe my nonexistent nose with my invisible hand. "For now. What happens if Thorn comes back?"

"We will cross that bridge when we get there," my demon says with a smile.

Even though I do not have a body, I still go through the motions of wiping my face clean of tears as if I have one. And maybe I do have some version of a body here.

"Can I ask a favor, though?" My demon asks as I wipe the ghostly tears from my fake face.

"Sure," I say with a shrug of my imaginary shoulders. "I don't know how much help I'll be without a body, though."

My demon chuckles as she replies, "But you have a body. It isn't substantial or solid, but it is what your mind conceives as a body, so it is real to you."

"It's still creepy," I say, feeling a shudder run through me. "I can't see myself, which makes it weird, and it's even creepier hearing you talk without seeing your mouth move."

My demon laughs, and I laugh with her.

"So, what kind of favor were you going to ask me for?" I ask as my laughter fades.

"Can you give me a name?" My demon asks sheepishly, shrugging her shadowy shoulders. "If I have a name, it will be easier to differentiate myself from this piece of Thorn I carry. It will make it harder for it to take over again."

"Oh. Umm…sure. I don't see why not. Let me think about it for a minute." I say.

"You aren't supposed to tell anyone my name, either. Except for the people you trust with your life," My demon says. "My name can have power over me, which could be dangerous if you give it to the wrong person. Like what happened with Thorn."

I nod an answer, still running through possible names in my mind. Then, one stands out to me. One that would be perfect for my demon, and a smile crosses my invisible face.

"How about Rose? You have a piece of Thorn inside you, but you are really a beautiful Rose."

I watch the shadowy smile form on my demon's face as her arm tightens around my shoulders. "I love it. My name is Rose."

"It really suits you," I say softly, wrapping my arm around her waist.

"I think so, too," She says with a smile. "Now, let's go home and hope Thorn stays dormant long enough to get us back to your body."

We walk like that in companionable silence this time, with her arm over my shoulders and me holding her around the waist. The ride through space and time is seamless, and none of those pesky memories come to haunt me. Before I know it, we are back in the bar's bathroom, and my invisible heart sinks to my non-existent feet.

My body is gone. Someone must have found me and taken me somewhere. My chest expands painfully as panic creeps into my departed soul. How long can my body live without it?

As if reading my mind, Rose says, "Don't panic, Mia. Your body can live without a soul. The only worry would be you would die without food or water, but if you were hooked up to an IV and a life support system, then you would be fine as long as they kept your IV bag full and the machines on."

"How long were we gone?" I ask worriedly.

"Only a couple of hours here. Time runs differently when you are in the middle of the space between dimensions," Rose explains.

"So, what are we going to do?" I ask, wringing my invisible hands nervously. "If Deklan found me, then my body is probably already hooked up to machines to keep me alive. But how long can I stay here without my body?"

"Technically, as long as you want," Rose answers. "Haven't you ever heard of spirits, ghosts, or apparitions?"

"Well, yeah. Wait, don't tell me ghosts are real, too?" I say with a huff. "What next? Vampires and werewolves?"

Rose laughs, a tinkling sound that I hope I hear more of in the future. "No, silly. Vampires and werewolves don't exist. But think about it. You are here, away from your body. You are invisible because soul-bodies are insubstantial, only a creation of the soul's mind. What do you think happens to souls that refuse to go into the underworld?"

I frown. "So ghosts really are souls of humans that have not passed into the afterlife like the myths say?"

Rose nods. "Yes. Many people stay for many different reasons. Eventually, every human soul ends up in the underworld. However, some souls here have wandered this dimension for hundreds, even thousands, of years, and their soul-bodies still hang on. They are completely aware of what is happening and who they are. They simply refuse to leave this life for one reason or another."

"So, we have plenty of time to find my body if we stay here?" I ask.

"Well, not exactly," Rose says with a nervous shrug of her shadowy shoulders. "I cannot stay in this dimension long without being attached to a human. Since you are technically not a human without your body, eventually, I will fade away and end up back in the Demon Dimension, and you will be alone here."

My heart palpitates with the fearful thought of Rose fading away and leaving me alone. "So, what do we do, then? Go to the Demon Dimension? We could find Harper."

"Yes, Harper may be able to help me keep Thorn subdued since he can keep the piece of Thorn he has from rising up and taking over," Rose says hopefully. "He could teach me his secrets."

"Maybe," I say. "But first, we have to go into the Demon Dimension and…"

"No, I won't risk you," Rose interrupts me. "Human souls do not last long in the Demon Dimension. If someone wants to kill a human soul, that is the way to do it. Hold them hostage in the Demon Dimension for an extended period, and they fade to nothingness."

Like Jeremy and Thorn tried to do with Sophia, I think to myself.

"Then maybe we should split up," I suggest. "You go back to the Demon Dimension and try to find Harper to see if he can help you, and I will try to track down my body."

"But you don't know how to travel well in this form," Rose says. "You have been holding onto me this entire time, so I don't want to leave you alone."

"Do you have any other bright ideas then? Because I don't know what else we can do," I say with a huff.

Rose runs a shadowy hand down her dark face, causing the blue glow coming from her eyes to dim dramatically. She pauses, looking around the dirty bar bathroom in disgust.

"Gross. You were actually lying on this floor," Rose says.

"Stop getting distracted and think," I snap as shivers of repulsion run through my soul-body at the thought. "You got us into this mess, so you need to find our way out."

"Fine. I will take you to the hospital where Deklan lives. He is more than likely the one to have found you, and he would have taken you there. I can teach you how to move on our way there, and then we can split up when we get there. I can enter the Demon Dimension while you look for your body."

I clasp my hands together, nodding enthusiastically as I respond, "That sounds perfect. My cousin has a mirror that leads directly to the Demon Dimension. I can show you where it is…"

"I am well aware of that mirror," Rose interrupts with a smirk. "Many demons in the demon dimension know about the mirror portal. You look for your body at the hospital, and I will find Harper in the mirror and ask him to help me with Thorn."

"Great, then let's get started," I say as she offers me her hand.

I take the offered hand as I pray to whatever God or Goddess is listening that we can find my body quickly before Thorn takes over again.

CHAPTER 16: DEKLAN

I am going to be sick. The knowledge that I do not even know where Mia's soul is settles in my chest like a bomb about to explode.

The thought of Mia being dragged somewhere through space and time, or through the Demon Dimension, twists my stomach in knots. The fact that I am helpless to stop it makes me want to hurl.

It has been almost twelve hours since I found Mia's body, soulless and lying on the bar's bathroom floor. Twelve hours of her body being fed and kept alive with machines. Twelve hours of Mia's soul wandering, lost, somewhere between here and Goddess knows where.

Unless her demon took her to the Demon Dimension.

A human soul can only last hours in the Demon Dimension before losing itself and eventually fading completely.

And it has been twelve fucking hours.

Mia's soul could be already gone.

No, I refuse to think that way. I will find her somehow. I have no idea where to begin looking, but I will never give up.

The mirror in the portal room (that is what I have come to call it now) pulses with light as I pace back and forth before it. Harper's visage is downtrodden, as is Sophia's, as she rocks in the reclining rocking chair, her arms wrapped around herself as if she were freezing cold.

Walking past the mirror for the millionth time, I run my hands through my hair, the pompadour long since fallen.

"Fuck, Deklan, you aren't going to accomplish anything with that infernal pacing other than pissing me off," Harper says gruffly from the mirror.

"Fuck you," I shout harshly, stopping in front of the mirror to glare at Harper. "This is your fault. I never should have let you talk me into trying to use sexual energy."

"I never told you to tear her heart out!" Harper shoots back.

"That wasn't my fault!" I shout. "She only heard one end of the conversation. If you would take me to the demon realm, I could find her and explain…"

"No! I already told you I'm handling things here. The angels need you there, and you need to look out for Mia's body."

"Her body is fine and hidden. I will never give up looking for her!"

Sophia shoots up from the chair, holding her arms tightly to her sides. She balls her hands into fists and stomps her foot hard.

"Would you two please stop fighting and try to figure out how to find my cousin!" She yells.

Harper huffs. "I don't know what else to do, Sophia. I have already talked to every demon I can find and searched everywhere."

"Well, search again," Sophia and I yell simultaneously.

Our heads whip around, and our gazes lock. The corners of Sophia's mouth quirk, and I can't hold the tension any longer. It comes out as a harsh laugh.

"Jinx," Sophia says almost humorously, making me laugh harder.

Finally, she cannot hold it any longer either, and her laughs join mine as we both release the fear, worry, and tension.

"I'm glad you both find it funny to yell at me," Harper says sternly, but his mouth is twitching too.

I run my hands down my face with a sigh, the laughter fading as I say, "Damn, I'm sorry, Harper. You too, Sophia. I'm just worried about Mia. I had to let it out somehow before I tore the place down."

"We are all worried," Harper says. "I'm sorry, too. We just need to all calm down and try to think of something."

"I told you, Harper. Take me into the Demon Dimension, and let me look for her," I say.

"And I told you that I will not risk you like that. We don't need something happening to you, too. Then who will watch Mia?"

I huff. "I am not going to fade away like some human, Harper. I'm a fucking angel."

"Fallen angel," Harper corrected. "But you can still get hurt or worse, especially with all these damn untamed demons running around."

"I would take Lucien and Jewel with me," I huff. "I'm not ignorant enough to go in alone. I know we always take trained demons with us when we go."

"But we need you here next to her body so you can fight that demon in case she finds her own way back," Sophia argues. "In fact, why are you even up here now? You should be down there with her."

"I tried, Soph. I watched her for hours but was too restless to stay. I feel too helpless just sitting there watching her body being kept alive with machines."

I sigh and ball my hand into my hair, tugging it roughly to alleviate the pain in my head. I run my other hand over my face, wincing at the roughness of my unshaven jaw. I do not even want to know what I look like right now, nor do I care.

"Look," Sophia says in a calming tone, her hand gestures matching her voice. "We cannot do anything right now other than wait. Harper has our demons scouring the Demon Dimension, and your hulk buddies are searching here. I cannot search since I am not one of those humans that can see spirits, but I can watch her body for you so you can join the search."

I take a calming breath as my eyes meet Sophia's almost-black gaze. "How will you control the demon if she comes back when I am not there?"

"I will take the mirror from the turret down there so I will have Harper with me to help."

My eyebrows raise in surprise. "You never take the mirror out of the turret. You would do that for me?"

Sophia nods. "Yes, Deklan, but not just for you. She's my cousin, so I am just as invested as you are. However, we must hurry. Tamara will be home from her vacation this weekend, and she still does not know about any of this. I would like to keep it that way."

Tamara is Sophia's one-eyed roommate. Ironically, it was Sophia who took her eye during Sophia's first psychotic breakdown. Tamara had come to visit Sophia in the hospital after Sophia had been found raped and beaten almost to death. Tamara had forgiven Sophia and offered to live with her to avoid Sophia being alone.

In any case, Tamara has been fed the stories everyone else believes to be the facts, which are...

Sophia was kidnapped by a fellow patient, Jeremy, in a jealous rage after finding out that Harper had fallen for Sophia and asked her to marry him.

Harper joined with law enforcement to find her and, right after Harper discovered Sophia's location and told one of the investigators over the phone, Harper had a heart attack from all the stress and passed away. In an ironic twist of fate, Jeremy had a seizure during class and died as well, right after Sophia was found and before the police could arrest him.

This is the story that the general public believes to be fact, and Sophia wants it kept that way, even to her best friend. I don't know how she will explain Harper's sudden reappearance to the land of the living if Harper ever gets back to his comatose body that Soph has hidden away. Now that I know that is what Sophia and Harper have planned, I wonder how they will pull that off.

"Of course," I respond to Sophia's pleading gaze. "I understand. I would never break your confidence, Soph. Not to anyone."

"Good," Sophia says with a smile and a satisfied nod. "Now, go find my cousin."

"I'll go check in with Jewel and Lucien and move to the other portal," Harper says, and this mirror darkens as his presence leaves it.

I turn and leave the room behind Sophia without another word, locking it securely behind me. I walk down the hallway to my room, my feet flying quickly. My adrenaline pumps through my body as I move down the hall, and my hands curl into tight fists at my side.

I grit my teeth to keep the scream of rage that has been building inside my chest from escaping out of my mouth. I reach my room and turn the knob, opening the door a bit harder than I had intended. It bounces off the wall with a resounding bang, and I flinch at the sound.

I stomp through my living room toward the bedroom, pausing to slam a fist into the door frame. The wood creaks, and the entire wall shudders. The frame held, absorbing my anger and giving me room to breathe.

I let out the scream I had been holding back, loud and hoarse like the drone of a tornado just before destruction takes over. The scream rages on until all the breath is gone from my lungs, and then I shrivel to the floor.

I gasp in a deep, aching breath, and it comes out in a helpless, rage-filled sob. I suck in another breath only to have it release on another sob, this one more heartbreaking than the first.

I never cry.

Not when my Goddess betrayed me; when I caught Luna in the arms of another angel.

Not when my jealousy got the better of me, and I took that angel out of existence.

Not when Luna sentenced me to isolation until she could decide what to do with me.

146

Not when she told me she loved me as much as she could, but she would never be faithful to one person because she was polyamorous.

Not when she said she could never be with me if I could not handle her lifestyle.

And not when Luna decided to banish me from her realm rather than kill me because she wanted me to suffer.

And especially not when she forced me to lead a group of people, knowing I would fail, which would make my suffering even greater.

And not when she recently told me that if I fail one more time, she will take me out of existence without blinking an eye.

No, I never cry. I survive, I get by, and sometimes, I even thrive. But I never cry.

So the sounds issuing forth from my chest, getting stuck in my throat, and spewing from my mouth are foreign to me. The liquid building in my eyes is unknown to me. The saltiness that runs down my cheeks and invades my mouth is strange to me.

"Get it the fuck together," I tell myself. *"It isn't over yet, and Mia fucking needs you."*

My knuckles dig into the carpet as I force myself to get up off the floor. I struggle to my feet and find my way to my bathroom. Leaning against the sink, I turn the cold water on and splash handfuls into my face.

The cold water helps as it washes away the unfamiliar tears from my face. I dry my face with the hand towel that hangs beside my sink and look at my miserable reflection in the mirror.

My emerald eyes are bloodshot and puffy. My skin is pale, contrasting sharply against the blood-red color of my goatee, which is in desperate need of a trim. The pompadour I usually style my hair into has been nonexistent for some time, and tendrils of bangs hang almost into my eyes.

All of my piercings are gone since I had been at work when this all went down, and I have not bothered to put them back in. My suit is wrinkled, my tie hanging loose and untied around my neck, and the shirt sleeves are rolled up to my elbows.

I look like shit. Not that I care. Right now, all I care about is finding Mia.

I run a hand through my red hair to tame it somewhat as I saunter back into the bedroom to find a pair of jeans and a T-shirt. If I am going to be running all over creation, then at least I will be comfortable.

After I am calm and changed, I leave my apartment and head back toward the 'secret mirror room' as it has come to be called. The padlock is still attached, which means Soph did not come back here. She must have gone to the turret to move the mirror down to the secret hospital room.

Or at least I hope that is where she went.

Cora gives me a sympathetic look as I reach the bottom of the stairs. I am not in the mood to deal with her today, so I don't make eye contact as I pass the desk.

"Where are you going to go?" Cora asks as I pass.

"Why do you even care?" I ask harshly, stopping momentarily to glare at the head nurse. "You're insanely jealous of Mia, so you would probably be happy if she was never found. Not that it would do you any good since I will never be with you."

I expect Cora to flinch at my harsh words, but she doesn't. Surprisingly, she smiles. It is a soft, humorous smile, and my anger quickly turns to curiosity.

"Oh, Deklan, you big Hulk you. I know you do not like me that way. Still, it is fun to flirt with you like I do with all the men I am fond of. And yes, I am jealous that I do not get to fuck you, but I would never wish anyone harm. I only want you to be happy."

Her words leave me speechless, and I can just imagine what I look like standing there gawking at her like an idiot. My mouth opens and closes like a fish out of water as I try to think what to say.

It isn't very often that someone renders me speechless.

I clear my throat and say, "Well, at least we know where we stand with each other."

Cora laughs. "Yes, we do. Now go find that girl and bring her home."

I do not respond.

I turn and stalk toward the door, but I feel lighter as I leave the hospital. My bike is parked in front where it always is, right under the corner covered by the hovering bottom of the turret.

I put on my helmet and mount the bike, but something deep inside my gut tells me not to leave. I glance back toward the front doors, wondering why my body hesitates to start the bike.

I assume it is because Mia's body lies on a stretcher in a hidden room inside the building. I remind myself that it is a body only. Mia's soul is gone.

I reach for the key, but again, my body hesitates. It takes all the willpower inside me to turn the key and start the bike. The engine's rumbling vibrating under me helps calm my nerves as I prepare to take off.

I shift into gear and ready myself to go, but my stomach roils violently, and it takes all my strength to keep the bike standing. I double over, my head on the handlebars and my arms wrapped around my stomach as I try to keep its contents inside my body.

I take deep breaths in, blowing them out slowly as I try to hold on while the nausea subsides. I turn off the engine, place the kickstand down, and dismount the bike. I take off the helmet so I can take in more air.

What the hell was that about, I wonder? The nausea still plays in the pit of my stomach, though it is more of a gentle rolling than a violent spinning. At least my stomach acids are no longer threatening to burn a hole in my esophagus.

I bend over and place my hands on my knees, holding that stance until I am sure I can walk steadily without yacking up my guts. I take in a deep breath and stagger toward the door. My legs are a bit shaky, and I feel as if I will suffocate if I don't get inside to the air conditioning.

It is a hot day. The sun is bright, shining down on the tiny garden on the side of the small driveway that leads up to the Victorian Mansion-turned-hospital. Rivulets of steam curl into the air from the blacktop driveway as I walk past.

I open the main door, and the cool air that flows out makes me catch my breath. It feels heavenly. I take a deep breath of the cool air as I enter the doors. Cora gives me a questioning look as I walk through the lobby towards the hallway that leads to the cafeteria. I ignore her and keep walking.

I don't stop until I reach the dining room-turned-cafeteria's glass doors, which lead to the side courtyard of the mansion. It is somewhat private as long as no one is on the turret's balcony looking over. I stare out of the glass at the multiple flowers, bushes, and the one bench in the smaller courtyard and think about how much I would love to sit with Mia on the bench and enjoy the sun's warmth.

If she would even sit with me.

Guilt tightens my chest and closes my throat. The last words I said to Mia should have been me reciprocating her feelings after she told me how she felt about me. Instead, it was an awkward silence and then a misheard conversation that made her believe I was only using her to keep my own ass alive.

It could not be further from the truth.

If I cannot get Mia back, I will accept my fate gladly. I will no longer be able to live in a world without Mia in it, anyway. I will be glad to let Luna wipe me from existence.

"Where the fuck are you, baby?" I ask to the empty air as I stare out the glass door. "Where the hell do I start looking?"

I do not expect an answer, so when the voice breaks the empty silence of the dining room, I almost jump out of my own skin.

"You're not going to find her standing around here."

I whip around to see Cora standing in the middle of the cafeteria, her arms crossed over her chest. Her blond hair is down, laying softly over her shoulders and standing out against her black scrub shirt.

My gaze is drawn down the blackness of her scrub pants to the stark contrast of her white slip-on nurse shoes, one of them tap-tapping against the tiled floor.

The sound of her voice pulls my gaze back to her blue-eyed gaze. "You should be out looking for Mia instead of brooding in the cafeteria about the suckiness of your life."

"Don't you think I know that?" I answer defensively. "I had my motorcycle started and everything, but something wouldn't let me leave."

Cora's stance relaxes. She drops one arm to her side and props the other with a hand on her cocked hip. "Look, I'm only trying to help you find Mia because that's what friends do. They help each other."

"You consider us friends?" I scoff. "I thought you just wanted to fuck me."

Cora eyes me up and down with a cocked brow as she answers, "I do, but that doesn't mean I can't be your friend as I admire you from afar."

The humor leaves her eyes, replaced by a serious look as she moves close, placing a hand against my chest as she says, "Think about it. She knows that either you or Mia would have come looking for her and, if you found her body, would bring it back here. So, try looking in all the places she would go if she returned here. Just ask yourself…if she gets away from her demon, where would be the first place she would go?"

My chest tightens with hope. Why had I not thought of that? Because I was too close and too emotionally invested in the problem. I know where Mia would go if she came here.

With a huff of frustration at myself for being an ass yet again, and a deep, calming breath, I step away from her touch and respond, "Cora, I think I owe you an apology."

Her eyebrows raise in surprise as she drops her hand and takes a step back, and she gazes at me suspiciously. "What for?"

I run a hand through my fiery hair. "I misjudged you. I took you for a self-centered, shallow woman who only wanted to fuck me."

Cora shrugs nonchalantly as she crosses her arms over her chest. "I suppose I deserved that. And I'll try harder not to eye you so much in the future."

With a dry laugh, I shake my head at her and answer, "Fair enough. Am I forgiven?"

Cora's eyes soften as she nods. "Of course you are, you big ole Hulk."

"I have decided that you are now one of the most awesome fallen angels I know," I tell Cora.

She scoffs and waves her hand dismissively, shooing me away as I turn toward the cafeteria door. I move quicker now that I have a solid destination.

And hope. Hope is always good.

If Mia came back here, my apartment would be where she would go. Even though she was angry with me when we were last together, my apartment is the only place she knows in this facility. I could tell when I had brought her here that she had never been here before that.

"Go get her, Boss," I hear Cora's voice call as I walk out the door.

Then, because I have the hearing of the Gods, even in human form, I hear her whisper, "She is a lucky girl."

I disagree. I am the lucky one. That is if she decides to forgive me.

CHAPTER 17: MIA

"**Y**ou're trying too hard," Rose says, her tone filled with suppressed laughter. "You don't flap your arms to fly. You are not a bird."

"Stop laughing at me and help me understand how," I shout in frustration.

"You are still thinking and acting like you have a body," Rose says patiently. "While your subconscious mind has manifested a spiritual version of a body for you, you are still just energy."

I frown in confusion, so Rose continues to explain.

"Think of a streak of electricity that must run through a wire," Rose says. "You are like the electricity. Now, imagine someone flipping a switch to turn on a light. You must travel through the wire from that switch to the lightbulb. However, you have no legs to run and no wings to fly. You are only electricity. How do you move? You just do it because you need to. You know the switch has been flipped, so you need to go to the light. That is how you must move through this world. You think of where you need to go and just go because you need to."

I screw my face up at my demon and huff in confused frustration. I can do this, I tell myself. I have no idea what my demon is talking about, but I have to try. It will be easy, like turning on a light.

Yeah, right.

I close my eyes and take a cleansing, calming breath as I try to envision myself as nothing but energy, moving and flowing through this world from destination to destination. I picture the situation Rose told me in my head, imagining the switch being flipped and me moving through the wire toward my goal.

I think about my goal, the beautiful mansion with the fragrant flower garden and roofed porch. I wonder if Sophia is out of her mind with worry over me. I laugh at the disappointment I will see on Cora's face when she realizes I have returned.

She would probably be happy if I never came back.

A strange, prickling sensation tickles my insides, pulling me from my thoughts and stealing my concentration.

"Dammit, I think I almost had it," I curse, stomping a ghostly foot on the ground. "I can't keep my concentration up with all these weird sensations running through this body."

"You don't have to," Rose says with a smile. "The sensations are good."

'What do you mean?" I ask confusedly. "Is there another way?"

"No, this is the way," Rose answers. "The sensations mean it is working. Look around. What do you see?"

Curiously, I look away from Rose to look at my surroundings. I gasp in surprise.

The Gothic Victorian mansion-turned-hospital looms before me in all its tall, dark glory. The circular driveway radiates heat from its surface, causing the flowers in the flowerbeds to seem as if they were wavering. The tiny walkway leading up to the covered porch stairs seems cooler in the shade of the porch roof.

A familiar blue street bike sits in the circular driveway in front of the house, tucked up in a corner under the turret. I am drawn to the motorcycle, remembering the feeling of freedom as I rode behind Deklan with the wind whipping through my hair.

As soon as my brain finishes the thought, the prickling sensation swirls inside me again. My 'body' is pulled toward the bike, floating through midair as I approach the huge, midnight-blue machine.

I finally get it.

I just have to 'want' to be somewhere, think about the place, and I automatically move to that location.

Excited, I picture myself sitting on the motorcycle, and the prickling sensation grows stronger. Instantly, I am straddling the bike seat, and I laugh in victory.

"I knew you could do it," Rose says as she appears beside me. "It isn't that hard."

"No, it isn't at all," I say. "I don't know why I was having so much trouble."

"Because you have no imagination at all, you sniveling simpleton," Rose says harshly.

I startle, my eyes widening at Rose's harsh and raspy tone. It is almost as if she is speaking entirely in another voice. Frowning, I turn to look at her, and my heart sinks in despair.

Her eyes flash, the colors alternating between cornflower blue and lavender purple as she stares at me with narrowed eyes.

"Rose?" I say uncertainly.

When she doesn't answer, I whisper, "Thorn?"

The demon's eyes glow lavender purple, and it smiles maliciously. Rose is no longer in there. The realization hits me, and the tiny hairs on the back of my neck stand on end. Fear radiates through my soul as the demon moves closer.

"Rose, please," I say pleadingly. "You can fight this. Come back to me."

But she doesn't. There is no sign that Rose is even trying to fight Thorn's influence. My non-existent heart thunders inside my chest, even though I know my body is just a manifestation of my subconsciousness. The fear pulsing through my soul makes it seem real all the same as I watch Thorn move closer.

"Rose is no longer home," The demon says sarcastically. "And you won't be either as soon as I find your body. Now, I will make sure you stay here like a good little soul while I go inside and find it."

The lavender eyes flash as I watch the demon draw closer, her eyes narrowing as she reaches shadowy arms out for me. I try to move, to get off the bike and back away from those grasping hands, but the fear paralyzes me, and I cannot move.

No…that isn't right…

I can move. I am not paralyzed. I just have to remember what Rose taught me before Thorn took her over again. I just need to calm down, envision where I want to go, and go.

The demon's eyes flash again, stealing my thoughts and wiping my concentration with the terror those eyes evoke in me. I shut my eyes tightly to block them out. Even though I know I don't have a body or eyes to shut, it works anyway. My mind manifests darkness as I think about closing my eyes, and I can better concentrate.

Now, all I need to do is picture where I need to go, somewhere inside the building and away from the demon. And, of course, the one place in the entire building where I definitely do not want to be is the first one that pops into my head.

It is the only place inside I know intimately.

The night I spent here with Deklan fills the forefront of my thoughts, and I can clearly see the heavenly bed we had slept in… fucked in…and fought in.

That glorious, extraordinary bed where whispered secrets take you away into a land of fantastical slumber and wonderous dreams flashes through my mind so brightly that my entire subconsciously manifested body tingles. The memory is so strong that I can almost feel the multiple orgasms Deklan had given me the next morning, and my imaginary stomach turns flip-flops. I am so caught up in the memory that I swear I can hear Deklan whispering my name.

"Mia?"

The pure emotion that my name carries through my mind in Deklan's voice has me opening my eyes, even though I am going to lose my concentration when I see the damn demon reaching for me.

But that is not what I see.

Instead, the image of Deklan's tortured yet relieved face looms before me. I blink several times, thinking maybe the demon has done something to my soul, and I am imagining his face to keep myself calm.

"Mia, thank the Goddess! I don't know how you managed to get back here, but we have to get you back to your body," My manifestation of Deklan says hurriedly.

Wait...what?

"Deklan?" I ask uncertainly, hope causing my tone to waver.

I look around at my surroundings. I am sitting on the edge of the bed, infused inside the filmy material that hangs from the canopy. It creeps me out, and I imagine myself standing to the side of the material instead of inside it. My body tingles again, and I instantly move, which puts me closer to Deklan's position.

Deklan reaches for me, moving as if he could cup my cheek in his hand. I can almost feel his warmth against my face, but I know it is impossible.

"How did you find your way back?" He asks, his tone calmer, soothing as if afraid I will disappear.

"You can see me?" I ask as the relief of being found fills me.

Deklan smiles, causing my ghostly heart to flutter. "I am an angel. I can see all forms of life, even the energy of souls. I would recognize your soul anywhere, Mia."

He pulls his hand away, running it through his blood-red hair before dropping it to his side.

"Unfortunately, I cannot touch you. You are incorporeal, even if your mind has manifested a body for you."

"That's what Ro...er my demon told me. She also showed me how to move in this form," I explain, stumbling over my words. I had almost given him my demon's name!

Deklan frowns confusedly. "You are on friendly terms with your demon now, even though she tried to steal you away and take over your body?"

"That's not entirely true," I say. "She was being controlled by another demon."

Deklan nods his head. "I am well aware. Where is she now?"

I frown in confusion. "I had to leave her. She isn't herself right now. And what do you mean, you are aware?"

Deklan huffs in frustration. "Mia, we can talk about this later. Right now, we need to get you back inside your body."

"So you know where it is?" I ask hopefully.

"Of course I do," Deklan says. "I'm the one who found your body unconscious on the bathroom floor. What were you doing in that bar anyway?"

Anger flares inside me, too hot to contain with or without a body. How dare he have the audacity to ask what I was doing in a bar when it was him I was running away from.

"First, it is none of your business what I was doing in a bar, and secondly, if you cop an attitude with me and keep trying to talk to me about anything other than finding my body, I will go find Sophia, and she can help me."

My tone must have conveyed the anger burning inside me because I notice Deklan backs up a step with every word I speak. I also notice that I had advanced on him with every step back, leaving me standing directly before him with my chest practically sinking into his.

Literally.

The effect is weird and creepy, so I instantly back away with a shudder.

A look of resignation falls over Deklan's features as he watches me back away, and his voice conveys the defeat reflecting in his gaze.

"Fine, Mia. I'll take you to your body."

He turns and walks away, leaving me to follow as best as possible. I am getting better at moving in this energy form. However, I still lag behind as we leave Deklan's apartment, move through the hallway, and head down the stairs to the reception area.

Cora gives Deklan a wink and smiles at me…

Wait…

Can she see me, too?

"Welcome back, Mia," She says in a friendly tone, doubly

surprising me with her improved attitude towards me.

She chuckles at my confused look and adds, "I can see you because I am an angel too. Didn't Deklan tell you?"

I shake my head in denial as my spirit automatically moves to the edge of the desk where I want to be.

"No, he did not tell me that. Thank you for the gracious greeting," I say, keeping my tone pleasant.

She gives me a small wave as Deklan disappears through the tiny door behind the desk, holding it open for me and waiting in silence.

Good. I didn't want him to speak to me. But even as I think it, I know it's a lie. The pang that fills my non-existent chest tells me so.

Sighing, I close my eyes in concentration, willing my spirit to follow Deklan through the door. The now-familiar tingling spreads through me as my soul moves. The sensation stays with me as I move while Deklan leads me through a large, sterile-looking hallway.

I look around in curiosity, noting the clean white walls and tiled concrete floors as we pass several metal doors, some with tiny, round glass windows. Deklan stops in front of one without a window and waits for me to catch up. His hand is on the knob as he watches me float down the hall toward him.

My first instinct is to stop, turn, and run away from that intense gaze, but obviously, my spirit has other ideas. The tiny spark deep inside me that is still attracted to the man, despite how incredibly furious I am and how much he tore my heart from my chest, still longs to be near him.

So, instead of running away, my spirit drifts right up to him, stopping inches from where he stands waiting. Once again, I find myself right up against Deklan's muscular form, so close that my incorporeal chest sinks into his stomach.

I swallow hard, willing my spirit to back up a few steps to look into his eyes, capturing his gaze with my own. His visage looks tortured, almost like he has recently suffered some great loss. He runs a hand through his tousled red hair and sighs defeatedly.

"Your body is close," He says, his tone matching his punished look. "Any moment now, you will start to feel yourself being pulled away. Just go with it. Don't fight it, and you will be back in your body before you can blink."

I nod, the words I want to say lodging in my throat when I try to speak. I want to tell him how much he hurt me, how angry I am at him for it. I want to tell him I never want to see him again.

But, for some reason, I cannot say the words.

Instead, I feel the pull like Deklan said I would and let myself fall into the sensation. As I feel myself being dragged away, I take a breath to speak while I still can.

"I hate you," I say in a whispered breath.

Deklan smiles a sad smile and breathes back, "I know."

CHAPTER 18: MIA

I don't know how long it takes to return to my body. I have no concept of time or space as I relax into the pull. The sense of floating is the best way I can describe it to myself in a way that my brain will understand. The pull is gentle yet insistent, like a soft current guiding me back to the shore. My skin tingles with a delicate, almost electric sensation, as if tiny sparks are dancing across my body. The air around me feels thick and velvety, wrapping me in a comforting embrace.

It could have taken minutes, hours, or even days. Time has no meaning in the void I have given in to, nor do feelings, emotions, concepts, or thoughts. The only thing that exists to me is peace and nothingness.

As the pull intensifies, I feel a gentle pressure, like a warm, invisible hand guiding me back into my body. My senses sharpen, and I become acutely aware of the physical world reasserting itself. The boundaries of my body solidify, and I feel the familiar weight of my limbs returning.

The first thing that comes back to my befuddled brain is sensation. I am cold, freezing cold, so my entire body shivers. The trembling wracks my body, tensing muscles I had forgotten I had during my trek in the spirit realm.

Discomfort comes next, flooding my body with the knowledge that I am lying on my back in an uncomfortable bed. My neck is cramped, my back flattened uncomfortably, and my legs twitch with the need to move. Dim light filters in through my closed eyelids, and my eyes begin to flutter beneath them.

My heart beats sluggishly at first, but as I become more awake and aware, it quickens and steadies. My breathing is slow and shallow. I take in a deep breath that releases with a stuttered sigh at the sharp pain that runs through my chest. My lungs expand painfully as I struggle to take in deeper breaths, shooting the pain through my entire body. I moan in discomfort, but the pain eases slightly with each deep breath.

After the pain eases and I feel more awake, I finally open my eyes. The fuzzy image of Deklan's worried face floods my view, and I blink rapidly to bring his face into focus. I swallow hard, and it hurts.

"Hey," I squeak out, and that hurts, too. My voice is rough and hoarse; my throat feels like someone rubbed sandpaper all over it, and it burns like someone lit it on fire.

Deklan's smile spreads across his face, and a myriad of emotions flow through his emerald gaze. Relief is most prevalent but is mixed with worry, causing a tightness around the corners of his eyes.

"Hey," He says back, and his voice reflects the emotions swirling in his eyes. "Try not to speak too much. They just removed the tube from your throat, so it will be sore. Also, you had an IV in your arm, so that may bruise later."

"How long did it take me to wake up after I got back into my body?" I ask, my throat burning with each rasping word.

I raise my arm up to look at it, groaning at the bandage plastered to the sensitive underside of my elbow.

"About an hour, now shut up and let your throat rest," Deklan fusses. He lifts his hand as if trying to touch my face, and I recoil. His visage falls into disappointment.

"I am only trying to help you sit up, Mia. I am not going to hurt you," He says as he grasps my shoulder with one hand and slides his other hand under my back.

"You already hurt me enough," I rasp sarcastically, flinching at the pain that burns along my esophagus as I try to speak.

"If you would stop talking, it wouldn't hurt," Deklan responds as he pushes me into a sitting position. "At least wait until you drink some water before you yell at me."

After Deklan ensures I am steady, he releases me and turns toward a table beside the bed. He grabs the bottle of water sitting on its surface and hands it to me. I snatch it from his grasp, remove the top, and take a huge drink, almost choking on it as the cool liquid slides past my burning throat.

"Easy, Mia. Drink it slowly," Deklan says as he gives me a couple of sturdy pats between my shoulder blades.

I groan in pain with each throat-scratching cough until they finally subside. The next time I take a drink of the water, it is a smaller sip. The cool water lubricates my burning throat, and eventually, the pain diminishes to a dull ache.

Then, the hunger hits, cramping my stomach and almost doubling me over in pain. The growling that roils in my chest is audible in the large room, echoing around where my arms are wrapped around my midsection.

"The doctors are fixing you a tray," Deklan says.

When I don't answer, he continues to speak.

"Mia," he whispers shakily. "You couldn't possibly understand how afraid I was for you."

I still say nothing, but I scoff disbelievingly.

Deklan sighs defeatedly, his shoulders slumping as he continues to speak. "It isn't easy for me to be open with anyone, but if you would only..."

"Let you explain? Let you speak? Let you tell me more lies?" I interrupt irritably. "You want me to listen to some lame excuse you came up with while I was out of my body? Well, don't bother. I may have to put up with you until we get Ro...my demon tamed, but I don't have to like the situation."

Deklan takes a breath to respond, but I cut him off before he can, adding, "Nor do I have to like you. After I get out of here, I'm going to find Sophia, tell her goodbye, then I am going home."

My throat burns again with the abuse as my voice rises, and I clear my throat loudly before taking another sip of water.

It helps.

The doctor brings me a tray of food, and my mouth waters despite its former dryness. The doctor shoulders Deklan out of the way so he can place the tray on the movable table, then wheels the table and turns it so it is sitting over my lap.

The food smells divine, and I inhale a deep, appreciative whiff. I use the fork on the tray to scoop up some of the mashed potatoes and bring them to my mouth.

They taste heavenly, salted and buttered to perfection.

"Mia, it isn't safe for you to stay in that abandoned building alone," Deklan says. "At least stay with Sophia in the Turret until it is safe."

I swallow my mashed potatoes and reply, "I'm not returning to that building. I'm going home to Phoenix."

Deklan's face falls. "Mia, you cannot go to Phoenix. How will I help you tame your demon if you are so far away?"

I ignore him as I take a bite of the fried chicken, followed by a nibble of the dinner roll. I close my eyes, enjoying the tastes of the delicious meal.

"Mia, please. Just talk to me."

"I'm trying to eat," I say over a mouthful of green beans.

"I won't let you go, Mia. You will stay here until you are safe with your demon, even if I have to hold you prisoner until then," He says, his tone dangerously low.

I continue to ignore him.

"Mia!" Deklan says loudly, igniting a fierce anger inside my chest.

I put my fork down, push the table away, turn on the bed, and swing my legs over the side. I glare up at him and find the same rage in his eyes as he presses his thighs against my dangling legs. He places his hands on the bed on either side of my thighs and leans in close, so close I feel his breath brush across my lips as he speaks.

His tone reeks with menace as he growls, "You will not leave here."

My hands tighten on the water bottle in my grip as I bring it up to my lips, forcing Deklan to lean back or get hit in the face with my water. I take a long pull from the bottle before I speak, coating my throat with the cool, soothing liquid.

"Fine, Deklan. I will stay long enough to let you help me with the demon, but I refuse to stay here with you. I will stay in my own apartment, and afterward, I am going home," I say, my tone matching the rage inside me.

Deklan does not budge, his face remaining taut and serious. "I will simply lock you in one of the solitary confinement rooms if you insist on leaving here."

Anger coalesces with the fire swirling in my gut as he stares at me with his livid, dark green gaze. How dare he? Who the hell does he think he is? He may have manipulated me and bent me to his will thus far with his lewd sex games, but now he is just being a controlling jerk.

"You are not my father," I say through gritted teeth, my tone venomous. "You will not tell me where I can and cannot go or what I can and cannot do."

Deklan's severe visage falls slightly. His furrowed brow relaxes somewhat, and his eyes soften just a tad. He takes in a deep breath as his shoulders relax ever so slightly.

His tone is slightly less vehement as he replies, "No, I am not your father, Mia. I am your guardian angel and know what is best for you even if you don't know yourself."

That statement only feeds my anger. How dare he presume to

know me? With a deep, angry growl, I fling the small amount of water left in the bottle at his scowling, unsuspecting face. I throw the empty bottle onto the floor and bring both hands up to his hard chest.

I push as hard as I can, causing him to stumble backward slightly, a look of surprised confusion taking over the anger on his now-wet features. I know only the element of surprise has him stumbling backward. I would never have been able to move the unyielding mass of Deklan's body otherwise.

No matter. I take advantage of his distraction to make my escape. Without his colossal form to hold me in place, I jump down from the uncomfortable hospital bed and bolt for the door that leads out.

I wobble slightly on my unsteady legs, the hours of laying prone taking their toll on my poor, unsuspecting muscles. But I push through nonetheless. I gain my balance and run, reaching the door just as Deklan manages to collect himself and chase after me.

The room beyond the door has monitors on one side, but I don't take the time to look. Deklan is right on my heels. I run for the other door on the other side of the room, hoping this door doesn't lead to some dead-end closet or pantry.

I huff in victory when I find myself in a hallway, but my relief is short-lived. Confusion settles in me, and I realize I am lost. I do not remember which way Deklan had led me down the hallway to get to this room.

There are several closed doors on either side of the hallway to my left and a bend in the hallway to my right. I hesitate for a hairsbreadth of a second, wondering which way I should go to get to an exit. My hesitation costs me, and I just barely get away from the brush of Deklan's fingers across my arm when I see him coming for me out of the corner of my eye.

I turn and run, not caring which way I am going. I only want to get away from this insufferable man. Yes, he saved me, saved my body. He brought me back to myself when my soul was lost. However, he also rejected me after I had laid my soul bare for him, opened up and made myself vulnerable.

Something I never thought I would ever do again.

But I did.

For him.

And he tossed me away like rubbish.

I remember hearing the tail-end of his phone conversation and what he had said. He only fucked me to keep me close, and he only saved me to save his own ass. The heart-piercing words play through my head in Deklan's deadpan tone...

"Because you and Harper knew I wouldn't fall for her since I am an unfeeling asshole, but I will work extra hard to help her despite my lack of caring since The Powers That Be would obliterate me if I don't tame that demon."

I don't know who he had been speaking to, nor do I care. The only thing that matters to me is the pain that those words had lanced through my soul.

"Mia, stop!" Deklan calls down the hall, his booming voice bringing me back to the present and out of my own head.

But I don't stop. I keep running even though I don't know where I am going. I just want to be away from him, away from his hurtful words, and away from this place.

"Mia, you're going the wrong way!" Deklan yells as I skid around the bend in the hallway to see a set of double doors at the end of the corridor.

I bolt for the doors, ignoring Deklan's panicked cries. I run past a few other doors on either side of the corridor but ignore them. I am running full out now, not intending to slow down as I crash through the double doors and run full speed into another hard, steel door.

Not thorough the door...

Into the door.

Thankfully, my hands were extended to push the door open ahead of me, or so I thought. The vibration of the unmoving barrier runs the length of my arms up into my shoulders as the rest of my body, moving too fast to stop, crashes into the solid steel surface. I have just enough time to move my head to the side so I don't break my nose on the unyielding, locked metal door.

Starbursts of pain shoot through my head as it bounces off the door, along with my body, and my arms wave in the air as I tilt backward. The sensation of falling flutters in my stomach as I soar back toward the set of double doors that still swing with the force at which I burst through them moments ago, and I close my eyes tightly in preparation for more pain.

However, the pain does not come.

Instead of hitting the still-swinging doors and falling to the floor, my body is stopped by the hardness of muscled flesh. Arms wrap around me, stopping my momentum and holding me steady against the firm body of my pursuer.

I struggle against him despite the starbursts exploding behind my closed lids and the pain erupting inside my head. I scream my frustration at being captured, at being hurt, but mostly at Deklan for tearing out my heart.

"Let me go!" I yell loudly as I continue to struggle and scream indignantly.

"Mia, just stop!" Deklan huffs into my ear between screams and heaving breaths. "You're going to hurt yourself."

"Yes, please don't hurt the body I will soon inhabit," a sly voice drawls aloud from the corner of the small space between the two doors.

Deklan's body tenses, his hold tightening around me as he backs up a step, pulling me with him. I stop struggling and look up to see my demon step from the shadows, and my heart sinks to see her eyes glowing purple instead of blue.

"Stay away from her," Deklan growls. "Or I will annihilate you where you stand."

The demon snickers maliciously as he responds, "Go ahead and try it."

One of Deklan's arms loosens around my waist, and I grasp that arm as I scream, "No! Don't, please!"

The maniacal laugh of Thorn coming from my demon fills the small space of the tiny alcove as I struggle to hold Deklan back from killing her.

"You see," the demon scoffs between laughs. "She won't risk hurting her precious demon."

"You are her demon, idiot," Deklan growls, his breath fanning the back of my ear as he pulls me closer to his body.

"In a matter of speaking," the demon says slyly. "I am a demon, but not the demon that belongs in this demon's body. At least, for now."

"I know who you are," Deklan growls angrily.

"Leave my demon alone," I shout as I struggle again in Deklan's hold.

"Mia, I have to protect...," Deklan begins, but I cut him off.

"I'm not talking to you. I'm talking to Thorn," I snap.

Deklan stops talking and remains silent.

Ceasing my struggles, I glare at the demon and continue, "You had your chance to help your human, and you chose to drive him deeper into his insanity. You don't deserve to be an inner demon."

"Then it's a good thing that I don't want to be an inner demon," Thorn says as he moves closer to me, his shadowy form blending with the shadows in the small space. "I have higher aspirations than that, dear Mia, and you know it. Jeremy knew it too, but your fucking cousin and that asshat Doctor Harper killed him before he could get me a body."

"What the fuck do you want, demon?" Deklan roars, but the demon ignores Deklan and continues speaking as it takes another step forward.

"All I need is to get back inside you where I belong, Mia, and then your body will be mine."

"You won't be touching her again," Deklan says, his tone low and threatening. "Not while I live and breathe."

Thorn lets out a low growl and moves slightly forward again, but his steps falter as the heavy, steel door that almost took me out creaks on its hinges and opens slowly. Deklan's hold on me tightens even more to the point that I almost can't breathe.

"You have to let the demon back inside, Mia," Sophia's thin voice carries into the small alcove. "You know damn well that you risk hurting Mia if you destroy her demon."

"No," Deklan argues as Sophia steps into the small space, moving between the demon and us. "I will keep her safe."

"How? You can't, Deklan. The demon is attached to her soul; you can do nothing about it. You can only put it to sleep for a while until we can figure out what to do with it," Sophia says.

"You," Thorn says, pointing a finger toward Sophia.

My blood runs cold. I have to get Thorn away from Sophia before he tries to hurt her, and I know he will if given the chance. But how am I supposed to get him away? The only way is to get Deklan to put the demon to sleep like he did before, but he isn't listening to me.

Sophia turns slowly toward the demon, turning away so I cannot see her face.

"What do you want with me, Thorn?" she asks sassily. "You don't want to tangle with my demons. You already tried that and failed, remember? So don't even try to intimidate me."

Surprised confusion fills me as I freeze in Deklan's arms. Sophia knows about Thorn? How? There is no time to get my questions answered, though. I need to get Thorn out of the way so he doesn't hurt my cousin.

"Deklan, just put the demon to sleep like you did before," I shout hastily. "Hurry before it tries to hurt Sophia."

There is a waver in the air on either side of Sophia's form as I struggle in Deklan's grip. Two shadowy forms materialize suddenly, one male and one female, wrapping Sophia in a swirl of darkness and shadow. They turn their glowing eyes on me; shining diamonds glittering from their shadowy faces.

"We won't let Thorn hurt Sophia. And we will try not to let him hurt your demon," they say in unison, their voices sliding through my mind like the softest silk.

Sophia turns back to me, her eyes narrowed in anger. "Mia, do you know what is going on?"

"Yes. My demon is being controlled by a not-so-dead piece of Thorn," I say, turning my eyes away from Sophia's furious stare.

I crane my neck to look at Deklan and say, "Just put it to sleep before anyone gets hurt."

"If I do that, the demon will be inside of you again," Deklan says in a low, tortured tone. "I don't know if I can protect you from it when it wakes again."

I slump in surrender in Deklan's arms. I close my eyes tightly to shut out the entire scene. With a defeated sigh, I lean my head back against Deklan's chest with my eyes still closed.

"Just do it," I say. "I won't need you to protect me when she wakes up."

"I'm not going anywhere, Mia," the demon taunts me, and I open my eyes to see Thorn glaring at me with his shining lavender eyes.

"I will see you again when I wake up, and you will…"

Thorn doesn't have time to finish that sentence before Sophia's two demons open their mouths and release a bright, shining light. The light crashes into Thorn's spectral figure, silencing his rant and sending a swirling vortex of shining shadow toward me.

I tense, preparing for the uncomfortable tingling sensation of my demon entering my body, and I breathe a sigh of relief when it is settled into my core. Deklan's arms loosen their hold, and I immediately step away from him when he releases me.

Sophia steps up to me, pointing a finger into my chest, and she says scoldingly, "You have some explaining to do, Mia. Why the hell didn't you tell me about Thorn if you knew?"

Sophia's demons each place a hand on each of her shoulders, their eyes glowing even brighter. Sophia's face takes on that far-away-look quality she gets when communicating with her demons.

After a few moments, she refocuses on me and says, "Jewel and Lucien want to know why you didn't tell us as well."

I huff and answer, "I just found out about it myself while I was being dragged through time and space."

Sophia frowns. "How did you find out?"

"My demon told me. She had a moment of clarity and told me about Thorn, and then she brought me back here so I could find my body. When we got to the hospital, Thorn took over again, and I ran away. I found Deklan in his apartment, and he took me back to my body. That is all I know."

I glance around the small space at all the eyes watching me. The scrutinizing looks everyone is giving me causes my heart to flutter erratically. This space is too small, and I find it hard to breathe. I break out in a cold sweat, and I can feel the edges of panic threatening to overtake me in the stifling confines of the small alcove.

I shift sideways, wrapping my arms around myself in a desperate attempt to stop the swell of emotions from consuming me. My breath comes in shallow gasps as I turn away from Deklan's scrutinizing stare and head for the swinging doors.

I have to get out of here. I have to escape Deklan, Sophia, and her creepy demons and figure out how to get Rose back. I will never be able to communicate with my demon with everyone around, especially if Thorn is still in control.

"Mia, wait!" Sophia calls out as I dash for the double doors.

Deklan moves too quickly for me to escape, blocking my way to the doors with his massive form, his arms crossed over his colossal chest.

"It is too dangerous for you to be alone right now," Sophia says.

"I'd rather be alone than with him," I seethe, glaring at Deklan angrily before turning back to Sophia. "I hate him."

"You don't have to like your angel," Sophia shrugs. "But you do have to put up with him long enough to learn how to control your demon."

"I don't need him," I say, and I can hear the desperation in my tone.

The panic attack looms close, and I try to stave it off. I close my eyes and try to control my breathing while my heart threatens to beat out of my chest. My vision blurs as I watch Sophia move toward me with worried eyes, her two demons sticking close to her side.

"Alright, Mia. Don't stress. You can stay with me tonight and talk about this in the morning after we are all a bit calmer. We can have a drink to calm our nerves before bed. What do you say?"

Sophia's tone is soothing, and she holds her hands out in a non-threatening gesture as she moves slowly in my direction. The panic must show in my features for Sophia to behave this way toward me.

Taking deep breaths, I close my eyes and force myself to calm down. The air is stifling and does nothing to alleviate the need to run, which swells in my chest.

"I just need out of this small space," I mumble as I back away from Deklan and the way out. "I just need out of here."

"Fine, then come into the turret with me. My living room is big, light, and airy, with a huge balcony. You can get some fresh air, and the view is gorgeous."

I open my eyes to see Sophia turn and open the massive metal door she had initially come out of, the one I got into a fight with and lost. She gestures toward the open doorway with an inviting smile.

I turn around to take one last glance toward Deklan, and the look on his visage almost brings me to my knees. His emerald eyes are filled with what I can only describe as immense suffering and grief. His brows are slightly raised and drawn together, his luscious lips slightly parted, and his jaws are flexed as if he is grinding his teeth.

He utters one whispered word and the utter loss in his tone shoots jolts of misery through my heart.

"Mia."

I almost go to him, almost wrapping my arms around him in a comforting embrace. I almost fall for the trap that he is trying to set. However, I don't believe it. I don't believe the emotions in his voice and face are real. It is an act, and it has been all along.

I heard him admit it with my own ears.

Shaking my head in torturous disappointment, I turn away from Deklan and follow Sophia through the door and into the turret, leaving Deklan and his act behind.

CHAPTER 19: DEKLAN

I watch as Mia walks out of my life for a second time, taking my heart with her like she did the first time. Only, this time, I think it may be for good. Even if I give her some space to calm down, I don't think she will believe my explanations of what happened.

My heart aches with a tearing pain as the loud bang of that metal door closing reverberates through the small space where I still stand, staring forlornly at the now-closed door. The pain is a reminder of that which I suffered when I was cast down to this accursed plane of existence.

Only this agony is worse.

I thought I knew what heartache was, what loss was. I thought I knew how it felt to have my heart torn from my chest and shattered on the floor.

I was wrong…so very wrong.

This is worse.

The pain is relentless, like a storm that refuses to pass. Every breath feels heavy, as if my chest is being crushed under an invisible weight. My heart feels like shattered glass, each fragment piercing deeper with every thought of what I just lost.

The torturous, helpless agony that consumes me bleeds into my core, making it hard to breathe. The physical pain in the center of my chest consumes me to the point that I can't think about anything else. Existence is irrelevant. There is only the pain.

I am lost in a void, unsure what to do next. My body is frozen in a state of distraught shock. I can't move, can't breathe, can't think of anything but the pain.

There is a hollowness in my chest, a sinking void of black nothingness that threatens to consume me in its icy embrace. My arms wrap around my torso, seemingly of their own accord. Slowly, I realize that I am still standing in the small alcove, staring at the fucking door as I hold myself tightly, trying to stifle the pain.

It doesn't work.

The metal door has cut me off from my life because Mia is my life. I can't live without her, and I refuse to keep existing unless she is mine. She awakened something in me and brought it back to life just when I thought there was no more life in me to give. She pulled me from the wreck I found myself in and lit that spark in me that allowed me to feel again.

And I refuse to give up and let it die again.

A determined resolve such as I have never felt before rises within me. I refuse to live without her. I simply refuse. The statement becomes my mantra as my body moves forward with purpose. It takes my brain a moment to catch up as I grasp the metal door handle and pull.

When my thoughts and actions come into balance, I realize that the door will probably not open since it will indeed be locked. Sophia always locks the door behind her.

Surprise and delight overtake me when the door pulls open without resistance. Sophia didn't lock the door. I wonder if it was on purpose as I enter and stride down the hallway toward the turret. She has never forgotten to lock it before, and Sophia certainly seems to be on my side regarding helping Mia. But is she really on my side as far as a relationship with Mia goes?

It doesn't matter. I refuse to live without Mia, and that's that. I will make her mine again, even if I have to force her like I did the first time. It will undoubtedly be more challenging this time, but I don't care. Mia is worth it.

I reach the door leading directly into Sophia's living room and pause. How do I want to go about this? Should I go in hard and rough like last time or take it slower this time? I am at a loss.

Last time, I was trying to lure out her demon, but this time, I am trying to make her mine, to make her love me.

No.

Not trying.

I will make her mine.

She wants me. I know she wants me. I can tell by the twitch of her skin every time I touch her, the way her eyes go out of focus when I say her name in that low, seductive tone she likes, or her breathy little moans she makes when my hands are wrapped around her throat.

I can tell by the way her pulse flutters in her neck when I get close to her, the smell of her arousal that drifts in the air when I call her a good girl, and the flush of her skin when I am about to punish her.

She wants me, but I want her to love me.

So, maybe a combination of both? I can go in hard and fast, kick up her arousal, and then make love to her until she is screaming my name into the heavens. After I fuck her anger away, maybe she will let me explain the tail-end of the conversation she heard.

Maybe she will even believe me.

Then I can tell her how I feel; maybe she will believe that too.

No.

Not maybe.

I will make her believe me. I will make her mine forever.

I place my hand on the doorknob and take a deep breath, readying myself to open the door, and burst into the room with guns blazing. But the sound of Mia's angry tones stops my actions short.

I suck in a breath, holding it in my lungs as I focus on my angel hearing to hear what she is saying through the closed door. The devastation in her tone has my heart palpitating with worry as I listen.

"How can this be happening," she says shrilly. "How can there be two pieces of the same demon? The demon that's supposed to be dead, might I add. I thought Harper cut his head off. Isn't that supposed to kill a demon?"

"Normally, yes," Sophia says in a calmer tone. "But Thorn was a very powerful demon. I'm not surprised that he found a way to leave behind pieces of himself."

"Pieces of himself? Thorn taking over my demon is a bit more than just a piece of himself," Mia says.

I can picture her standing there with her arms crossed over her chest, the petulance on her features.

"I just found out about it myself, so I am not clear on the entire situation," Sophia says with an irritating huff. "But we can ask Harper about it tomorrow. You need to eat, rest, and regain your strength for now. Thorn will be less likely to try to take you over if you are healthy and rested."

"I'm not a child," Mia says. "I don't need everyone telling me what to do."

"You are acting like a child, so apparently, you do need someone to tell you what to do," Sophia says, and I hear the beginnings of anger in her voice. "You won't sleep. You give your guardian angel a hard time, and how long has it been since you ate something?"

"I ate just before I ran away from that insufferable angel. Besides, he is the one that gives me a hard time," Mia scoffs sarcastically. "Did you know that he…"

Mia stops abruptly, and I strain to hear through the door, wishing I was a fly on the wall inside the room.

"He what?" Sophia questions.

I press my ear close to the door and hold my breath, anticipation of hearing the next words from Mia dancing over my skin. Is she going to tell Sophia about our sexcapades? Or will she tell Soph I crushed her heart with my unwillingness to confess my feelings for her?

Mia's voice is barely a whisper as she says her next words…

"He…well he…" She stops, causing me to tense in preparation for what she will say. However, Mia does not speak next.

Sophia's tone is comforting, dropping to a whisper to match Mia's as she says, "You can tell me, Mia. What did Deklan do?"

The tension soars through my entire body as I wait for Mia's response. It feels like an eternity before I hear Mia's strained voice say, "He forced himself on me."

Anger flares through my chest. Did she really say what I thought she said? I never forced Mia to do anything she did not want to do. I would have stopped at any point during my demands of Mia had she told me to and been serious about it.

As a matter of fact, I had stopped at one point when she told me to wait. I had stopped and waited until she had consented to proceed, even though it strained every nerve and muscle in my body.

But she never told me to stop. She may have hit me, ran, and said the word 'please' a lot, but if anything, she was begging me to keep going. Her hits were barely small slaps, and her attempts to run were not very convincing.

It was the reactions of her body that told the real story of how she felt about what I was doing to her. The way her skin heated at my every touch, the flush of her cheeks whenever I had her at my mercy, and the way she said my name was all proof that she wanted everything I gave.

And I will give it all to her again to prove she wants me.

Soph's surprised gasp carries through the room, halting my intent before I can turn the knob and storm into the room. I grit my teeth and force myself to listen before barging in. Surely Sophia will defend me.

"That's a serious accusation," Sophia says, but her tone isn't accusing. She sounds calming and attentive as she asks, "Can you tell me more?"

Okay, so she didn't defend me. However, she didn't get angry and demand my head on a pike either, so I continue listening, my curiosity at Sophia's intent overriding the anger.

"He did dastardly things to me!" Mia says in a more demanding tone. "He tied me up, and then he…well, he…he made me watch while he…"

"Did you tell him to stop?" Sophia asks, interrupting Mia's tirade.

"Of course I did!" Mia says forcefully.

"Did you mean it?" Sophia asks curiously.

There is silence, and I imagine Sophia staring Mia down, forcing her to answer honestly.

Finally, Mia's voice comes through, resigned and unsure. "I fought and kicked, but he just kept…doing what he was doing."

Sophia's tone is soft and careful as she says, "Are you sure you didn't like it just a little bit?"

There's another pause, a longer one this time, and then Mia's defeated tone fills the silence.

"I did like it, alright? Is that what you want to hear?" Mia answers with a huff.

"Only if it is true," Sophia says. "It's alright to feel that way, Mia."

"No. No, it isn't alright. I didn't want to like it, but I did." The pain in Mia's tone almost brings me to my knees as she continues, "How can being humiliated feel so good? How can I like that? I must be some kind of freak."

Sophia's tone is light, and I can almost hear the smile she surely has on her face as she answers, "You are not a freak, Mia. Many people enjoy sex games. For many, it is an outlet to take out their anger and frustrations toward each other in a way that makes them feel good. It takes explicit care and adoration toward another person to be able to make them feel good while taking out their frustrations on them at the same time."

There is silence while I wait tensely for Mia's reaction.

"I never thought about it that way. He certainly made me feel good despite being humiliated. It was the most intense orgasm I have ever had," Mia says softly.

The smile that blooms on my face hurts my cheeks, but I can't seem to stop it. The hope that blossoms in my chest lightens the pain that previously consumed me. I can finally breathe, and I let out a long, quiet sigh.

"And how do you really feel about Deklan?" Sophia asks, catching my attention once more.

Every muscle in my body tenses in anticipation of Mia's answer as I press so close to the door that I'm in danger of busting it open. I hold my breath, waiting for the words that will either break me entirely or give me the ambition to reach my goal of owning Mia completely.

"I hate him," Mia says, but my heart doesn't sink in disappointment.

The tone of her voice was the same as it always was when she would utter those words, when she meant something else entirely, even though she didn't know what she meant.

Hell, I didn't know until just this second, the realization hitting me like an F5 tornado. She was saying she loved me. Every time she had said those words to me, she had been telling me how she felt. The recognition brings on its heels another understanding of my own. When I answered with 'I know,' I was saying I loved her too.

That's the drive I needed to spur me into action.

I twist the knob and barge into the room, piercing Mia with a look that I hope she understands as I say firmly, "I know."

The tiniest hint of understanding passes through her surprised, chocolate-drop eyes as they land on me when I enter the room. Her mouth drops open in stunned silence, and she raises a hand to cover her open mouth.

I see the triumphant smile stretch across Sophia's face out of the corner of my eye as she says, "And on that note, I'm going to bed. You two have fun!"

"Wait, Sophia!" Mia says urgently, dropping her hand from her face. "Don't leave me alone with…"

Mia's voice trails off as Sophia ignores her and keeps walking until she disappears down the hallway that trails around to the bedrooms, leaving us alone in the large circular room.

Mia moves to follow Sophia, but I block her way, moving faster than even I thought I could. She almost collides with me but stops just short of touching me. Her ample breasts press so close to my upper stomach that I can feel the heat from her skin through my t-shirt.

I bring my hands up and grasp her by the shoulders before she can turn and bolt, my fingers digging into her skin slightly as I hold tight. She still wears the scrubs that the doctors had put on her body, and the feel of her naked flesh in my hands sends sparks of longing running through my veins. The teasing peak of her breasts from the low-cut neckline sets my loins on fire, and I can't seem to pull my gaze from those bronze mounds.

"Deklan," she whispers in a torturous tone, low and soft, almost like a prayer.

The sound of my name slipping from her lips in such an agonizing way has my heart stuttering in my chest. My eyes lift to hers, and a low, angry growl slips from my chest.

"I am not a rapist," I say through gritted teeth. "You wanted every single thing I did to you, whether you knew you wanted it or not. Your body craved it just as much as mine did."

A small whimper escapes Mia's full lips, igniting the lust curling through my bones. I watch her throat bob as she swallows, my fingers desperate to curl around her neck and watch the desire fill her eyes as I squeeze. But I resist.

My voice is a growl of pent-up anger as I rasp, "Bad girls get punished, Mia. Do you want to be punished?"

As she shakes her head, a tear forms at the corner of one almond-shaped, chocolate-drop eye.

"Then you better eat your words and tell the truth," I spit out harshly, my voice low and growly.

Her throat moves with another hard swallow, and her voice is breathy and wavering as she replies, "You...you...heard that?"

"I heard everything," I ground out through gritted teeth.

Every muscle in my body is taut from holding back my desire to grab her throat, pull down her flimsy scrub pants, and fuck her until she begs me to stop.

Or not to ever stop.

"I...I...Deklan," she stutters as I lean closer into her, squeezing her shoulders to just this side of too hard.

She whimpers, causing my dick to jump in my jeans and push painfully against the zipper. I lean down so close that her breasts are pinned against my chest, causing the fabric of my shirt to rub against my skin as I move. The friction is delightful, sending tendrils of need curling through me.

"Spit it out, Mia," I say, my gaze darting to her luscious mouth with salacious desire.

I want to feel the heat of her mouth clamped around my hard cock as I wrap a fist in her silky, black hair. I want to watch her almond eyes as she gazes up at me while she sucks my cock. My dick throbs with need as those images flash through my brain.

"Deklan, please," Mia whispers tremblingly. "I didn't mean…"

"Then why did you say it?" I ask roughly, interrupting her feeble excuses with a firm shake.

Her eyes widen, and I watch the uncertainty in her visage drain away, replaced by a slow, smoldering rage. Her spine stiffens, her muscles tense in my tight hold, and her chin lifts defiantly.

She takes a breath, and her tone becomes more steady, her voice louder as she says, "Why does it matter to you anyway? I am nothing to you but a way to save your own ass."

Her anger ignites the rage swirling in my gut, and I release a fury-filled growl from my chest.

"That isn't true, either, angel. Your mouth is just full of lies today."

Her spiteful look falters briefly, but she covers it quickly and spits out, "I heard you with my own ears."

"You didn't hear what you think you heard, angel. I have tried to tell you that, but you refuse to listen…"

"And I won't listen," Mia shouts, twisting against my hold. "You're the liar, not me!"

"Mia," I ground out, trying to keep my grip on her shoulders without hurting her.

I am about to force her into a chair, hold her down, and make her listen when a bright, blinding light fills the space around Mia's body. The surprise and unexpectedness of the brightness causes my grip on her arms to loosen, and she pulls free of my grip.

She careens backward, the bright light following her as she stumbles, her arms waving in the air for balance. She steadies herself as the light fades into a mess of shadowy tentacles that wrap around Mia and hold her in place.

The rage in my gut spills out through my entire body, burning like molten lava through my veins as I watch Mia's demon take form out of the writhing mess of shadows. It pierces me with its glowing cornflower-blue stare.

"Leave Mia alone," it shouts, the female voice of the demon echoing through the large room.

The anger fades suddenly, replaced with startled confusion.

Mia gasps audibly and shouts, "Oh, thank the Gods! Rose!"

Then Mia slaps a hand over her mouth and turns her wide-eyed stare on me. My confusion grows.

Rose? Has Mia named her demon? When I found her wandering spirit, Mia said she had dealings with her demon while she was out of her body. If the blue, glowing eyes were any indication, I would guess that her demon is close to being tame.

But how?

Then, the flashing blue eyes change, switching between cornflower blue and lilac purple. The demon stumbles, shaking its head as if trying to shake something off.

"Oh no," Mia whispers, squirming out of the dark tendrils' grasp and backing away from the demon with both hands covering her open mouth.

My eyes narrow as anger consumes me again, finally catching on to what is happening.

Thorn is taking over.

The name of the demon that tortured and raped Soph and trapped my friend in the Demon Dimension swells in my brain like poison, festering in my thoughts and feeding my rage. Every muscle in my body tenses, my heart races, and my hands are drawn into fists at my sides.

Thorn…the name runs through my mind like sludge, gathering in the corners and sticking there. It clouds my judgment and sparks my desire to smite the demon with no mercy and no thought of anything else. My hands rise to the position, gathering the energy blast in my arms and hands, like loading a shotgun and readying it to fire.

The sound of my name being called repeatedly plays in the background of my mind, but I am too focused on my task to pay attention to it. I am staring down the demon who hurt my friends, preparing to send him into the afterlife where he belongs. His purple eyes flash, narrowing into a glare that pierces through the light shining at the end of my hands.

The light I am about to release straight into his smug face.

"Deklan, please don't!"

Mia's voice breaks through my barriers, filling my awareness with an alarming tone.

"Please, don't take my demon!"

"Deklan, stop, or you'll kill Mia!" Sophia's voice joins Mia's, and her words break the rage-filled trance.

I was a second away from releasing the devastating blast that would have taken out the demon, but I stopped. The demon smirks victoriously as I ball my hands into fists, pull the energy back, and shake out my hands to ward off any residual energy. I tamp my rage with a long, drawn breath and run a hand down my face.

"When will you get it through that thick head that I am not going anywhere, you stupid angel?" Thorn says as he stalks toward me.

"Oh, you're going somewhere, alright," I snap as I stand my ground. "As soon as we figure out how to separate you from Mia, you're dead."

Thorn laughs, drawing closer to me with every cackle. "You will never separate me from Mia. And as soon as I take over her body, I will call all the other pieces of myself together, ripping away the lives of those who carry it."

"Harper," Sophia whispers, her tone coated in desperation.

Thorn's menacing laugh fills the large room as he draws even closer to me, and my smirk grows wider. Let the demon touch me. He is in for a rude awakening. All that unused energy crackles in my veins, and I will release it on him as soon as I convert it from smiting to sleeping energy.

Of course, Thorn was never properly tamed or taught anything but how to be an evil asshat. He will never know what I am doing as long as I can keep him distracted long enough.

Nervousness flows through me when Thorn moves closer, that devilish smirk spreading across his shadowy features. I need more time to prepare the sleeping energy before he can touch me.

But then the sound of redemption has me taking a relieved breath.

"I wouldn't touch that angel if I were you, Thorn." Harper's voice says, filling the room and eliciting a delighted gasp from Sophia. "Didn't anyone ever tell you that demons can't touch angry, power-filled angels without being put to sleep?

"Why did you have to ruin it?" I huff, turning to the mirror at my back. "I was just going to let him touch me."

I smirk inwardly at Harper's attempt to keep Thorn talking, knowing that Thorn won't believe us, and will try to grab me anyway. But not before I turn the energy around.

The mirror Harper appears in hangs on the wall and is usually covered by a black drop cloth, but Sophia must have failed to recover it after she brought it back from Mia's hospital room. Harper's image wavers slightly on the mirror's surface as he smiles from his prison.

"I was feeling generous," Harper shrugs with a crooked smile, then his smile fades as he pierces Thorn with an angry stare. "But I won't be generous for long. Go ahead, touch him if you don't believe me."

Thorn hesitates, stumbling to a halt only feet away from me. I back toward the mirror and Harper.

"You good, Boss?" Harper asks as I draw closer.

That throws me for a loop, but I keep my features calm. I am not Harper's boss, but Thorn doesn't have to know that.

"I should be asking you the same," I answer. Then, in a low whisper that the demon can't hear and without moving my lips as much as possible, I turn to the mirror and breath, "What are you playing at?"

Harper just gives me a knowing look and slyly gestures toward the room with only his eyes. I turn and take in the entirety of the room, breathing a sigh of relief when I see Sophia hustle Mia toward the circular hallway that leads to the bedrooms. Thorn is paying them no mind since he focuses solely on my movements and Harper's visage in the mirror.

"I'm fine," Harper says aloud. "I felt Thorn's presence through that tiny spark of him inside me, so I thought I would investigate. Glad I did."

"You expect me to believe that when I make an angel angry, it will put me to sleep when I touch them?" Thorn asks with a sarcastic, disbelieving scoff.

"Something like that," I answer with a sly smile, playing along with Harper's game as I stop next to the mirror.

I glance over my shoulder at Harper in the mirror, gesturing with my thumb toward Thorn.

"Get a load of the uneducated demon," I say to Harper, snickering and shaking my head.

Thorn lets out an angry growl. "You won't be so smug when I get what I want. After I take your girl's body, will you still want it? I'd be happy to play sex games with you, Deklan. I'm not picky about gender."

My laugh stops abruptly, the grin fading as I turn my attention back to Thorn. "I would never let you touch me in that way, and I certainly won't let you take Mia's body."

"How are you going to stop me?" Thorn asks as he smiles widely and starts to fade.

But I am too fast. Thorn stopped too close to me. He has underestimated me.

Again.

I jump into action, surging forward and grabbing the demon before he can fade. I release the sleep energy I had been preparing as Harper and I have kept him busy talking, pushing it into Thorn through the hand I have wrapped around his wrist. Thorn screams in frustrated rage as his image fades and Thorn is put back to sleep.

"I just put that fucker back less than an hour ago," I say breathlessly. "It's getting harder and harder to keep him out, and Mia isn't making it any easier since she is refusing to rest."

"You have to keep her healthy," Harper stresses. "The weaker her body is, the more control the demon has."

"I know, Harper. I know," I say in a defeated tone. "I think it's best if I leave. Maybe Sophia will have better luck. Her health is more important than my hurt feelings at the moment."

Harper nods as his image begins to fade. Before he can fade completely, he says, "Everything will work out fine, Deklan. I believe in you."

Pride swells in my chest at Harper's words. It makes me happy that Harper believes in me despite our past.

I only wish I believed in myself half as much.

CHAPTER 20: MIA

I know the instant my demon returns to me. The sensation of butterflies fluttering around in my stomach tells me. I'm glad she is back and hope she will be herself again when she reappears.

Also, I am nervous that she may be mad at me when she reappears. I had been so happy to see Rose earlier that I blurted out her name in front of Harper and Sophia, but I don't think either noticed.

Especially not since Thorn made himself known.

Thorn.

The name fills me with a simmering anger that I won't be able to deny much longer. My sweet demon wants nothing more than to learn and grow, and Thorn has taken that away from her. I would protect my demon if I knew the secret to keep Thorn at bay.

But I don't. Only Deklan does.

My heart lurches at the thought of Deklan. It is confusing that I should be concerned about him despite my anger. However, the idea that Deklan could be hurt or worse, by my own demon no less, as Sophia and I hide out in her room has my heart twisting with worry.

I assume it is safe since I felt my demon come back to me, but that doesn't mean Deklan is unhurt. The irrational urge to run to him, to see for myself that he is okay, is overwhelming but I don't want to take any chances. I turn to Sophia, and a shiver runs up my spine as I see the worry on her face.

"I'm sure they have it handled," I tell her, patting her hand comfortingly. "I felt my demon return to me, so it is no longer a threat."

Sophia tries a weak smile, but it doesn't reach her eyes. "You're probably right. I'm just worried about Harper after what Thorn said."

"You mean about calling the pieces of himself back?" I ask. "I wonder who else has a piece of Thorn."

Sophia frowns thoughtfully. "What do you mean, Mia?"

My brows raised in surprise that Sophia failed to catch what I had, but, then again, she was so focused on her worry for Harper...

I could see where she would have missed it.

"Thorn said *pieces*...as in more than one. He said the people who carried them would lose their lives, so there has to be more than Harper carrying pieces of Thorn," I explain.

Sophia's eyes widen as realization dawns on her face. "Oh, shit. You're right."

"Who else was around when it all happened?" I ask.

Sophia taps a finger on her lips, rolling her eyes toward the ceiling in a thoughtful expression. "Let's see...Only my demons, Harper inside of Thorn, and me. Jeremy was already dead at that point."

"It has to be one of the demons. If it was you, one of your demons would have noticed by now," I say matter-of-factly.

"Yes, they would have," Sophia agrees. "And they would have noticed it in themselves as well."

"Unless it's such a small piece they have not noticed," I suggest with a shrug.

"Oh, we would have noticed that," a sarcastic male voice flows through my brain.

"Hi, Lucien," I say dryly. "What has given me the honor of hearing your esteemed voice today?"

Sophia snickers at my sarcasm as Lucien appears before me, his narrowed sapphire eyes glowing brightly.

"I only came to tell you it is safe to leave the room," Lucien says. "Deklan is gone. He said to let you know he would check on you later."

A sting of pain shoots through my heart, but I quickly school my features.

Feigning nonchalance, I answer, "Fine, whatever. He can go to hell for all I care."

"Hell does not exist, human," Lucien says.

I narrow my eyes angrily. "It's an expression, demon. Do all demons take things so literally?"

Sophia snickers. "They are slowly learning about metaphors and expressions."

Lucien turns to Sophia and says, "That is all I need to say. I will speak with you later, master."

"Oh, for fuck's sake, Lucien, how many times do I have to tell you to stop calling me master?" Sophia says in frustration.

Lucien turns toward me with a sly wink, which Sophia does not see, but his deadpan tone does not change as he answers, "Sorry, Sophia. I forgot again."

Lucien disappears in a swirl of smoke and shadow, and I scoff at the demon's attempt at humor. I shake my head at the wisps of smoke remaining in Lucien's wake.

"What?" Sophia asks.

"Nothing," I say, holding back a smile as I think that perhaps Lucien was trying to make me feel better. Squashing the feel-good emotion in an attempt to hold on to my anger, I ask, "Where am I sleeping? I think I'll take a nap."

Sophia eyes me suspiciously, but she does not comment. Instead, she turns toward the door that leads back out to the hallway.

"This way," she says, gesturing for me to follow.

She leads me out into the hallway and to the left, further around the circular corridor. We pass a few doors on the right before stopping at the last one on the left.

"This room hasn't been slept in for a while," Sophia says as she turns the knob. "This is the room I stayed in after Harper locked Jeremy away and before Harper and I became lovers."

"When you didn't know which one to trust, and Harper kept you here to keep you safe from Jeremy," I added, remembering the story Sophia had told me...

Back before, when I thought the demons didn't exist and Sophia was batshit crazy.

I gasp when I see the beautiful four-poster bed sitting diagonally in the left corner of the room. The coverings are done in blue to match the curtains, which flow over the big window that overlooks the garden. The vast expanse of the hardwood floors and smartly positioned furniture gives space to the room.

The matching dresser sits against the far right wall next to a door that I assume is the closet. There is a small vanity with a bench sitting against the back wall next to the window and beside the bed.

The care that must have gone into decorating the room gives me a new appreciation for Harper's attention to detail where Sophia was concerned. Sophia's favorite color is blue, and she loves gardens.

"The room is beautiful," I breathe as I voice my thoughts aloud. "Harper cared a great deal about you, didn't he?"

"The room wasn't like this at first," Sophia answers. "I had to earn some things since I was such a shit in the beginning and brain washed by Jeremy. But, yes, Harper did care about me from the beginning."

Sophia pauses momentarily, her tone saddening when she continues, "I only wish I had realized it sooner; then maybe he wouldn't be stuck in the Demon Dimension."

I place a comforting hand on her shoulder. "I know it will work out, and I wish you all the happiness in the world. You deserve it."

Sophia pats my hand with a sad smile. "Thank you, Mia. I wish the same for you. Just don't be too late for Deklan like I was for Harper."

And with that, she turns and walks out of the room. What did she mean by that? Deklan cares nothing for me like Harper does for Sophia. I am nothing but a means to save Deklan's ass from extinction. Maybe Deklan has everyone fooled, which leads me to wonder who he was talking to on the phone that day in his office. I had assumed it had been Sophia, but now I am not so sure.

I sigh loudly as I shuffle over to the bed, intending to lie down and take a short nap when a chill runs down my spine, and the fine hairs on the back of my neck stand at attention. The dreaded feeling that someone is watching me floods my system, and I turn rapidly to look behind me.

Nothing or no one is there. Only the faint outline of my shadow wavering on the wall beside the vanity greets my eyes. Still, that creepy sensation that someone or something is watching me permeates my senses.

The sense of dread that flows over me prompts me to turn and run, but that desire is stopped abruptly when the sight of my shadow peeling off the wall and walking toward me paralyzes me with fear.

The lights in the room flicker rapidly, and my heart matches their rhythm. My lungs scream for oxygen, and I realize that I have been holding my breath. I suck in blessed air, and my exhale becomes a terrified scream when my shadow draws near enough to touch, and its arm slowly reaches for me.

"Mia! It's only me," a soft, female voice flows through my mind.

My scream gets stuck in my throat at the sound of Rose's voice in my head, and the fear flowing through me is replaced with profound relief.

"Thank fucking goodness. You scared the fucking shit out of me, Rose, but I am so glad to see you anyway," I gasp aloud as I grab my chest in an attempt to keep my heart inside my body.

The hand that was reaching for me touches my shoulder, and the icy touch of my demon is a comfort. Her eyes glow a light shade of blue as she forms more solidly before me. She continues the conversation aloud.

"After your angel put Thorn to sleep, I awoke and felt your distress. The force of Thorn is so strong. I don't know if I will ever be strong enough to overcome it."

Rose's tone is worried and stressed, causing my heart to skip a beat as she draws me into a frigid hug. She is so cold, the cold of the grave, the cold of death. However, the iciness matches my mood at the moment, so I do not mind.

"You're not mad at me for accidentally revealing your name?" I ask against her icy skin, my face pressed into her shoulder as she hugs me tightly.

Rose scoffs a light laugh. "No, Mia. Your angel should know my name. He is sworn to help and protect us, after all. And Sophia is your family. I can feel the trust you have in her. If you trust her, then so do I."

I smile against Rose's shoulder, and the sudden urge to cry overcomes me. The tears prick at the backs of my eyes as a burning lump forms in my throat. My chest tightens, and every muscle in my body tenses when I try to hold back the sob that threatens to break free. My heart kicks up a beat, and my breath comes in ragged gasps.

"It's alright, Mia. Let it out. I'm here," Rose croons as she sways slightly with me in her arms. "I know you're hurting. A good cry will help relieve some of the pain."

"I don't even know why I want to cry," I say, my voice coming out in a shaky, choked tone. "I'm happy that I was able to get back to my body and that you are back. I have no reason to cry."

"Yes, you do," Rose says softly. "Deklan."

Just the sound of his name sends shockwaves of longing and sorrow through my bones.

"He hurt you, Mia. You were falling for him, and he hurt you," Rose says in a whispered tone.

A sob escapes my burning throat. My chest feels about to burst, and it hurts when I try to draw in a shaky breath.

"You are hurt, and it is okay to cry when you're hurt," Rose says, tightening her hold.

The damn bursts.

Tears stream from my eyes as wracking sobs break free, filling the air with the grief-stricken sound. The tightening in my chest is somewhat relieved with the release of so much agony, but the dull ache of my heart still resonates through my soul as the abused organ thumps hard in my chest.

Tears fall like rain, unbidden and free, each drop a testament to a heart that continues to break with every sob released. Rose pats my back comfortingly as I cry, making cooing noises and swaying slowly as she holds me. She doesn't say anything or shush me. She just lets me cry until I seem to run out of tears, and my sobs turn to tiny, hiccupping gasps.

Somehow, after coming out of my crying stupor, I find myself crumpled on the floor with Rose kneeling beside me, still holding me against her cold, shadowy chest. The only shreds of evidence left of my crying fit are the sniffles wracking my nose and the trembling of my body as the adrenaline wears away.

"Feel better?" Rose asks when I wipe my almost-dry eyes with the backs of my hands, squirming out of her grasp as I attempt to sit up.

I nod but only manage to squeak out a barely audible, "Mmhm."

"Good. Then, let's get out of here," she says as she steadies me and helps me up from the floor. "I will help you get back to your apartment."

Alarm bells sound off in my brain as I attempt to reorient myself after being on the floor for God knows how long. I really do want to go home and be alone for a while to evaluate my emotions and let the whirlwind of everything sink into my mind, but what will I do if Thorn comes back? I can't defend myself against a powerful demon or help my demon defend herself, either.

The only person who can protect me and my demon is Deklan, but I don't want to be around him right now. I also don't want to be alone with my demon, but how do I tell her that without hurting her feelings and backtracking on all the progress we have made?

What the hell am I going to do?

"Mia?" the whispered tone of my demon pulls me out of my own head.

I look into those glowing sapphire eyes and smile sadly as I say, "I'm fine, Rose. Just thinking."

"Trying to figure out how to tell me you're scared of me?" Rose asks softly.

My eyes widen, and I shake my head emphatically as I try to explain. "No, I'm not scared of you, Rose. I promise. I'm just..."

Rose interrupts me with an understanding shrug. "You're scared

Thorn might come back. I understand, Mia. You don't have to be afraid of hurting my feelings."

I frown in confusion and reply, "How are you doing that? Can you read my mind or something?"

Rose scoffs a laugh. "Not technically, but I am part of you, Mia. So I can feel what you feel, and some thoughts flow through to me in vague forms. However, knowing the circumstances, it isn't hard to decipher into words."

"So, what do we do? I want to get out of here, but I don't think I have that option right now." I sigh disappointedly.

"Look, Mia, I think Thorn should stay away for a while now since Deklan gave him a good shot of sleeping energy this time. Plus, you need a few days away to recuperate and get your emotions in check. Then, you can face Deklan with a renewed sense of fuck-you-buddy vibes and tell him where he can stick it."

"Or where he is no longer allowed to stick it better yet," I laugh, the humor easing the pain clutching my heart a bit more.

"That's the spirit," Rose says with a giggle. "Now, come on. I have a trick to show you."

"Oh?" I respond with a curious raise of one eyebrow. "What is it?"

"You'll see," Rose says with a sly smirk.

She turns and floats through the door of the room. I laugh and shake my head, opening the door and following her into the hall. She is looking at the door expectantly when I open the door and step out and then seems surprised when she spots me.

I watch humorously as realization dawns in her eyes, and she slaps her shadowy forehead with a spectral hand. "I forgot you aren't in spirit form any longer. You physically have to open doors."

I laugh again, but then my laughter stops abruptly when I hear whispered voices echoing through the circular hallway.

"You have to go talk to her," Sophia's voice hisses. "Your very existence is on the line as well as hers."

"Mia isn't going to listen to me any longer," Deklan's whispered tones answer. "And I am not going to force her anymore."

"Damn right you won't," I hiss under my breath.

Turning to Rose, I add, "How are you going to get me out of here without getting spotted by those two?"

"I'm not telling you to force her," Mia's voice carries down the hallway. "I'm simply saying…"

Rose taps my arm, interrupting my concentration.

She smiles deviously and says, "That's the trick I wanted to show you. We will walk right past them, and they won't see us."

I frown in disbelief. "How?"

"Welll…," Rose drawls out, pausing dramatically.

"You have to do something. Explain what happened, and maybe she'll forgive you," Sophia says.

However, I don't have time to ponder the meaning of Sophia's statement since I am more focused on what Rose is whispering to me.

"Demons have this ability to hide their master in darkness and shadow, causing them to be virtually invisible to anyone not paying attention, and I am strong enough now to use the ability."

"Wow," I say, my eyes widening in amazement.

Deklan's voice echoes down the hallway, but I don't take the time to listen to his response. Instead, I turn my full attention to Rose and block out Deklan and Sophia's conversation.

"When did you discover you were strong enough to use it?" I ask Rose.

"When I snuck up on you just now," Rose answers snarkily.

I bark out a laugh. "And you nearly gave me a heart attack."

"Those two are distracted by their intense conversation, so if we are very quiet and sneaky enough, we can slip right by in shadow without them seeing us," Rose says with an impish grin.

I don't even take time to think about it. Nodding, I say, "Let's do it."

Rose smiles and places a finger to her lips, gesturing for me to be quiet. I mimic zipping my lips with two fingers as I return her smile. She gestures for me to follow and turns toward the sound of the voices. Nervously, I trail behind, walking softly on the tile floor of the hallway.

Thankfully, I am still wearing the hospital slippers that were on my feet when I sprinted from the sick bay room earlier, which are nothing but socks with grips on the bottom of them. I'll worry about shoes once I am out of this place.

I keep my attention averted ahead, my heart speeding up as we get closer to the living area where Deklan and Sophia's conversation continues. I do not listen to the words of the conversation since I am too focused on walking silently. I clutch my hands to my chest as I walk to keep them from shaking, and I try my best to steady my breathing and quiet my gasping inhalations.

Rose gives me a wink over her shoulder, and then I feel a tingle of sensation cross over my entire body. I shudder from the cold that creeps into my skin, and my eyes widen in fascination at the dark tendrils of shadow that snake their way around us as we continue to move silently toward the end of the hall.

When we reach the living room, where Deklan and Sophia stand in the middle of the room talking in whispered tones, I am shaking from the cold of the shadows, but confident that we cannot be seen through the cloud of darkness I am walking in with my demon.

The conversing couple comes into sight as we draw ever closer to the exit door leading out of the turret, and my eyes are automatically drawn to Deklan's bulging biceps. The ink running down his arms catches my eye as my breath catches in my throat. A shudder of desire runs through me at the sight, causing me to clench my thighs together as I walk.

My stupid, traitorous vagina flutters with the need to be filled, and I berate my lady parts in my mind as I follow close behind my demon. What the hell is wrong with me? I am so devastated by Deklan's betrayal. My heart is shattered into a million pieces, but my body still wants him.

I can still feel the remnants of his body against mine and remember how his massive cock filled my trembling pussy. I can still taste the urgency of his kisses as he fucked me and hear the tone of his darkly sensual voice when he told me what a good girl I was. My body still needs him even as my heart and mind reject him.

I give him one last longing look. I long to run my fingers through that mess of fiery hair as I gaze into those emerald eyes, calling his name as he...

No! I must get him out of my mind, out of my system. I need to get back to my apartment and be alone. I need to get away. I need air and room to breathe, and I need to be able to think without his presence suffocating me.

We are almost to the door, Rose still moving steadily even as I falter and hesitate as his head whips around suddenly. My breath lodges in my throat as he looks directly at me, but I can tell from his blank expression that he doesn't see me. Then, his visage crumbles, and my heart drops to my feet as I take in the sight of Deklan's tortured face.

My mind was so occupied with trying to remain quiet while fighting the sensations of longing that overtook me that I didn't hear a single word he had spoken to Mia as I snuck past him. Now, I wonder what was said between them. What had put that devastating look on Deklan's handsome visage? Why did he look…destroyed?

That is the only word I can think of to describe the utter torment on his features.

The soft touch of Rose's hand on my arm startles me, and I slap a hand over my mouth to stifle my gasp. She is frowning at me, asking with her eyes what is wrong, why I stopped moving.

I remove my hand from my mouth and shake my head, giving her an I'll tell you later look and gesturing for her to continue to move.

We are feet from the door. I can taste the freedom. I don't look back again as Rose ever-so-quietly opens the door, and we slip out unnoticed. Rose keeps us hidden as we make our way through the maze of hallway and out into the main entrance, exiting through the door behind Cora's desk.

Even Cora is oblivious to our presence as we sneak by her, make our way to the main door, and leave my cousin's mental facility behind.

Even though I know this is for the best, I can't help but feel that I'm leaving behind a little piece of myself, and I wonder if I'll ever get it back again.

CHAPTER 21: DEKLAN

The strangest feeling comes over me as I stand in the living room of the turret, arguing with Sophia about whether I should go talk to Mia. The fine hairs on the back of my neck stand at attention as an icy tendril of sensation trails its way down my spine. I jerk my head around to look behind me, but nothing is there.

"Deklan, if you don't go talk to her, you could possibly lose her forever," Sophia says, bringing my attention back to the conversation.

My heart throbs with devastation at the thought of living without Mia in my life. I have already decided to not live without her, no matter what that means.

I turn back to Sophia. "What do you expect me to do when she doesn't listen to me?"

Sophia sighs in defeat. "I don't know. I do know, however, that she was hurt, and it will be next to impossible for her to trust anyone ever again.

"It was a miracle that she even opened up to you in the first place, and you ruined it with your cowardice."

"I know that," I shout angrily. "Don't you think I feel guilty enough already?"

"Then go talk to her and do something about it, idiot!" Sophia shouts back. "Tell Mia you love her and explain that stupid phone call to her. Force her to listen if you have to."

Panic surges in my chest as I think about the last time I tried to voice my feelings aloud, then guilt overtakes the panic. Isn't that why this entire situation is happening to begin with?

Still, the panic I feel at talking about my emotions aloud is overwhelming. "Do I really have to say it aloud?" I ask.

"Oh, for fuck's sake, Deklan. Are you going to tell me that you aren't head over heels in love with her?"

I swallow the lump in my throat and try to breathe around the panic in my chest. I open my mouth to deny it, but Sophia lifts a hand in a silencing gesture.

"Don't try to lie to me. It's written all over your face every time you look at her," she says sternly.

If it's that obvious to Sophia, then why was it so hard for Mia to believe? Breathing around the panic, I shakily respond, "Yes, I love her."

I wait for my throat to close up and my heart to beat with anxiety, but it doesn't happen. Surprisingly, the panic subsides as I stand and wait for it to surround me. It does not return until I think about what Mia's reaction will be when I admit my feelings to her.

My slowly building confidence deflates, and my tone reflects my insecurities as I say, "But she is not in love with me."

Sophia runs a hand down her face as she makes an angry sound. "Fine. Look, we don't have time to argue the fact right now. Just do me a favor and go talk to her please."

"Fine. I'll go talk to her," I say with a huff.

I turn and stare toward the hallway. Fear churns in my gut as I think about storming down that hallway, barging into Mia's room, and telling her how much I care about her as I beg for forgiveness.

Will she reciprocate my feelings, or has she had a change of heart? It would certainly be what I deserve since I have done the same to her. The threat of rejection sits so heavy in my chest that it feels like a tangible thing hanging in the air before me.

I shuffle toward the hallway slowly, not wanting to accelerate my impending doom. I know my heart will shatter when Mia tells me she doesn't want me anymore. My life will be over.

Steeling myself for the worst, I come to the door at the end of the circular hallway and lightly tap on the door.

"Mia, can I please talk to you?" I ask, trying to be polite before I just barge in and force her to listen to me.

There is no answer.

"Mia, we can do this the easy way or the hard way, no pun intended," I shout through the closed door, trying a bit of sarcastic humor to lighten the mood.

Still no answer. There is only silence on the other side of the door.

"Mia, I'm coming in there whether you let me in or not, so you might as well let me in quietly so we don't disturb Sophia."

Nothing.

I can only guess Mia is being stubborn, but I have had enough.

"Just remember you asked for it," I say before twisting the knob to see if the door is locked before having to break it down.

I am utterly surprised when the door opens. Okay, maybe she is asleep? Yes, that must be it.

Defeatedly, I move closer to the bed. My fingers itch to wrap around her pretty little neck, causing my dick to throb with need. I want to fuck the anger out of her until she screams my name and begs me to never stop. The vice around my chest tightens the closer I come to the bed and the possibility of that vision coming true.

But my blood freezes in my veins when the bed comes into full view, cutting off my thoughts and stopping my heart.

The bed is empty.

My hand balls into a fist as I stalk over to the en-suite bathroom door and turn the knob.

"The longer you hide, the worse your punishment will be," I growl as I open the door, but my voice echoes in the empty room.

Where the fuck did she go?

Panic threatens to choke me, but I tamp it down and swallow the lump in my throat. I draw in a deep, cleansing breath as my heart stutters and begins to beat a furious rhythm. I take a few more deep breaths, but it isn't calmness that floods my body.

It is rage.

Pure, unadulterated, righteous rage.

The anger rips from my body in the form of a scream as I pound my fist into the door frame. I turn suddenly, slamming the bathroom door behind me. That beautifully stubborn, ignorant girl has snuck out again.

I grab fistfuls of my hair, growling in frustration. Doesn't she understand how much danger she is in right now? Our relationship aside, she needs to get it through her head that she needs me right now.

Turning back to the door, I let go of my hair and make my way back to the living room where I'd left Sophia, but she is gone. She probably went to bed after I left the room, but I am not going to take time to look for her. Besides, it isn't her I am after.

The fury churns in my gut as I leave the turret and stalk down the long corridors that lead to the door into the receiving room. When I get my hands on Mia, I am going to…

Thoughts of how I will punish her thaw some of the anger flowing through me, replacing it with a dangerous desire that melds with the anger and creates a dark, carnal lust that threatens to consume me. My dick flexes inside my sweatpants, growing semi-hard as my mind wanders to the sight of Mia spread out on my bed, her wrists and ankles tied to the bedposts as the canopy surrounds us in a filmy embrace of erotic secrets.

I shake my head to clear it. I can't get sidetracked by that right now. I have to find Mia, and I know where she might be. I leave the turret and head toward the stairs, not even stopping to talk to Cora when I burst out the door behind her desk. I take the stairs to my apartment two at a time.

I have to get dressed, get to that fucking abandoned building that Mia bought, and drag her back to the hospital.

I know that's where she is. Where the fuck else would she go?

I think back to only moments ago when I stood arguing with Sophia in her living room and that strange sensation that had come over me. I bet it was Mia sneaking past me, but how had I missed her? There was only one explanation, and it had my feet moving faster than ever. Her demon had helped her, and now Mia was alone with that damn demon that could turn into Thorn at any second.

I reached for my bike and started it while mounting it simultaneously. I don't even bother with the helmet. I rev the engine a couple of times before taking off down the circular driveway toward the road. Surely, Mia hadn't planned on walking all the way to town. It is nearly five miles. I will probably find her on the road somewhere before I even get to her building.

The fury drives me to go faster, my hands tightening around the bike's handles as it speeds down the road faster than I have ever rode these roads before. I ignore the alarm bells going off inside my brain, telling me to slow down before I kill my fool self. I have to get to Mia. I have no time to slow down.

I come to the end of the tiny country road and still haven't seen Mia. I veer my ride to the right toward the highway, watching both sides of the road for any sign of the raven-haired temptress. There is still no sign of her when I reach the exit onto the main highway that will take me into town, and my heart races with worry.

I slow down for the ramp, knowing the curve here is steep and I will be in danger of tipping the bike if I don't. However, as soon as I get off the exit and onto the main highway, I let my blue demon fly.

My mean machine tears down the highway faster than I have ever ridden it before. The motor roars as the bike eats up the road until I come to the turn-off that will take me to Mia's building. My fury rages as I wonder if Mia made it safely home and, if so, how Mia could have made it here so quickly.

She must have gotten a ride, and it would have been a stranger since Mia doesn't know anyone here besides Sophia and her father. Could she have gotten a ride from her father?

I hope so because the thought of her hitching a ride from a stranger sets me off, and my blood boils to a raging inferno as I park the bike in the abandoned lot of the building. Surely, she would not have been that stupid. Anything could have happened to her. She could have put herself in mortal danger by getting into a vehicle with someone she didn't know.

I could have parked right up against the main entrance like I did last time I was here, but I needed a minute to cool off. I don't trust myself to interact with her when I am this angry. So, I stalk across the parking lot, pacing around for what seems like an eternity before I feel ready enough to face her without wanting to choke her out for real.

I enter the building, and, of course, it isn't locked. I storm past the dilapidated desk, up the hallway toward the stairs, and take them two at a time, making it to the second floor in seconds. I pause to look around, not sure where to go at this point.

She has done some cleaning up here, so the hallways are not as cluttered and the broken chairs that had been scattered about the now-polished tiled floors are gone. Since her office is up ahead, I decide to look there before heading for her apartment is a few doors down.

The silence is deafening, the only sound bouncing off the beige-colored walls coming from the clop of my boots on the tile floor. My heavy breathing, and my thumping heart fill the silence, carrying on a fast beat that throbs through my eardrums.

A different sound catches my attention, and I stop in the middle of the hallway to listen. A glimpse of light from further down the corridor draws me toward it, and I follow. The closer I get to the light, the louder the sound becomes. It's as if someone, or something, is trying to tear down the entire building.

She has got to be in her apartment. At least, that is where the noises are coming from. Banging, scraping, things being thrown against a wall, and angry footsteps building up into a crescendo of what sounds like furious violence against inanimate objects, making me walk faster with every thump and bang.

Finally, I spot the source of the light from underneath a closed door further down the corridor.

The door to Mia's apartment.

The sounds grow louder the closer I get until I hear a mumbling, cursing voice mingling with the other sounds.

"Fucking superior fallen angels...doesn't think about the feelings of others...wish I had never known about their existence...hate them all...packing my shit and leaving," are some of the snippets I can hear as I draw closer to the door.

I can tell it's Mia's voice, even though I am still feet away, and she is mumbling under her breath. My enhanced angel's hearing allows me to hear it as if I am already in the room.

Even though her tone is angry and her words are hateful, the sound of her voice still makes me smile, and some of my anger dissipates at the anticipation of seeing Mia again. Especially since I now know she is safe and her demon still sleeps.

Unless it is the damn demon that she is speaking to and not herself.

That thought has me quickening my pace so that it only takes a mere second before I am at the door and turning the knob. The door is unlocked, so I throw the door open. It bangs off the wall and almost comes back to shut again, but I stop it with my foot as I barge into the...

The room is messy and destroyed. The simple sofa, which is all the furnishings Mia had in her living room, is piled with books, files, and boxes. Clothing, shoes, and other random items are strewn across the floor, piling out of an open suitcase held by a furious Mia.

Her angry gaze lands on me as I come bursting into the room. The look of shocked surprise that takes over her features almost makes me laugh, but more than that, it burns my loins with a desire for her so strong it almost makes my knees buckle. She is fucking magnificent when she is mad.

Her chocolate eyes shine with a fire that makes them seem almost black. Her raven hair flows over her shoulders, tendrils framing her face and falling across her cheeks. The furious color that has crept into her cheeks, highlighting her face, makes her skin seem to glow. It makes her seem practically magical.

I can tell she has dropped the suitcase because of how she grips the handle with both hands and the angle at which it still dangles in her grasp. The lid had fallen open, and the contents of the suitcase had tumbled out in front of and around her. It must have happened just before I had burst into the room, hence the angry cursing I had heard in the hallway.

"What the fuck are you doing here?" Mia seethes through gritted teeth. "Why can't you just leave me alone?"

The rage in her tone pulls my own anger back out of its box, and my hands ball into fists at my side.

"How the fuck did you get back so fast?" I ask through clenched teeth.

"Not that it's any business of yours," she seethes. "But I caught a ride with someone. They saw me walking and picked me up."

My eyes widen in disbelieving rage. "Mia, for fuck's sake. Don't you know how dangerous that is?"

"You mean more dangerous than having a damn demon living inside you and being stalked by a falling angel?" she shoots back.

I stalk toward her, pushing out my massive chest threateningly. "If you would stop running away, I wouldn't have to stalk you."

"And if you would just leave me alone…"

I interrupt her mid-sentence, taking another step closer. "You know I can't leave you alone, Mia. And if you would fucking listen…"

"No!" she interrupts me right back. "No, Deklan, I will not listen to your…"

But I don't give her a chance to finish her statement. I interrupt one more time, tired of playing her games. Before she even knows what is happening, I jerk the damn suitcase out of her hand and grasp her upper arms in my large grip. Clothing is trampled under my feet, and my grasp is almost bruising on her arms, but I don't care. Mia is going to listen to me one way or another.

She struggles furiously in my hold. "Let me go!"

I pull her in closer, ignoring her struggles and angry cry. "No, Mia. You will listen to me whether you like it or not!"

Her tiny hands ball into fists, and she begins flailing on my chest. I have had mosquito bites that hurt worse. She drops her weight, trying to fall out of my grip, but I only hold her tighter, pulling her in against my body as her feet drag on the floor.

I release her shoulders to get a better grip on her, and she uses the momentary freedom to turn and try to slip away. But I am too fast. I grasp her around the waist, pulling her back to my front and trapping her arms against her sides. I pick her up off the ground, her legs flailing wildly in her struggles.

Her furious screams ring through the empty room, but I know no one is around to hear them. I quickly turn my face to the side to dodge the back of her head when she throws her head back in an attempt to headbutt my nose. I turn back as her head connects with my shoulder, effectively trapping her head between my strong jaw and massive shoulder. My mouth lingers close to her ear.

My tone is low, rough, and dangerous as I growl in her ear, "Mia, I am warning you, if you don't stop fighting, I will punish you, and you won't like this punishment."

She instantly stops and sags defeatedly in my embrace. Her chest heaves against my hold with her heavy breathing, and I can feel her rapid pulse throbbing against my chin.

A low, defeated sob escapes her lips, and her voice is shaky when she replies, "Fine, Deklan, do with me what you will. But this time, I will not be willing."

The fury running through my veins ignites into molten lava. The fierce growl that escapes my chest scares even me.

I growl into her ear, "I am no rapist, Mia, despite what you told Sophia. But I will force you to listen to what I say, you stubborn, infuriating woman!"

The laugh that rings out is cruel and forced. "I won't believe anything you say to me."

"I never said you had to believe it, but you will listen," I say as I keep my grip on her with one arm and bring the other hand up to clamp across her mouth.

She thrashes her head against my shoulder, trying desperately to loosen my grip on her face, but I hold firm. I lift her further off the ground, her legs still kicking furiously as I carry her across the room to the sofa.

"If you will just stop your infuriating struggling and listen to what I have to say, I'll let you go so you can sit down," I growl into her ear.

"Mmff hmf mmm mmm hmm," she screams against my hand.

"Is that a yes? Just nod your head," I say as I shake her just a little to emphasize my words but not to hurt her.

She yells one last muffled scream of fury, and then her entire body slackens. She nods her head as she slumps in defeat against my hold.

"Good. About time. It's not like anyone was going to hear you anyway," I say as I release her, turn her around, and push her down onto the sofa.

She falls onto the cushion with a loud, irritated huff, plucks up one of the throw pillows, and holds it tightly to her chest. She curls her legs up, sitting cross-legged as she glares at me.

I ignore the glare and kneel on the floor directly in front of her, placing my hands on her knees as I gaze directly into her chocolate-drop eyes.

"Mia, what you heard the other day at the bank is…"

Mia interrupts me, hashing out each word in a bad imitation of my voice.

"Because you and Harper knew I wouldn't fall for Mia since I am an unfeeling asshole, but you also knew I would work extra hard to help her despite my lack of caring since she-who-shall-not-be-named will obliterate me if I don't tame Mia's demon," she repeats my words, verbatim.

"Do I need to cover your mouth again?" I ask harshly, leaning in threateningly.

She huffs and shakes her head vehemently.

"I know what I said. I am trying to tell you that what I said is NOT how I feel. I was simply stating what Harper and Mia had said to me before, and I was only repeating it because I was being nagged by the other person on the other end of the phone because that isn't how things ended up, and I thwarted their plans."

I said it all in one breath, trying to get it all out before Mia can interrupt me again. I suck in air to feed my starved lungs and wait for her reaction.

She doesn't say anything at first and only stares at me with that righteous fire in her eyes. Then, her expression softens just the tiniest little bit, igniting a spark of hope deep inside my chest.

She raises one eyebrow. "Who told you those things and why?"

I swallow, taking a deep breath and centering myself before answering, "Sophia and Harper."

"Why?"

"It wasn't without reason," I confess, and raise a silencing hand when Mia opens her mouth to respond, cutting her off before she can.

"Buuut, that was in the past. I admit I fooled around a lot when I first came here. I was hurt and confused, and I thought by sleeping with every human woman I could, I might be able to hurt my Goddess as much as she'd hurt me or at least gain her attention once more.

"When I realized I was wrong and she paid no attention to my sexual antics, I went on a binge of drinking, partying, and basically trying to forget my Goddess ever existed. Or maybe I was trying to forget that I ever existed. I don't know which one I was going for."

I pause, preparing to breathe through the pain that is about to wrench its way into my chest at the memory, but I'm surprised to find that it isn't so bad. The relief that Mia is finally listening to my explanation and the hope that she may forgive me overshines the grief of losing my Goddess.

I think about what that might mean, and then I think about how I felt when Mia walked out on me earlier. The pain that slices through my chest at that memory is far worse than the pain I had suffered after being cast aside by my Goddess. What does it mean?

I had loved Luna with a fierceness that knew no bounds.

Or, at least, I thought I had. Now, I am beginning to wonder...

"Why were Sophia and Harper nagging you about it?" Mia asks, cutting into my thoughts and bringing me out of my reverie.

"They were worried about you," I answer. "Your demon was beginning to manifest, and we needed a way to bring it out so I could put it to sleep long enough to explain inner demons to you, get you to believe me, and, finally, teach you how to tame it.

"We didn't have much time, so Harper felt that sexual energy would be strong enough to draw it out. Harper knew I wasn't looking for a relationship, and Sophia swore you wouldn't be either. Therefore, the logical thing would be for me to work my charms on you, sleep with you, and draw out the demon. Plus, we could both have a little fun before getting down to the serious stuff."

I paused to clear my throat, noting the twitch in the corners of Mia's mouth.

Before I can continue, she chimes in, "Work your charms on me, huh? Did you mean to punish me into submission? Is that how we were supposed to 'have fun'?"

I shrug. "Same difference."

The small smile that tugs at Mia's lips flares the hope inside my chest even brighter.

"Well, it didn't work," Mia smirks. "At least, the demon part anyway. I did have fun, I guess."

I chuckle. "You guess?"

Mia's smile widens, strengthening the hope in my chest.

"So, they were upset that the plan didn't work. Is that the only reason they were fussing at you?"

I take a calming breath and answer, "No. They were fussing because what you heard me say is what they said to me when we devised this crazy plan. They were upset because they didn't predict you would fall for me..."

I hesitate, the tiniest pause as I watch Mia's eyes widen in anticipation of what I will say next.

"Or that I would fall for you. They were upset because we fell for each other, and then both of us got hurt."

Her mouth drops open in disbelief. She frowns, closes her mouth, then opens it again. She takes a breath as if she is going to speak but then closes her mouth again and releases the breath through her nose in some semblance of a snort.

"You didn't fall for me. You only pretended to so you could keep me close and save your own ass," Mia says, her eyes taking on that angry glare once more.

I growl in frustration, running both hands over my face before reaching out and grasping both of her wrists. I pull, dragging her upper body toward me until her face is close to mine. I lean my forehead against hers, locking my gaze with hers. The throw pillow falls freely to the floor.

"Mia, didn't you hear a fucking word I have said? I told you that the one-sided conversation you overheard is not how I feel. I fell for you, dammit. That is why Sophia was yelling at me about it. Why is that so hard for you to believe?"

Her eyes dart back and forth between mine as she answers, "Because, Deklan. You're a fucking angel, and I...well..."

Anger flares in my gut, and I pull her wrists, driving her forehead harder against mine.

"Mia, so help me if you say you are nothing, I will take you over my knee right now and spank you mercilessly until you scream your safe word, and then I will fuck you until you understand how wonderful and perfect you are," I ground out through gritted teeth.

She scoffs disbelievingly, but she doesn't utter another word.

"Mia," I whisper pleadingly. "Please believe me."

Mia pulls back, and I let her, releasing her wrists as she sits back up and takes a breath. "Then why didn't you tell me how you felt after I had told you? Why did you shut me out?"

It was my turn to take a breath, running a hand through my hair as I sat back on my heels.

"Because I am a coward," I confess, turning my gaze to the floor in shame. "You were so brave, and I was a coward. I was scared out of my mind to admit my feelings to you. I didn't want to get hurt again. But now I'm not scared to admit my feelings anymore. Now, I'm more afraid of losing you."

Mia scoffs. "Afraid of losing your life, you mean. You only care about saving your own ass."

That's it. I have had enough of this conversation. If words aren't going to convince her, then I will have to resort to other tactics. Mia will be mine one way or another.

CHAPTER 22: MIA

Deklan growls in frustrated anger and rises onto his knees. Shivers run through my spine at the sound, sending shockwaves of desire coursing through my veins. How can I want him so bad when we are so angry at each other? Does he want me like I want him?

He answers my silent questions by grabbing my shoulders and pulling me into him before I can react. His mouth crashes into mine with another furious growl. I am too stunned to act at first, but then I push at his chest and struggle to get away from him.

If he thinks he can just take me like he has done before, he has another thing coming. No matter that my heartbeat speeds up at the assault or that my vagina pulses with need. Just because my body has no willpower to resist his charms doesn't mean I have to fall in line as well.

I try to turn my head, but he traps my face between his hands and continues kissing me. He pulls me further toward him, and there is no way I can get away from him now. The only things preventing me from falling off the couch and into his lap are my hands pushing at his chest, and that proves problematic.

The sensation of my hands on his chest, the massive muscles jumping under my palms, has my nerves quivering, and not in a bad way. My body definitely still wants him, and I cannot understand why.

His tongue probes my lips, begging for entrance, but I deny him. I struggle against him, letting out an angry sound as I try to pull my legs out from under me so I can gain purchase to get away. I have to resist this hold he has on me. I have to get away.

But Deklan is relentless, pulling me further into his lap and off the sofa as he holds my head in his hands and continues his assault on my mouth. His mustache tickles my nose as he kisses me more forcefully until I have no choice but to open or cut my lips on my teeth.

His tongue invades my mouth as he wraps me in his embrace and falls back, pulling me fully off the sofa and on top of him. Before I can react, he rolls me over and traps me beneath him. His legs pin mine to the floor, and he grasps my wrists, one in each hand, and pins my arms down over my head, all without breaking his assault on my mouth.

I try to continue my struggles, try to hold onto my anger and frustration, and try to quench this burn of passion that threatens to consume me with every touch. But the smoothness at which he has imprisoned my body has my lady parts on high alert. His lip ring rubs against the sides of our mouths, shooting tides of passion through my soul while his mustache and goatee tickle my skin with primal sensations.

What the hell is wrong with me? Am I a glutton for punishment? Why does my body still want him so much? Whatever the reason, I am powerless to stop it.

Wanton desire runs through my entire body as my inner walls quiver with the need to be filled, and I am tired of fighting. With a frustrated groan of surrender, I open and kiss him back.

My tongue battles against his in a desperate war of passion and desire. A small whimper escapes my throat and joins the fray of lips, teeth, and tongues. I start to struggle again, but this time, I am struggling to move against Deklan's body in a desperate attempt to quench the burning need for friction.

My hips buck up against his, driving his groin into mine. He is still wearing jeans now. He must have changed out of the sweats he had been wearing when I woke up in that hospital room this morning. I, however, have not taken the time to change yet, and am still wearing the scrubs. I had been too focused on my anger and doing some packing to prepare for my departure.

However, now, I am thankful I have not changed because the material of the scrubs is so thin. The thick, rough material of the jeans against the thin material is just the friction I need to send that little bundle of nerves into a happy place inside my pants.

Deklan breaks the desperate kiss to trail hot, eager kisses down my jawline and the sensitive spot on my neck, just under my ear. I moan with pleasure and writhe underneath him, rubbing against his jeans again. Deklan bites that spot, sending a shockwave of heat and longing into my core.

Another eager moan escapes me as Deklan pumps his hips against me, meeting my thrust as he licks the spot where his teeth had been seconds ago. Then his mouth travels lower, biting along my breasts through the scrub top as I cry out with every nip.

I struggle against his hold on my wrists, overpowered by the need to weave my fingers into his hair, holding his head while he tortures my breasts. The wet heat from his mouth penetrates the flimsy scrub top material as he continues to nip and bite until he comes to my nipple.

"Deklan, please," I whimper when he nibbles at my nipple through my shirt.

He raises his head to look at me. "Please, what?"

My breathing is erratic, and I am sure Deklan can hear my heart trying to tear its way through my chest. My blood is pumping furiously through my veins, and my entire body is quivering with need. I try to calm myself enough to answer, but my reply still comes out in a breathless, shaky tone.

"Please let go of my hands so I can touch you."

Deklan's throat works as he swallows, and dark desire churns in his emerald gaze. "Only if you tell me you believe me and that you forgive me."

I pull at the hold he has on my wrists and rasp, "Do you want to fight, or do you want to fuck?"

"Oh, I am definitely going to fuck you, angel. The question is, do you want to fuck first or fight first? But no matter what, I am going to fuck you so hard you will be screaming my name and begging me to let you cum."

His words send desire surging through me, and I writhe underneath him as I respond, "What are you waiting for, then? Fuck me, Deklan. We can deal with the rest later."

He growls and releases my wrists, trailing a burning line of sensation down my arms with his fingers. One hand slides into my hair, tangling it around his fingers and tugging lightly until I gasp. His other hand continues to travel down until he reaches the hem of the scrub shirt, dragging it up and freeing my breasts.

"Mia, you are so perfect," Deklan says, his hot breath rolling over my nipple.

He cups my breast and lavishes it with kisses, suckling the nipple into his mouth and biting lightly. I take advantage of my hands being free by curling my fingers into his hair as my other hand grasps his huge bicep, digging my fingernails into his skin. He releases my nipple with an audible pop and then moves to my other breast to lavish it with the same attention.

"Tell me you still want me," he says after releasing the other nipple.

He shifts his lower body, freeing my legs and settling between them. I can feel how hard he is through the thin cloth of my scrub pants when he brushes against me.

"Tell me," he insists as he thrusts his hardness against me.

I hiss in pleasure and wrap my legs around his waist, clenching him firmly between my inner thighs as I hoarsely cry, "I want you, Deklan!"

He thrusts again and growls, "Tell me you forgive me."

"Ahh," I cry as his cock, begging release from his jeans, grazes against the sensitive bundle of nerves through my thin scrub pants.

"I will forgive you if you solve one problem for me," I say with a gasp.

"Anything," Deklan says desperately. "Tell me what I can do."

"Too many clothes," I rasp as Deklan writhes on top of me, rubbing himself against me and lighting the tiny bundle of nerves above my entrance on fire.

Deklan smiles ravenously as he lavishes kisses along my breasts and up to my earlobe.

"I can solve that," Deklan breathes into my ear before sucking the lobe into his mouth.

He releases my earlobe and raises onto his knees, pulling out of my grasp and eliciting a whimper of protest from my lips. He makes quick work of my shirt, tossing it to the side like discarded rubbish. He pulls the scrub pants down my legs, hissing in pleasure at the sight of my black lacy panties.

The scrub pants join my shirt on the floor, and I lay under the smoldering look of Deklan's emerald gaze, naked except for the scrap of lace that covers my secret place. It cries out for Dekan's touch, longing to be filled by his massive member, and I whimper with longing as I stare up at my tattooed guardian angel.

"You are a fucking Goddess," he whispers, his eyes roaming up and down my body. "No one can compare to you, angel."

His words send rockets of desire coursing through me, and I writhe on the floor. He strokes a hand from the top of my stomach to my belly button, his hooded, lust-filled eyes following the movement. His tongue darts out and licks his lips as his hand travels lower, stroking over the lace of my panties to a wide, wet spot that sits over my entrance.

"Mmm, baby, you are so wet for me," he growls, slipping a finger in through the side of my panties to stroke it up and down my quivering lips.

The touch of his bare skin against my pussy lips sends an electric sensation through my core, causing me to cry out in pleasure and thrust against his hand, wanting more.

"Am I forgiven now?" he asks as he drags his finger through my lips, grazing over my clit and then pressing teasingly over my entrance.

I am too far gone to speak, so I answer with a breathless moan and nod of my head as he pierces me with that dark, smoldering stare.

"Good girl," he purrs. "Are you ready for me, baby?"

I nod again, squeaking out a yelp of desire as his finger swirls around my swollen clit. He pulls his finger out of my panties, using both hands to drag them across my thighs, past my knees, and down past my ankles. He tosses them away onto the pile with my discarded shirt and pants.

He grasps my legs, one in each hand, and thrusts them wide apart, baring me to his gaze. The heat in his smoldering eyes practically burns me as he takes me in, and the growl that escapes his throat has my walls quivering frantically with need.

"I am so crazy for you, baby," Deklan says, the hunger in his emerald gaze making me shiver. "Never forget that."

I swallow hard and nod, still unable to speak, especially after he removes his shirt and tosses it aside, baring those rock-hard muscles and decadent tattoos to my view.

My gaze travels over the muscled planes of his chest and the dark, curving lines that color his skin. I take in the roses on his chest, hidden in all the black patterns drawn across his shoulders, and I marvel at how masculine the feminine flowers look drawn on Deklan's huge muscles.

My eyes move lower past the tattoos, down to his rippling stomach. They follow the trail of curling hair that runs down from his belly button and dips inside the waistband of his jeans.

I wait for him to take off his pants and bare that magnificent cock to me, but he doesn't. Instead, he leans down, lying flat on his stomach between my legs and propping his upper body on his elbows. He grasps my hips with both hands, raising my hips and bringing his face close to my opening.

He blows his hot breath across my sex, and I try to be disappointed that he has denied me his wonderful member. But the electric sensation of his hot breath across my lusty vagina eats through my core, dragging a scream of pleasure from my lungs. The scream grows louder as the heat of his breath is replaced with the wetness of his tongue. Deklan licks me with one long, sure stroke from the bottom of my wide-open pussy to the top, where the little bundle of nerves waits for attention.

He swirls his tongue around the little bundle once, twice, three times before moving back to the bottom and doing it all over again. I grasp his hair with one hand, grinding against his mouth, begging for more. His hands move to cup my ass, holding me in perfect position for more of his tongue's torture on my pussy.

He comes to the top again with one long stroke, but this time he sucks my swollen clit into his mouth, holding it there while he tortures it with his tongue. He releases the sensitive bud, gives it a lick, and then sucks it back in again.

The sensations shooting through my body are driving me wild with need. My back is bowed off the floor, my hips thrusting as I grind my pussy against Deklan's face, and little moans and screams of desire fill the air around us.

The building of an orgasm has my inner walls trembling as Deklan continues his assault on my pussy with lips, teeth, and tongue. It builds torturingly slow as I push his face into me and grind against him, desperate for more friction to build the orgasm faster.

But there is no need.

"Cum for me, Mia," Deklan rasps against my pussy.

He pulls one hand out from under my ass and then slides two fingers into my opening while he swirls his tongue over my swollen clit.

That's all the coaxing my lady parts need. The orgasm spills over the edge, milking Deklan's fingers with the hard throbs of my pussy walls. He continues his assault while my orgasm rides me, crashing through me like ocean waves as his fingers pump in and out of me and his tongue plays over the sensitive bundle of nerves.

"Deklan!" I scream as I ride the sensations to their crescendo, bowing my back even further from the floor and throwing my head back as my eyes roll into the back of my head.

Wave after wave after wave runs through me, pulsing my inner walls around his fingers and shooting pleasure through my entire body.

Finally, the delicious sensations begin to ebb as the orgasm fades, and my pussy walls settle from intense, hard throbs to small, delicate flutters.

Deklan removes his fingers from inside me and sits back up on his knees. He releases the button of his jeans, sliding the zipper down and reaching into his underwear to pull out his massive cock. He doesn't even take off his jeans, only pulls them, along with his underwear, down to mid-thigh before sliding into place between my legs. He reaches between us and positions his head against my opening, rubbing it over my entrance and across my clit before sliding the head inside.

I cry out and thrust against him, begging for more even as he slides further into me. He lowers himself slowly, inch by inch, until finally he is sheathed fully inside me. He grinds his hips against me, sending waves of pleasure through me.

Surprisingly, another orgasm begins to build in my core with the movement, and I begin to thrash against Deklan as he moves back out of me. He pushes into me again, but this time, he lowers his entire body onto mine, propping himself on his elbows so I don't take all of his weight.

He pumps his hips, pulling out of me and then sliding back into me. He grinds against me before pulling out and repeating the process. His head falls to my shoulder, his heavy breathing flowing across my skin as he continues pumping in and out of me.

He picks up a rhythm, not too fast but not slow either. His groans and sighs of pleasure light a fire in my veins, and my whimpers coalesce with his.

"Yes, Mia... Fuck, you feel so good," Deklan breathes against my neck as his rhythm grows faster.

My hands have a death grip on his hips, and I dig my fingernails into his flesh as he rides me.

"Fuck yes," he hisses, thrusting harder and faster the harder I dig in. "I'm close, baby. Cum for me, Mia, one more time."

It's as if he has a switch inside me that is activated by his commands. Deklan tells me to cum, and that is all it takes.

"Deklan!" I shout as the waves crash through me with an intensity so fierce that my fingernails draw blood from Deklan's flesh.

He hisses as if in pain, but I hear a groan of satisfaction follow the hiss, and then he comes apart inside me, his cock throbbing in time with my fluttering pussy walls.

"Fuuuck, yes," he cries out, and I feel his seed fill me inside as my pussy walls milk every last drop from his cock.

He remains inside me as our orgasms fade, resting his head against my shoulder as his breathing slows. His heart beats so hard against his chest that I can feel it against my chest, keeping a rhythm with my thumping organ. We lay like that for some time before Deklan pulls out of me and flops onto the floor beside me.

He drags me against him, wrapping me in his arms as he breathes into my ear.

"You are mine, Mia. I will never let you go again. I fucking love you," he says.

"And I hate you," I whisper back softly with a smile.

Deklan chuckles, a light, happy sound. He turns and props himself on one elbow, looking down at me with what I can only describe as love in his emerald gaze.

"I know," he responds with a wink.

CHAPTER 23: MIA

We end up in my bedroom after two more rounds and a shower. It is well into the evening, and I am starving. I suggested we eat at Sophia's…er…my father's restaurant and Deklan quickly obliged.

"I would love to meet your father," he says as I rummage through my large cedar chest, where I keep some of my father's old clothing, trying to find something for Deklan to wear. "Especially since he will be my father-in-law soon."

My heart skips a beat at Deklan's words, and I spin around to glare at him. "What the fuck makes you think I would want to marry you?"

"Oh, I don't know…maybe the six orgasms I just gave you. Or it could be my persuasive tactics and charming personality," he answers, playfully slapping my ass when I bend back over to resume my search.

I let out a sound, something between a scream and a hiss of pain, as I turned and flipped him the bird.

"Fuck you, Deklan!"

"You already did that," he answers with a smirk.

I toss the navy blue polo shirt I had just found at his head. It hits the mark, and he laughs as it slides down his face. He catches it before it can hit the floor.

"I can just wear my jeans if you can't find any pants," Deklan says as I stomp over to the closet.

"Fine, wear your jeans. I still have to find something for myself regardless," I say as I open the closet door.

"Or we could stay here and have some more fun," Deklan suggests.

I shoot him a glare over my shoulder as I say, "You are the one who is always fussing at me to eat and rest."

"Touché. At least wear some pants."

I scoff as I turn back to rummage through the clothes in my closet as I ask, "Any particular reason your Highness wants me to wear pants?"

"I have my bike," Deklan says.

My heart speeds up with excitement, and I dig through the hanging garments until I find my favorite jeans and a cropped t-shirt that shows off my stomach. I dress quickly while standing in the large walk-in closet. I grab my sneakers off the shoe rack in the closet, slip them on, and then come out of my closet, ready to leave.

Deklan shoots me a smoldering glance as I shut my closet door, his emerald eyes roving lustfully over my body. He comes up off the wall where he had been leaning, striding casually over to me and taking one of my hands into his.

"Mia, you are a vision," He says before placing a tender kiss on the back of my hand. "But if anyone looks at you the wrong way…"

He lets the statement stand, but I can see the heated fury in his eyes when his gaze lands on the exposed skin of my stomach. He releases my hand and runs his hand down the plane of my waist to my hip. He grips my hip and pulls me into him, lowering his face to mine and capturing my lips with his.

Amazingly, even after tons of intense orgasms, a bit of carpet burn, and a sore vagina, my body is ready for more. My heart races in my chest, and my inner walls flutter with longing. I curl my hands around the back of Deklan's neck and pull him in for more.

He growls low and deep in his chest, deepening the kiss and squeezing my hips tighter in his grasp. He pulls me in even closer, and I gasp in astonishment against his lips when I feel his erection scrape against me through the fabric of our jeans.

I moan with longing and grasp a handful of his blood-red hair, pulling him even tighter to me. I want more, want him all. I want every inch of me touching every inch of him, and it still wouldn't be enough. Deklan Maleck has consumed me, and I am now his, heart and soul.

He pulls away, breaking the kiss with a breathless sigh as he places his forehead against mine.

"If you want to eat, we need to stop this, or we will starve to death in bed," Deklan says.

I laugh breathlessly. "At least we would die happy."

Deklan laughs then, placing a chaste kiss on my forehead and releasing me from his hold. He grasps my shoulders and turns me toward the door, patting my ass as he herds me forward.

"Come on, you insatiable vixen. Let's go eat."

Thirty minutes later, after Deklan rode me around on his bike when I begged him to let me ride longer, we were seated in my father's restaurant, ready for a good meal.

And maybe a shot of good bourbon as well.

We hadn't been greeted by a server yet, so I looked around the large dining room, hoping to flag one down. There weren't many patrons here this time of night since the place would be closing in an hour, and I wondered if the servers were all in the back taking care of side work and closing duties.

"Wait here a minute," I say to Deklan as I lay my menu down and slide out of the booth seat. "I wanna go see if my father is around."

"What would you like me to order you to drink?" Deklan asks before I can walk away.

"Get me a tea, preferably sweet," I answer.

Deklan nods, and I turn toward the swinging doors leading into the server alley and open kitchen area. I open the doors to find two servers, one filling the ice bin and the other sweeping the floor. They both look up as I enter the room.

"Miss Mia, we didn't hear anyone come in the front doors," Pheobe, the blond female server says as she leans the broom against the expo counter where the food comes out of the kitchen and is prepared to go to the tables.

"I think that dang electronic bell is broken," Harley, the male dark-haired server says as he hoists the full bucket up and dumps the ice into the ice bin attached to the soda fountains.

"What can we do for you, ma'am?" Pheobe asks with a smile.

"I'm here with…with a friend, and we are hungry," I say, returning her smile. "If one of you could take care of us, that'd be great."

"Of course," Pheobe answers. "I can certainly do that. Harley, will you finish up while I take care of Miss Mia and her date?"

"Friend," I correct her quickly.

Pheobe smiles wider, shooting Harley a quick, knowing look as she says, "Sorry, her friend."

Harley clears his throat and nods, the corners of his mouth twitching as he answers, "Sure thing, Pheebs."

I look back and forth between them with a frown. "It's not a date."

Pheobe nods rapidly and says, "We believe you."

I know she's lying by the sly roll of her eyes as she glances to the side at Harley quickly and then back to me before she thinks I notice.

But I notice.

However, I let it go for now. I am too hungry and anxious to talk semantics. I simply turn and walk back out with "Pheebs" right on my heels. I make it back to the table and slide in across from Deklan.

"Did you find your father?" Deklan asks, glancing over the top of his menu.

"Oh, I forgot to ask about him," I say, glancing at Pheobe questioningly.

I did not mention that I forgot to ask for my father because I was busy avoiding questions about Deklan and my relationship.

Pheobe points toward the door to the back as she says, "He's in the office with some man."

I frown. "Who?"

She shrugs and answers, "I have no idea. Never seen him before in my life."

Curiosity gets the better of me, and I slide out of the booth again. "I'll be right back. Bring me a sweet tea, please."

I glance at Deklan to explain, but he simply waves me off.

"Go, find your father," he says. "I'll order dinner."

I don't question it. I'm not picky, so I'll probably eat anything he picks out. I'm more interested in finding out who is with my father.

I enter the double swinging doors once more, expecting to see Harley finishing up the cleaning duties, but no one is in the server alley area. I look through the open kitchen area toward the hallway that leads to the office. I can see the door from this angle, and it's closed.

I move to go around the expo line into the kitchen when a noise from behind catches my attention. I turn quickly, my heart racing at the sound, and sigh in relief when I see the kitchen printer projecting paper.

The office door opens, and my father, Vincente Dominguez-Jose, sticks his head out and yells in his thick Latino accent, "Harley, where you at, boy? I heard the kitchen printer."

I gasp, startled at my father's loud tone, but I recover quickly. I smile broadly when he spots me and give him a small wave.

"Hi, papa," I say softly.

"Mia? Hija, is that you?" he asks as he slowly comes into full view, shutting the office door behind him.

His black hair is slicked back on his head and probably gelled down so it won't move. His neatly trimmed goatee twitches as his lips thin into a smile. His smiling, almost-black eyes take me in as he moves further into the hall.

He's wearing his usual black chef's pants and a t-shirt with a soiled apron over it, covering his large, muscular frame that still looks as if he could be in his thirties instead of late forties. Of course, the lack of wrinkles on his face contributes to that as well.

"What are you doing here, mi vida?" my father asks, and alarm bells go off in my head at my dad's cautious tone.

Frowning, I move closer to him and answer, "I was hungry, so I came here with my friend to order some food. Is everything ok?"

"Si, si mi amor, everything is fine," Vinny answers, glancing nervously toward the closed office door as he speaks.

"Who do you have in your office?" I ask casually.

Papa smiles wider, wringing his hands as he says, "You'll see soon enough. Go back out to the dining room. I'll be out there soon. We were going to come to your place and see you, so your visit could not be more perfect."

I frown. "Papa, who's in there?"

The office door opens, and Vinny smiles broadly as he turns around to face the door.

"Hello, Mia," a familiar voice drawls. "Such a wonderful coincidence that you would come to eat on the same night I come for a visit."

My blood runs cold, and my breath freezes in my lungs. I had not heard that voice since I left Phoenix, and I had hoped never to hear it again. He steps toward me with that familiar smile that had always meant he was happy to see me.

But that was before he had betrayed me the night before our wedding with my maid of honor.

The picture flows through my mind as clearly as the day it happened. It's as if I am reliving the entire scene over again, and the pain, anger, and confusion come flooding back into my soul.

The surprised look on their faces is what I remember most. Brandon's blonde hair had been tousled and hung down in his eyes, hiding his raised eyebrows. His blue eyes held shock and guilt as he stared at me standing in the doorway. He was still sank to the hilt inside my best friend, his arms bulging with the effort to stay above her.

Amanda lay under him with her head thrown back in ecstasy, her auburn hair flung around the pillow underneath her head. She had raised up with a questioning look when Brandon had stopped pumping in and out of her, and that look turned my way to see what Brandon was looking at. Her brown eyes widened when she spotted me, and she instantly began pushing at Brandon's chest and trying to squirm out from under him.

A lot of cursing, blame-throwing, and half-hearted apologies coalesced in the still air as I stood there, my world and heart crumbling at my feet. Brandon instantly began making excuses, but they fell on deaf ears.

I walked out on Brandon that night after I told him the wedding was off and told him never to contact me again. I had not heard from him again before now.

"What the fuck are you doing here?" I ask, my tone low and dangerous.

Vinny turns and stares at me with confusion in his almond-shaped brown eyes. I had never told my father about what happened with Brandon. The only thing anyone other than Brandon, Amanda, and myself knew was that the wedding had been postponed indefinitely due to an emergency in Brandon's family.

It hadn't been a lie. The morning of the wedding, Brandon's grandmother had passed from a heart attack, so the wedding was postponed because of that. I had just failed to mention to everyone that indefinitely meant forever.

"He came here to surprise you," Vinny whispers, pulling me back to the present.

Brandon's smile never wavers as he says, "I miss you, Mia. I thought I would visit you since we haven't seen each other in so long. Aren't you glad to see me?"

"Not particularly," I answer. "I would have been happy to never see you again."

"What's gotten into you, girl?" my father asks, crossing his arms over his chest. "Is that any way to talk to your fiancé?"

The wedding had been postponed for six months, and it had been another six months since we had left. Brandon had been absent from my life for an entire year, and Vinny had never mentioned Brandon or asked why he had never come for a visit.

"Papa, Brandon and I broke up long before we ever came here. We broke up the night before our wedding," I explain, cursing myself for not telling him sooner.

"Now that just isn't true, sir," Brandon says, striding toward me menacingly. "We just had ourselves a little fight, is all. I thought you'd be ready to forgive me by now."

I move closer to my father, hoping he doesn't fall for Brandon's smooth demeanor and fake smile. I touch Vinny's arm and step beside him, not one to cower behind someone else but needing the reassurance that someone else is there just in case. Vinny pats my arm reassuringly.

"Why did you think I would forgive you for sleeping with my best friend the day before our wedding," I say, giving Brandon my best intimidating stare.

Vinny gasps audibly beside me. Now he knows, and I wonder what he thinks of Brandon now. Vinny had always liked him before, but I bet his opinion has changed drastically.

"We can talk about this," Brandon says, stopping a few inches before me and reaching for me. "You still wear that ring on your left hand, I see. Surely, that must mean something."

I jerk away from him, moving closer to Papa and keeping my features impassive. He is sorely mistaken if he thought that would get a reaction from me. I don't even flinch as I stare him down. In fact, I let the corners of my mouth lift in the tiniest hint of a smile. The look of complete fury that passes over Brandon's features is fleeting, and I can tell he tried to hide it. But I saw it nonetheless.

I reach toward my left hand with my right one to remove the ring that still sets like an obscene reminder on my finger. I watch his face closely, searching for any of the fury I saw in his eyes. He is up to something. I know he is.

His eyes dart down to my hands, and the fury I saw returns as he sees what I am about to do. An angry growl escapes his lips, and he surges forward, grabbing for me.

Vinny pulls me away from Brandon's reaching hands just as I am about to slide the ring from my finger. Brandon's fingers graze my elbow, and I jerk away, but the movement stops me from taking off the ring.

"Leave me alone!" I hiss, stepping even further back.

"You need to leave my restaurant," Vinny says as he steps in front of me, putting himself between me and Brandon. "Before I call the police."

"I just want to talk to Mia, Vinny," Brandon says smoothly. "I don't want to cause any trouble."

"You keep trying to touch me," I seethe. "I don't want you to touch me."

Brandon throws his hands up in surrender and says, "Fine. I won't touch you, then."

"Leave," I say, backing away from him further.

His hands are up, but he still tracks my movements, stepping forward as I step back.

"I'll leave when you agree to talk to me," he says calmly, but I am not fooled. I saw that momentary flicker of fury in his gaze.

"Papa, go to the office and call the cops," I say forcefully, leaving no room for argument.

He nods and pierces Brandon with an intimidating look. "You touch her, you die."

But he doesn't listen. The moment the office door closes, Brandon is on me. I back away, but my hip hits the expo table that separates the server alley from the open kitchen. Brandon grabs me by my shoulders, bringing my face so close to his that I can feel his breath across my face as he speaks.

"What makes you think I'll let you get away?" he asks with that malicious smile on his face.

"What do you want after all this time, Brandon?" I ask through gritted teeth. "You didn't bother to talk it out before. Why now?"

"I heard about your dear cousin Sophia inheriting that doctor's fortune," Brandon says. "Your dear daddy sure likes to brag to his friends about his darling niece."

"What's that got to do with me?" I seethe through gritted teeth.

"Everything. Your cousin is going to give me the money I ask for," Brandon says with a malicious smile.

I scoff. Brandon has no idea what he is getting into by threatening me or Sophia. He will be in for a rude awakening when he faces three angry demons.

I am about to tell him how much he will regret messing with me when the double doors leading into the server alley are opened forcefully, flying open so hard that they hit the wall and bounce back as if to close again. Brandon releases me and jumps back at the sound, probably thinking the police have arrived.

I turn to see the doors being stopped from closing again by a pair of large, heavily muscled, and heavily tattooed arms. My heart soars as Deklan steps into the server alley. I am standing on the other side of the expo line, and Brandon has taken several steps away from me. I begin to move toward the end of the line, where I will be free to run to my guardian angel and away from Brandon.

"What's going on in here?" Deklan asks with a worried frown as he steps into the room. "I heard Mia yelling."

I had not realized I had been yelling, but given the circumstances, it didn't surprise me. I reach the end of the line and almost lunge myself at Deklan, but I am stopped by a pair of hands catching me around my waist.

Deklan turns and spots me struggling to break free from Brandon's hold, and my blood runs cold at the look in Deklan's eyes when he sees another man with his hands on me.

I had not told him about Brandon. Deklan knows I was hurt, but I don't know if Sophia had told him the details. I had not told him anything. However, now was not the time to go into a lengthy explanation, and by the look in Deklan's eyes, there would be no time before Deklan tore Brandon apart.

"Deklan, this is Brandon, my ex-fiance," I say calmly, even though I still struggle to pull away from Brandon's hold.

Deklan stalks toward us with murder in his eyes, and I am surprised that Brandon hasn't released me yet and run screaming from the massively muscled, tattooed fury that draws ever closer.

"I suggest you let my woman go, boy," Deklan growls, the rage in his tone matching the fire in his eyes. "Before you bite off more than you can chew."

"She isn't your woman," Brandon says, backing us toward the hallway. "She never broke up with me, and I have come to reclaim what is mine."

I have heard enough. I'll show this lying asshole what I'm made of.

I stop struggling and suddenly go limp, which does the trick by surprising Brandon just long enough to distract him. Quickly, before he can recover, I slam my head back and grunt with satisfaction when the back of my head hits something hard. Brandon releases me suddenly, crying out in pain mixed with rage. That had never worked with Deklan, so it brings me a morbid sense of satisfaction when I turn to see the blood pouring from Brandon's nose.

"When I kicked you out of my house after finding you with my best friend, that qualified as a break-up," I yell at Brandon.

Brandon raises his gaze to mine, holding his nose with one hand, and the utter wrath in his eyes sends a wave of fear through me.

"You fucking bitch," he growls as he lunges for me, grabbing at me with his free hand, causing me to stumble back in an attempt to scramble away from him.

But he doesn't make it to me. Brandon's efforts to grab for me are stopped by a mountain of a man who inserts himself between me and Brandon. Deklan grabs him by his shirt collar and lifts him off the ground. His feet dangle in the air as Deklan moves until he slams Brandon's back against the wall.

Deklan leans in close to Brandon's face and says in a low, menacing tone, "Touch her again, and you'll find out my unique skills in dentistry. Maybe you'd like a new set of dentures?"

"You don't understand, man," Brandon says pleadingly. "She's lying to you. She has done this before."

"Shut up," Deklan seethes. "You're the one who was putting your hands on her."

"I was just trying to keep her from running like she always does," Brandon says as he tries to pry Deklan's fingers from his shirt. "After she left home, people began to tell me stories of her trysts with other men."

Deklan shakes Brandon roughly and says, "Don't talk about Mia that way."

"Look, man, I didn't initially believe the rumors of her infidelities either, so I came here to talk to her. Now you are saying she is your woman, so what am I supposed to believe?"

"She is my woman, and you won't touch her again," Deklan says, shaking Brandon again.

"But she never broke up with me," Brandon says. "Just look if you don't believe me. She is still wearing my ring."

Fuck. I had started to take it off but had gotten distracted. Why hadn't I taken it off immediately and thrown it at him? Because it was my grandmother's ring, that's why. I was going to take it off and put it on my right hand to show him I meant business but I had gotten distracted.

I see the recognition in Deklan's eyes, and I see his gaze turn cold as he starts to listen to Brandon's words. And why shouldn't he? Hadn't I run out on him several times already? And I was still wearing the ring, just as Brandon had said.

This is not good. I can feel the walls closing in, painting a picture of me that isn't true. And everything seems as if it is. I am wearing the ring, and I have not said a word to defend myself. Shouldn't Deklan know me better than that after everything we have been through? If not, then he doesn't deserve me anyway.

I watch in devastation as Deklan slowly lowers Brandon to the floor and lets him go, nodding toward the door as he says, "Get the fuck out of here and don't come back."

"Good luck with that one. She'll tear your heart out when she's tired of you. I know from experience," Brandon says and then scrambles for the door.

He doesn't look back and almost knocks Harley, who is just entering the doors from the dining room, down in his haste to get out.

"What's going on in here?" Harley says, confused. "I just got back from a restroom break."

Vinny comes out of the office and moves down the hall, walking briskly toward the kitchen as he says, "Hija, I have phoned the authorities and they are in the parking lot. Oh, hello, Deklan. What are you doing here? Is Sophia with you?"

But none of this registers in my brain. The only thing that fills my soul at that moment is the look of complete betrayal and hatred on Deklan's face as he locks his gaze with mine. He ignores Vinny's questions and speaks to me instead.

"Let me see your left hand," he says, the muscles in his jaw working furiously as if he is gritting his teeth hard.

"Deklan," I say pleadingly. "Please, you don't believe…"

"Let me see," Deklan says harshly, cutting me off.

I swallow hard and raise my hand to his gaze, the ring catching the light like a beacon of doom. Deklan's eyes darken, and his visage turns savage.

"Is what he said true?" Deklan asks through gritted teeth.

Does he have to ask? Hurt and anger radiate through me at Deklan's question. I raise my chin and glare at him defiantly, but I refuse to answer. I am nothing to him if he doesn't know me better than that.

"I'll take your silence as a yes, then," Deklan says, his voice wavering with anger and…

Hurt?

My eyes widen as I look into his eyes. No! That isn't why I didn't answer. However, Deklan doesn't give me a chance to explain. The pure hatred radiating from his gaze pierces my heart like a thousand knives, shredding it to pieces, and then he turns and walks out the door.

"Mia, what's happening? Are you alright?"

My father's words barely register in my mind. I crumble to the floor in devastation as my world shifts. Is this how Deklan felt all those times I walked out on him without a second thought? If so, I certainly deserve my fate.

"Mia? Mia!"

The world around me blurs even as I hear the sirens and my father calling my name. Something inside me turns dark, and I welcome the darkness. I sink into it, welcoming it with open arms as the cold seeps into my bones and the cold tiled floor hits my back.

The numbness of nothingness settles in as my eyes drift shut. Nothing is left except darkness, the cold, and the absence of lucid thought. If this is what dying feels like, then I welcome it.

I don't want to live anyway without my angel.

CHAPTER 24: DEKLAN

I have never experienced complete and utter devastation as I had experienced when I saw that ring on Mia's finger. I had barely made it out the door without falling to my knees in grief. I don't even remember how I had made it home. My mind and body had been so numb, paralyzed by anguish and betrayal.

Why I had never noticed it before, I don't know. Probably because I was too busy noticing everything else about that perfectly deceiving body while I fucked her senseless.

It infuriated me that the fuckhole Brandon had enlightened me to Mia's cheating heart, that he knew her better than I did. Why had I not seen it before? The red flags were certainly there, but I had been blind to them despite having gone through this before. Why had I not learned my lesson the first time?

The memories of that night play relentlessly through my mind. It had been an entire week ago. It feels like an eternity, and yet it feels like only yesterday. I have not eaten since food has lost all flavor, and I have tried drowning my sorrows with alcohol like I did before. However, It only made the incessant grief that surrounded my soul worse when the intoxication took hold.

Sleep offers no respite on nights when I am able to sleep. Most nights, I lay awake, filled with this suffocating loneliness I suffer.

Just like tonight.

I lie awake, staring at the ceiling, feeling the emptiness beside me where Mia would be if only I had not walked out on her, let her speak, and continue her lies. But then our relationship would only be a sham.

Sure, in those rare moments of distraction, when I would have Mia spread out underneath me, writhing and calling my name, I could almost forget about Brandon and his claim that Mia was still his. I could even forget about Luna and how she had destroyed me.

But afterward, when Mia was no longer in my grasp, the agony would return with a vengeance, reminding me that my heart was still broken and Mia would never be able to help me mend the pieces because I no longer trusted her.

I sigh, the sound carrying through the empty air like a foghorn. The silence in my apartment is deafening, amplifying the ache that never seems to fade. I try to clear my mind, to stop thinking of the woman who could never be mine, and find some semblance of normalcy. But the nagging pain is always there, lurking in the background of my already shattered heart, digging the pieces in deeper, if it is even possible. Brandon's parting words come rolling back through my mind.

"Good luck with that one. She'll tear your heart out when she's tired of you. I know from experience."

Even Soph had told me that Mia wasn't looking to settle down, and now I am drowning in an ocean of grief, struggling to stay afloat while the weight of Brandon's words pulls me under.

But soon, none of this will matter any longer. Not my grief, not my failures, not even the fact that Mia may still be in trouble since Thorn still inhabits her demon. It is all out of my control and soon to be forgotten in the extermination of my existence from this life. Luna will soon send me into oblivion when she finds out I have failed.

And there will be no afterlife for my soul. Angels that are punished with death do not get to have an afterlife, not even in the lowest circles of Hades that are reserved for cruel and wicked souls.

And all for a woman.

Again.

Sighing in frustration, I rise from the bed to pace around the room, pulling at my scarlet hair with both hands. How could I have been so stupid? Sophia and Harper tried to warn me, but I didn't listen. This is entirely my fault. I can't even fault Mia. She was only taking what I freely offered. Of course, she didn't have to lie about falling for me and tearing my heart out.

The silence in my apartment is broken by a loud banging on my door, and I frown, wondering who could be bothering me. Sophia's voice rings through the silence, answering my question.

"Deklan, get your ass out here now! Uncle Vinny is here, and I am unhappy with what he told me!"

Sophia's words float through the muddled mess that is my brain, snapping me from the haze I have let myself drift into. Had Sophia said Uncle Vinny was here?

Fuck. I hadn't told Sophia yet about what happened. I had been too busy holed up in my room and wallowing in self-pity. I should have known Vinny would say something, and it only took him a week.

She bangs on my door again, and I curse silently to myself. With a heavy sigh, I stroll toward my bedroom to get some clothes. I may as well get dressed and let her in or suffer the consequences. After all, this is her hospital, and she has a key to every door here. If I don't open the door, she will be even more pissed off for having to dig out the keys.

It's never a good day when Soph is pissed off.

"Deklan, you better let me in, or so help me, I'll have the hulks bust your door down instead of using a key!" Sophia calls as if reading my mind, banging on the door again.

"I'm coming! I just have to get dressed," I yell back, stumbling at the sudden pain that wrenches through me from my unused throat.

"Sophia, let the man get dressed," Vinny says, his voice muffled by the closed door.

I don't even bother fixing my hair or brushing my teeth. I simply shuck off my sleep pants, pull on a pair of sweats and a T-shirt, and then answer the door.

Sophia's eyes are alight with unbridled fury when I sling open the door and glare at her.

"What?" I say roughly and wince at the pain.

Sophia's arms are crossed over her chest, and the tension radiating from her is so thick that it's almost palpable. But then her gaze takes me in, and the rage lessens.

"You look like shit," she says with a frown.

"Yeah, well, I feel like shit," I say, my voice gruff and throat burning from dryness and lack of use.

The anger in Sophia's gaze disappears completely and is replaced with empathy. Her arms fall to her sides, and she shakes her head.

"Oh, Deklan, you poor fool," she says. "Come on, let's get you some water, and I'll cook you something to eat."

"Soph, you don't have to…"

"Shut up, hulk, and go sit at the table."

I do as she says, and thirty minutes later, we are sitting at my kitchen table. Vinny has a mug of hot coffee in one hand and a fork in the other, shoveling a huge bite of eggs in his mouth.

Sophia sits beside him, sipping on a cup of coffee, while I, sitting beside her, push my eggs around on my plate with my fork. My water sits beside my plate, only half empty and forgotten.

"Eat," Sophia orders. "Or, at least, drink the rest of your water."

I shake my head. "I'm fine. My throat feels better, and I'm not hungry."

"You really do love her," Sophia says with a sigh.

I shrug, running a hand through my hair. "It doesn't matter. She doesn't love me."

A small bit of the anger returns to Sophia's visage, and she pokes a finger at me as she says angrily, "Of course she does, you idiot. She's suffering as much as you are right now."

"Sophia, you don't know what you're talking about, ok? Didn't Vinny tell you what happened?"

I look over at Vinny as he finishes off his coffee.

"Tell her, Vinny," I say, sitting back in my seat and crossing my arms over my chest.

"I'm sorry, Deklan, I don't know what happened," Vinny answers. He stifles a burp with his hand and then continues, "I went to the office to call the police, and the dispatcher had me stay on the line until the authorities showed up. It was over by the time I came out."

I frown, trying to remember if I had seen Vinny in the kitchen area or not. I had been so consumed with rage at the sight of Brandon's hands on Mia that I hadn't noticed. I had just assumed he'd been there since it was his restaurant.

"That's what I came here to ask you," Vinny continues, pulling me from my thoughts. "Mia broke down after you left but wouldn't tell me what happened. She wouldn't say anything to the authorities either, only that her ex came to find her and harass her. She wouldn't even press charges."

I scoff. "Yeah, that's because she's still with him."

Sophia cut in, "What? No, she's not. Who told you that?"

"Brandon did," I answer. "I didn't believe him at first, but then he talked about her running away all the time, which she does, and that she was still wearing his ring, which she was."

"That's a lie. Mia called off the wedding," Sophia argues.

"Actually," Vinny says with a contrite shrug, placing his fork on his empty plate. "Their wedding was postponed at the last minute because Brandon's grandmother had a heart attack and died the morning of the wedding, and they never rescheduled it. I never knew why and never bothered to ask. I felt it wasn't my business. However, I did hear her accuse Brandon of being unfaithful just before the wedding."

"Brandon said she had been the one that had been unfaithful, and more than once, during their engagement," I supply, adding to Vinny's argument as I pinch off a piece of bacon. I pop the piece of bacon in my mouth and chew.

"Oh my fucking God!" Sophia shouts, and the fury is back in her eyes. She slams both hands on the surface of the table.

"Watch your mouth, young lady," Vinny snaps.

I hide a snicker behind my hand, disguising it as a cough that quickly becomes real when the bacon goes down my throat the wrong way. I scramble to get a drink of water as Sophia shoots me an evil glare.

Some of the pain in my chest eases. It's been a while since I've smiled or laughed.

Sophia takes a calming breath and says, "Sorry, Uncle Vinny. I was just upset because both of you are wrong, and poor Mia is suffering for it."

Vinny frowns and I harumph in disbelief, putting down the now-empty glass and crossing my arms over my chest once more.

"What do you know about it?" Vinny asks Sophia. "Was Sophia telling the truth about Brandon?"

"Of course she was. The wedding would have been called off anyway," Sophia says, shooting me another angry glance. "She wasn't the unfaithful one."

"Why didn't she say anything to me?" Vinny asks.

I only roll my eyes disbelievingly. Of course, Mia would project her unfaithfulness on her fiancé. It was becoming increasingly clear that Mia was a master manipulator.

Even better than myself.

But I listened to Sophia's explanation anyway, figuring it would be entertaining to find out what Mia had told Sophia about the ordeal.

"She knew you liked Brandon and didn't want to upset you, so she just let it slide after it went so long without you asking. She hoped you would simply just forget rather than be angry with her for breaking it off with him."

I scoff. "That doesn't make any sense. Why would Mia think her father would take a man's side over hers?"

Vinny looks toward her for an answer, his eyebrows raised questioningly. Sophia pats Vinny's hand on the table and takes a deep breath before answering, "Because Mia has always felt that you treat everyone else better than you treat her."

This time, Vinny scoffs, waving a hand dismissively as he says, "That's ridiculous. Why would she think that?"

"Uncle, do you remember when Mia and I were little and were always fighting?"

Vinny nods his head, and Sophia continues, "Well, we fought because you always told me how proud you were of me, but you never said that to Mia. Mia was extremely jealous," Sophia says.

Vinny frowns, pulling his hand away from Sophia as he says, "That's simply not true."

"Uncle, Mia graduated college with honors, and you barely gave her a pat on the head, yet I won employee of the month at my first job, and it was an entire celebration with a party and everything. Don't you see how that would look to Mia?"

A pang of guilt shoots through my heart. Mia never told me any of this. She never told me how left out and despondent she felt living with her father. Of course, I never really asked about her past. In fact, I never really asked her about herself at all or made any effort to get to know her. I had been a shitty...boyfriend...lover...whatever. I had been shitty to Mia. I return my attention to the conversation as guilt overwhelms me.

Vinny's frown deepens as he responds, "Surely Mia knows how proud I am of her. She is my daughter."

"But you never told her you were proud of her," Sophia argues. "You never even showed it. Did Mia get a party after her graduation?"

"Well...not a big one like yours...but..."

"And did Mia get a check for a hundred bucks to celebrate her first job?"

"No...She lived with me, so I always gave her money."

"And did Mia get a ribbon-cutting ceremony when she opened her business?"

"That was set up by your mother. I attended so I could visit and celebrate with you."

Sophia huffs in frustration and says, "But you still celebrated. You didn't celebrate when Mia opened her business."

Vinny looks defeated as he stares down at his empty plate. He breathes a heavy sigh and answers, "I guess I took a lot for granted. I always thought she knew how proud I was of her."

"No, Uncle, she didn't," Sophia answers sympathetically. "So you see why she would think you would take Brandon's side?"

I swallow hard. Had Brandon been the liar after all? He had been so convincing, painting a picture that made Mia seem guilty, especially with the ring and her habit of running away. But had it been the truth? Had I just walked out on the best thing that had ever happened to me over the deception of a douchebag?

What have I done?

"What happened?" Vinny asks softly, his voice low and hushed.

I give Sophia my full attention, preparing myself for the blow. I know the guilt will punch me in the gut hard after hearing this.

"Mia caught Brandon with her maid of honor, Amanda, the night before the wedding. She walked in on them when she went to Brandon's place after her bachelorette party. The fucked-up thing was that she was upset that Amanda bailed on her party due to a last-minute headache, and she was coming to Brandon for comfort."

The room went deathly silent when Sophia finished speaking. Vinny continues staring at his plate while I pull at my hair and run both hands down my face.

I break the silence by asking, "What about the ring? She still had his ring on her left finger."

"She's always worn that ring on her left finger," Sophia answers. "Our grandmother gave it to her, put it on her finger herself, and she's never taken it off."

Sophia pauses, piercing me with a quizzical look as she asks, "Did Brandon make it seem like that was his engagement ring to her?"

I don't answer and only nod, my gut twisting with nausea at Sophia's shake of her head.

She rolls her eyes and says, "She had Brandon's ring layered over that one, but she threw his ring at him the night she walked out on him."

"He was so fucking convincing," I say in a whispered tone. "His eyes were so serious."

"Most narcissists are. They are master manipulators," Sophia responds.

"Fuck!" I yell as I slam both fists on the table hard enough that I hear a faint groan from the wood.

The sudden outburst of temper startles Vinny and Sophia, but neither of them makes any comment. I place my elbows on the table and lower my head, covering my face with my hands.

"What am I supposed to do now?" I mumble, my voice muffled from my hands covering my face.

"I'll tell you what you're gonna do," Vinny says, finally picking his head up as he runs a hand through his messy hair. "You're gonna do the same thing I'm gonna do. Go beg for her forgiveness and never take her for granted again."

"You do that, Uncle Vinny. But, you," She points a finger at me and pierces me with an angry glare. "You are not gonna do anything."

I frown, balling my hands into fists as I slide them from my face. "What do you mean? I'm not just going to sit here and do nothing. How can I now that I know she's innocent and that I was an idiot for believing that dipwad? I'm going to go get her back."

"No, you're not," Sophia says firmly. "You both have fucked up, not trusting the other and thinking the worst of each other. You both will end up hurt worse than you already are."

I shake my head in denial as I respond, "No. No, it can't be over. She's all I can think about, Sophia. She consumes me, heart and soul, and I will never be happy without her."

"Nor will you be happy with her, Deklan," Sophia argues. "You will never learn to trust anyone if you can't let go of the past and learn to put your faith in someone else. It's obvious from your actions that you have not done those things yet."

I start to argue, slamming a fist on the table again, but the soft, musical voice that fills the room stops me, causing my heart to race erratically.

"She's right, Deklan, my angel," the voice says.

No. She can't be here now, not when I have decided to win Mia back again. I'm not ready to be wiped from existence yet.

Vinny goes pale, which is a feat for such a dark-skinned man, and he slides out of his seat and falls to his knees, mumbling something in Spanish.

"¡Le amor de Dios!" he says in a shocked tone.

"For the love of God," Sophia translates, and her tone matches Vinny's as she stares in the direction he is looking. She moves to stand beside Vinny with her mouth hanging open.

I don't have to follow their gazes to know who they see. I would know Luna's voice anywhere, but I am curious to see how she has presented herself to humans. I turn in the direction of their stares to see her brilliant smile light up her already-glowing face as she looks down at Vinny from her stunning ten-foot height, her head almost brushing the ceiling.

Her white wavy hair flows around her face and shoulders as if in an invisible wind, and her angelically blue eyes shine brightly with happiness. She is dressed like the clichéd Goddesses one sees in books and fairy tales, with the white flowing dress and a gold roped belt tied around her waist. A wreath of flowers adorn her head, filled with Angel's Trumpets and Evening Primroses.

She is the epitome of a moon Goddess in all her glory.

"¿Quieres decir Diosa?" She replies to Vinny in her sing-song tone.

"You mean…" Sophia begins, but I cut her off.

"You mean to call me Goddess," I translate. "I know Spanish too, remember?"

Sophia only nods as she stares open-mouthed up at Luna, who takes up the entire side of my dining room. I sigh as if I'm bored, trying hard to show nonchalance even though my heart threatens to burst from my chest.

So many emotions run through me, too many to process simultaneously. Fear that my time in this existence is up, sorrow that I didn't have time to apologize to Mia, and nervousness over whether or not Luna will make Sophia and Vinny watch my demise.

But the one thing I don't feel is grief or regret like one should feel when seeing a former lover they supposedly loved with everything in them. What can that mean?

"Can you make yourself appear normal-sized so you stop scaring my guests to death?" I say to Luna in a mildly annoyed tone, trying not to show the conflicting emotions warring in my gut.

"Of course," Luna says. "I did not mean to scare anyone."

Her form shrinks to human size instead of giant, and she primly sits at the table. She holds her hand down to Vinny with a kind smile.

"Please, sir. Rise to your feet. There is no need for supplication when I am not your Goddess," Luna says to him as she offers him her hand.

Vinny's throat works with a hard swallow, and he answers, "I did not mean to offend you."

Her tinkling laughter fills the room as she replies between giggles, "Dear Vinny, I am not one of the jealous Gods or Goddesses. You are free to worship whichever one of us you choose, and I would never be offended by that. In fact…"

She pauses, piercing me with her hard stare across the table as she says, "I would be proud of anyone who chooses to follow their own path instead of the one they were coerced into following."

Vinny accepts Luna's offered hand and stands, bending to kiss her hand before dropping it and returning to his seat. Sophia inches toward me as Luna's gaze grows harder and never leaves my face.

"Luna," Sophia says, moving in as close to me as she can get with her hands out pleadingly. "Please don't take Deklan from us. I know he messed up again, but give him a chance to redeem himself. He may not have completely helped Mia, but her demon…"

"Sophia," Luna says, interrupting Sophia's tirade.

Her voice is soft, like a whispering breeze, but strong enough to stop everyone from talking simultaneously.

Luna's smile returns as she addresses Sophia. "I am not here to take Deklan. Now, can we all sit, please?"

I raise my eyebrows, hope flaring in my chest as Luna continues.

"I'm here to, hopefully, knock some sense into him," she says, piercing me with that stare once more.

"Oh," Sophia says, scooting away. "I'll just go sit down then."

"What? You're not here to smite me into oblivion?" I ask, using sarcasm to cover the fear of losing the hope that flows through me.

"No," she says deadpan, her angry gaze never wavering from my face.

"Then why are you looking at me like that?" I ask as Luna continues to stare at me accusingly.

She doesn't answer at first but simply waves her hand. Wine glasses full of some reddish-purple drink appear, one in front of each person at the table. Vinny and Sophia gasped in surprise, but I had expected it the minute she began waving her hands. Luna always liked to have a glass of red wine during visits, especially if it was a friendly visit.

The gesture made my hope grow, and I genuinely began to believe that Luna would let me live. But she had a lesson to teach me first, as was the norm for a God or Goddess. Forgiveness and salvation…with a "moral of the story" lesson to learn.

"What I said before about people choosing their own path and others trying to coerce them down a different path?" Luna asks and then takes a sip of wine.

Yep, just as I suspected. *The moral of the story is this, children…*

Luna gazes at me expectantly over the rim of her glass as she takes another sip.

"Yes, I remember what you said," I answer. "What about it?"

"Essentially, that is what you were doing to me when you wanted to force me into monogamy. I am not a monogamous person, Deklan."

I swallow, hoping Luna won't obliterate me for what I am about to say. But I have waited a long time to say it, so I do.

"Luna, I would never force you to be monogamous. However, you should have at least been honest with me." I pause, shaking my head in disappointment as I run a hand through my hair. "Being lied to is what hurt the most. I am not polyamorous. Had you been honest with me from the start, I could have told you that, and we could have avoided all this heartache."

Luna's eyes soften, and she takes another sip of her wine.

She sighs and responds, "You are right, Deklan. I should have made myself clear from the beginning. While I did not lie, I did not communicate properly either. I am sorry. I am sorry for everything, Deklan."

My eyes widen in surprise. I hadn't expected an apology. Was a Goddess admitting she was wrong? This was not the lesson I was expecting.

"I...I...I don't know what to say, Luna," I admit. "You have surprised me."

"Gods and Goddesses are not perfect. We are not nearly as messy as humans, but we do make mistakes. However, the lesson we must learn from all this is..."

Ah, there it is. I knew there was a lesson somewhere. I hide my snicker as I continue to listen to Luna's speech.

"We must let go of the past to move forward, just as Sophia so eloquently said. Forgiveness is an important part of letting go."

So it was the old cliché *let go of the past* lesson. I could deal with that. It was better than being exterminated like a parasite.

"It may take me some time, Luna. If you had only told me before we fell into a relationship, I would still be in the Divine Dimension, worshiping you like I was before I fell for you," I say.

Luna smiles widely and responds, "You never fell in love with me. You were simply infatuated. You are in love with Mia, and if I had not banished you to this dimension, you never would have met her."

I frown, gulping down the rest of my wine before saying, "You know about my feelings for Mia?"

"Of course, Deklan. I watch all my followers, even the fallen ones."

I drop my head and run a hand through my hair, sighing in defeat. "I wanted to stay mad at you forever, but you make it hard to hold a grudge."

I raise my head to see her smiling at me, her luminous icy blue eyes alight with affection, which grow brighter as I say, "You are a good Goddess, Luna. Just because we are no longer lovers does not mean I stopped following you."

She finishes her wine and rises from her chair. I looked around to find that Sophia and Vinny had slipped out while I had been focused on my conversation with Luna. They had taken their wine with them as well.

"What are you going to do about Mia then?" Luna asks, pulling my attention back to her.

I stand, my voice full of determination as I say, "I'm going to get her back, of course."

"In that case, I give you my blessing and a little gift that you will discover later," Luna says with a mysterious smile.

"Discover later? What does that mean?" I ask.

"You will know when the time comes," she answers, confusing me more.

I walk over to her and offer her a hug.

She takes it, hugging me back, saying, "Be good to her, Deklan. Humans only last so long, so give her a good life."

I smile and say, "I will. That is if she will have me back."

"She will," Luna says assuredly.

I release Luna and nod, watching as Luna's image fades away, leaving a trail of stardust in her wake. I turn toward my bedroom, heading for my in-suite bathroom and the shower.

I need to make myself presentable. I am going to get my girl back.

CHAPTER 25: MIA

I can't escape the memories. They haunt me, replaying in my mind like a cruel, endless loop. I can almost feel Deklan's hands on my body, the tender way he touched me. I can still see the way he looked at me with love in his eyes. I remember our playfulness, the witty banter, me telling him I hate him but meaning the opposite. I can still hear him say 'I know' in my head...But then all the sensory memory become sharp reminders of what I no longer have.

The more recent memories of the fight I had with my fucking ex come blazing in next. He had wanted to ruin me, and he had won. Deklan had believed his lies, and I had flown the white flag and let Deklan believe it. I hadn't even tried to defend myself because I was too full of my pride, thinking that if Deklan believed that of me then he didn't deserve me.

But had I not done the same to him? I had believed the worst of him when I had heard half of a conversation, and I hadn't given him the benefit of the doubt. So, of course, he would believe those things about me after everything I have put him through, and after everything he has been through before me.

I don't know much because Deklan hasn't told me, but what I do know is that he was hurt by his Goddess. She had hurt him badly, and I am no better. I had stood there and let him believe the worst without explaining the situation.

Pain lances through me as I recall the look he had given me when I refused to answer his questions. Complete and utter devastation had filled those emerald eyes when he had seen the ring on my finger, and then it had quickly changed to pure hatred. My chest tightens with misery at the memory. It's as if my soul is being torn apart, piece by piece, leaving behind a hollow shell.

Thorn may as well take this body now. It is damaged and broken. My heart has been shattered, and my mind has been lost to my misery.

My cowardice, pride, and stubbornness lost me the one man who could have saved me, and the regret eats at me constantly.

But It has been an entire week, and Thorn hasn't shown his face. Maybe Thorn is gone and I won't have to worry about it. I wonder if Deklan would still help with my demon if Thorn shows his face again.

I wonder if he even still cares. Either way, I am not sure I can take being around him and seeing the hate in his eyes when he looks at me. No, I can't do it. I can't stay here. I have to go back to Phoenix and damn the consequences.

I will just deal with everything on my own as best I can. And if not, then Thorn will have a fight on his hands before he takes this wretched body.

"But what about me?" Rose's voice drifts through my gloom-filled brain. "I can help you fight."

"Rose! Oh, thank goodness, Rose. I was beginning to think Th…"

"No! Don't say his name! It may bring him out," she says alarmingly.

"I was beginning to think he had done something bad to you," I finish, leaving out the name.

"It's strange, actually," Rose says with a thoughtful frown. "I can't feel him at all right now. It's as if he is gone, but how is that possible?"

I shrug. "Maybe Deklan finally put him to sleep for good. That last blast was a doozy."

"Maybe," Rose says disbelievingly. "I'm not going to let my guard down, though. Who knows what he has up his sleeves? Based on what you told me about the last time he tried to take over someone, he will stop at nothing to get what he wants."

"That is very true," A cold, calculating voice says, startling me to the point that I almost stumble as I whip around at the sound.

Icy tendrils of dread slither up my spine as my eyes lock on another shadowy figure across the dimly lit room, his eyes glowing with a malevolent violet light that pierces the darkness. A sinister, shadowy grin stretches across his face, revealing a gaping abyss that threatens to suck the happiness from the world.

Rose darts to my side, her arm wrapping around my shoulders in a protective embrace. The coldness of her shadowy touch offers a fleeting comfort, but the frigid terror emanating from Thorn's evil visage makes my heart pound wildly in my chest. His presence seems to suck the warmth from the room, leaving an oppressive chill that seeps into my bones.

The air grows thick with an unnatural silence, broken only by the sounds of my heavy breathing. Thorn's shadowy form flickers and shifts as if he is not entirely bound to this world. His eyes lock onto mine, and I feel an overwhelming sense of doom as if his gaze alone could drag me into the abyss.

"How is this possible?" I whisper raggedly, moving closer into Rose's embrace.

"I don't know," Rose whispers back, tightening her grip on me.

Thorn flickers again as he moves closer to us, wavering unsteadily as he gains ground. Rose moves us back, stepping before me and shoving me behind her.

"What do you want, demon?" Rose asks bitterly.

"I want what I have always wanted," Thorn answers evilly. "I want a body of my own. One that is not made of darkness and shadow. One that is made of flesh and bone."

"You want to be mortal?" Rose asks in a disbelieving tone.

"When I am done, I will not be mortal," Thorn answers disdainfully. "I will still be immortal, but I will have a body. I will be able to feel and touch. I can enjoy the sensation when I…shall we say interact…with my victims. I have long desired to feel the heat of blood in my hands, the sharpness of broken bones against my skin, and the trembling of their bodies caused by the terror I invoke."

Thorn's words slither through my mind as terror and dread coil through my body. Nausea roils through my stomach, and I retch at the unbidden pictures my mind summons. I can't let Thorn do that to my body!

"You won't touch her!" Rose hisses threateningly. "You might be stronger than me, but I'll die defending my human."

Thorn laughs maliciously, sending tendrils of dread through my nerves. His form flickers again as he moves ever closer, and I back away slowly, digging my fingers into Rose's shadowy back and dragging her with me.

"I don't want your puny human," Thorn snorts contemptuously. "How am I supposed to rip someone apart with my bare hands using that tiny, weak little body?"

I frown in confusion. "That doesn't make any sense. You have been after my body ever since I knew of your existence."

"You know nothing, human," Thorn snaps, his form shifting out of focus as if he is beginning to fade away. "Your insignificant body was only a means to an end. I have much higher goals to attain."

"Fine," Rose says as she moves backward with me still cowering behind her. "If that's the case, then go away and leave us alone."

"Ah, you see, it isn't quite that simple," Thorn says with a deceitful smile. "While I have grown strong enough to manifest independently, I am still attached to you. Hence the flickering."

He stresses the fact by blinking in and out as he runs a hand up and down his body in a showing gesture before continuing, "Therefore, you must come with me, and we must take your annoying human as well since you cannot be far from her side because you are so weak."

Terror and panic radiate through my entire being as Thorn moves ever closer, reaching out those shadowy arms toward Rose. My back hits the wall, and I cannot back away further. I watch helplessly as Thorn grabs my sweet rose by her throat, opening that terrifying abyss of a mouth and letting out a sound such as my ears have never heard before.

The demon's scream pierces the air, a bone-chilling cacophony that seems to come from the very depths of hell. It's a sound that defies nature, a blend of guttural growls and high-pitched wails that reverberate through the room. It is filled with an unholy rage, echoing with the torment of countless lost souls that have fallen victim to this vile demon.

It claws at my ears, making my blood run cold and my heart pound in terror. The very air seems to vibrate with the malevolent energy of the scream as if the fabric of reality itself is being torn apart by the sheer force of the demon's fury.

Rose's form begins to disintegrate in Thorn's wicked grip, her shadowy darkness wavering and flickering like Thorn's had moments ago. Her mournful cry tears through the cacophony of Thorn's scream, inciting an anger inside me that spurns me into action.

"Let her go!" I cry so loud that it drowns out the demons' screams.

I lunge forward, grabbing at Thorn's shadowy form in an attempt to tackle him to the floor. It doesn't work, but it does take him by surprise, distracting him for a split second as I topple empty-handed to the floor beside him.

It's enough for Rose to slip from his grip and dive for me, grabbing my wrist and hurtling me through the ripples of time and space faster than I can blink. She doesn't even take the time to rip my spirit from my body. I had no clue that a person could go into the void between dimensions in physical form, but apparently, it can be done.

I had experienced it before, but never in the flesh. The sensations of being here in spirit do not compare to being dragged through the void physically.

It's as if I'm being torn apart and reassembled in a relentless, chaotic storm. The world around me disintegrates into a maelstrom of blinding light and impenetrable darkness, twisting together into a nightmarish vortex. My body is weightless, yet every fiber of my being is stretched to its limit as if the very essence of reality is ripping me apart.

The sensation is a harrowing blend of painful torment and sheer terror. My heart pounds with a frantic, almost aching intensity. The air around me roars with a deafening, otherworldly howl, drowning out all other sounds as time fractures and splinters, moments elongating into agonizing eternities before snapping back in an instant.

The harrowing presence of Thorn's pursuit looms like a shadow at the edge of my consciousness, his malevolent intent driving us to flee faster and faster through the ever-shifting, nightmarish landscape of space and time.

A sudden, bone-chilling cold grips me as we hurtle through the chaotic storm. The air thickens, and an oppressive darkness closes in. I feel Thorn's malevolent presence before I see him, a suffocating weight that presses down on my chest, making it hard to breathe.

Thorn materializes before us in an instant, his shadowy form flickering and shifting like a living nightmare. His eyes, glowing with a sinister violet light, lock onto mine, and I feel an overwhelming sense of dread. His grin stretches wider as we come to a sudden stop, inches away from his looming form.

With a swift, predatory motion, Thorn's clawed hand shoots out and grabs me. His icy touch sends a jolt of frigid terror through my body. The world around me blurs and distorts as his grip tightens, pulling me closer. I can feel the raw, malevolent power radiating from him, a dark energy that seeps into my very soul.

Thorn's low, guttural growl echoes in my mind, filling me with a sense of hopelessness.

"You cannot escape," he whispers, his words dripping with malice.

The shadows around us seem to come alive, writhing and twisting as if eager to consume me. He pulls, jerking me from Rose's grip and into his dark, surprisingly solid form. I start to panic, but Rose appears beside me almost instantly, her presence a beacon of hope in the encroaching darkness. Her eyes, filled with determination, meet mine as she wraps her arm around my shoulders, her touch a comforting cold.

"Hold on," she urges, her voice steady despite the terror surrounding us.

Rose's eyes glow brilliantly, a shining diamond-colored beacon in a dark void. She thrusts out her free hand, and the intensely bright light that is in her eyes emanates from her palm, creating a protective barrier of light that pushes back against Thorn's darkness. Thorn cowers, and she pulls me away from his grip, wrapping me in her protective embrace and moving me away from him.

Hope fills my chest. My demon is becoming stronger having learned a new power, and for a moment, it seems like we might escape. But Thorn rises, brushing off Rose's valiant attempt at vanquishing him as if brushing an annoying insect from his shoulder. His malevolent grin widens as he recovers and stalks slowly toward us. Rose starts to turn with me in her arms, trusting the barrier to hold and give us time to get away. But Thorn casually flicks his wrist, shattering Rose's light barrier like fragile glass.

"No!" Rose cries out, her voice filled with desperation as she tries to shield me with her own body.

Thorn effortlessly swats Rose aside, sending her sprawling into the void. Her anguished scream echoes in my ears as she disappears into the darkness.

"Rose!" I cry out in anguish as I helplessly watch her disappear from sight.

"Don't worry," Thorn drawls maliciously as he grabs my wrist and pulls me to him. "She will catch up eventually."

"No, please!" I beg as Thorn drags me deeper into the abyss, the last remnants of light and hope fade away.

The terror is all-consuming, a relentless force that threatens to swallow me whole. I am trapped in Thorn's grasp as he drags me away, caught in the clutches of a demon whose very presence is a nightmare-made flesh.

The last thought that flits through my mind as reality fades away is of Deklan and the all-consuming regret that I may never see him again. I will never get to tell him how much I miss him and never want to be away from him again.

I don't know how long we travel through the slats of time before we finally come to a stop, and Thorn carelessly flings me down onto a hard surface. I can tell from the looming feelings of disorientation that we are still somewhere amid nothingness, but somehow, it is different.

I no longer have the sensation of being torn apart and reassembled or feeling confused and weightless. I feel more solid and in control but still weak, as if I am caught between existence and nonexistence. Somewhere along the way, I had closed my eyes, and the darkness now suffocates me. Inch by inch, I open my eyes and take in my surroundings.

The floor I was so carelessly tossed upon is hard tile, like the floors in Sophia's hospital. Exactly like them, I realize as I take in the smoky gray, swirling pattern intermingling with the black main color of the tiles. It's the same pattern of the floors in Deklan's apartment and Sophia's living space in the turret.

I pick myself up into a sitting position and open my eyes wider. The dimness of the room surrounds me as I take in the white tiled wall in front of me, just like the tiled wall of Deklan's bathroom. Frowning in confusion, I turn my head to take in more of the room, and a bone-chilling cold consumes me to my soul.

There is no furniture in the room save for one tiny bed against the far wall and a recliner that sits close to the other wall, close to a full-length, extravagantly framed, antique, broken mirror. The shattered pieces lay scattered along the floor before the large mirror, glinting in the tiny shards of light in the dim room.

The mirror is cause for concern, but what lies on the bed makes my heart race with cold-blooded terror.

Since I had never met him in person, I would not have recognized him without having seen Sophia's pictures throughout her living space in the turret and in different places in the hospital. She has pictures of him everywhere: on the walls, sitting on shelves and tables, and the large one in the reception area of the hospital, which is the centerpiece of his memorial.

Harper. He is still alive. At least, I think he is. I watch closely for the rise and fall of his chest or any minuscule movement, like the slightest twitch of a finger, as I struggle to stand.

If Harper is here, then that means Thorn has brought me into the Demon Dimension. This is the one place I definitely don't want to be. I am human, which means I will not last long here, and who knows what effects it will have on me since I have been brought here physically.

I make it to my hands and knees shakily, crawling toward the bed as I see Harper's chest rise. Relief floods my system as I watch him breathe, but I wonder why he is not conscious.

"What the hell have you done to Harper?" I yell as I turn around, but then realize that Thorn is nowhere to be seen.

I am yelling at an empty room. He had just dumped me here, but he is not here. Time has no concept, so who knows if I have lain on that floor for hours or minutes. Certainly, enough time for Thorn to leave me here alone with Harper, but where had he gone?

I turn back toward the bed, forgetting about Thorn momentarily and focusing on Harper and his current state. I manage to reach Harper's side, my fingers trembling as I touch his cold skin. It is not a normal cold. It is the cold of death, the cold of the grave, and my heart stutters as I begin to shake him gently. He doesn't respond and only takes a deep, rattling breath.

"Harper?" I say softly, shaking him once more.

There is still no response other than a fluttering of his eyelashes as he struggles to open his eyes. I catch the fleeting color of black as his eyes open and shut rapidly, and my heart sinks to my feet.

Is this the body that Thorn wants? Is Thorn trying to take over Harper's body as I watch helplessly?

A soft, warm light fills the room, and I turn to see Rose materialize beside me. Her presence fills me with relief and brings a fleeting sense of hope. I can tell she is hurt, but she valiantly hobbles toward me with resolve.

"Rose," I whisper, my voice cracking. "We need to save him. I think Thorn is trying to take over his body."

Rose touches my shoulder gently as she says, "I understand you want to help your cousin's friend, but we don't have much time. If you don't get out of here soon, you will start to die. It's bad enough when a human soul is here, but you being here physically…I'm not sure what's going to happen."

"Rose, please. I can't just leave him here. Sophia would never forgive me, and I would never forgive myself."

Rose sighs in defeat and nods, her eyes filling with determination.

"Alright, I will try. I can recreate that barrier from earlier inside Harper, stronger this time…hopefully."

She kneels beside Harper, placing her hands over his chest. A faint glow emanates from her palms, and Harper's breathing steadies as his body soaks it in. I watch in fascination as the faint glow becomes brighter, lighting up Harper's body and shining like a beacon of hope in the dim room. But just as quickly, the light flickers and dims.

Thorn's dark energy is overpowering.

"I can't break Thorn's hold," Rose says, her voice strained. "He is too strong."

I place my hands over hers, feeling the warmth of her magic mingling with my own desperate energy as I say, "You can do it, Rose. I know you can."

My touch seems to strengthen Rose, and the light grows brighter again. We focus on Harper, Rose's magic filling him while I silently will him to fight against Thorn's influence. For a moment, it seems to be working. Harper's eyes flutter open, and he gasps for air. However, my relief is short-lived as a shadowy figure flickers and appears at the foot of the bed, his malevolent grin sending chills down my spine.

"You think you can save him?" Thorn sneers. "How naive. He's fighting, yes, but it's only a matter of time before he succumbs. He's not coming back."

With a wave of his hand, a surge of dark energy flies through the air, shattering the light Rose had built up around Harper's body and blasting us back. We fly across the room, and I cry out in pain as I hit the wall, slumping to the ground. Rose hits the wall beside me, almost hitting the already-broken mirror. She scrambles to her feet amidst the broken shards of glass and runs toward Harper's body, but it's too late.

Thorn's power is too strong.

Thorn makes a graceful dive through the air, straight into Harper's body. Harper's body convulses several times, an unworldly sound coming from his open mouth as if the hounds of hell are howling all around us. The convulsing stops, and Harper lays still for a moment before rising to a sitting position and swinging his legs over the side of the bed. His eyes glow with a violet, otherworldly light. Thorn's laughter echoes through the room, and the eerie sound comes from Harper's mouth as Thorn takes control of Harper's body.

Rose scrambles to my side, her shadowy visage panicked as she takes in my crumpled form. A sense of overwhelming dread courses through me as I realize I can't move my body, and I look up at Rose helplessly.

"Rose, help me," I plead, tears streaming down my face. "I think I might be paralyzed."

Rose looks injured and weak as well as she slumps to the floor beside me, piercing me with a pained expression of panicked dread.

"We… we have to find a way to get you out of here."

"You are not going anywhere," Harper says, but it's Thorn's voice that comes from his mouth. "I have you to thank, Rose. I can complete my plan even faster now that I know humans can travel through the realms physically. Thank you for showing me that."

"You know what else can travel through the dimensions physically? Angels," Rose shoots back. "And her angel will come looking for her at any minute."

But Thorn only laughs sinisterly.

He points at the broken mirror and replies, "No one will find you now since the portal has been broken, so we have all the time in the world. Well, some of us do."

He waves a dismissive hand toward me and continues, "I have to have all the pieces of my soul back simultaneously to take complete control, and there is one more piece I must fetch. But for now… "

He pauses, smiling sinisterly as he prowls toward us in Harper's body. "For now, I feel I am strong enough and have enough control over this body that we can have some fun before I go fetch it."

CHAPTER 26: DEKLAN

The emptiness of the previously abandoned building looms around me as I look up to the second floor, searching for the lights that should shine from one of the windows. If Mia is here, that is where she would be. Either in her apartment or in her office.

The entire building is eerily silent and dark, and trepidation trickles across my nerves. Maybe she is asleep? Yes, that's it, I tell myself to calm my racing heart. She is probably asleep. However, somewhere deep down inside my gut, I know I am lying to myself.

Something is very wrong.

I can feel it coalescing inside my chest, cutting off my air and making it hard to breathe. Hastily, I shake off the feeling and enter the building, practically running toward the stairwell and taking the steps two at a time. I hurry down the long hallway toward Mia's apartment, stopping for only a second to glance in the door of her office.

The office is empty, and nothing seems amiss.

I continue to her apartment and almost hit my knees when I step inside. I can feel the malevolent energy still present in the small space of Mia's living room. A demon has definitely been here, and it was a strong one.

However, it doesn't feel like Thorn. No, this is much worse. The energy I feel now is more akin to the energy of a Higher demon, and, if I am right, that is utterly not good.

Higher demons are spirits of humans, like most demons. However, higher demons have been brought into the demon realm whole, not broken like the inner demons.

While an inner demons' entire existence is to atone for their sins, higher demons have no purpose. They can appear as human as they choose, creating havoc among the unsuspecting humans they encounter. However, they are bound by their Goddess.

They were followers of Lilith in their human lives, and have been brought into the Demon Dimension to serve out their eternity by worshipping Lilith in the afterlife as they had in life. They are powerful in their magic but mostly harmless since they are happy to serve their Goddess and have some extra perks. However, some will do almost anything to get a chance at another life.

Perhaps Thorn found a way to convince a Higher demon to help him with his crazy schemes, and if this is the case, a simple call to Lilith will help me sort this out.

I tell myself this to calm the overwhelming panic that threatens to take me over, stealing my air and causing my heart to explode from my chest. Especially since Mia's body is nowhere to be found.

My heart to falls to my feet in misery and dread as I search the entire apartment and find it empty except for Mia's bed and dresser in her bedroom and the abandoned sofa in the living room.

Where did they take her body? It will do no good for Lilith to help get her soul back if there is not a body for Mia to return to.

My mind reels with anxiety and dread, and too many thoughts flow through my brain...

I have to tell Sophia. I need to get my band of angels together, which means calling a meeting. They can help me find her body. Then, I'll have to tell Vinny, which will probably destroy the poor man. Should I call for Lilith? Maybe, possibly, call Luna? How am I going to find Mia's body? What the fuck am I going to do?

So many emotions are running through me that I can't focus on one thing. My heart runs like a rabbit through an open field, and my breathing is ragged and uneven. If I don't calm down, I may have a panic attack.

Can angels have panic attacks?

If the way I am feeling right now is any indication, then yes, yes we can. I need to calm down.

I pace the empty room, sucking in deep breaths as I walk. This isn't helping. The frustration and anxiety in my chest only grow to an almost painful point, doubling me over and bringing me to my knees. Suddenly, a searing pain shoots through my head, and I clutch it, gasping for air as a scream of pain escapes my throat.

Images flash before my eyes behind my closed lids; faces of people I know and strangers alike, each one shadowed by a dark, writhing presence. My body is still kneeling on the floor, but it is as if my spirit has been hurtled across the planet.

My senses pinpoint each face that flits through my mind, and a thousand locations surround my thoughts, leading me to the places where the faces await my call.

What the fuck is happening to me? My chest expands with intense anxiety, but suddenly, my goddess's words echo in my mind:

"I give you my blessing and a little gift you will discover later. You will know when the time comes."

And suddenly, I know. This is it. This is the gift she spoke of. It is a power reserved for specially picked fallen angels. Different Gods and Goddesses call them different things. Luna calls hers "hunters", and it is considered a great honor to be given this role by one's Deity.

However, I have no time to dwell on the honor I should feel for having been given this gift because the power consumes me and drives me further into my mind.

I can see the inner demons living inside humans, each one a unique entity. Some are calm and controlled, their humans have learned to harness their power. But others are wild and untrained, causing chaos and suffering. These are the ones who need help, the ones I can see most clearly, and the ones I will need to find and assign them an angel to help.

The knowledge is overwhelming, almost too much to bear. My heart races and a cold sweat breaks out on my forehead. Fear grips me in an all-consuming fire of misery. What if I can't handle this power? What if the power consumes me?

The weight of the responsibility I have been given presses down on my shoulders, making it hard to breathe. But then, amidst the fear, a spark of excitement ignites. This is a gift from my goddess, a chance to make a real difference. She is giving me a second chance to show I am still a true follower. She is giving me a second chance to show her I still care, even though I am in love with another.

I force myself to focus, taking deep, steadying breaths. The power surges within me, wild and untamed, like a storm threatening to break free. My heart pounds in my chest, each beat echoing the chaos inside. I close my eyes, trying to center myself, but the fear is overwhelming.

What if I can't control it? What if I hurt someone?

Sweat beads on my forehead as I struggle to harness the energy. It feels like trying to hold onto a live wire, the current threatening to slip through my fingers at any moment. I grit my teeth, pushing past the terror that claws at my mind. I can't fail. Not now.

Slowly, I begin to find a rhythm. I focus on my breathing, each inhale and exhale a lifeline pulling me back from the brink. The power responds, its wild edges softening just a fraction. I force myself to concentrate, to see each person as an individual.

The initial terror begins to fade as I focus in on one face at a time and realize I can do this. The fear is replaced by a sense of purpose.

I can do this. I was chosen for this.

I close my eyes, take a deep breath, and let the power guide me. I smile deviously as I realize I now have the means to find Mia, and the demon that took her will not win. With this power, I can find anybody or any spirit that is or has been attached to an inner demon.

I focus in on my new power and let it take me to the one face that is focused in the center of my mind. Other faces blur past rapidly until one comes into sharp focus. My heart stutters an uneven rhythm when I finally find her.

Mia...

She is crumpled in a heap on the floor against the wall. Her face is pale, her chocolate eyes wide with fear, and beside her stands Harper, a malevolent grin twisting his features. Her demon kneels beside her, hovering protectively as she stares up angrily at Harper's form. Confusion blooms in my chest at first, but my new power takes over and shows me the truth...

Thorn has left Mia's demon, reuniting with the piece of himself that had resided within Harper. Thorn has taken over Harper completely, but I can tell, thanks to my new gift, that Harper is still in there, battling to cast Thorn out.

What's worse is that Mia has been taken into the demon realm bodily, and her spirit is suffocating inside her for having been dragged into the Demon Dimension. I had no idea that was even possible.

Rage surges through me, hotter and more intense than anything I've ever felt. Thorn has taken Mia, the one I love, the one I had been searching for my entire existence. I just had not known it until now. The realization lights a fire of determination inside me.

I will save her despite Thorn's presence feeling like a high demon. That is why I had felt that presence in Mia's apartment. Thorn's powers have grown, and they will grow even more since he found one of his pieces.

What will happen when he finds the last piece?

I can't let that happen. I force myself to focus even harder, casting my doubts aside. My vision sharpens, and I can feel the power coursing through my veins, guiding me. I hone in on the scene with Mia again, and my blood runs cold.

I see the dark tendrils of Thorn's influence wrap around Harper, suffocating his spirit. I also see the look on Harper's face, being controlled by Thorn, as he looks salaciously at Mia lying on the floor. The sight fuels the rage burning within me, activating a fierce determination to save her.

I rise to my feet, my legs trembling but resolute. The room around me fades away as I focus solely on Mia, Mia's demon, and Thorn. I can feel the power growing, expanding within me, giving me the strength I need.

I know what I must do, but first, I will let Sophia know what's up. It will hurt her to know what has happened, but she deserves the truth. I don't know if I can save Harper, but I have to try.

I only hope I won't be too late.

With a determined breath, I step forward, ready to confront Thorn and save Mia and Harper, no matter the cost.

As I move, the power expands, becoming slowly stronger as it sharpens my senses. I can hear the faint whispers of shadowy demons that don't have humans to inhabit yet all around me, experience the coldness of their presence, and feel their longing to be assigned so they can begin their process of retribution.

Is this the power of a Hunter as well? Or is this something more that Luna has gifted me? Whatever the case, I have no time to speculate, so I push their whispers aside, focusing on the warmth of Mia's essence and the light that still flickers within Harper. I won't let Thorn extinguish that light, and I won't let him hurt Mia. Not now, not ever.

I have Mia's location pinpointed in my mind, and I hold onto that information through my internal struggle. The power still threatens to overtake me, but I push against its hold, willing it to bend to my will instead of the other way around.

I stuff the locations of all the other humans with demons into a box in the back of my brain, ready to be opened and explored when needed. I imagine the box turning into a filing cabinet, sorting out each individual person into their own file. My supernatural mind will be able to sort through the files quickly, honing in on any individual without all the prep work of before.

With that cacophony of knowledge handled, I push outward, creating a shield around me that blocks out shadowy whispers from entering my conscious thoughts.

My world instantly restores, shifting and flickering around me until I find myself standing in Mia's living room. The air around me is still and silent once more, but I can still feel the coil of energy inside my gut, twisting and writhing patiently, waiting to be unleashed.

I take a deep breath and take my phone out of my pocket, willing my nerves to calm as I dial Sophia's number. She answers on the first ring.

"Deklan?" She breathes into the phone, her voice panicked and squeaky. "How did you know I was getting ready to call you?"

I frown in confusion. "I didn't. I just…"

But Sophia cuts me off with a hurried, "You need to get here now."

The panic I had fought off only seconds ago returns with a vengeance.

"What's wrong?" I ask urgently, the cold sweat breaking out along my forehead once more.

"It's the mirror," She cries, her voice quivering with a mixture of rage and misery. "It's broken."

CHAPTER 27: MIA AND DEKLAN

MIA

Harper, controlled by Thorn, draws nearer to my position, where I still lay crumpled on the floor. A mix of fear and anger surge through my veins as I watch him approach, knowing it's not really Harper but horrified of the man all the same.

The dangerous intent in his violet-glowing eyes sends sparks of dread curling down my useless spine as I try to move away. My body remains unmoving despite my desperate attempts. Rose worriedly helps me even as she tries feebly to fend off the demon.

"Back off, Thorn!" Rose cries bravely. "You already have what you need, so leave Mia alone."

Thorn laughs maliciously, rubbing his hands together as he says, "Oh, I am not done with Mia yet. I still need her for my bargaining tool."

"What else could you possibly want?" I ask, my voice wavering.

"I want what I have always wanted," Thorn drawls. "And I almost had it before Sophia and Harper stuck their noses in my business. It's poetic justice that they will help me get it after all."

Thorn continues to advance, his tone growing more villainous as he continues, "Once all the pieces of myself are joined and I become whole again, I will be unstoppable. I will be more powerful than even the Gods and Goddesses. They will have no choice but to hand control of the Demon Dimension over to me."

"Rose, get out of here if you can," I whisper, wincing at a spark of pain that shoots through my arm. "Go find help. We can't let Thorn get away with this."

Thorn's evil grin on Harper's face turns my stomach into knots as he responds, "My dear, I already have. I may not be able to fight both of Sophia's demons at once to get to Sophia and take back the part of my soul that lies dormant inside her, but Sophia will gladly call off her demons and hand over her life to save yours. Especially when I tell her I will do wicked things to you before I kill you...and I will make her watch."

My blood runs cold as I hear his words pouring from Harper's mouth. He will kill me anyway; I know it. He may threaten Sophia with my life, but he won't let us go even if Sophia complies. A whimpering sob escapes my throat as Rose suddenly comes up from the floor despite her being injured.

"Why don't you just die!" She screams as an unholy, bluish light shines from her eyes and surrounds her.

She lunges herself at Harper's body with a guttural demon scream, swiping clawed, shadowy hands at his face. He dodges and turns, and Rose moves with him, her light shining through the dimness of the room as she continues her assault.

Thorn simply laughs, holding out his arms and dancing around to block and ward off the blows. Purple lights dance from his eyes, surrounding him and colliding with the light surrounding Rose. Her light flickers, fades, and dies.

Rose growls with frustration and anger, bending over and ramming her shoulders into Thorn's stomach. Hope fills my chest as I watch Thorn stumble back a few steps at the assault, his purple eyes flickering in surprise.

He takes the hit, and I wait for Thorn to go down with Rose's forward momentum and her cry of victory. But her whoop is cut short when Thorn recovers quickly, refusing to go down. Rose's momentum is stopped suddenly, her breath leaving her body in a whooshing sound.

Rose stumbles, but she doesn't go down either. However, my relief is short-lived when I see the vicious intent in Thorn's eyes, and I cry out a warning as I see Thorn's hand raising.

But my warning comes too late. I watch in horror as Thorn's hand comes down, batting Rose's form away from him like swatting a fly. She flies through the air, landing on the bed across the room. Thorn holds out a hand and shoots purple energy from his palm. It surrounds Rose, and her scream of pain pierces my heart almost as painfully as it rips through my eardrums.

"No!" I cry as I watch her form flicker and fade away.

"What did you do to her?" I ask desolately.

"She isn't dead if that's what you're worried about," Thorn says. "But that blast will keep her away long enough."

"Long enough for what?" I ask meekly, terror coursing through me.

"For me to play with you before I go get Sophia," Thorn says, turning back toward me with a sinister grin.

Dread snakes its way up my spine, icy fingers massaging each vertebra, freezing the breath in my lungs. Thorn begins to move toward me again as I lay on the cold, hard floor, my body refusing to obey my desperate commands to move. Every muscle and bone screams in agony, fear, and exhaustion.

I try to scream, but no sound escapes my open mouth. Thorn's footsteps echo ominously in the dimly lit room, each step bringing him closer. My heart pounds in my chest, a frantic drumbeat of terror pulsing through my eardrums.

I try desperately to crawl, to drag myself away with my arms, but my limbs refuse to move. The more I struggle, the more helpless I feel. Tears blur my vision as I watch Thorn's predatory movements loom larger and larger. His eyes are cold, devoid of mercy, and his lips curl into a cruel smile.

"Please," I whisper, my voice barely audible over the sound of my own ragged breathing. "Please, don't."

Thorn's laughter is a chilling sound, sending shivers down my spine. He reaches out, his hand closing the distance between us. I try to scream, but no sound comes out. My throat is dry, my voice stolen by the sheer terror of the moment. Thorn's hand is inches away now, and I can feel the frigid cold of his presence, the malevolence radiating from Harper's body because of Thorn's invasion.

In that instant, time seems to slow. Every second stretches into eternity as I lay there, helpless and afraid, realizing that I am with this cruel demon in Harper's body, alone and unprotected. My mind races, searching for any possible escape, but I can't think through my panic.

As his hand finally reaches me, I close my eyes, bracing for the inevitable. He grabs the collar of my shirt at my shoulder, dragging me roughly across the tile floor. My body jerks violently with spasms at the sudden movement, shooting torrents of pain through every muscle and bone.

I scream in anguish, trying feebly to gain control of my body. It's no use. My body refuses to obey the commands of my brain, and yet the pain tells me I am not completely paralyzed. I don't understand why my body won't work.

He pulls me through the entire length of the room to the bed. He keeps hold of my shirt as his other hand grabs a handful of my hair and pulls me off the floor. I scream in pain from the ripping sensation in my scalp that sends burning agony through my head.

He ignores my screams and tosses me roughly toward the bed, cackling like a maniac as I bounce on the mattress from the force at which he throws me. I land on my back, gazing helplessly up at Harper's body as Thorn controls him.

"Where's your precious angel now, whore?" Thorn sneers, distorting Harper's face into a cruel visage. "You won't be going anywhere with that binding spell I put on you."

So that's why I cannot move. Terror shoots through my body, sending goosebumps all over my flesh. He can do whatever he wants with me, and there isn't anything I can do to stop it.

He reaches for his belt, unbuckling it slowly as he smiles lecherously down at me and says, "I have always wanted to fuck a woman while inside a human body. I came close once, but I was only cloning the body. It wasn't the same. I wasn't technically in a human body."

My heart threatens to burst from my chest, and my breathing becomes ragged as he slowly slides the belt from his pants and continues to speak.

"Of course, I am not technically in a human body right now, either. Just the spirit of one."

A whimpering sob escapes my throat as tears stream down my cheeks. Pain and agony radiate up my spine, but Thorn continues to ignore my pain as he tosses the belt to the floor.

"However, the human spirit can experience the same sensations as its body, so it is the same in a way. I have been told that sex is more intense for humans since the human body is more sensitive to touch and sensation than a shadowy demon body."

My head hurts where my hair has practically been pulled from my scalp. My body is useless, and all I can do is lie here where Thorn threw me and watch as he unbuttons and unzips his pants.

"Hopefully, Harper's spirit experiences sensation like his body did. It will be interesting to test it on you, my dear."

Tears stream down the sides of my face. There is nothing I can do to stop this. I am going to have to endure Thorn's abuse.

"My old master used to tell me that there was nothing like pounding your dick into a tight pussy and listening to the screams. He used to tell me that Sophia's pussy was his favorite."

He pushes his pants to the floor, leaving on his boxers. He steps out of the pants and starts unbuttoning the dress shirt, starting at the top and working his way down as he continues, "I wonder if your pussy is as good as your cousins?"

My breath is coming in short, uneven bursts as panic consumes me, choking me in its embrace as Thorn shucks off his shirt and moves closer to the bed.

"I'm gonna fuck you good, Mia. I'm gonna fuck you until you scream, and then I'll fuck you some more. I wanna see how good that little pussy is, and I wanna hear you scream."

"Please," I say, choking on a sob. "Please stop."

But he doesn't stop. He looms over me, moving ever closer as my panic and fear consume me. The fear is overwhelming, a suffocating blanket that threatens to consume me entirely. All I can do is hope, pray, that somehow, this nightmare will end or that Deklan will find a way to save me.

If he can even find me, and if it isn't too late…

DEKLAN

My motorcycle whips into the hospital driveway, and I am barely stopped before I throw down the kickstand and leap from the bike. I burst through the doors and run for the stairs, unable to take the spiral stairs quite as fast as a regular staircase, but I certainly give it a good try.

I make it to the top landing and have barely begun my trek down the hallway toward the mirror room when two shadowy figures suddenly materialize before me.

I stop suddenly, jerking to a violent halt with my hand on my chest.

"Jessuss H Christ on a fuckstick! How many times have I told you two NOT to scare me like that!" I say between ragged breaths.

"Stop whining you big baby," Lucien scoffs humorously.

"I'm sorry, Deklan, but there is no time to be delicate," Jewel says more kindly.

A third form wavers in the air behind them, coming into focus much slower than the first two and not as solid. The new demon is smaller than the other two, and her eyes do not glow as brightly. However, they glow a dull cornflower blue color. Not red. Not purple.

Confused, I ask, "Who is your new friend?"

This time, Jewel scoffs as she answers, "You don't know who she is?"

"I was always under Thorn's influence when Deklan was around," the new demon says.

I think about how lovely her voice sounds as she continues to speak, and memory slowly comes into my brain.

"But it was because of Deklan that I could come out without Thorn. Deklan always put him to sleep so I could interact with Mia. He helped even though he didn't know he helped."

My heart skips a beat as I take a second look at the new demon's shadowy face. The face is the same, only softer and not full of malice and hate. The voice is different, though. Softer, sweeter, and definitely more feminine. And, of course, the eyes are different.

My heart fills with hope. If her demon is here, then…

"You're Mia's demon," I say, trying desperately to remember what Mia had called her.

The demon smiles and nods.

"Where's Mia?" I ask, trying hard to keep the anger out of my tone. "She was with you before. Did you leave her there?"

Her smile fades, and her eyes grow hard, the blue light sparking like lightning. "Of course, I didn't leave her! Thorn has taken over Harper's body. He has her in the hidden room behind the mirror in the Demon Dimension. I tried to save her, but…wait, how did you know where Mia and I were?"

I surge forward without answering, intent on getting into that room and through the portal, but Lucien's loud voice stops me. "Thorn has broken the mirror. We can't get in through the portal and don't know how to get there through the Demon Dimension."

I stop and whip around.

Mia's demon continues the story. "He cast me out while I was trying to save Mia, and I don't know how to get back."

"Not even I know where that hidden room is inside the Demon Dimension," Jewel adds. "It is Harper's secret, and since Thorn has taken over Harper…"

A sly smile spreads across my face as I interrupt Jewel. "I don't need the portal or Harper to find that room. Like I said before, I know where Mia is."

The demons look confused, so I explain, "My Goddess visited me and gave me a gift. I'm a Hunter. I can track Mia down anywhere in the multiverse."

Mia's tiny demon still looks confused, so Jewel quickly explains, "A hunter has the ability to track down any demon or human that has a demon in the entire multiverse. It is a special gift given by the Gods and Goddesses to certain followers."

Mia's demon's eyes light up.

"That's good, very good. We must go tell Sophia," the demon says. "She's in the mirror room right now."

I turn back around and move toward the mirror room again.

"Yes, very good," Jewel agrees as she turns and follows. "We will have the element of surprise in our favor since Harper nor Mia knows about this power. Thorn won't be suspecting that you will know where he is."

"And we must take Sophia with us," Mia's demon says.

We all stop again, turning on the tiny demon with anger on our faces. Our voices coalesce together as we all speak at once.

"Hell no, we are not taking Sophia," I say.

"Fuck no," Lucien says.

"I will never let that happen," Jewel says.

Mia's demon holds out a hand, waving it back and forth to get our attention as she says, "Please, let me explain."

"There isn't an explanation in this entire multiverse that would make me want to take Sophia with us," I say, crossing my arms over my chest.

"But we have to if we want to protect her," Mia's demon says.

I frown and start to ask how that is possible, but Lucien beats me to it.

"How in the fuck will taking Sophia with us protect her from Thorn?"

"Thorn wants Sophia. She holds the last piece of his soul," the demon says.

"Fuck!" Lucien screams. "I told her I felt like something has been off for a long time. She kept brushing me off, fussing about how I worry too much..."

"Lucien!" Jewel screams, cutting him off. "Shut it! She's having a hard time right now."

"I told Lucien to stop worrying," Sophia's voice calls out from down the hall. "He never listens."

We all whip around, startled by the sound. Sophia stands in the hallway before the open door to the mirror room, leaning against the door frame as if ready to fall over at any moment. Her hair is disheveled, lying in frizzy, black waves over her shoulders. Her skin is pale, her dark brown eyes dull, and I can tell from the red rims she has been crying. She sniffles, as if confirming my suspicion, and her entire body seems to vibrate.

The light in the hallway skirts around Sophia's form, chased off by the darkness that leaks from the open door and surrounds her in its embrace. She holds her arms around her midsection as if warding off a blow, looking like she is going to double over at any moment.

"Sophia," I whisper, holding a hand out to her as I draw nearer. "What's happened?"

I grab her shoulder and pull her to me, pulling her out of the darkness and into the lighted hallway. She falls into my body, and I wrap her in my embrace, hugging her to me as if she were something precious. I can feel her trembling against me as she buries her face into my shoulder.

"Sophia, I don't mean to upset you," Lucien says. "But isn't it my job to worry about you?"

"I know, Lucien, but that's not what has me so upset right now," Sophia says against my shoulder.

She releases a shuddering breath before adding, "It's the mirror…Harper…oh Goddess!"

Then she is weeping uncontrollably in my arms.

"Please…I…need…to…go…to…him," she stutters out between hiccupping sobs.

Her demons are instantly there, one on each side of me. They each place a hand on her shoulder, offering comfort and letting her know they are there. They give me a knowing look and nod simultaneously.

I sway gently, rocking her comfortingly in my arms as I rub circles along her back and shoulders and whisper reassuring words soothingly. I let her cry for a moment until her cries turn into hiccups and sniffles, and then I push her out to arm's length. I hold onto one shoulder, using my free hand to tilt her face up to look at me.

I lock my sympathetic gaze to hers as I softly say, "Sophia, you must be brave. I can take you to Harper, but there are things you need to know first."

MIA

Harper's hot breath heats the skin of my cheek as his breathing turns ragged. He lies on top of me, his weight suffocating me as one hand holds a handful of my hair and the other hand squeezes one breast painfully.

His erection presses against my panties through his boxers as he ruts on top of me, making sickening noises that cause nausea to roil in my stomach. Fear and dread course through me with each push of Harper's body against mine, and the terror ratchets up as his hand releases my breast and runs down my body toward my hips.

Tears roll down the sides of my face as I shake my head back and forth, the only thing on my body that seems to obey my brain's commands. Wracking sobs consume me, suffocating me even more as my lungs scream for more oxygen than I am providing. My heart beats painfully against the backs of my ribs.

"Well, this is not as much fun as I thought it would be," Thorn's voice complains through Harper's mouth. "Don't get me wrong; that body is sexy as fuck. But you are rather boring."

I reign in my sobs enough to ground out through gritted teeth, "What, am I supposed to do parlor tricks for you?"

Thorn laughs cruelly as he reaches for the hem of my panties and says, "You could put up a fight."

"I can't," I choke out. "I can't move. Release me from this spell, and I'll show you a fight."

"Oh, yes," Thorn says, rising to his knees. "I forgot about the spell."

I take in a relieved, gasping breath as the absence of his weight frees my lungs to draw in deep. He snaps his fingers, and the sensation of my limbs coming back under my control feels like a constricting band suddenly snapping, freeing me from its hold.

Thorn slouches back over me, and I go into instant motion.

Bending my knees and bracing my feet against the lumpy mattress,

I buck my hips violently once, twice, and a third time, launching Harper's body off me. I ignore the pain in my body as I come up off the bed quickly and get to my feet.

I almost fall to my knees from the agony that wracks my bones and the stiffness that grasps my muscles, but the adrenaline coursing through me allows me to shake it off and keep going. I scramble across the floor but come to an abrupt halt as a hand clamps over my ankle and drags me back down.

I fall hard with a thud, pain shooting through my hip where it strikes the ground. I cry out in pain, screaming in agony as sharp nails dig into my flesh.

"Where do you think you're going, darlin?" Thorn asks from the floor where he had landed.

Thorn's iron grip on my ankle is unyielding, pulling me back every time I try to lunge forward. The small room feels like it is closing in on me, the walls pressing tighter with each desperate breath. The coldness of the place seeps into my bones through my naked flesh, and a shiver of apprehension runs through me as I am pulled back closer to Thorn.

He laughs maliciously. "See, isn't this more fun?"

"Let go!" I scream, my voice cracking with fear and frustration.

I kick out with my free foot, trying to dislodge his hold, but he only tightens his grip, his fingers and nails digging into my skin.

"You're not going anywhere, Mia," he growls, his voice a low, menacing rumble.

His eyes through Harper's face glow violently with that violet light, filled with a dangerous determination that sends chills down my spine. I twist my body, reaching for anything I can use to break free. My fingers brush against a long shard of glass, and I grab it, ignoring how it cuts into my palm. With a new surge of adrenaline, I slash at Thorn's hand, hoping to make him release me without hurting Harper's body too bad.

He yelps in pain, his grip loosening just enough for me to yank my ankle free. I scramble to my feet and stumble forward, nearly falling, but I can't stop. I have to get away. I have to escape. I can feel the sharp sting of broken glass under my bare feet, but the pain is nothing compared to the terror gripping my heart.

I frantically look around the nearly empty room, spotting a door only a few feet away, but it feels like miles. I can hear Thorn scrambling to his feet behind me, his curses filling the air.

"Come back here, fucking whore. You won't get far. Come back, and I promise I won't be too rough."

Thorn's tone sends waves of horror coursing through me as I push myself harder, my lungs burning, my heart pounding in my chest. Just a little further. Just a few more steps. I can make it.

I have to make it.

But I don't make it.

I slip on the tile floor, my legs flying from under me. I land on my back in a stream of blood that had obviously come from me. I am bleeding everywhere; from my feet, my palm, and even my knees where I tried to crawl through the glass earlier.

And now, I am bleeding from my head as it cracks against the hard floor. Stars burst through my vision as waves of dizziness wash over me. Nausea curls through my stomach as I quickly roll miserably to my side.

I have to get up.

Thorn is upon me before I can get back to my feet, looming over me and laughing maniacally, sending shards of icy terror shooting through my veins.

"You look beautiful lying in all that blood. Maybe I'll just take you right here on the floor."

I scream as Thorn grabs for me, grasping my hips and yanking me to him as he sinks to his knees. I kick out, but Thorn dodges my kicks, wrestling himself between my thrashing legs and pinning me to the floor with his hips.

He grasps both wrists in one large hand and holds them to the floor over my head, trapping me underneath him. He uses his free hand to grasp my chin, forcing me to look at him.

"I have had enough playtime. Now, time to get real," he says viciously.

I whimper with fear, wondering what is taking my angel so long.

Afraid that he may not be coming at all.

CHAPTER 28: DEKLAN

"Are you ready?" Mia's little demon asks Sophia. We are in the mirror room, standing despondently before the blank mirror. It isn't broken on this side, but the portal no longer works. Now, it is simply an elegant, antique, beautifully decorated mirror.

Our reflections show the determination, anger, and worry on all our faces, even the shadowy faces of the demons. Mia's demon has her hand resting on Sophia's shoulder, her feet wide apart, and her face set in a determined visage.

"Are you sure this will work?" Sophia asks, her voice shaking with nervousness.

"It worked with Mia," the demon answers.

"We have to try," Jewel says. "We don't know what effect the Demon Dimension will have on a human body since the body is more fragile than the spirit."

"Are we going to talk about the elephant in the room?" Lucien says, his tone sprinkled with annoyance. "Or are we just going to ignore the fact that an untrained demon already has blue eyes and a power that no other demon has ever had? Are we just going to blindly trust that she can drag Sophia into the Demon Dimension, body and all?"

"We don't have time to discuss this right now," I snap heatedly. "Mia may be in trouble. I have to get to her, and Sophia has to go with us. It worked with Mia, so it will work with Sophia."

"But she was under duress. How do we know that she can do it on purpose?" Lucien argues.

"Hush, Lucien," Jewel scolds. "Let her at least try. That power may be just what we need now to save Harper. If anyone can get through to him, it's Sophia. If he finds out she is there physically, he will go through hell to save her, which means..."

"He will fight Thorn's hold on him," I finish for Jewel and then turn to Mia's demon. "Now, can you do it or not, demon?"

"I have a fucking name, and you can all stop talking about me as if I am not here," the demon says snappily. "I may be young, but I know what the fuck I'm doing."

Lucien snickers. "I like her. I could use a baby sister."

She shoots Lucien a glare and says, "Sorry, Lucien. I don't want an annoying big brother."

I choke out a laugh, covering it with a cough. It hurts my heart even though I laugh because it reminds me of Mia's sassiness.

Jewel elbows Lucien in the side, stressing the demon's name as she says, "Leave *Rose* alone, dammit, and let's get going."

I slap a hand to my forehead. "That's what her name was. I have been wracking my brain, trying to remember what Mia called you."

"Can we get going, please?" Jewel huffs impatiently.

"Yes, sorry, Jewel. Let's get going," I say, running a hand nervously through my hair.

"Lead the way, boss," Lucien says to me with a sarcastic wave of his hand.

I look toward Rose, who nods and grasps Sophia by both shoulders. I nod back and step forward, feeling the air around me grow colder as the fabric of reality begins to tear. The void between space and time opens before us with a commanding wave of my hand, a swirling vortex of darkness and shimmering light. The sensation is both exhilarating and terrifying, as if the very essence of existence is being pulled apart.

Leading the way, I glance back at my companions. Jewel, her eyes glowing with fierce determination, stands ready. Lucien, ever the silent guardian, balls his shadowy hands into fists, his gaze fixed on the path ahead. Rose, her name so cleverly suited to her delicate frame, clutches Sophia tightly. Sophia's eyes are wide with fear, but she is trying not to let it show. I can tell by the twitch in the corner of one eye.

We step into the void, the sensation of falling and floating all at once overwhelming our senses. Time loses meaning here; seconds stretch into eons, and moments flicker instantly. We traverse this liminal space, the void between dimensions, for only a moment, or maybe an eternity, before I feel the tug in my gut signaling we are close to the dead land of the Demon Dimension.

Lucien steps forward and waves his hand much as I had earlier, and the Demon Dimension begins to take shape before us, the air growing thicker, charged with a dark energy that hums with malevolence. The space before us shimmers and wavers, and I can see blurry images coming into focus through the opening portal. Blobs of dark color loom in the distance, and my nerves tense at the sight of the jagged mountains of the demon dimension appearing over the land before my eyes.

More of the landscape becomes visible, twisted with barren, burnt plains and rivers of molten lava. Steam rises from the rivers, permeating the dense air with ash and smoke. The sky slowly comes into focus, a perpetual twilight that casts an eerie glow over everything the dim light touches.

Finally, the portal is fully open, and I take my place back in the lead as we emerge from the void, our feet touching the scorched earth of the Demon Dimension. The ground trembles beneath us as if acknowledging our arrival. Shadowy demons rise from the darkness to greet us, their eyes gleaming with anticipation of fresh meat.

Lucien and Jewel step forward, coming up beside me and putting Sophia and Rose behind us.

"All of you, back off," Lucien says with a dangerous glare. "We have business here, and then we will be gone. Leave us in peace, and there will be no trouble."

"And if we don't?" One of the shadowy forms asks, slithering forward to stand before us.

A bright, white light begins to glow around Jewel, her eyes matching the glow. Lucien's eyes also glow a sparkling diamond shade, the color surrounding his head like a halo. My light is brighter than theirs, bright and pure white, shining like a beacon in a dark, cold world.

The shadowy, unknown demon snickers. "Is that supposed to scare us?"

"No, but this might," I say, and I release the one thing that hasn't been out in quite some time.

They don't exist on Earth, but I am always aware of their presence in the other dimensions. They are stiff from being contained for so long, and the muscles are weak from misuse. However, they do not fail to come bursting from my shoulder blades, spreading to their full twenty feet spread from one wing tip to the other.

The feathers are silky soft and white, and the tops rise over my head even at full spread. I pull my wings up and give one strong, wind-filled flap, sending the shadowy figures sprawling away from us across the tattered, burnt ground.

They scramble to their feet and scatter like the loose feathers that had come out and floated free with one great flap of my huge wings. I turn to my companions, a sense of purpose filling me as I pull my wings in and settle them folded on my back. They loom over me like a protective old friend.

"Enough of this," I say, my voice steady despite the energy it had taken to flap my unused wings only once. "Let us continue our journey."

They all look at me as if I had sprouted another head instead of a set of wings. Their eyes are wide, and their mouths hang open.

"What? Have you never seen an angel with their wings out?" I ask.

Sophia clings tightly to Rose, her head shaking vigorously and her eyes a mix of fear and curiosity.

"No, I haven't," she answers. "I have, also, never ventured outside the hidden rooms when I was in the Demon Dimension with Harper."

Jewel comes up beside Sophia, her diamond eyes glowing as she adds, "The combination of your massive wings and the vast expanse of the Demon Dimension must be both awe-inspiring and terrifying for Sophia."

I nod in understanding, softening my gaze as I say to Sophia, "Just stay close. We will protect you while we find the hidden room."

Jewel leads the way this time, her eyes scanning the twisted landscape for any signs of more trouble-making demons. Lucien follows closely, his presence a comforting shield against the unknown dangers that lurk in the shadows. Both of their lights still shine, lighting our way through the twilight-darkened land.

I follow, giving instructions on which way to go whenever we come to a turning point or if they stray from the path my power is leading me on.

Mia's demon, holding Sophia protectively, speaks softly to her. "This place may seem frightening, but remember, you are not alone. We will find the room, save Mia and Harper, and fix the portal."

Sophia nods, her eyes becoming more curious than fearful. She looks around, taking in the jagged mountains in the distance and the river of molten lava at our side. The air is thick with suffocating heat, rising from the lava and swirling around us. Dark energy hums in the stifling air, writhing with a malevolent force that makes her shiver visibly.

I watch her over my shoulder as we move deeper into the Demon

Dimension, watching for any negative signs that the land may be wreaking havoc on her body. Shadow demons rise from the darkness once more, but they keep their distance this time. When I am sure everyone is safe for the moment, I close my eyes, focusing on the power within me that allows me to sense the inner demons and their humans.

A familiar presence tugs at my consciousness…

Mia.

She is close, and I can feel her fear and pain. She's hurt, and anger floods my system at the one that hurt her. Her face blurs into existence in the darkness behind my eyelids, and the anger flares to a white-hot rage.

Her face is pale and tear-soaked, and one side of her face is scratched and bruised. She is lying on the ground, a puddle of blood spreading from under her. I can't tell where the blood is coming from, and fear spreads through me at the sight, mingling with the anger that threatens to consume me.

"Get off me! Leave me alone!" She is screaming at the naked figure on top of her.

Thorn is using Harper's body to…

A scream of fury escapes me, causing my companions to jump. I know where Mia is; if I hurry, I can stop it before it is too late. I take the lead, pushing ahead of the glowing demons in a dead run. I shout over my shoulder as I move.

"This way," I say, my voice filled with urgency. "Mia is in trouble. We must get to her now!"

We quicken our pace to a full-out run, the sense of urgency driving us forward. Sophia's grip tightens on Rose as she runs with us, her eyes filled with fearful determination. She knows that finding this hidden room is the key to saving Harper and Mia.

A shimmering light dances above the overhang of a scorched hillside as we reach the ridge, stopping just short of the five-foot drop. I jump down easily, turning to find the entrance hidden against the cliffside. The door shines with a dim, foreign light, and I am surprised it remained hidden for so long. How could no one see this light shining in a perpetually dark land?

"This is it," I say, turning to my companions.

They give me confused stares.

"What, is it buried underneath the burnt dirt?" Lucien asks.

I frown. "What do you mean? It's practically shining, and you can't see it?"

"We don't see anything shining," Sophia says as she clings to Rose.

How can they not see it? I want to ask, but the urgency to get to Mia drives me ever forward. I approach the door, running my hands over its surface. Could it be some kind of trick or trap? Or is this just part of my new abilities to find the lost souls that have inner demons?

"What if this is some kind of trap?" Lucien asks, reflecting my thoughts. "Maybe Thorn sensed the angel's presence and set a trap."

"We don't have time to speculate," Jewel says hurriedly. "We can protect everyone if it is a trap. Deklan, just open whatever door you see, and let's get to Mia."

Jewel is right. I will have time later to speculate this new, strange ability. Right now, Mia needs me. She needs us all.

I take a deep, preparing breath and open the door.

CHAPTER 29: MIA

"**I** have had enough playtime. Now, time to get real," Thorn says viciously as he covers my body with his.

Fear courses through me as he raises his free hand and snaps his fingers. My entire body trembles so violently that my teeth chatter. My heart pounds, threatening to burst from my chest. The sound of Thorn's fingers snapping together rings through my ears as my body goes still again, my limbs refusing to work. I scream a sound of fury mingled with frustration and pain, but it doesn't stop the evil demon.

He rises to his knees, grasping the waistband of his boxers and pulling them down. I thrash my head, the only thing I can move, and scream as his hands latch into the waistband of my panties, the last barrier between my nakedness and Thorn's throbbing penis.

He rips them away and covers my body with his once more, settling between my legs as I lay helpless, his binding spell rendering my limbs useless.

"Get off me! Leave me alone!" I yell, but he ignores my demands, biting at my breasts and rutting over me like he had done before, only this time, there is no barrier between his throbbing dick and my opening.

His swollen member brushes over my lips, sliding ever so slightly between them but not reaching my entrance. I close my eyes tightly, screaming my fury and fear against his violation of my body.

"I'm gonna fuck you, whore. I'm gonna fuck you hard, and it's gonna feel so good," Thorn whispers against my neck as he bites his way down to my breasts.

"Stop, please don't do this," I beg, opening my eyes to see him reach between us and grasp his throbbing cock.

"Please, no," I wail as he slides the head of his cock between my lips and lines it up against my entrance.

I let out a whimpering sob and squeeze my eyes shut, preparing for the violation. But the painful thrust of his cock into my vagina never comes.

Instead, I hear a loud banging sound, like a gunshot…

Or a door slamming against a wall, I think hopefully.

Time seems to stand still as the sound reverberates throughout the room. The sound of my rapidly beating heart pounds in my ears, my ragged breathing keeping time with the rhythm.

Suddenly, I feel nothing. The pressure of Harper's body over mine is gone, and I wonder if I have lost sensation in my body. I crack open my eyes to see Harper's body being hurled through the air, a scream of pure rage filling the air above me. Huge, white wings fill my vision as the figure above me turns its back to me, and I gasp in awe at their beauty.

"No! Don't hurt him, please! It's not his fault!"

Sophia's voice calling out through the room surprises me, and I struggle to rise to a sitting position. But, of course, I am still trapped by the binding spell.

"Someone help me, please," I call out into the room, my voice wavering with a combination of relief and fear. "I can't move. Thorn put a binding spell on me."

"Oh, well, that's easy enough to break," a soft feminine voice says.

A shadowy form fills my vision, but this demon isn't mine. She is larger, her form fuller, and her eyes shine like diamonds instead of sapphires. She snaps her fingers, and the snapping band sensation fills me once more. With a whimper of relief, I finally sit up, covering myself with my arms and hands.

"Thank you, Jewel," I say.

"Here are your clothes," another demon, this one male, says as he hands me my jeans and shirt.

He looks everywhere but at me as he says, "The panties were torn. I'm sorry."

"Thanks, Lucien," I say shakily as I take the clothes from his shadowy hand.

"Are you alright?" Rose says, coming into my line of vision. "I brought back help as fast as I could."

I wince in pain as I try to pull my pants on over my bloody feet and legs. My head hurts, I am sticky with drying blood, and every muscle and bone in my body hurts. Am I alright?

"No, Rose, I am in pain, I'm scared, and I am confused as to what is going on at the moment," I answer, waving an arm at the fight going on in the corner between my winged hero, Harper who is being controlled by Thorn, and Sophia who is yelling at the winged form.

"Who is that, anyway?" I ask, gesturing toward the large, white wings. "I want to thank him for saving me."

Lucien lets out a gruff chuckle, and Jewel giggles. Rose looks uncomfortable as she helps me pull my jeans over my hips. I frown.

"What?"

"I'm sure he would love for you to thank him," Lucien says sarcastically. "After this is over and you forgive him for being stupid, you can thank him all night long."

Jewel laughs harder, and Rose shakes her head disapprovingly as she helps me pull my shirt over my head.

"Would you two leave her alone?" she says.

Sophia's wail brings our attention to the fight, and I scramble to my feet, fully dressed. The winged man and Sophia have Harper, who is still controlled by Thorn, trapped with his back to the wall. He holds a huge shard of glass in his hand, holding it to his wrist.

"Come one step closer to me, angel boy, and I'll cut this body until it is rendered useless," Thorn says.

Angel boy? No, it can't be. Deklan doesn't have wings.

"You aren't even in his body, you idiot," the winged man says. "Harper was trapped here in spirit. That piece of you simply fused with Harper's spirit."

Icy heat flows through my veins, and I don't know if I am angry, turned on, or both at the same time. His voice is unmistakable to me. I would know it anywhere. It haunts my dreams and is burned into my memory.

"No matter," Thorn says, sneering at Deklan with intent. He slides his gaze to the side, toward where Sophia stands. "I'll just take her body, then."

"You won't touch her," Jewel and Thorn say together, moving to stand beside Sophia.

I try to move, to stand beside Deklan, but my body sings with pain at every step. Deklan must have sensed my presence moving toward him because he casts a glance over his shoulder at me and slightly shakes his head.

I stop feet away behind his intimidating winged presence, and my heart soars when he throws me a wink and a smile before turning his attention back forward.

"You forget, boy," Thorn says to Deklan, pointing a finger toward Sophia. "I have one more piece of my soul to call, and when I do, she will die unless I am inside her."

A growl of anger and frustration rumbles through the room, but Thorn ignores it and continues, "Unless you want to save your friend instead. When I rip myself from Harper, he will die. So, choose, angel. Which one of your precious friends would you like to save? The human or the witch?"

I swallow hard as Sophia turns and locks gazes with me. She turns to Deklan, her voice a trembling whisper as she says, "Let him take me. Save Harper."

"No," I breathe.

"We won't let that happen!" Lucien screams angrily.

Thorn presses the shard of glass more firmly against Harper's wrist, casting us all an evil glare through Harper's eyes. "You must choose, angel boy. One or the other."

"There is no choice," Deklan says, his voice tinged with fury. "The one that lives won't live at all. You will take their body as your own, so they will be you. There is no way to save either of them if I choose."

The suspense of the moment is palpable in the air. Everyone seems to take a breath, letting Deklan's words sink in. He's right. There is no way to make a choice. No matter what, they both die. But the wink and smile Deklan gave me fills me with hope, despite the direness of the situation.

He has something up his sleeve, I know it.

"What is it going to be, gang?" Thorn asks with a victorious smirk. "Who will you choose to save? One dies and one lives, but as my vessel. Choose one, angel boy."

There is a moment of silence, and my gaze locks with Sophia's worried eyes. Then, Deklan surprises us all.

"How about both?" he says, moving with blinding speed as he rushes Thorn and grabs him by the throat before any of us can blink.

Deklan's hand around Harper's throat begins to glow a blinding, brilliantly pure, white light. It flows around Harper's body, surrounding it, and its energy fills the room with comforting warmth. Deklan's wings spread out, filling the room from one side to the other. They are too big, and the tips of each one bend to accommodate.

The scream that erupts from Harper's throat is unnatural, guttural, and unlike anything I have ever heard before. It invades my ears, making me want to cover them like I do when the demons scream, but this scream is different. Instead of inflicting pain, it inflicts a sense of dread that runs through my soul.

I watch with wide eyes, my heart pounding with a mix of fear and worry for Harper. The light from Deklan's hand invades Harper's open mouth as he screams, filling him up inside and spilling from every orifice in his body. Light streams from Harper's eyes, nose, mouth, and ears, lighting up the room in a blinding show.

"Don't hurt him!" Sophia wails as she starts to move, but her demons hold her back.

Deklan turns his head, glancing over his shoulder at something on the opposite side of the room. "Get them out of here!" he yells.

I look over to see Rose, who I had momentarily forgotten about with everything else going on, standing in front of the unbroken mirror. The glass glows with the remnants of her power, and the beginnings of a new portal starts coalescing and swirling inside its newly repaired surface.

She hurries over to me and grabs my hand, leading me over to Sophia. We duck under one of Deklan's massive wings, and I brush my fingers over it as we pass. I see the wing shutter, and Deklan shoots me a heated look. His wings must be sensitive.

I can see the effort and strain on his face as he refocuses his attention on holding Harper's neck in his grip and pours his light energy into Harper's body. I start to pull away from Rose and go to him, but Rose tugs at my hand and pulls me with her.

"Hang in there, master," she whispers softly. "Just reach out and grab your cousin, and don't let go."

Master. Did Rose just call me master? But there is no time to ponder on what that means now. Instead, I do as she says, grabbing and holding Sophia's wrist tightly. Sophia struggles, but I refuse to let go. Rose grabs her other wrist and we pull her with us, me on one side, Rose on the other, and Sophia struggling against us in the middle. We make it to the mirror, and Rose jumps through, pulling us through the portal and out the other side.

"No! Take me back this instant!" Sophia yells at my demon.

Rose only shakes her head. "Deklan ordered me to get you out. I'm not taking you back in there."

Sophia places both hands on the mirror, wailing Harper's name as we watch Deklan pour his energy into Harper's spirit, trying to eliminate the evil presence inside him.

Thorn will die today, and I can only hope Deklan can save Harper as well. I hold my cousin to my side and pray.

CHAPTER 30: DEKLAN

Pulling a demon from a body should have been simple. It's one of the new powers I have come to discover I have. When Luna had said that I would know what to do when the time came, she wasn't wrong. Every time a situation came up where I needed something, I just knew what to do.

Just like now. I now know I can pull demons from bodies if needed, which would have been helpful when I had first met Mia. But, better late than never. I have the power now, and now is when I need it the most.

However, I am finding it particularly difficult to pull Thorn from Harper's spirit. Thorn is now more powerful than ever, having been reunited with the piece of himself that had been inside Harper, and he is putting up a heck of a fight. I am struggling to hang on to my power, and Thorn is stubbornly refusing to come out. I have blasted massive amounts of light energy into Harper to make Thorn give way, but Thorn is still in there, digging in his heels and refusing to let go.

I was glad I had had Rose get Sophia out of here. Goddess knows how hard it would have been to drag Thorn out of Sophia if he had gotten his clutches on her and reunited with his final part. The amount of power Thorn has now is scary enough.

Sweat beads on my forehead as I continue to pull against Thorn's presence, pulling it up ever so slightly more toward Harper's crown chakra, where Thorn will be forced out, and Harper will be free. My invisible arm of power pulls more forcefully as I pour more light energy into Harper's spirit, and my physical arms shake with the effort. Every muscle in my body sings with tension, my heart pounding a fierce rhythm in my chest.

My hand on Harper's throat tightens as my body shakes with adrenaline. Thorn is still screaming as he resists the pull, and light still pours from Harper's orifices. If I let my hold slip the least bit, Thorn will settle back in and be even harder to pry out. I hold on with everything I have.

I think about Mia's parting touch as I pull on my reserves of strength and pour it into my efforts. Her fingers had brushed against the sensitive under-feathers of one wing, sending electric currents through my body and strengthening my power.

Her touch had made my heart soar with hope and happiness, which was the fuel I had needed. She had wanted to come to me, I could see it in her eyes. She had even started toward me, but then Rose had pulled her away. The heartbreaking look she had given me had increased the hope flowing through me, which fueled my resolve to pull Thorn out even more.

Now, the determination to get back to Mia keeps me going, even though my muscles quiver from the strain, and my power is weakening ever so slightly. I can't let go, can't give up. I have to get to Mia.

"She made it through," I hear Lucien say. "Let's go, Jewel. Deklan needs help."

My mouth quirks with the start of a victorious smirk as the two demons step up on either side of Harper, each grabbing an arm as their eyes glow with power. With the addition of their light energy to mine, it should be easier to pull Thorn out.

Thorn's scream of pure rage as the two demon's energies fuse with mine is music to my ears. I yank harder on my metaphysical link on Thorn and feel him slide further out, coming ever closer to the top. I tug and tug, every muscle in my body straining with the effort, even though it is mental instead of physical.

The burn of so much energy inside Harper's spirit makes me cringe, and I wonder if there will be anything left of my friend to save once we get this stubborn spirit out of him. Nevertheless, it does not deter me from pulling ever harder on Thorn's presence, feeling him slide further, closer and closer to that crown chakra.

I can hear Sophia screaming from the other side of the portal, and I can only imagine how it looks from her point of view. I can practically feel her fear at the sight. I know it looks bad, with light pouring out of Harper's body and that unearthly scream tearing through the air. The room is bathed in an eerie glow, shadows dancing wildly on the walls. Harper's face contorts in agony, his eyes wide and unseeing, as if he's caught between two worlds.

Finally, I feel the final slip of Thorn's spirit as I pull him out of Harper's body. It's like trying to grasp smoke, the essence of Thorn resisting, writhing in my grip. My heart pounds in my chest, each beat echoing the slipping of Thorn's spirit as I pull him through Harper's crown chakra. Sweat beads on my forehead, trickling down as I concentrate all my energy on this one task.

I keep a hold on it, feeling the cold, malevolent presence of Thorn's spirit thrashing against my will. The air around us seems to thicken, charged with a palpable tension. Keeping a firm hold on Thorn's spirit, I release Harper from my grasp and watch as his body goes limp, the light dimming from his form. Jewel, with a look of fierce determination, steps forward and catches him just before he collapses to the floor.

Harper's body is heavy in her arms, his breathing shallow and ragged, but alive. I breathe a sigh of relief as the room falls into a hushed silence, the only sound the faint, lingering echo of that unearthly scream. I stand there, panting, wobbling slightly, my body trembling from the exertion, knowing that we've just crossed a dangerous threshold.

Lucien grabs my arm as I go down, exhausted from pulling so hard for so long. My wings slide back inside their sheath, and I feel relief at not having their weight on my shoulders. However, I still hold onto that piece of Thorn for dear life, watching it manifest into a shadowy form with glowing, ultraviolet eyes. The death grip I have on Thorn's neck tightens as his true form comes into full view.

"Now, Thorn, this is what's going to happen," I tell Thorn with a rough shake as Lucien helps me struggle to my feet. "I am going to fetch that other little part of your soul and exterminate it. Meanwhile, Jewel will have the honor of killing your ass here."

Thorn does not respond, but I see the defeated fear in the dimming of the purple light. I also see the resolve, but I see that too late.

I don't see Thorn's true intent until he reaches out in a last-ditch effort to cause pain. He swipes a clawed hand at Harper's unmoving body lying motionless in Jewel's arms. It is so quick that she has no time to react. The blood flowing from the scratch marks on Harper's neck is the first indication of Thorn's final attack.

Then I heard the mortified, mournful, tortured screams from Sophia and Jewel, and I knew what Thorn's intent was. He wanted to cause as much pain and sorrow as he could before he left this world, and icy dread runs through my body when I think he might have succeeded.

"If you still want the privilege of annihilating this piece of shit, then you better get him now," I say to the still-screaming Jewel through gritted teeth.

Lucien takes Harper from her, and the anger flashing in those diamond-colored eyes burns through the now panicked demon in my grasp. She goes instantly calm, but it is a dangerous, killing calm. Thorn starts to struggle as Jewel latches into the back of his neck and drags him from my grasp.

"Let's get him out of here, now!" I scream at Lucien as I wrap Harper's limp spirit body in my arms and take him from Lucien's hold.

Lucien doesn't resist; only hands Harper over and follows me through the portal. Thorn's tortured, agonized screams follow us out of the Demon Dimension and into the room on the other side of the portal, but I don't look back to see what Jewel is doing to him.

When we come out the other side, I ignore the satisfaction on the faces staring into the mirror. I ignore the thrill Mia's presence always sends, skirting through my senses. I pay no attention to the sad, hope-filled look she sends my way as I carry Harper's spirit through the room. And I don't respond when Sophia begins barking orders, telling Lucien to ready the staff in the room where Harper's body is.

I keep walking until I reach the reception area, and Cora's mouth hangs agape when she sees the figure I carry in my arms. She places a hand over her mouth, her eyes wide with...

Shock? Surprise? Fear? Maybe a combination of all?

"Get the door," Sophia's voice snaps, spurning Cora into action.

She opens the door and stands aside to allow us to enter. My feet don't stop. Two of my fellow hulks are waiting to open the monitor room door, and the other hulk stands beside the open secret door.

I rush toward that door, but Harper's spirit is torn from my arms before I can get there, ripped away by an unseen force that drags him through the ripples of space and back into his physical body.

I enter the room just in time to see the doctors huddled around his body, waiting for that initial gasp of life so they can begin taking the tubes from his throat and the monitors from his body.

I come up to the bedside, hope filling my chest. I can feel the spark inside his body now, tiny and weak but there all the same. I wait expectantly, but nothing happens. My heart sinks as I feel the spark getting weaker instead of stronger.

"Harper, dammit, you better not leave me here alone," I ground out, grabbing one of his hands in mine. "I need you here. Sophia needs you here."

"I'm here," a breathless Sophia says, grasping Harper's other hand as she worms her way between the doctors on the opposite side of the bed.

I glance up at her and give her a comforting, confident smile.

The spark flares, strengthening slightly at my words and growing brighter at Sophia's touch. My heart pounds with worry and hope. I plead silently to whatever Gods and Goddesses may be listening, but Harper's body remains still.

However, the spark inside remains, so I don't give up hope. Even late into the night as I sit by Harper's bed, waiting for that first gasp of breath that tells us he will be alright.

The gasp that never comes.

CHAPTER 31: MIA

Weeks have passed since Thorn's demise and Harper's release from the Demon Dimension. I have not been home to my apartment, content to stay in the Turret with the now-healing Sophia. Deklan pulling the last piece of Thorn's spirit from her body took a toll on her. It doesn't help that she never rests, content to sit by Harper's bedside with Deklan, whom I still haven't spoken to since that day.

Except in my thoughts throughout the day and in my dreams at night. Sometimes, I sneak down the hall to the monitor room and ask whoever is there to let me in the secret room. I steal in quietly without him knowing, and just watch him sitting by his friend's bedside, watching Harper's body and the monitors with worry, hope, and a bit of fear.

My heart bursts with…love. Yes, I admit, I am in love with my angel.

If he is still my angel.

Now that my demon is doing well and working with me, I may not need a guardian angel anymore. But I still need him. I still need Deklan, and I am afraid I have ruined the best thing that has ever happened to me.

Today has been worse than most days. I received bad news from my company in Phoenix. We lost a big account today due to a client's death, and her family chose not to continue with us. Then, Dad called to say he received bad news at his doctor's appointment today.

It wasn't life or death, but enough of a concern to cause worry. He will have to watch what he eats from now on and stop smoking those infernal cigars he likes, or it could get bad.

I feel defeated after today and want to feel Deklan's comforting touch more than ever. The desire to be in his presence is overwhelming, and my ears long to hear his voice. It is almost too much to bear.

Gathering my courage, I decide to make another trip into the secret room. This time, maybe I will be brave enough to speak to him instead of just silently observing him.

Yes, that is what I will do. I don't even bother getting dressed; the pink silk, short-sleeved sleep shirt and matching silk shorts provide enough cover for my comfort. I pad barefoot to the living room of the turret.

The sun has set, bathing the room in a warm, golden glow that has me sucking in a breath at its beauty. I make my silent way down the hallway to the monitor room as I have done a hundred times before. The hulk in the room smiles familiarly at me as I enter, pushing the button that opens the secret door without me having to ask.

I approach and pause just outside the secret door, my heart pounding in my chest. The familiar sounds of the monitors and the soft hum of the machines fill the air, a constant reminder of Harper's fragile life as he hangs on by a thread.

I take a deep breath, leaning against the cool wall, trying to steady my nerves. My mind races with memories of Deklan; his smile, his laughter, the way his eyes would light up when he saw me. His touch, how it burned me from the inside, and how it felt to have him inside me.

The love in his eyes when he looked at me and the way I never recognized the emotion until it grew within myself. But those memories are tainted by the pain and misunderstanding that drove us apart.

I close my eyes, gathering my courage. I know I need to do this, to face him and try to mend what was broken. But the fear of rejection, of seeing the hate in his eyes again, holds me back.

Minutes pass, and I force myself to take another step forward. I peek into the room and see Deklan sitting by Harper's bedside, his emerald eyes fixed on him with a mixture of worry and hope. His shoulders are slumped, his ruby red hair disheveled, and he runs a hand through it as I watch.

The sunset light shines through the single window in the room, bathing Deklan in a wash of crimson, making his red hair seem even redder. I ache to run my hands through it, soothing him with my touch. My desire to have him look at me with that love light in his eyes once more is debilitating.

His skin, usually slightly tan, looks more gold than bronze in the light, his muscles rippling as he shifts in his seat. The urge to run my hands over his skin and feel those rippling muscles under my fingertips almost brings me to my knees. The thought that he might not want me touching him right now tightens my chest.

His short-sleeved, plaid button-up shirt is wrinkled as if he'd slept in it, and his jeans are dingy as if he'd worn them for a couple of days. My heart goes soft at the thought of Deklan suffering over his friend's condition. His eyes never leave Harper's body as he sits watchfully by Harper's side, and the sight of him, so dedicated and caring, makes my heart ache. He used to be that way with me once, and I threw it all away.

I take another deep breath, my hands trembling. I know I can't delay this any longer. I have to face him, to tell him how I feel, no matter how difficult it might be. Finally, I step into the room, my voice barely a whisper.

"Deklan," I say, my voice trembling. He turns to look at me, his expression turning unreadable.

"I... I wanted to talk to you," I continue, stepping closer. "I know things are...complicated, and I haven't spoken to you since..."

I pause, gesturing toward Harper as I draw closer to Deklan's unmoving presence.

"But I need you to know that I still care about you. More than ever, in fact. And I hope you know that what Brandon said was never true."

I stop and take a shuddering breath as Deklan's eyes harden slightly. He stands up, moving towards me as I stand frozen in my tracks. My heart pounds with tension when he stops inches before me.

"Why now, Mia?" he asks, his voice tinged with bitterness. "After everything that happened, everything we went through, you didn't even try to explain yourself at the time. Why now?"

I swallow hard, feeling the sting of his words. "I thought you should have believed in me," I admit. "When my ex told you those lies, I didn't want to defend myself. My pride got in the way, and then when you believed him anyway, I was hurt and confused."

He scoffs, crossing his arms. "Hurt and confused? That's your excuse?"

My breathing turns shallow, my chest tightening. It feels as if every breath is a struggle as I rasp, "Please, I know it comes late. But I want to explain now..."

He interrupts me, his eyes hardening and his tone strained as he says harshly, "I already know the truth, but I had to hear it from others. You let me think you were cheating on me, Mia. You didn't even try to fight for us."

Tears well up in my eyes as I fight for each breath, trying not to sob as I respond, "I was scared, Deklan. Scared that you would hate me no matter what I said. There was so much hate in your eyes when you left, when you walked out on me…"

"Well, you were right about one thing," he snaps, interrupting my tirade. "I did hate you in that moment. You betrayed me, the same way my Goddess had betrayed me. And then I found out the truth from Vinny and Sophia, but by then, it didn't matter. The damage was done, and I didn't think you would have me back. Hell, I didn't even know if I even wanted you back. I didn't know if we would ever be able to trust each other."

I step closer, reaching out to touch his arm, but he pulls away. "Deklan, please. I never stopped thinking about you. Even when you thought the worst of me, I still cared about you. I would have taken you back. I…"

I falter, the words refusing to come as Deklan's eyes refuse to look my way, and I am afraid of what I will see when he does. I swallow hard, swallowing the words I was about to say. Tears stream down my cheeks, dripping from my chin and onto the floor.

He finally meets my gaze, his eyes filled with a mix of anger and pain. My breath catches in my throat. At least it isn't hate in his emerald gaze.

"I never stopped thinking about you either," he admits. "I crave you every day, needing to feel your touch and hear your voice say my name. But that isn't going to be enough to fix this. Not after everything we've been through."

We stand there for the barest moment, the weight of our past misunderstandings hanging between us. I break the momentary, awkward silence.

"Can we start over?" I ask, my voice barely above a whisper. "Can we try to fix this? I can have my demon misbehave, and you can come to my rescue."

Deklan chuckles, his expression softening slightly. He reaches out, grasping my hand in his and causing my heart to soar with hope.

"I do want to try again," he says. "But it won't be easy. We have a lot to work through, and we have to learn to trust each other."

"I know," I reply, the hope swelling in my chest. "But I'm willing to try if you are."

As we stand there, hand in hand, a sense of peace washes over me at Deklan's touch. I know it's going to be okay. No matter the challenges, I know we'll face them together. Deklan's eyes fill with something I have only dreamed of in the past weeks since we parted ways. That familiar heat fills his emerald gaze, sending shards of desire shooting into my core.

"We can start right now if you want to come to my apartment with me when Sophia comes to relieve me," he says, his voice dark and seductive.

I shiver with anticipation and answer, "Are you going to punish me for being such a bad girl?"

He chuckles, his grip on my hand tightening as he draws me into his hard, muscled body.

He leans down, placing his lips next to my ear, and whispers, "Baby, it's going to take a lot of punishment to make up for what you put me through. Are you sure you're ready to take on the challenge?"

"Oh, yes," I whisper, shuddering in his arms as rampant desire courses through my veins. "I want it. I want all of it. I want all of you."

Deklan growls deep in his chest, brushing his lips over my cheek as he brings his mouth to mine. However, before he can press his lips to mine in an earth-shattering, lets-make-up kiss, the monitors hooked to Harper start beeping erratically.

We break apart, Deklan rushing to Harper's side as a shuddering gasp comes from Harper's body. Harper thrashes in his bed, trying desperately to pull the tube from his mouth as he starts to choke.

"I need help over here!" Deklan calls anxiously, grabbing Harper's hands and attempting to hold him down while calming him.

Suddenly, the room is a flurry of movement, doctors running toward Harper's bed, unhooking machines and holding him down while they attempt to remove the tube from his throat.

Voices coalesce together, all of them straining to stay calm and gentle as they fire off orders at Harper.

"Sir, remain calm, and let us help you."

"Don't try to talk, sir, until your throat can recover from the tube."

"Stay still, sir, while we get that tube out of you."

The doctors fuss over Harper, working around Deklan's vigilant form until the monitors and tubes are removed from his body, save for the I.V. that has been feeding him. They move away from the bed after giving a few instructions and advice to Deklan, and I see the steady rise and fall of Harper's chest as he breathes on his own.

Deklan raises questioning emerald eyes to me, and I nod with a comforting smile. He looks back to Harper just in time to see his eyes fluttering open. He looks around, disoriented, and then his gaze locks onto Deklan's.

"Harper!" Deklan exclaims with a relieved sigh. "You're awake."

Harper's voice is weak, but he manages to speak. "You two get a room."

Then his eyes flutter back closed as a smile spreads across his peaceful face.

"Really?" Deklan scoffs. "You come out of a fucking coma to tell me to get a room?"

The smile on Harper's face grows wider even as his eyes remain closed. Deklan chuckles as he shakes his head, and I laugh with a mixture of relief, hope for the future, and complete and utter love for my angel.

CHAPTER 32: DEKLAN AND MIA

DEKLAN

Sophia comes bursting into the room, tears of relief and joy streaming down her face. She hurtles herself across Harper, his grunt and wince of pain ignored as she rains kisses upon his face.

Harper is smiling, but I can see the pain in his eyes. His hands tremble as he holds Sophia to him and takes the loving abuse. His dark hair is disheveled and sticks out everywhere, but Sophia doesn't seem to care. She also does not seem bothered by Harper's full beard and the weakened state of his body, all factors that can be fixed with a shower, shave, and weeks of workouts and gym time.

"I thought I was going to lose you forever," she manages to get out between kisses. "I was so scared. Never scare me like that again."

"I don't plan to, baby girl," Harper rasps, his voice hoarse and scratchy from unuse.

"Soph, Soph…" I say, but she is too engrossed in Harper to hear me. She runs her fingers through Harper's hair and smooths her hands across his beard and down his chest.

"Sophia!"

"What?" she cries, shooting me an annoyed glare. "Can't you see I'm busy welcoming my fiancé back to the land of the living?"

"About that," I say. "We have a lot to discuss, mainly what we will say to the public about Harper's rise from the dead. Also, I'm pretty sure you're suffocating him right now."

"Oh!" she exclaims, rising from Harper with a chagrined look. "I'm so sorry, babe, I just got excited."

"It's fine," Harper croaks, his twisted features and strained voice saying it was not fine at all.

I grasp Sophia by the shoulders to help her stand, turning her to look at me as I say, "He has a long way to go, Soph, but we got this."

"Yeah, babe," Harper croaks. "It'll only be a couple of months of physical therapy and a few weeks of getting used to solid food again."

She nods with tear-filled eyes, grasping Harper's hand as if afraid he will disappear. "I'll take care of you," she says through her tears.

"We will take care of each other, love," he says.

"But for now," I continue, releasing Sophia's shoulders. "I need to speak with Mia alone. I have a lot to discuss with her as well."

I hear Mia gasp behind me at how I had said the word *discuss,* and I smile darkly. Sophia catches the look and smiles knowingly, wiping tears from her face.

"Well, be safe, and don't kill each other," Sophia says with a wink. "And take care of my cousin."

"Deklan," I hear Harper's weak call and immediately go to his side.

"Hey, bud," I say with a smile. "What's going on?"

"I might need your help," Harper says, his voice weak and scratchy.

I frown. "With what? Anything you need, just ask."

"Well," Harper says with a quirk of an eyebrow. "I have this demon, you see. And since she has vanquished this powerful demon that had been giving us all hell, she is just full of herself, and I need help smacking her off her high horse."

By the time Harper finishes, Jewel has appeared by his bedside, rolling her eyes with her shadowy arms crossed over her chest. My booming laugh rings through the room, and Sophia laughs and cries simultaneously.

"Seriously, Deklan," Harper says as the laughter dies. "Thanks. You really came through this time. Thanks for bringing me back."

I pat his shoulder with a nod and say, "You'd do the same for me, man."

"You know it," Harper says with a smile.

I turn to the other occupant in the room, who'd stood quietly by the entire time. She gives me a shaky, uncertain smile as I lock eyes with her. Her chocolate-drop eyes stare deep into mine as I stalk toward her, and I can see the excited anticipation radiating from them.

"Shall we go upstairs to my apartment?" I ask with a seductive smirk.

I watch her throat work as she swallows, and her eyes take on a dark light. Her chin quivers as her tongue darts out and licks along her bottom lip, sending my thoughts spiraling over what she could do with that tongue. "Yes, please," she answers.

It was the *please* that has my dick jumping in my pants as I picture her under me, begging me to let her cum as her pussy milks my cock.

Goddess, how I had missed her.

I reach her, bending low to whisper in her ear, "I missed you, Mia. I'm going to take you upstairs and show you how much."

I smile deviously when I hear her breath hitch, and I kiss the racing pulse on her neck before I rise and take her hand, leading her out of the secret room, through the monitor room, down the hallway out of the turret, and up the stairs to my apartment.

I whisper hurriedly, "Harper is awake," at Cora as we pass.

I smile when I hear her sharp breath and a following *yesss!*

My body hums with anticipation as we climb the stairs. This is the moment I have been dreaming of since I had realized my true feelings for Mia. It had been the day of Luna's visit, when I had been all gung-ho about getting Mia back after discovering the truth. Much of what Luna had said had made sense then, but I had not put much thought behind it. I had been solely focused on Mia.

Then everything happened, and I had many hours to think about everything while I sat at Harper's bedside. One thing I had thought a lot about was how much I loved Mia. Enough to let her go if need be. If we couldn't learn to trust each other, then it would only cause us more heartache in the long run. If this was going to work, it would take both of us learning how to apologize and how to forgive.

Now, with her hand warm in mine and my heart racing with anticipation of having her in my arms, I couldn't imagine ever giving up on us. I couldn't imagine my life without her.

I will never let her go again.

We reach the door to my apartment, and I turn when I feel a tug on my hand. I turn to see Mia looking at the closed door with wide eyes. I give her a confused look as I draw her to me.

"Mia?" I ask, my heart lurching. Please, for the love of all that is holy, don't let her be having second thoughts.

She looks up into my eyes as I draw her near, but there isn't any doubt or concern in her eyes. Instead, she looks…happy…almost glowing.

"I was just remembering the last time I was in your apartment," she says with a naughty smirk. "You couldn't keep your hands off me, and we almost ended up late for work. How is your job going, by the way?"

Relief floods my system as I return her smirk with one of my own, pulling her in even closer. I hold her to me with my hands on her hips, leaning my forehead onto hers.

I chuckle as I answer, "Clark thinks I have a family emergency going on, which is partially true. He has given me another month to sort everything out before I give it another go."

"You'll do fine," she says with a soft smile. "Now, about that day…"

"You remember everything, do you?" I ask with a laugh.

Mia smiles. "Mmmhmm."

"So, you remember the good morning sex, the two spankings, and the quickie in the shower?" I rattle off.

Her smile widens. "I absolutely remember that heavenly shower. I was also thinking about the night before," Mia coos, running her fingers up the buttons of my shirt as she presses her forehead more firmly against mine in a nuzzling motion. "How passionate you had been when you made…"

Mia hesitates, biting her bottom lip and clearing her throat. I finish the sentence for her and am no longer afraid to say the words.

Softly, I finish, "When I made love to you."

She pulls her head back and stares into my eyes with an uncertain look. "Did you…umm…after…er…before we fell asleep?" Mia stutters, her eyes darting side to side as she refuses to look at me.

I smile as I watch the blush creep up her neck and into her cheeks. "Did I whisper I love you before I fell asleep with you in my arms?"

"Yes," she whispers, ducking her head to hide her gaze.

"Yes. Yes, I did." I answer.

"And did you love me then?" Mia whispers, almost too low for me to hear, fear rising in her chocolate orbs as she slowly raises them to look up at me.

I bring my hands up to cup her face, pulling her to me and placing a soft kiss on her lips before answering, "Yes, Mia. I did and still do. I am totally, head-over-heels, completely and forever in love with you, and I have been for a long time. I was just too afraid to say it, but I'm not anymore."

The fear and uncertainty leak away, to be replaced with a combination of happiness and relief.

"Oh, Deklan…"

"You don't have to say it back right now," I interrupt her, giving her a dark, lust-filled smirk. "I would rather you take me in my apartment and show me."

Her eyes go dark with desire as she runs her hands down my chest and says, "As you wish, my angel. But I do have one request."

I raise my eyebrows questioningly as I say, "Anything for you, Mia. Just ask."

She smirks mischievously as she replies, "Can you bring those wings back out?"

I throw my head back and laugh.

MIA

Disappointment flows through me when Deklan explains that his wings don't exist in this physical plane.

Damn.

They had been so beautiful, so soft, and I had longed to run my hands all over their massive planes and get lost in the sensations. I tell him that, and a dark, dangerous growl escapes Deklan's throat, running a shudder of ecstasy through my entire body.

He lowers his face to mine, looking at my lips with intent as he says, "Maybe one day I'll get permission to take you into the Divine Dimension for some playtime,"

"They would let you do that?" I ask breathlessly as he wraps a hand in my hair and tugs lightly.

"They have been known to let lovers play," Deklan rasps in my ear while nibbling on the sensitive flesh of my neck.

"That would be lovely," I say with a shudder.

"You are lovely," he responds huskily, backing me up with a hand on my chest.

He pushes me up against the still-closed apartment door, pressing his hips against me until I feel his erection pressing against my belly through his jeans.

"Can you feel how hard you make me, Mia?" Deklan rasps in my ear.

I swallow so hard the gulp is audible over the sound of my pulse racing. He presses his hips more firmly against me, running his hands down my arms until he reaches my wrists. He brings my arms up, traps my hands against the door over my head, and then captures my mouth with his.

The kiss is gentle yet demanding, filled with the pain and agony of the past two weeks mixed with heat, lust, and the love we have found for each other. His hands hold my wrists firmly while his hips keep my body pressed against the door. My hands ball into fists, trying to hold on to my sanity as Deklan uses lips, tongue, and teeth to kiss me senselessly.

Every nerve and cell in my body is on fire with ecstasy, burning for his touch, his kiss, his everything. I yearn for his naked skin against mine, the want so intense I writhe against him with a soft moan. The moan vibrates against our joined lips, eliciting a growl from deep inside Deklan's chest that rumbles against my breasts. The sensation is erotically sensual, pebbling my nipples against the soft fabric of my silk sleep shirt.

He breaks the kiss, lavishing kisses across my cheek and neck, freeing my mouth. Before he can claim my mouth again, I say breathlessly, "Deklan, we need to go inside."

"Here is fine," Deklan says between kisses, and he continues his assault on my neck.

"Deklan! We're out in the hallway," I say with a chuckle.

I am flattered he is so caught up in me that he forgets where he is, but I would rather not let the entire hospital see us in the hot throes of passion.

He raises his head to look at me, his eyes hooded and wanton. I watch as recognition floods his gaze, and he looks to each side of us. He slowly raises off me, letting go of my wrists and smiling sheepishly.

"Guess I just got carried away, baby," he drawls adorably.

My heart melts.

I grab the belt loops of his jeans and pull him back into me as I say, "That's alright, my angel. Why don't you open the door so you can carry me away to your bedroom?"

"As you wish, babe."

He leans down, grabbing my ass and lifting me off the ground so suddenly that I barely have time to grab his shoulders and steady myself. I wrap my legs around his waist as he settles his hands on my thighs and turns with me in his grasp.

He uses one hand to turn the knob and open the door to his apartment as I hold on. He carries me through the door, kicking the door closed behind us. He captures my lips with his once more, holding me tight in his arms as he moves us through his living room and into the bedroom without breaking the kiss.

He breaks the kiss to move the filmy material aside and toss me onto the bed. I let out a delighted squeal as I land, and dodge to the side when I see him dive onto the bed. He lands beside me, grabbing for me as he bounces once, but I scramble away, laughing.

"Aww, baby, it's too late to run away now," he says as he lunges for me.

"It's never too late," I say breathlessly as I scramble toward the other side, avoiding his grasping hand.

"Are you gonna be a bad girl?" he asks, sitting up and reaching through the hanging canopy for his bedside table.

"Depends," I say, sliding off the other side of the bed, moving the material aside, and preparing to run.

I freeze, however, when I see what he pulls from his bedside table's drawer. He smiles deviously as he holds up the device, and I shudder at the memory.

"Are you sure? Only good girls get rewards," he says slyly, holding the device hanging from one finger.

He moves his hand forward, giving the stringy panties a good swing. The little butterfly on the front flies forward, revealing the silver pod attached to its underside. Deklan holds up his other hand to reveal the control that operates the tiny orgasm-maker. I swallow hard.

"Come here," he orders, his tone dark and hungry.

I move between the material and the bed, around to the side where he sits, and he grabs me when I get within his reach. He pulls me to him, fitting me in the space between his legs, and begins unbuttoning my sleep shirt. He dips his head to follow his fingers, biting at each piece of skin revealed as he peels off the shirt.

He captures the nipple of one breast, sucking it into his hot mouth and pulling an ecstatic moan from my throat. I grab handfuls of his scarlet hair, throwing my head back as I relish in the feel of his mouth on me. Every nerve in my body sings with pleasure, and every muscle quivers with anticipation of what he will do to me next.

His hands grasp the waistband of my sleep shorts and pull them down my legs. They fall to the floor, and I step out of them and kick them away. Deklan pulls away from my breasts and sits up, looking me up and down with desire written all over his handsome face.

"Fuck, baby, you're so damn beautiful," he says huskily.

I start unbuttoning his shirt as I say, "You're not so bad yourself, but you are wearing too many clothes."

The need to feel his naked skin on mine is unbearable, and my fingers fumble clumsily as I try to hurry. He bats my hands away and hastily unbuttons the last buttons, pulling the shirt off quickly as I start on his jeans. He raises his hips to allow me to pull the jeans down, and then he kicks them off quickly.

He sits on the bed before me, naked and glorious, and my lady parts do a little happy dance at the sight of his throbbing, hard dick. He pulls me to him, wrapping me in his embrace and capturing my lips with his.

My body hums with wanton desire so intense that the first touch of his naked flesh against mine is explosive. Shockwaves of electric pleasure shoot through every fiber of my being, and I moan my pleasure into his kiss.

His return growl of lust rumbles from his chest, vibrating against my breasts and heightening the sensation. His hands travel down my back to my buttocks, squeezing the checks with his big palms. He breaks away from the kiss to pick the butterfly up from where he had dropped it on the bed beside him.

"Put it on," he says breathlessly.

I quickly obey, bracing myself for the push of the button. But he doesn't push the button. Instead, he pats the bed and stands.

"Lie on the bed," he commands.

I do as he says, every muscle in my body trembling with anticipation. He towers over me, standing at the side of the bed while I lay on my back staring up at him. He holds the remote up in my view as he smiles deviously.

"Say my name, baby. Say my name as you ask me to make you cum," he says commandingly.

My breathing is erratic, my heart fluttering frantically. My voice is breathy as I gasp, "Make me cum, Deklan."

"Good girl," he drawls but still doesn't push the button, even though I had tensed and prepared for it.

"Deklan," I rasp.

He runs a hand up one leg, pausing at the apex of my thigh as he pierces me with his gaze.

"I'm gonna make you cum so hard for me, baby," he says and then shoves a finger into my entrance.

My hips buck automatically as I cry out in pleasurable surprise. He pushes another finger inside me as I writhe, and then he begins pumping in and out of me with the two fingers.

"Fuck, Deklan!" I cry.

"You like that, baby?" he coos.

"Yes, yes!" I scream, pumping my hips in time with his thrusts.

"Then you are going to love this," he says.

He pushes the button, and I am not prepared.

The sudden vibration of the tiny silver pod, combined with the sensation of Deklan's fingers pumping in and out of me, rips an orgasm from my core, sending it crashing through me with the force of a hurricane.

I scream his name over and over, grinding against his hand as the orgasm takes me to a place where only pleasure exists. My pussy walls pulse and throb, squeezing his fingers so hard I am afraid they might break. I don't know how long the sensations tear through me before they start to fade, leaving me a breathless heap of useless bones on the mattress.

Deklan pulls his fingers out and pulls the butterfly panties down my legs, tossing them to the side. He leans over and kisses my stomach tenderly, causing the muscles to flutter under his touch. He kisses his way up, lavishing each breast and nipple with attention before coming to my lips.

"Such a good fucking girl," he whispers against my mouth, causing me to whimper when he pulls away without kissing me. My disappointment fades as I feel the mattress give under his weight. I turn my head to see him leaning toward me, positioning himself over me and balancing his weight on his elbows.

He spreads my legs apart with one knee, then positions himself between my legs. He reaches between us with one hand and positions his throbbing cock at my entrance. He pushes himself inside inch by delicious inch, piercing me with his gaze as he sheathes himself inside me.

I am filled by him; body, soul, and heart. His emerald eyes stare into mine as he makes love to me slowly, tenderly, and completely. Our bodies meld together as our orgasms take us simultaneously, and as our cries of bliss coalesce together, our souls connect until we are one in our pleasure.

Finally, we lie in comfortable silence side by side in Deklan's heavenly bed, surrounded by the filmy canopy, the heat of our lovemaking, and the scent of sex. We are breathless, spent, and satisfied.

Deklan captures my hand in his, breaking the silence when he says,

299

"Marry me, Mia."

My heart stutters as my head jerks to the side. "What the fuck did you just say?"

He chuckles and turns to me, piercing me with his gaze. "Marry me."

"Are you fucking crazy?" I ask incredulously. "We have a lot of work to do to get to that point, don't you think?"

His gaze turns serious, and he responds, "I know we do, but we can do it while we are married. This is what I want, Mia. I want you, only you, forever."

I narrow my eyes at him with a huff. I see the tension in his gaze as he waits for my response. I raise an eyebrow as I smile sardonically.

"I can't marry you," I say with a humorous smile.

Deklan frowns, but his lips quirk in the corners as he asks, "Why not?"

"Because I hate you," I say.

His laugh rings through the room as he answers, "I know."

ABOUT THE AUTHOR

Rebecca Jose lives in a small town in the heart of Kentucky. She has three grown kids, a multitude of "adopted" kids, eight grandkids, four dogs, and a parrot. She enjoys her job at a local historical sight in Harrodsburg, Kentucky.

When she is not working at her job or home on the computer, she enjoys her time with her husband, grandkids, and family. Her dream is to create many stories for many readers, and she hopes that people will enjoy her stories for years to come.

THANK YOU FOR READING AND FOR BEING A FAN...

REBECCA JOSE XOXO

FOLLOW HER ON SOCIAL MEDIA …

TIKTOK…https://www.tiktok.com/@REBECCAJOSE4080

FACEBOOK…https://www.facebook.com/rebecca.maggard.79

TWITTER…https://twitter.com/Rebeccajose8

INSTAGRAM…https://www.instagram.com/mymeshara/

GOODREADS…https://www.goodreads.com/author/show/21408581.Rebecca_Jose

www.ingramcontent.com/pod-product-compliance
Lightning Source LLC
Chambersburg PA
CBHW060950030726
47503CB00003B/812